A *Journey*
through
HEAVEN

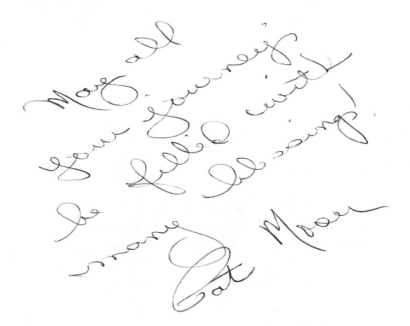

May all your journey's through life with be more

Pat Moser

Patricia Moser

ISBN 978-1-0980-0864-2 (paperback)
ISBN 978-1-0980-0865-9 (digital)

Christian Faith Publishing, Inc.
832 Park Avenue
Meadville, PA 16335
www.christianfaithpublishing.com

Printed in the United States of America

Luther

Luther opened his eyes, blinking rapidly to bring them into focus. Instantly, he knew something was different today. He had such a weird feeling, one he couldn't remember ever feeling before. He was in a nursing home; that much he knew.

"I know exactly where I am and everything that's going on around this place. They can't fool me, by golly! Maybe I'm not as senile as they think I am," he chuckled.

Luther, however, wasn't always sure who all these people were. He knew they worked at the nursing home, but he couldn't remember their names. Sometimes they looked familiar, sometimes not. He had to admit that he did get confused at times.

But one thing was for sure—he always knew when he was hungry and when it was time to eat. Luther loved to eat. The food was good most of the time. He also knew he enjoyed sitting out in the hall watching people go by. He figured they all thought he was just an old man who had lost his mind.

What was that word they used? Alzheimer's? That was it. I can't be too far gone if I can remember a fifty-cent word like that. Yep, they can't fool me!

His name was Luther Wayne Yeager. He was ninety-three years old. And this is his story.

*****

The nursing home wasn't really all that bad, and by now Luther even thought of it as his home. He had a nice room with a large window and a big TV he would watch when there was nothing else to do. Most of the time, though, he thought the shows were really dumb. Whatever happened to *the Ed Sullivan Show*? And *Jackie Gleason*? Where were they? Now they were good shows.

Luther loved baseball and enjoyed watching the televised games. He even remembered watching the Phillies, his favorite team. He almost went to a World Series game once. The Phillies should have been there, but they lost so many games in a row; they got knocked out of contention. What a bummer that was.

But today—well today—he just wasn't sure. He knew he wasn't in his room, yet he was in a bed. Had they moved him to a new room in the middle of the night? Why? He felt anxious; he wanted to get up. Normally, he had to wait for a nurse to come and help him, but today he felt like he could actually get out of bed on his own.

He sat up, a miracle in itself, and felt none of the usual aches and pains. He was even able to swing his legs over the edge of the bed. "Wow! I couldn't do that yesterday."

Now what was going on? Where was that music coming from? He never heard music in his room before. He thought back to the good old days when music was music and not this hip-hop crap the young kids played today. Listening, he felt like dancing, and by damn, he felt he could do just that. He vaguely remembered dancing with a very pretty girl, right before the war. Wow, that must have been seventy years ago, maybe even longer.

All of a sudden, he started remembering lots of things that happened a long time ago. Memories were coming back to him and he was getting lost in them. In his mind, he was seeing familiar faces and places. He wasn't sure who they were, but somehow he knew they had been important in his life. He was beginning to feel dizzy with memories whirling about in his head.

Where exactly am I? he asked himself. He wanted to get out of bed and look around, but he was afraid. Even though his legs felt stronger, he didn't want to fall and end up face down on the floor. But who knew when someone would come in to check on him? He decided the best thing to do was to just stay put.

His thoughts began to drift and swirl wildly in his head. He soon saw a woman—a very pretty woman. Somehow he sensed she spent a lot of time in a kitchen preparing meals. He saw a little girl with long brown hair on a swing in a backyard. Who were they?

Next, he found himself at a picnic. He noticed a young boy standing idly by. There were many people there. All of the women were sitting under a big oak tree talking and laughing; some were rocking small children. The men were standing near a barn door looking at a tractor. A group of young girls were chasing one another and acting silly. Some boys were playing baseball. One of them asked if he wanted to play. Luther said sure.

Was that boy me? Luther wondered. But it couldn't be; they called him Wayne. His name was Luther, although his middle name was Wayne. He was very confused. He remembered joining in the ball game. He remembered hitting the ball and running like crazy to first base. "Run, Wayne, run. Keep going," he heard. He ran all the way around the bases, and when he was just about to cross home plate, the catcher on the other team tagged him. He was out.

Now the boys were booing him and telling him he couldn't play with them anymore. Luther picked up his hat and ran toward the cornfield. The next thing he knew, his foot caught on a rock and he fell. He started to cry. "It wasn't my fault."

Soon, one of the women walked over to him. She hit him across the back of the head and he froze in fear. He made no movement when she told him to get up and to stop crying and acting like a baby. He was afraid of her. She was awfully mean, this woman.

This was all too confusing. He wasn't even trying to think of his past, but somehow these images were popping into his head. Why? And why now? Some of these thoughts weren't very nice and he wished they would just go away.

Well, Luther thought, it was obvious that no one was coming to his room to help him get up. On impulse, he decided he would stand up and find out where he was. Slowly, he put his feet on the floor and found himself standing. He didn't feel shaky. In fact, he felt pretty good.

He glanced around the room. It was a nice-sized room. Against the far wall was a chair. The bed was big and comfy, with a sky blue down comforter on it the same shade as the painted walls. Plaid curtains framed the windows. Luther started walking—actually walking unassisted. Another milestone. He walked toward the window and looked out at a courtyard below with lots of green grass. There were white chairs with big fluffy yellow pillows on them. Luther thought it would be nice to go out there and sit down. But how?

Just then, there was a knock at the door. Before he had the chance to say anything, the door opened and a beautiful young girl came in. He smiled. Luther never ignored a beautiful woman. This lovely young girl had cream-colored hair that shaped her oval face. She wore it long, with a ribbon across the crown. Her eyes were a deep piercing blue that seemed to glisten when she turned toward the light.

"Welcome, Mr. Yeager," she said. "We are so happy that you are here. My name is Marianna."

Luther just stared at her, feeling totally tongue-tied. He couldn't say a word. Here was this beautiful young woman standing in his room, saying she was happy he was there, and he couldn't make any words come out of his mouth.

"Are you okay? Is there anything I can get for you? Maybe a glass of water?"

"No," Luther said. He wasn't thirsty. "Tell me. Where am I?"

"Why this is your home, Mr. Yeager. Make yourself comfortable and someone will be here to see you very soon." And just as quickly as she came, she was gone.

What did she mean that this was his home? He didn't remember this place at all. How did he get here? How was it that he could now stand and walk and remember things? He had a lot of questions, but who to ask? Well, he figured, if she could open that door and walk in and out, so could he. And that's just what he would do. He would go out that door and find that girl, Melissa...no...Maryann...no. Oh, what the hell was her name, anyway?

Luther was still unsure of his footing, as he leaned against the wall for balance and support. But he felt so good, so sure of himself.

He could actually walk without any help. Things were very strange around here. He had to get out of this room and find someone, anyone. He felt he was going crazy.

He opened the door and heard voices. *Thank goodness,* he thought. *At least there were other people here.* When he saw the large open area directly in front of him, he was amazed. People were walking, talking, and even riding bikes. The grass was greener than any grass he had ever seen. The sky was a startling blue. Big white fluffy clouds floated by. He felt like he was outside, yet he was sure he was inside. People looked as if they were having a good time. He wanted to walk over to them and find out about this place. A man walked by and said hello. Luther said hello in return and started to ask about this place, but he was already out of sight.

He looked to his right and his left. Doors exactly like his lined the hallway as far as he could see. If he walked away from his door, he knew he would never be able to find it again. How could anyone find their way back? How ridiculous was this? He wondered if other people were inside those rooms, afraid to come out.

He thought about going to one of the doors and knocking to see if anyone answered. If he went only one door down, he could find his way back. But what if his door slammed shut and locked? He had no key. He decided to prop the door open. He looked around his room and found a pillow to put by the door so it wouldn't close. He then walked to the door to his right and knocked. No answer. He decided he would try the door to the left. He knocked. He thought he heard voices inside, but no one came to the door. He knocked again, louder this time. Still no one came. Defeated, he hung his head and went back to his room. The door was still open and he went inside feeling totally helpless. Lifting his chin, he noticed that it was different. There was another room there now with a chair, a table, and a TV. Luther knew this room wasn't there before. He was positive of that. He thought maybe he should go back to bed and try waking up again, realizing this must be a strange dream. A very strange dream, indeed.

But rather than going to bed, he felt pulled toward the nearby chair. He went over to it and sat down. This was by far the most comfortable chair he had ever sat in. The room was like a small living room. There was this great chair with the TV across from it and the table with the lamp on it. This room was also painted sky blue. They must have had a sale on blue paint at the hardware store, he thought, since everything was painted blue.

Henry

Luther noticed the pretty girl was standing by the table. *Now how did she get here? I thought she left.* Her name was Marianna; he remembered now. *See, I'm not totally over the hill yet.* She smiled gently and informed him that someone would be there shortly. "Okay," he mumbled. She told him that before; he remembered. Once again, as quickly as she came into the room, she was gone. Maybe, when someone came, that is, if someone actually was going to come, he could find out just what was going on here and exactly where he was.

There was a remote on the table next to the chair. Assuming that this was for the TV, he pressed a button near the top. After several attempts, the TV came to life. There were clouds floating all over the screen. Nothing else. There were two other buttons on the remote, an arrow pointing up and an arrow pointing down. He pressed the up arrow. Nothing happened. He pressed the down arrow. Nothing happened.

"Wonderful," he grumbled. "Of all the rooms in this whole place, I had to get the one with a TV that doesn't work and no way to contact anyone to complain about it. There isn't even a phone in the room."

Then, all of a sudden, a picture appeared. The word MENU scrolled on the screen in giant letters. *Okay,* he thought, *now we're getting somewhere, as long as this isn't a computer or something.* He had tried a computer some time ago and didn't have much success. Surely, this had to be easier.

He tried the arrow buttons again and this time a page appeared on the screen. It was a picture of a dining room with many, many tables. The room was very elegant. All the tables were covered with a heavy linen tablecloth and napkins at each place setting. Fresh flowers adorned each table. Each tablecloth was a different color. Luther didn't think it was possible to come up with so many different colors, but there they were, colors other than sky blue. A nice change. Some of the tables had four chairs, others had two, and a handful had only one chair. Luther wondered what that was all about. Did it mean that if you were bad, you were banished to a solitary table? Would that person have to sit by themselves? Hopefully he would soon find out—sooner rather than later, he hoped, because now he was getting hungry. He couldn't remember when he last ate or what he had to eat. Luther loved food; he was ready to try this place out.

Luther was startled by a loud rapping on the door. "Huh," he muttered. "Guess I fell asleep. Must be those fluffy clouds floating by on the TV screen." Luther swore they did something to you; they were mesmerizing.

Luther shuffled to the door and opened it slowly. This time, an older man came in.

"Hello, Luther. Welcome," he said. "It's nice to have you here. My name is Henry and I'm here to escort you to the dining room."

Henry was very tall and slender. He wore what Luther thought was a butler's suit. He was bald on the top of his head, with tufts of gray above his ears and around the back. He had a dimple in his chin, but was clean-shaven.

Luther looked at Henry wondering if there was something familiar about him. He didn't think so. In desperation, Luther asked, "So, Henry, please tell me where I am."

"Why, Luther, I thought Marianna told you. This is your home."

"Sure, Marianna. Yeah, she did," Luther replied. "But where exactly is this home?"

"These are things you will learn all in due time. For now just enjoy yourself. Follow me. It's time for our evening meal."

"Evening meal? But I just woke up. How can it be evening already?" Luther was puzzled. "So tell me, Henry, am I dead? Is this the hereafter? Weird things have been happening and I really want to know."

"As I said, Luther, you will find out everything you need to know when the time is right. All in due time, Luther, all in due time. For now are you hungry? The food here is fantastic."

Before Luther could say anything more, Henry was leading him out the door.

"Wait," Luther said. "How will I find my way back to this room? All these doors look alike. I won't know where I am."

"There are no two rooms alike, although there are many dwellings in our Father's house. Don't worry, you won't get lost." Luther wasn't too sure about that. Maybe the interiors were different, but the outside doors were all the same. Luther was beginning to worry.

Once outside of his room, things looked much brighter. There were tiny lights all along the walkway. Was it evening? He couldn't really tell. People were walking in the same direction as Henry was leading him. Luther assumed they were all going to the dining room. Everyone was all dressed up. The men wore suits and ties and the women had on fancy dresses. He looked down at his clothes and noticed that he too had a suit on. He knew he didn't have that on earlier, and he didn't remember changing. Now how did that happen?

Soon they arrived at what looked like the dining room Luther had seen on his TV. People began sitting at the various tables. Henry led Luther to a table toward the back and against the far wall. It was a table for one.

"Surely I'm not going to sit by myself," he said, "not for my very first meal here." Henry helped Luther get seated and told him this would be his table for dinner. "Why do I have to sit by myself? There are other tables with just one person. Couldn't we all sit together? How will I get to know anyone? I don't want to sit here." Luther pouted.

"All in due time, Luther, all in due time."

"Damn, that sure is a popular saying around here," Luther grunted. Luther figured he would have to find out who was in charge around here and make a few suggestions as to how to run things. Strange that no one else seemed concerned about this solitary seating arrangement.

The dining room was quite large. The tables were covered with tablecloths of varied colors, just like he saw on the TV. His tablecloth was bright orange. The flowers in the vase were vibrant poppies. He saw a pink tablecloth with pink roses and a green one with a flowery vine. There were open patio doors on the one side that looked out onto a garden. Obviously, this is where they grew the many flowers. Luther had never seen such a variety of flowers in his life. Soon a young man came by and asked him what he would like for his evening meal. Luther had no idea; no one had given him a menu.

The young man smiled and said, "You must be new here. We rarely have menus. You order whatever you want. So what are you hungry for tonight?"

"It's not possible for you to have every kind of food for every person in this room. What if I wanted something out of season, or something exotic and very unusual?"

"Not a problem, Mr. Yeager. Whatever you wish, I will have prepared as to your liking."

"Okay," Luther said. "I can play along with this. Well, for starters, how about a shrimp cocktail? Then I would like a big juicy steak, medium rare with lots of onions and mushrooms. And how about a baked potato covered with butter and sour cream. And a tossed salad with bleu cheese dressing. How does that sound?"

"Wonderful, sir. I will have it ready for you in no time at all."

And before Luther could even unfold his napkin, the entire meal was placed in front of him. *How did they get the steak grilled so quickly?* He wondered. *How was it possible for everyone to have their meals made-to-order?* The service here was fast, way too fast.

Luther practically inhaled the shrimp cocktail. It tasted wonderful. Then he cut into the steak with his knife and it seemed to melt away like butter. He took a bite. This, he thought, was possibly the very best steak he had ever eaten. He finished off his meal with a piece of apple pie topped with a big scoop of vanilla ice cream. When he first entered the dining room, he didn't think he was very hungry, but when the food arrived, he devoured it like someone who hadn't eaten for a year. The meal was fantastic. Luther hadn't had a steak this tender or potatoes with so much butter and a salad with unlimited dressing for too far back to remember. The doctor said he could no longer eat that way because of his cholesterol. He wondered what his doctor would have to say now. Luther would probably catch hell the next time he saw him. He didn't care; it was worth it. He grinned as he took that one last bite of his apple pie.

When Luther finished eating, Henry stopped by and told him he would now escort him back to his room. Luther tried to remember the various turns they had taken, but he was totally lost in no time. He didn't even realize that they were going an entirely different way until they arrived in front of his door, coming from the opposite direction. He was sure Henry was trying to trick him.

Once back in his room, Henry told Luther that he should get ready for bed because tomorrow would be a busy day. Luther felt as if he had just gotten up, but obviously he was wrong. He had hoped to wander through the gardens or sit on those chairs outside, but Henry was gone and Luther believed there was no chance of finding his room again without him. How did he do that? Show up and disappear. He definitely was a strange fellow.

He went into the bathroom and found a pair of pajamas neatly folded, sitting on a small stool next to the shower. There also was a towel, washcloth, a bar of soap, and a toothbrush. He stepped into the shower and the water came on automatically. The temperature was perfect. It was the most refreshing shower he ever had. After he dried off with the big white fluffy towel, he put on his new pajamas and brushed his teeth.

Luther didn't really feel tired even though Henry had told him to get ready for bed. He actually felt invigorated and full of energy. He sat down in the chair and turned on the TV. This time, a picture of his bedroom appeared on the screen, with the same crazy clouds floating around. He guessed there would be no watching TV tonight. He tried to get the remote to do something else, but it didn't move. Obviously, it was bedtime whether he wanted it or not.

Suddenly, he felt very tired and went into the bedroom. The comforter on his bed had been turned down. He crawled into bed, and before he even knew it, he was in a deep sleep.

George

Morning came and Luther woke up feeling exceptionally good. He didn't know what or where this place was, but he felt like he was thirty again. He looked around the room, trying to become familiar with it. He remembered his room in the nursing home. It was very nice and he felt safe there. He felt safe in this new room too. It was just all so confusing. He wanted to remember his life. There were times when he felt he remembered something, but most of the time, it was a blur.

Luther noticed some clothes on the chair—a pair of pants, a shirt, underwear, shoes, and socks. He assumed he was expected to wear them today. But how did they get there? He didn't remember seeing them there the night before. This place was strange. He hoped he would get answers to his questions today. Henry had said today would be a busy day. *What was that all about?* he wondered.

Luther had just finished putting on his shoes when he heard a loud knock at his door. Henry walked in carrying a large tray of food.

"Good morning, Luther. I trust you had a pleasant night's sleep?"

"I slept like a baby," Luther replied. "I remember getting into bed, and the next thing I knew, it was morning. Henry, tell me what's going on around here? Where am I? And why is it that I feel so much younger?"

"Luther, I know you have lots of questions and I think today you will get some answers. But first you must have breakfast. I brought ham, bacon, eggs, home fries, toast, and coffee. Two sugars, right?"

"Sounds great, but I'm not allowed to eat that kind of food anymore. My doctor wouldn't be very happy hearing about the meals here. And how do you know what I take in my coffee?"

"Luther, one of the advantages of living here is that there are no restrictions as to what we can eat."

"Really!" Luther exclaimed. "So why are we eating breakfast in my room? Can't we go to that nice dining room?"

"I thought today we would save some time and eat here. By the way, how do you like your room?"

"My room is very nice, but this isn't the nursing home where I used to live. Just tell me where I am. This is all so confusing."

"All in due time, Luther, all in due time." Luther just rolled his eyes.

Breakfast was finished and Luther was amazed that he just had another fantastic meal. Between last night's steak and the breakfast today, he couldn't remember ever eating meals so delicious. They were awesome! Whatever this place was, he was glad to be here.

"Okay, Luther, it's time for you to meet George."

"George? Who's George?" Luther asked.

"Come with me. We don't want to keep him waiting."

When Henry opened the door from Luther's room, there was a golf cart sitting outside. The scenery and surroundings looked totally different from yesterday. There now was a lake nearby and mountains in the background. Luther wanted to ask Henry about the change in scenery, but didn't. He had seen the look on Henry's face and knew the only answer he was going to get—"All in due time."

Henry drove the golf cart around the lake. It was so beautiful. The water shimmered with ripples from the reflection of the sun. They drove around a golf course where people were already playing. Luther loved golf and he thought he remembered learning how to play. He didn't think he was very good, but he was sure he enjoyed being out where the action was. Luther would have loved to be out there among all those golfers. Maybe he would be able to eventually. But first things first. He had to meet this George, whoever he was. Someone in charge, perhaps someone with quite a bit of authority.

After about a ten-minute drive, they stopped in front of a large office building. There were quite a few golf carts parked in front. Luther didn't notice any cars, so maybe golf carts were all that was needed. Henry parked in the designated area and led Luther into the building. There was a large lobby with elaborate walls. They looked as if they were made of gold. And the floor was marble or granite. He wondered what this place had cost to put together.

"This way, Luther. George's office is right down this hall."

Luther couldn't get over all that he was seeing. The carpet was very plush and the hallways were lined with famous paintings. They soon came to a door with the number 1 on it.

Henry opened it and they walked in. There was a door on the opposite wall that was closed. Henry and Luther sat down on the only two chairs in the room. Luther wanted to ask Henry many questions, but he was too much in awe to open his mouth.

After a short wait, the door opened and out walked a man who Luther assumed must be George. He was very tall with long light brown hair that waved slightly around his ears. His eyes were a deep, piercing blue. He looked to be in his late thirties or early forties. He wore navy blue pants, a white shirt, and a sports coat. No tie. He had a pair of glasses on a chain around his neck. He looked over at Henry and Luther. He smiled, showing very white straight teeth.

"Ah, Henry, so good to see you again," he said as they shook hands. "And you must be Luther. So nice to meet you. I am George." Luther took George's extended right hand and noticed he had a firm handshake. Luther liked that in a man. "Please come in. Let's sit on the sofa and get acquainted. Henry, I'll call you when we are finished."

"Yes, sir," said Henry. "See you later, Luther."

Luther followed George across the room and sat on the sofa, as indicated. It was very comfortable. He sank easily into the plush cushions. George sat on the chair opposite him with a coffee table between them. A side table had a bouquet of flowers in an oriental vase.

George said, "Luther, I am sure you have been wondering what is going on here. Let me assure you that this is all very natural, very real. All of our guests feel this way when they first arrive and now they can't imagine living anywhere else."

"George, will you answer me one question, please? Am I dead?" he stuttered. "Is this heaven?" he asked in a soft, shaky voice. As nice as it was to be here and as good as he felt, Luther was afraid what the answer would be.

George crossed his right leg over his left and sat back in the chair. He seemed to be contemplating what to say. After what seemed an eternity, he looked over at Luther and smiled. "Interesting question, Luther. What makes you think this is heaven?"

Luther wondered if George was avoiding the question, or wasn't sure how to answer it. A simple yes or no would do. He hoped he wouldn't get the answer that Henry always gave him—all in due time.

Luther finally spoke. "It's very confusing. I feel like I'm thirty but I know I'm ninety-three. I was in a nursing home. I know they thought I didn't understand anything they said, but actually I heard everything, and most of the time, I knew what they were talking about. I don't remember much of anything before being in the home though. I thought I would live there for the rest of my life. But suddenly, I am here and things seem to happen like magic. The food is wonderful and it's prepared in seconds. The scenery changes every time I go outside my door. I don't know what to think, unless I've really lost my mind and I'm daydreaming all this."

"Luther, you have good observation skills, I will tell you that. Your physical body has reached the end of its life, the life you lived on earth. I don't like to use the word died or any terminology associated with death. Here we don't think about whether we are alive or dead. We live here eternally in our Father's house. This is one of many sections here, the place you come to first after your life on earth has ended. Some people stay here for all of eternity. Others move on to other areas. Everyone comes here when their earthly life is over. It is here that we evaluate one's previous life. There are challenges here that must be met and questions about decisions you made in your lifetime that must be answered. For many people, this is a wonderful reenactment of their lives. For others, it is heartbreaking and awkward.

"Luther, this may all seem very confusing to you, but I can assure you that in time you will understand. You are new here, and it will take time. We don't age here, nor are we any particular age. We are not the age we were when we left our earthly life. You will have the opportunity to see friends and family who may see you as they remember you. You too, Luther, may see individuals from your past as you remember them. Time here is irrelevant. Did you notice that there are no clocks or calendars? Here, life is perfect. We get the proper amount of food, sleep, activity, and sustenance that is needed."

Luther was stunned. Without really answering the question directly, George said he was dead, even though he didn't like to use that term. Now he had come to heaven even though George actually never used that word either. So Luther just assumed that heaven was where he was. How had his life ended? What would he learn about his earthly life? He guessed he was going to find out, but it all seemed a little scary and uncertain.

Luther pondered. So if George was in charge, did that make him God? And if he was God, why did he go by the name George? He decided to ask. What did it matter? If this was a dream, he would wake up at some point. If all this was real, he had no choice but to follow along.

"So, George, if this place is heaven, then are you God? Or maybe...Jesus?" Luther was surprised at his boldness.

A funny grim came on George's face as he said, "Luther, I am many things to everyone here, but you only need to know me as George. If you choose to believe that I am God or Jesus, that is your prerogative. I will tell you this, we are going to be spending a lot of time together. Your life was quite interesting. You will learn a great deal about yourself and the meaning of the life you lived on earth. There are going to be things that we discuss and look at that you will not like. Some things you will have to explain and answer to. Some of these things will be relatively easy. Others will be painfully difficult."

"Am I going to remember my past, my childhood, my parents, and other family that I must have had? Everything?"

"Yes, Luther, everything. Before we are finished, you will know your entire life even better than you actually lived it. We will begin our work together soon. I will have Henry bring you to me when it is time to begin. In the meantime, there are activities here that you may want to participate in. Anything you can imagine is possible here. Henry will tell you all about them. So, for now, do you have any other questions before you leave?"

"Well, yeah. I was trying to adjust the TV in my room and it didn't seem to be working. Could it be broken? And I ate supper last night at a table by myself. Can I sit with others? I want to meet people here and make friends."

"I could suggest that you be assigned a dinner companion. I will look into that. As to your TV, I assure you that it is working as it should. Now, Luther, Henry is outside waiting for you. Please enjoy your time here and I will see you soon."

And with that, George was out of the chair and opening the door for Luther to leave. Henry was already outside waiting. How did George contact him? He said he would, but Luther never saw him press any buttons or anything. Another mystery. Luther walked out more confused than he could ever imagine. He wondered if they had a bar at this place. He really could use a good stiff drink.

Joe

"So, Luther," Henry began, "you seem confused. I know this is all very different and new to you. I've been in your shoes. My advice is to just take things one day at a time. Enjoy the things that you can do here and let the rest take care of itself."

"Henry, this George mentioned things to do. Maybe if I kept myself busy, I wouldn't think about all this and try to understand it all right now. What do you think?"

"That may be an excellent way to look at it. There are many things to do. I know you were looking at the golf course we passed. Did you play golf?"

"I used to but I wasn't very good at it. At least I think I played. What else is there to do?"

"Luther, from what I know about you, I believe you would enjoy the golf here. There is also bowling, and in the evenings, we have a variety of card games. Pinochle was your game, I believe. There are several swimming pools and tennis courts too. When we get back to your room, I'll show you how to find the schedule of activities. Right now, it is lunchtime and I have a surprise for you."

Suddenly, Henry made a sharp turn to the left and they entered a beautiful garden. There were tables set up all along a patio around a big pool. Henry led Luther to a table near a rosebush with the largest roses Luther had ever seen. The table was set for two and he told Luther he would be having lunch there. Luther felt good seeing the two chairs, assuming he would have a lunch companion. Having someone to talk to and see what they had to say about this place would be great. Just then, a man came over and Henry introduced him to Luther.

"Luther this is Joe and he will be your lunch partner today. I'll see you back to your room after lunch."

There was something familiar about this Joe. Luther was trying to recall how he could have known him. Joe was smiling and said to Luther, "Hey, good to see you. Glad we're having lunch together. It's been a long time. I doubt if you remember me." Joe was a tall man, over six feet; he had gray hair with some traces of his original coal black hair. He wore dark horn-rimmed glasses, jeans, and a T-shirt. *A casual guy*, thought Luther.

"You look familiar, but where or how would I know you? I just got here and I don't know too many people."

"Well," grinned Joe. "It's this way. It don't matter when you get here because there will always be someone you knew. You and me, we used to work together at Gallagher's Plastic. We worked under Frank Banner. Remember him? He was our lead man on the 12–8 shift. When he left, we both went up for his job and I got it. You were madder than a hornet when you found out. You were so mad you went to the big boss, Ray Miller, and told him I was stealing money out of the lunch slush fund. You even planted my lunch box nearby. You remember my lunch box, the one my kid made me with the horses on it? You made it really look like I did it. The boss was so mad he fired me on the spot and then you got the job. Ring any bells there, Shorty?"

Shorty? Why did he call me that? Then he remembered. It was the nickname the guys called him at Gallagher's because he was the shortest guy who worked there.

Oh no! It was Joe Wozneski! Luther wished he could slide right off the chair and hide behind the rosebush. He remembered everything that Joe said, and sadly, it was all true. He had really wanted that lead man job and felt he should have gotten it. When he heard that Joe got it, he was mad, really mad. He didn't think anyone knew about the lunch box he had moved. He lied to the boss when he was asked about it. Everyone thought Joe had a weak moment and had really stolen the money. Luther got the lead man position and Joe

21

was out the door. Luther didn't even feel bad about it. He was just happy that he got the job he felt he deserved. Now here he was, sitting across from Joe. Joe didn't seem to be mad about it.

"Look, Joe, I'm sorry about that. I don't know what else to say," Luther said, feeling about as low as anyone could feel.

"Hey, no problem, Shorty. I managed. When I went home that night and told my old lady that I got canned, she picked up the kid and walked out the door. Went to live with her parents. She said she wasn't going to live with a no good bum like me anymore. I didn't even get a chance to talk. I tried to find another job after that, but it wasn't easy. I was labeled a thief and no one wanted to hire me.

"Finally, I found work as a janitor in the paper factory. Took a hell of a pay cut. I hardly got to see my kid anymore because I couldn't afford to pay child support. The house we lived in was repossessed and sold, and I ended up living in one of those shelters for a while. Believe me, they ain't pretty. Rough group of characters there. Yeah, my life wasn't the same after that. It took me twenty years to get back on my feet again, and by that time, my kid was grown and didn't want anything to do with me. I tried to contact him once. But he hung up on me. Finally, I met Gail and she was an angel. She was the first person who treated me like I was a human being. She said I had a kind face and she knew I was a good person. She even believed me when I told her what happened at Gallagher's. I don't know why, but I sure was glad she did. She even got me a job at her dad's lumber company. We saved our money and were able to buy a little place. Lived there till I came here. Gail still lives there."

Luther was feeling sick; he wanted to get out and get out fast. When the waiter came by to take their orders, Luther said all he wanted was a glass of water. He wanted in the worst way for lunch to end so he could go back to his room. He never knew what had happened to Joe after he left the plastic plant. And now he knew that all that had happened was his fault. If he were Joe, he would have wanted to take a swing at him, but not Joe. He quickly got up and walked away as fast as he could. He hoped he would never run into Joe again.

Somehow, and he had no idea how, Luther found his way back to his room. Henry had told him this would happen, that he would just know. He hadn't even waited for Henry to show him the way. He was never so glad to get inside and sit down, away from everything and everybody.

Sitting alone in his room, Luther slowly began to remember everything about that incident with Joe. Luther felt sad for him, but it seemed Joe did okay. What a shame about his kid, though. He should have, at least, listened to his dad's side of the story.

Suddenly, the TV went on, scaring Luther. There was George, front and center on the screen.

"Hello, Luther. I heard you aren't feeling well. What seems to be the problem? I thought you would have enjoyed lunch today since you had someone to eat with. Joe did show up, didn't he?"

Luther was puzzled. How did George do this? How could he talk to him through the TV? Certainly no privacy in this place. "Yeah, he showed up and I'm sure you know all that happened. Why of all the people here did you pair me up with Joe for lunch today?"

Looking very serious, George said, "Yes, Luther, I know exactly who Joe is and what his relationship is to you. I also know that you remember the incident as if it happened today. Well, it was exactly forty years ago today, as a matter of fact. Do you remember? Joe remembers. It was on that day that his entire life changed. Unnecessarily changed, I might add. What you did that day was unspeakable. Luther, you need to analyze all of your actions while you lived on earth. You will have to answer for them before you can move on to the next phase of your journey here. This was your first one."

"I get you now. I have to…what's the words they use…atone for my sins. Is that it?"

"That could be one way of putting it. I am not going to dwell on this transgression. You did apologize to Joe and he accepted your apology. Perhaps this is a way of teaching you how your actions affected other people. You went on with your life as if nothing had happened. You got the job that was meant for Joe. In your defense, you did a decent job as lead man. However, Joe would have done a better job. Think about that. But enough of this. I think you realize the mistake you made and have atoned for it. I will see you in my office tomorrow morning after breakfast. Henry will bring you. After tomorrow, I expect you to be able to come on your own whenever you are summoned. Have a good rest of the day, Luther. Until tomorrow." And with that the TV screen went blank.

Luther was beginning to figure out just what was to be expected of him. He simply had to atone for all the bad things he had done on earth. He couldn't remember much, so for now he had no idea how many sins there were. A lot? Surely George didn't expect perfect people to come here. No one was perfect. Well, maybe George. We were all sinners on earth. Luther began to feel a little better.

He decided that he would try to forget about Joe and go outside and walk around. He spent the remainder of the day checking out the golf course, the tennis court, and the swimming pools. He ended up at the bowling alley where someone challenged him to a game. He eagerly accepted.

Bertha

Luther ate breakfast alone the next morning, much to his delight. Although he would have liked to have someone to talk to, he didn't want it to be Joe or anyone else from his past that he might have had a problem with.

After breakfast, Henry took him to George's office. This time, the door was open. Luther walked in and found George sitting on the arm chair, close to a window.

"Is it all right if I come in now, George?"

"Ah, Luther, come in. I have been expecting you. I hope you had a pleasant night. I understand you went bowling yesterday and did rather well."

"Yes, George, I did. It was fun."

"Now, Luther, let's get down to work. I am going to take you on a journey through your childhood. As we proceed, you will begin to remember certain things. This is okay. It is what is supposed to happen. You will eventually remember all the events of your life."

George walked over to an opening in the ceiling in the far corner of the room and pulled down a screen. He pushed a button and the lights went out and the curtains closed. Soon images began to appear on the screen. There was a couple sitting on a sofa surrounded by children. The woman was holding a baby.

"Luther, do you recognize any of these people?"

Luther stared at the screen and looked at the face of each person. Suddenly, he knew this was his family and that he was the baby in the woman's arms. *That must be my mother*, he thought.

"These are my parents and my sisters and brothers, right?"

"That is correct," said George. "You were born on March 6, 1919, to Bertha and Warren Yeager. You were the youngest of their seven children. This picture shows a happy family, but as you will soon learn, it was far from that. Your mother was very unhappy. She was tired of having children. Your oldest sister, Mildred, was already married and living away from home, with a child of her own. Your next oldest sister, Marion, was engaged to a very nice young man named Earl. They were planning on marrying that summer.

"Elizabeth was living away from home with a family she worked for. The mother was a professor at the local college and had hired Elizabeth to watch her children. Doug and Marge were in school and Gerald was two years old when you were born."

As the story unfolded on the screen, Luther learned about his parents and siblings.

*****

Bertha tried to take care of her two young boys, but she became more and more bitter with each diaper she had to change. She was terrified of Warren. Quite often, he would stop at the local bar on the way home from work and would be drunk when he stumbled into the house.

When all the children were in bed, he wanted to have his way with her. Bertha resisted as she was afraid it would result in yet another unwanted pregnancy. She did her best to stay away from Warren, but most of the time, she was unsuccessful. Warren's reasons for drinking were to forget a miserable homelife. He had a wife he knew hated him and detested taking care of all the children. The older children were easier to handle, but when the babies needed attention, she just went crazy, yelling and screaming. Warren wanted to avoid all of that as much as possible and he found comfort at the local bar.

It was an endless cycle in the Yeager household until Bertha found a friend in the next-door neighbor, Horace Hinderfield. Horace was a wealthy man who made his money in banking and was also an attorney. Not all of his banking was, shall we say, on the up and up, but he was very careful to avoid being caught with anything that would be incriminating against him. He was a shrewd attorney with a good law firm. Horace was married, but his wife lived in another part of town. It was an unusual arrangement, but it seemed to be what they both wanted; it seemed to work. Mrs. Hinderfield was happy with this as long as she had a hefty allowance dropped off at her residence each week. Horace was only too happy to oblige.

Horace often heard arguing and yelling in the house attached to his. He sensed that the lady of the house was unhappy. One day, as Bertha was hanging laundry on the outside wash line, he came out on the back porch and watched her. Unknown to her that he was even home at the time, she hung the laundry singing just under her breath. The older children were in school and her young boys were taking a nap.

Horace thought Bertha was very attractive. To get her attention, he cleared his throat a few times. Bertha jumped when she realized she was not alone in the backyard. Horace immediately apologized for startling her. He asked if she would like to join him on his porch for a lemonade. At first, Bertha refused, knowing that it would not be very ladylike to have any kind of drink with a strange man when her husband wasn't around. But Horace was very persuasive and insisted since it was a warm spring day and she looked exhausted.

Bertha finally decided to accept his offer and for the next hour found herself sitting on her neighbor's porch. She was enjoying a lemonade and intelligent conversation for a change, not the usual baby talk she had to listen to every day. She didn't realize how long she had been sitting there until young Gerald appeared at the back door calling for her. Startled, she looked up and realized that he must have crawled out of bed by himself and had somehow managed to get down the steps without falling. She quickly excused herself and went back into her house. She realized and knew, all too well, that she had to go back to her humdrum life, in her house, with children and with Warren.

Bertha didn't tell Warren about her afternoon with the neighbor when he came home that night. She didn't want to disrupt his good mood. For once, he had come home right after work without stopping at the bar. Bertha had made pot roast for dinner and the family sat and enjoyed a peaceful evening meal together. This was so unusual that Bertha actually found it refreshing, relaxing. The older children, sensing a calm atmosphere in the household, shared stories about their day at school. Marion was home that night, not having a date with Earl. After the meal, Marion helped clean up and do the dishes so Bertha could tend to her two young boys. Bertha silently wished every evening could be this calm, this pleasant, but she knew it was too good to be true.

That evening when Bertha and Warren went to bed, he rolled over, gave her a kiss, and said good night. *Thank goodness*, she thought. Bertha had a hard time falling asleep, however, as she recapped the events of the afternoon and evening. Exhaustion finally took over and she slept.

The next morning, she said goodbye to her husband and older children and sat down with her second cup of coffee. She was day-dreaming of sitting on the porch and sipping a cool lemonade with Horace. She thought back to the wonderful evening with her family. Somehow, the two scenes were running together and she felt torn at the thought of being that happy all the time. She was soon brought back to reality when her youngest started crying. It was back to the real world, she thought, as she climbed the stairs.

Throughout the day, Bertha found herself looking out the back door and toward the neighbor's porch. She was hoping to see Horace again. She wanted to thank him for the wonderful afternoon the day before, but she never saw him. Suddenly, she had an idea. She would bake a cake for her family and she would make an extra one for him. After all, there was nothing wrong with that. She was just being neighborly and obviously there wasn't a Mrs. Hinderfield to bake any cakes.

After the cakes were baked and iced, she wrapped the smaller one in foil and tied a bow around it. When the boys went upstairs for their nap, she took the cake to Horace. She hoped that he would be home, but if not, she would leave it between the doors.

Bertha combed her hair and took off her apron. She wanted to be sure she looked nice. She took the cake and knocked on Horace's back door. There was no answer. She knocked a little louder. After a few minutes, she realized that he wasn't home. She placed the cake between his back doors. She was disappointed that she didn't get to see him again, but she hoped he would find a way to thank her.

An entire week went by and she never saw or heard from Horace. Life in the Yeager household returned to the normal routine of kids, Bertha yelling, and Warren coming home drunk. Bertha pined even more for Horace. She wondered where he was, what he was doing, and why he hadn't contacted her.

She decided to look between the doors to see if he had taken the cake. She was horrified to find it still there. No wonder she hadn't heard from him. He wasn't home. She hoped he was all right and hadn't been injured and in the hospital, or something even more serious. She had no way of contacting him. She took the cake out from between the doors and threw it in the trash. Suddenly, she felt so alone, so hopeless, and so helpless.

Another week went by. By then, Bertha had given up on ever seeing her neighbor again. She knew he was there at times, because she would hear a radio playing through the thin walls in the living room. Unfortunately, the sounds were in the evening when Warren was home and she couldn't venture out.

She asked Warren one evening if he knew anything about the neighbor. He told her his name and that he was a lawyer. She already knew that. He told her that he travelled a lot with his job and wasn't around much. He also told her something she didn't want to hear. He said he had heard that he had a wife, but Warren didn't know where she was. He guessed that perhaps she was travelling on her own. Bertha didn't want to believe any of this. Horace was a wonderful person. If he had a wife, why wouldn't she want to be with him? But then she also wondered why Horace lived in the house next door if he was that wealthy. Yes, it was a clean neighborhood, but certainly not one that a wealthy person would want to live in. Perhaps it would be best if she just put him out of her mind altogether. But try as she could, she found that impossible. The dreams, both during the day and at night, were what was keeping her sane. They were all she had in life anymore. The rest was the never-ending housework, too many demanding children, and a drunken husband.

Bertha and Horace

"All right, Luther," George said. "I've told you a good bit about your mother and there is much more to tell. What are you thinking right now? Do you want me to go on or would you rather I stop?"

"Well, it sounds like my mother had a pretty rough life and that my father didn't treat her very well. I don't remember my mother at all. Please don't stop. I want to know as much as possible about my past."

"Okay, Luther, let's continue." And for the next several days, Luther met with George and was told more about his mother.

*****

A month passed before Bertha finally saw Horace again, walking toward his front door. She became so flustered she didn't know what to do. She wanted desperately to talk to him, but then, what would she say? She had to think fast because he was almost at the door.

She opened her door as if looking for the mail. She feigned surprise when their eyes met, as if she was just noticing him. "Hello," he said. "How are you today?" She said she was fine and that it was good to see him again. He told her he had been away on business and then had to visit an ailing relative in upstate New York. She told him she wanted to thank him for the lemonade and conversation they had several weeks before. He looked pleased and said they should do that more often. Bertha flushed and said that would be nice.

Horace let her know that he would be home the next afternoon. Perhaps she could find time for another lemonade? Bertha knew she would find time, somehow. They said goodbye with promises to meet the next day. Now Bertha once again had a spring in her step and a smile on her face. She couldn't wait until tomorrow. And then she'd ask him about Mrs. Hinderfield.

The rest of Bertha's day was like a dream. She imagined being alone with Horace, just the two of them, with no children, no dinners to fix, and no household chores. That night, Warren came home drunk as usual. He wanted Bertha close to him in bed. When she refused, he started hitting her. She fought back, wrestling his fists back to his side of the bed as best as she could and dodging when she couldn't, until he passed out. When she was sure he was asleep, she pulled the blankets over her head and muffled the sounds of her crying so her children wouldn't hear and finally fell asleep.

The next morning, she put her two youngest in their room to play, closed the door, and went into the bathroom for a soothing bubble bath. This was something she never did; she never had time for such luxuries. But today, she was going to make time. She had gotten up early that morning and made the evening meal so she would only have to warm it for dinner. She dabbed perfume behind each ear. She put on her best linen dress, one of the few she owned. She rarely wore them, mostly just to church.

She didn't dare linger too long in the bathtub because of the boys. She thought she could take the chance that they wouldn't get into too much trouble. When she was finished, she played a few games with them and fed them their favorite lunch while constantly checking the clock. She hoped to put them down for a nap around one. Then she could visit Horace. She figured with such a poorly constructed house with thin walls, she would hear them if they cried while she was next door, at least she hoped so.

It was almost two o'clock before the boys settled down for their naps. She tiptoed downstairs, walked out her back door, and knocked on Horace's. He opened immediately. He looked so handsome and elegant in his three-piece suit. He invited her in and asked her to join him in the parlor. The furniture was beautiful and looked expensive.

The upholstery was a fine, rich brocade in deep colors of blue. There was a marble table at the front window with a Tiffany lamp centered on it. Bertha felt as if she were in Buckingham Palace getting ready to meet the king. There was a side table with bottles of brandy and whiskey on it. Horace asked if she would care for a glass of sherry.

Oh my, she thought, *having a glass of alcohol in the middle of the afternoon. How daring!* She never thought of having any kind of an alcoholic drink at any time, especially with a man who was not her husband.

Horace told her that whenever he was home, he would often watch her as she hung the laundry in the backyard, or when she took her two little boys outside to play. He told her he thought she was the most beautiful woman he had ever seen. Bertha blushed; she was so flustered she almost dropped her glass of sherry. She had to say something; she had to regain her composure.

"Why, Mr. Hinderfield, I don't think Mrs. Hinderfield would think very kindly of you talking to another woman like that." She lowered her eyes; she couldn't look at him as she anxiously waited for his response.

Horace laughed and shook his head. He said he didn't think Mrs. Hinderfield cared what he said to anyone, man or woman. He told her that he had a loveless marriage to a woman who was very greedy. All she cared about was money and what she could buy with it. He told Bertha that she lived across town and that he rarely saw her. He wanted a divorce, but she wouldn't agree. Not that she loved him or wanted to remain married to him, she just didn't want the repercussions of what people would say about a divorced woman. He went on to tell her more about their marriage and his terrible wife.

Bertha felt so sorry for him. She wanted to comfort him; she wanted to tell him she understood. She decided to tell him the truth about her marriage, about Warren and how he would come home drunk at night and then demand to have his way with her. She said she had too many children and she felt overwhelmed. She told him that Warren made good money, but with what he spent at the bar, there was very little leftover to pay the household bills. She knew that wasn't necessarily true. Warren made good money, and although he did spend too much time and money at the bar, he made sure that the household bills were paid and that his wife and children had the things they needed.

Horace was horrified at what Bertha was telling him. He admitted there were times he could hear them arguing. Now he knew why. He reached out and touched her hand and said they were two lonely people trapped in unhappy marriages—a very sad situation. He said he would have loved to have children, but his wife didn't want to go through childbirth and have little brats, as she called them, running around and cutting into her socializing time.

Bertha thought Horace's wife sounded like a very spoiled and conceited person. Horace was better off living alone than to put up with all that. Bertha felt his hand on hers; it felt so warm and soothing. She knew she should pull it away, but she so longed for a kind touch from someone. She wanted the moment to go on forever and have time stand still, right then and there. She was with a man who was caring, handsome, wealthy, worldly, and wonderful.

Horace stood up and took Bertha's hand and pulled her to her feet. He wrapped his arms around her and kissed her ever so gently. Bertha wanted to run away and stay there all at the same time. She knew this was wrong, but it felt so wonderful. At that moment, she heard her youngest child crying and knew she had to leave. Quickly, she ran out the back door and into her own kitchen. Her face was flushed and her heart was racing so fast she was sure it was going to explode. She ran up the steps to the room the boys shared. Both boys were crying uncontrollably. She tried to calm them. Gerald told her that his baby brother woke up and was scared, so he stayed with him.

Something snapped in Bertha. She suddenly realized that she felt no love for either of these children. In fact, she found herself wanting nothing to do with them. In reality, she knew she had to, but it was a burdensome chore, not a joy. She would do what she had to do, but absolutely no more. She changed a diaper and took the boys downstairs and put them in their playpen. She gave each boy a cookie and went upstairs to change into her every day dull, drab dress. She sat down on the bed she shared with Warren and cried. She cried for the woman she was and the woman she now longed to be. She knew which woman she had to be and that was the most painful thing she could imagine. She wanted to run away, but there was nowhere to go. She would have to live with the memory of the touch of Horace's hand and his kiss as she faced her daily drudgery of a life with Warren and these children.

The Tap on the Wall

Bertha was thirty-seven years old and she felt ninety-seven. She married Warren when she was seventeen and had her first child a year later. She had known Warren her entire life. He was four years older than her and had lived around the corner. He was best friends with her brother, Daniel, and was often at their house. When he was there, he always made time to see if Bertha was around so he could say hi to her.

Warren was painfully shy, but when he was around Bertha, he felt different. Bertha was a beauty. She was just about five feet three inches tall and had the bluest eyes that could match the sky on a bright sunny day. She had light brown hair that she always wore in a braid down her back. She had dimples on both cheeks that really stood out when she smiled. It was that smile that had won Warren's heart. He knew he wanted to marry her from the first time he saw her, when he was nine and she was five.

Secretly, Bertha had a crush on Warren too. He was older and more mature than the boys in her school class. She loved it when he came over to the house to see Daniel. She never knew he felt the same way about her. One day when he was getting ready to walk in the door, Bertha was walking out and they ran right into each other. They were touching heart to heart and neither wanted to break apart. Bertha was sixteen and Warren was twenty. By now Warren had a good job at the oil refinery. Without even thinking twice about it, Warren asked Bertha if she would like to go for a soda one night after she got home from school. That was all it took. They were inseparable from then on.

They planned a wedding for the summer after her seventeenth birthday. They married in her parent's backyard with their families there to witness this happy occasion. Warren had been saving his money ever since he started working at the refinery and was able to secure a loan on a house on Fourth Street. This was his wedding present to his bride. Her parents helped furnish the house with excess things from their house, and along with some great deals at the local furniture company, they were ready to start their married life.

It was perfect. Bertha was now Mrs. Warren Yeager and she couldn't have been happier. Warren was married to the woman he had loved his whole life and they were starting a new life together. Within two months of their wedding, Bertha realized that she was pregnant. Both she and Warren were so excited, perhaps Bertha a little more than Warren, for he was hoping to have a little more time alone with his new bride before sharing her with children.

When Mildred was born, Warren's heart immediately melted. He now had two beautiful girls in his life to love. Bertha loved being a mother and life was good. By the time Mildred was three months old, Bertha discovered she was pregnant again, another girl Marion, then another girl Elizabeth, and soon after a son Douglass. Before long, Margaret was born and Bertha was totally overwhelmed with children. She told Warren she wanted no more children as it was so much work to care for the five they already had. Warren agreed, but he just couldn't leave his beautiful wife alone. Bertha went through three more pregnancies, losing each one. She was advised not to have any more children for health reasons.

However, that was not to be. Gerald was born two years later, followed by Luther two years after that. There were now seven children in the family. There was constant chaos. The older children were always being asked to help out with the younger ones. They, of course, resented this, but usually did as they were told. By the time Luther was born, Mildred was married and had an infant son of her own. Bertha didn't have time to help Mildred with her child because she was too busy taking care of her own children.

*****

A week after Bertha had that small glass of sherry with Horace, they became lovers. She would sneak over to his house whenever the opportunity arose. Horace found himself working from home more and more during the week, or at least that is what he told them at his law office. Bertha lived for the afternoons she could spend with him.

She wasn't home one day when Marge and Doug came home from school. They walked in the house and heard their little brother crying upstairs. At first, they thought their mother was with him, but when the crying continued, they called for her, but there was no answer. They went upstairs to calm him, wondering where their mother could be. Gerald told them she wasn't home. Just then they heard the back door close. Bertha was home. She had lost all sense of time with Horace and didn't realize how late it was. She was flustered when they asked where she had been. She told them she was next door helping the neighbor. She said he had tried to bake a pie and it spilled out all over the oven and started a fire. He had come knocking on her door to ask what to do. It seemed like a reasonable excuse. She made a mental note to be more careful of her time in the future.

One day, Marion did not go to work at the local department store in town. She told her mother she was ill and was staying home. Bertha had planned on being with Horace that day and knew now she wouldn't be able to. About two in the afternoon, there was a tapping on the living room wall. This wall adjoined the wall in Horace's living room. Marion heard it and wondered what it was. Bertha knew all too well it was the signal for her to go over. Horace always tapped on the wall to let her know he was finished with his work. Bertha said she had no idea. Before Bertha could stop her, Marion, in her pajamas and robe, went out the front door and knocked on Horace's door. He yelled to come in because the door was unlocked. He didn't turn around in time to see that it was Marion and not Bertha before asking why she was coming in the front door when she always came in the back. Needless to say, it was an awkward moment for both of them when he realized who was now standing in his living room. Marion had suspected something was going on and now she was certain of it. She went home to confront her mother. Bertha said she had no idea what had just happened, but guilt was all over her face.

The following week, Horace and Bertha realized they would have to do something about their situation, because neither of them could continue keeping the relationship a secret. They were both going to get a divorce so they could be together. Bertha knew as soon as she told Warren she wanted a divorce, she would have to leave. Horace was going to tell Amelia, his wife, and he didn't care what she said. He was going through with the divorce even if he had to pay her a fortune. They decided that if a divorce wasn't possible, they would leave town, go as far away as possible, and just live together.

Bertha decided to tell Warren the following night. Everything went wrong. When he came home from the bar drunk, he started hitting her. She took a frying pan from the kitchen and hit him on the head with it. She wasn't even thinking that it could have killed him; she just wanted him to stop. Fortunately for her, he passed out in a drunken stupor on the kitchen floor.

Early the next morning, Bertha woke Marion and asked her if she would call in sick again so she could watch her two younger brothers. Bertha was adamant despite Marion's protests about getting fired if she missed another day of work. Bertha then woke up Doug and Marge and told them they were going away with her. Since Horace wanted to have children, they decided they would take Marge and Doug with them. Bertha had already packed a suitcase with some of their things and a suitcase for herself. Horace told her not to worry about taking much for either herself or the children because he would buy them all new things when they were settled somewhere.

Marion

"Well, Luther," sighed George. "I do believe this is enough for today. We have met every day for the past week and I have told you about your mother. There is much more to tell you about her, your father, and your early life. We also need to discuss other parts of your past."

"George, if it's all the same to you, I would really like to continue. I need to know these things."

"Yes, you do, but no more for today. In fact, I would like you to go out and have fun. There are so many things that you can do here. I want you to try and not think too much about all of this. You will need to process it in your mind, but give it time to settle. And since there is more to the story, don't try and reach any conclusions until you hear everything. We will meet again in a day or two."

Luther found himself out of George's office before he even realized he had gotten off the sofa. His head was swimming with all that he had been told. He definitely wanted to know more. He had the impression that since he was the youngest of all his brothers and sisters, obviously his parents were not alive and that perhaps they were here somewhere. He wanted desperately to see them and talk to them about the things he learned.

Back in his room, he sat in his chair and allowed George's words to fill his head. He was trying to figure out when all of this took place. George told him he was born in 1919, so his mother would have left sometime in the early 1920s. He didn't know how old he was when she left. Did she come back for him and Gerald? What about Elizabeth? Not much was mentioned about her. Come to think of it, there wasn't much mentioned about Mildred either. He knew she was married and had a son. Her son would be his nephew and would have been older than he was. That was strange. He was an uncle before he was even born.

He was trying so hard to imagine what his parents, brothers and sisters, and even his nephew looked like that he never heard his door open. Suddenly, he looked up to find a woman standing in the doorway. She looked familiar, but he wasn't sure who she was.

"Hello, Wayne."

"Hello," Luther said. She called him Wayne, the name from his childhood. "Who are you? Do I know you or, maybe I should say, how do you know me?"

"Wayne, I'm your sister Marion."

"Marion, my sister?" Luther felt every emotion possible hitting him all at the same time. "Come in and sit down. You called me Wayne. That's the name I used to go by. I've been Luther for so long I've forgotten."

"Wayne, stand up and give me a big hug. You always were and always will be Wayne to me. I know you started going by Luther after Millie died, but you're Wayne to me."

"Millie? Who is that?" Luther asked, trying hard to remember. *Was Marion referring to our sister, Mildred? Did we call her Millie?* Luther was getting frustrated and mad that he couldn't remember these things or remember who these people were.

"I guess you haven't gotten that far with George yet. Don't worry, you will."

"But I want to know now," Luther shouted in a demanding voice.

"You never did have any patience," Marion added throwing her hands in the air. "It was one of the things that used to annoy Millie so much. I guess you never changed. Wayne, come with me. I want to show you some things here that you haven't seen yet."

"Marion, if it's all the same, I don't want to walk around. I left George a little while ago and he was telling me about our mother. I wanted him to tell me more, but he said I will have to wait for another day. Tell me about her? I want to know now. And about

Millie too." Luther was almost shaking as he stood there, staring at Marion.

"Wayne, calm down. You always had a temper, and like I said, you were the most impatient man I ever knew. I used to think it would give you a stroke or something. I guess that didn't happen, though I can't figure out why. Daddy had a temper, but yours was worse than his. Mother had one too. I guess it's no wonder you have one. It was in your genes. Come on, let's walk. I'm not taking no for an answer."

Luther reluctantly started for the door with Marion following behind. If she wanted to walk, then they would walk. He was so confused and he wasn't getting answers to his questions from his sister.

Marion held his arm as they walked. It was good for them to be together again. Marion always felt more like his mother than his sister, and he remembered that feeling. Slowly, memories were coming back to him. He remembered a time when someone tucked him into bed and actually kissed him on the forehead. It was Marion. It was the only time he ever remembered having someone put him to bed.

They walked over a bridge and through a garden of vegetables where people were pulling weeds. Some were cutting off green beans and picking tomatoes. Luther guessed that it must be summertime since some of those crops were ready. He asked Marion about it and she started to laugh.

"My dear brother, here every day can be any season we desire. Today at this spot it is summer. Tomorrow if you walk this way it could be winter with people skiing down those hills over in the distance."

Marion was short and stocky. Her once brown hair was now showing more gray than brown. She had a pair of glasses hanging from a sash around her neck. Her complexion was ruddy as if she had worked outside most of her life in all kinds of weather. She wore a wedding and engagement ring on her left hand. On her right hand, she wore a large ruby ring. Her fingers were on the chubby side and chapped. She had earring hoops in each ear with a tiny ruby at the end closest to her lobe. She walked with a slight limp. It didn't seem to slow her down though.

41

They walked in silence just enjoying each other. It had been many years since they had been together. Finally, Marion stopped and asked, "Wayne, do you remember when you told me I was stupid and didn't need all the insurance policies I had?"

Luther was taken aback by her question. Of course, he had no recollection of saying that. "Marion, what are you talking about?"

"It happened one day when I came to visit you and Millie. I was still driving at the time and Millie invited me to come and go to a band concert. I was going to renew a life insurance policy and thought I would bring it along so you could look it over for me. I trusted your instinct, Millie's too. I wanted to make sure I was doing the right thing by renewing it or if I should just cancel it. You didn't even look at it. You said you didn't know why I had so many policies. You said it was just stupid and that if I had read everything these people talked me into buying, I would realize that I was just throwing good money down the drain. You were being rather nasty about it. Millie gave you one of those looks she was so good at giving and told you to settle down. You got mad and stormed out of the room. I didn't know what upset you so much. It was my money to do with what I wanted. I thought about going home right then and there, but Millie, God love her, told me she wanted me to stay. I was glad I did because we had a good time at the concert. When you came back, you acted like nothing had happened. I was hurt, but I got over it."

"Marion, I seem to have done or said things that I can't remember. George told me I have to face the things I did while I lived on earth and make amends for them. I can only say that I'm sorry. Now will you tell me who this Millie was? Was she my wife? And what happened to her? Is she here now? I would like to see her."

"Yes, Millie was your wife, but that's all I'm going to say. Let's keep walking. There's something I want you to see."

For the next twenty minutes, they walked in silence, commenting only on the beauty of a flower, the sound of a bird, or an unusual cloud formation. Luther kept wondering about Millie. He hoped he would see her. Finally, Marion stopped and told her brother to look over to the left.

Sitting on a park bench was a woman, all alone with her head down. She was looking at something that she was holding in her lap. It appeared to be a handkerchief.

"Wayne, do you see that woman over there?"

"Yes."

"She is our mother, Bertha."

The Exodus

Three days later, Luther found himself in George's office again. He had been summoned there by a message on the TV screen. He was anxious to go because he was hoping that George would continue to tell him more about his mother. He couldn't get over the image of her sitting on that park bench looking very sad. He wanted to go to her, after Marion told him who she was, but Marion said that couldn't happen. She didn't elaborate why.

"Luther, you are looking good today. How have you spent the past several days?"

"Well, I had three meals with a man named Harry. I don't think he was anyone I knew. He talked a lot about what he did for a living. He was a dentist and was very wealthy. He travelled all over the world. He introduced me to several people he knew and they were very wealthy too. One was a lawyer and the other owned his own business. I enjoyed being with them.

"I went to the bowling alley and made friends with some of the guys there. It was really noisy with balls rolling down lanes crashing into pins and shouts from bowlers excited about getting a strike or upset at yet another split. Joe and some guys from my old bowling team at Gallagher's were there. Joe had just rolled his third strike in a row and all his teammates were giving him high fives. He must have been having a good day. He always was a good bowler, but I had a higher average. I walked in the opposite direction so I wouldn't have to see them. I saw a couple of guys on lane 82 and they invited me to bowl with them. That was a lot of fun, and in one game, I had seven strikes in a row. That was better than Joe did. We bowled three games

44

and my high score was 273. The guys were nice and invited me to come back again. I think Joe and the other guys saw me, but I didn't want to talk to them."

*****

George smiled as he thought about Luther and Joe at the bowling alley. He had watched the event on his TV monitor. He was curious to see if there would be any interaction between Luther and his old teammates, especially Joe.

"Hey, guys, guess who's here?" Joe said to his friends. "Remember Shorty Yeager from productions level two? I had lunch with him last week. Well, I should say *I* had lunch. When Shorty realized it was me, he hightailed it out of there. I guess he suddenly remembered everything that happened. I don't hold no grudges anymore. Right? We ain't supposed to here. What happened, happened. Can't change it."

"No shit," said one of the other guys. "I haven't thought about him for what, fifty years. He got away with that one with you, Joe. We all really thought you stole the money. Couldn't believe it, but everything pointed to you. Shorty had a temper, I remember that. I guess he did a fair enough job as lead man as long as you watched what you said to him. I know when he retired, no one really missed him. Said he wanted to travel with the missus."

"Don't think they did much travelling," said Ronnie White. "I heard his wife was killed in a car accident a few months after he left the plant."

"Hey, can we get back to the game? Maybe we run into him and maybe we won't. Don't make no difference to me," added Larry.

*****

Luther continued to George. "And I met my sister, Marion. That was nice. I remember a little about her now. We went for a walk and it was nice being together. She took me to a park and pointed to a lady sitting on the bench. She said she was our mother. I wanted to

45

go and meet her, but Marion wouldn't let me. Now that I know she is here, do you think I can see her? I would like to talk to her."

"Very interesting, Luther. I took note of the order in which you told me the events of your days. I can only assume that they were in the order of importance to you. Meeting influential people who are wealthy is important to you, isn't it? It makes you feel important and people you would like to be with. Bowling was second and getting a higher score, beating your bowling friends. And last was seeing your sister. I am surprised, even though I shouldn't be, that your sister wasn't number one. The wealthy men you met were okay, but Marion is family. And I might add that right now she is the only family you have here, or at least the only family you now know. Luther, do you remember what your social status was? Were you wealthy? Did you have an important job such as these men you just met?"

George noted that Luther didn't seem to even notice when his order preference was pointed out to him.

"I worked in a plastics factory, and from what Joe told me, I was a lead man. I guess that didn't come anywhere near to being a dentist or business owner. I think I travelled and I would have had to have money to do that. Maybe I was just good at saving."

"Oh my, Luther, we have a long way to go here, but that will have to happen at a later time. We are concentrating on your early life now. Would you like me to continue telling you about your mother?"

"Yes, I would."

"When we left off, your mother had taken your sister Marge and your brother Doug and went away with the man who lived next door, Horace Hinderfield. She left behind her drunken husband, your father, sleeping on the kitchen floor and you and your brother Gerald. Marion was told not to go to work again so she could stay home and take care of you both. You and Gerald were, of course, too young to understand anything that was going on."

*****

Marion was furious with her mother. Where was she going with Marge and Doug? Why did they all have suitcases? She knew if she told her girlfriend Stella to tell her boss that she wouldn't be coming to work again, she would probably lose her job. But what else could she do? She couldn't leave the boys home alone. Her father was of no use still sleeping on the kitchen floor. How could he not hear all the noise in the house? Two little boys crying, Marge and Doug wanting to know what was going on, and Marion yelling at her mother.

Bertha stood her ground and told Marion that she was leaving and she was taking Marge and Doug with her. She said she had had enough of their father coming home drunk every night and she could not stand to change one more diaper or clean up one more spilled glass of milk. She wished Marion good luck in her upcoming marriage to Earl and hoped that she would have a good life. Bertha actually liked Earl and was glad that Marion had found a good man who would take care of her. As for her daughter, Mildred, she too had a good man and they seemed happy. Mildred was doing a good job as a wife and mother. Elizabeth was living with the Whitneys. They had offered her a room in their home with the understanding that she would help with some of the domestic work, but her primary duties would be to care for their children. Elizabeth seemed fine with this arrangement, and Bertha was happy to have one less child in the house.

It was just the two boys who needed constant care. Bertha knew Warren couldn't handle them, but she wasn't going to let that stand in her way of happiness. She had finally grasped the golden ring and nothing was going to stop her. Bertha knew Marion wouldn't abandon the boys and would probably take them to her home and raise them as her own. Earl was a farmer and could use two good farm hands as the boys grew older.

With her mind at ease, Bertha, Marge, and Doug walked out the door and into the car that was waiting at the curb. Marion knew right away who the car belonged to. She also knew that there was something going on with her mother and that man. Bertha used to tell Marion what a nice man he was and how she would make an extra dessert for him since he was all alone. Marion had asked her what she saw in Horace; her daddy was handsomer. Marion knew her mother was leaving all of them and going off with him. But why was she taking Marge and Doug with her? Were they her favorites? How could a mother leave two little children, one still in diapers? No decent mother did that. She guessed that answered her question.

As hard as it was to admit, Marion felt her mother was not a decent human being. Maybe they would all be better without her. But what about Daddy? He had to go to work every day just so he could pay the bills. She watched as Bertha, Marge, and Doug got in the car and drove away.

A New Life

Inside the car, Marge was crying and Doug was trying to make sense out of all the confusion. He wondered if they were being taken to school; if not, where were they going? And why were they going with Mr. Hinderfield from next door? And why did they have suitcases?

They drove for about an hour and finally stopped in front of a hotel. It was a grand place with Roman columns surrounding a beautiful open porch. People were rocking on chairs in the cool breeze. Hanging baskets with flowers hung from the roof. It was all so beautiful.

When they walked inside, a huge chandelier sparkled so brightly they had to look away as the brilliance almost blinded them. None of them, except for Horace, had ever been in such a grand place before. Maids were walking around with big feather dusters. The carpet was so plush that Marge took her shoes off to let her feet sink into it. Bertha reprimanded her and she quickly put her shoes back on. Horace was talking to a man at the front desk. The man looked over at Bertha and the children and frowned. Clearly, he felt the three of them were not the caliber of other guests at his hotel. Horace gave the man a stack of money and that seemed to be more than enough to change his attitude.

Soon they were ushered into an elevator and up they went, up and up to the very top floor. Marge and Doug had never been in an elevator before. It was both scary and exciting. They shut their eyes and held their breath.

When the door to their room was opened, the children cried out in delight. It was so big they were sure their entire house could have fitted inside. There was a huge fireplace between two massive windows that went from ceiling to floor. The curtains were a rich gold tapestry over white sheers. Several chairs and small tables surrounded the fireplace. But there were no beds. Where were they to sleep? Doug wondered. Just then, a maid came in with an armful of towels and asked if everything was satisfactory. Doug immediately asked where the beds were. The maid scowled at him, thinking a child should be seen and not heard. She told him they were in the bedrooms, of course. Where else would they be?

She opened a door on the left side of the room. It was another large room with two big beds. They had pretty bedcovers on them and each bed had a canopy. Marge had always dreamed of having a bed with a canopy. She was thrilled.

There was a bay window overlooking the street below. A huge dresser with a gilt mirror above it was against one wall. There was a wardrobe closet that had a funny smell. "What is that smell?" Doug asked. The maid saw their puzzled looks and pitied these uncivilized people. She mentioned that it was a cedar closet. That meant nothing to Marge and Doug, but it was obvious that Bertha was more than impressed with her surroundings. The maid asked if she could unpack their bags for them. Marge was about to say yes, getting into this fancy way of living, but Bertha quickly said that the children had to be responsible for their own things. And she added that she too preferred to put her things away. Actually, she didn't want the maid to see their ragged clothes. Horace had promised to buy them all new things, and she couldn't wait to get rid of the rags that were all she could afford on Warren's paycheck. Of course, if he hadn't spent so much money in the bar, they could have afforded better, but she didn't want to even think about that anymore.

Doug was still wondering where he was supposed to sleep. He figured this room was for his mother and sister, but surely, he wasn't expected to sleep in there. Before he had time to ask, the maid told him to follow her. She quickly led him to a room on the other side of the big room. This room was smaller, but still much bigger than the room he shared with his two younger brothers at home. He noticed that the bed did not have a canopy for which he was grateful. That would have been too sissified for him. The bed had a navy bedcover with two pillows. It actually looked like it should be a boy's room. It had a smaller dresser with a plain mirror. There was also a wardrobe closet. A window looked out onto the main street, but it wasn't as big as the one in the other bedroom. That was okay. Doug didn't mind. There was a desk with a lamp on it and Doug thought that would be a good place to do his homework. He was hoping they would be going to school. He actually liked school and enjoyed his studying. He wanted to go to college and had good enough grades, but he knew the opportunity would never happen because his parents didn't have enough money. Perhaps he could be lucky enough to get a scholarship somewhere.

Out in the big room, Bertha was dancing around like she was royalty. This was the life she always wanted and now she would have it. She knew she would have to talk to Marge and Doug and explain just what was happening. She was hoping Horace would join them soon so they could tell the children together. She wasn't sure what their reaction would be. She wanted to tell them in a way that they could understand it was all in their best interest.

*****

Horace and Bertha eventually divorced their spouses and married exactly one year and two days after they ran away together. Horace paid a great deal of money to his wife, and she finally agreed, saying she was planning on moving to Europe where no one knew her. Horace didn't care where she moved as long as she signed the divorce papers. Horace arranged for a lawyer to handle Bertha's divorce. Back then, it was more difficult for a woman to obtain a divorce, but as they say, with the right lawyer and enough money, anything was possible. Fortunately, Horace had both.

Marge and Doug were very confused at first, but being much like their mother, they were now enjoying the finer things in life. Things they could never even dream about suddenly became part of their everyday life. Bertha told them that their father was a drunk and that she was afraid he would come home one day and seriously harm her and possibly the children as well. Marge and Doug were aware that their father came home drunk. They knew their parents argued more nights than not. Concerned about their younger brothers, they questioned what was going to happen to them. Bertha assured them that Mildred and Marion were going to be taking care of them. But as far as their father was concerned, he could rot in hell. It was over.

The children now went by the name Hinderfield, telling everyone that their mother's new husband was their father. Bertha assumed the role of a widow whose husband had died in a horrendous traffic accident. Bertha told Marge and Doug it would make Horace immensely happy if they called him Papa. This they did, and by doing so, they were each given generous allowances. They were sent to an excellent private school and became friends with other children who lived as they now did.

After their marriage, Horace and Bertha moved into a grand Victorian house in the best part of town, fifty miles away from their old neighborhood. No one knew their past. Horace had a position at a prestigious law firm. His credentials were impeccable, and within five years, he became a senior partner. Doug and Marge were enjoying their school, new friends, and new lifestyle, and Bertha was living the life of her dreams.

Bertha enjoyed the privilege of having domestic help in her home. It gave her the freedom to go into town and shop in the finest stores. She slowly made friends and became active in the local garden club. Actually, she wasn't all that interested in anything that had to do with gardening, but it was a way to get into that sacred inner circle of the rich and elite.

Bertha, Horace, and the children attended the local Episcopal Church regularly and became one of the best contributors. Money was never an issue and Horace had been wise enough to save his money and didn't get caught up in the Depression.

When Doug graduated from high school, he was accepted into Harvard University to follow in his "father's" footsteps of becoming a lawyer. Upon Marge's graduation, she was accepted at a nursing school in Philadelphia. Both children now had bright futures ahead of them.

Bertha and Horace lived out their lives in their big home, eventually welcoming a daughter-in-law and then a son-in-law and three grandchildren. Bertha never gave one thought to Warren or her other five children. It was as if they had never existed. She had totally disowned them.

*****

George looked at Luther, knowing what he had just told him about his mother was something no child should ever hear.

"I know you have a lot to absorb right now. I want you to know I am always available if you need me. It is difficult to hear these things."

"I can't believe any mother could do that," Luther said, wiping tears from his face. "And so she went on to live the life of luxury, not caring what happened to the rest of us. George, what happened to my father after all this?"

"That is another story for another day. And we will get to that. It is important for you to know the other side of the story as well. It will help you here."

"Just what is this thing that I need to do?"

George rubbed his chin with his thumb and finger, wondering how to best answer that question. He knew Luther was going to have to answer to his own parental relationship with his child. He knew that right now Luther had no idea he even had a daughter and that many of the things his mother had done would be similar to the way he would treat her. They had to proceed carefully. But first, Luther needed to learn about his father.

"Luther, I will tell you this much. You will need to learn lessons from the behavior of your parents and that will help you here. I don't want to say anymore for now. Please trust me. I know that what has to happen will be painful, but you will not be alone. There is always someone here to talk to and help you make the right decisions so you can move forward. I'm sure you have a lot to think about now and that is exactly what I want you to do.

"You may feel hatred toward your mother and that would be a natural reaction after what I just told you. Try to go beyond that and see things from a different prospective. It may not seem possible now, but you will have to eventually forgive your mother and your father as well."

"How can I forgive a woman who did what she did? I told you I saw her in the park. Marion pointed her out to me. I want to see her and talk to her and hear her try to defend herself. I just don't know what to do. I don't understand."

"Luther, it is possible you will see her as you explore places here. If this should happen, I very strongly advise you not to tell her who you are. After all, she has a task of her own as well, and it may hinder her readiness to accept what she must do."

"I sure hope her task is to realize what she did and how she abandoned her children when they needed her the most—and all for money. They say money is the root of all evil and in her case that is very true."

"Luther, that is indeed a good saying, one that I want you to remember and heed. That very saying may help you with what you need to do. Now, if you have no further questions, I will let you go. I understand there is going to be a carnival near the ball field today and I believe you will enjoy that. Go and have some fun."

Luther said goodbye and walked out of the office. He wasn't sure he could have fun and still think about his mother. Damn that woman!

Krissy

Luther wasn't about to go to any carnival today. As much as he wanted to have fun, he didn't think there would be anyway he could just now. He just couldn't get it out of his head that his very own mother did the things she did. He was just about to walk into his room when he heard a noise coming from the other end of the hall. It sounded like a bike going really fast. He no sooner turned his head when he was almost run over by a little girl on a scooter.

"Hey there, little miss, slow down. Are you supposed to be riding that thing in the hallway here?"

"Sorry, mister. I'm going to the carnival and I took a shortcut through the hall. Please don't tell anyone I was inside or I'll get in trouble. Hey, are you going to the carnival?"

"No, I'm going to pass on that today. I don't really feel up to something like that. But you go and have a good time. Your secret's safe with me."

"Gee, thanks. Well, have a good day whatever you decide to do." And off she went down the hall.

She appeared to be about five years old. Funny, she was the first child he had seen since arriving here. Obviously children die too, but this little girl was the first little one he had seen.

Suddenly, she stopped riding and headed back the hallway. She stopped at Luther's door and knocked. When he opened the door, he was surprised to see her.

"I thought you were in a hurry to get to the carnival. What brings you back here?"

"Mister, it just wouldn't be right if you didn't go to the carnival, so I came back to ask if you would go with me. We can have lots of fun. I was there last year and it was super and they said it would be even more super this year. So come on. Let's go."

Luther started to protest, but saw the determined look on this little girl's face and knew it was a battle he would lose. Then he thought that maybe a carnival was just the thing he needed to take his mind off his mother. After all, George did say to have fun today.

"Okay. Okay," he said as she started pulling on his arm. "But we have to walk there. I don't have one of those contraptions to ride on."

"I guess we can do that. What's your name? Mine is Krissy and I'm six years old. How old are you?"

"Well, hello to you, Krissy. My name is Luther and I'm ninety-three years old."

Krissy was a pretty little girl with long brown hair. It was tied back in two ponytails. She had the largest brown eyes Luther had ever seen. She was wearing bright pink shorts and a T-shirt that had a panda bear on it and sandals without socks. She parked her scooter outside Luther's door and took his hand, and off they went to the carnival. Krissy was practically running and Luther had to jog some to keep up with her. Funny thing, he didn't seem out of breath. It felt funny to run again.

They talked on the way there. Krissy told Luther all the things that were at the carnival. They had all kinds of rides from Ferris wheels to merry-go-rounds and much, much more. And when she told him about the many different kinds of food there, his mouth started to water. He soon realized that he hadn't eaten anything since breakfast and that was several hours ago. Somehow, he just knew he was going to have a good time today and this little girl was going to be the reason.

When they arrived, Luther saw that everything Krissy had told him was true. There were all kinds of rides as far as the eye could see. There were food vendors everywhere. The day was perfect for a carnival. There were big white fluffy clouds in a sky as blue as can be. Luther didn't know what the temperature was, but it felt perfect.

They decided to each get a cheeseburger that was loaded with all kinds of goodies—lettuce, tomato, cheese, pickles, onions, and some kind of sauce that made it delicious. Krissy wanted French fries with hers. Luther wanted iced tea and Krissy got a soda. They found a blanket under a tree and sat down to enjoy their lunch. Krissy spread napkins down on the blanket and started devouring her food. Luther couldn't help but laugh because she soon had sauce all over her face and running down her chin. She took a napkin and wiped her mouth and then wiped some sauce from Luther's chin as well. He didn't even realize that the sauce had drizzled down his chin too.

Luther was curious about Krissy and wanted to know more about her. "So tell me, Krissy, how did you get to be here? I haven't seen any other children before, and as I look around, I see lots of kids here. Some around your age and some older."

"I don't really come to this side of heaven very often," Krissy said after she took a long swig of her soda. "I live on the other side, the one you go to when you are done talking to George and studying with him. I used to talk to George, but I didn't have to study anything. He's a very nice man, you know."

"Oh yes, he is and he is very smart too," said Luther.

Krissy looked off into the distance, watching the roller coaster as it made its big fall into a pool of water. "I want to go on that with you later. When I was born, I had a bad heart and one day it just stopped working and I died. I came here to heaven. My parents were very sad and they cried a lot. I was a little scared when I first came. Then I saw other children and soon I felt better. I have a special friend named Anna. She talked to me and showed me everything and made me feel better. She's an angel. I always come to this side of heaven when the carnival is here. One year, I couldn't come because I didn't do all my chores. Boy, after that, I made sure I did everything I was supposed to do so I didn't have to miss it."

"You have chores to do here?"

"Oh yes. George and Anna both told me that even though this is heaven, I still have to make my bed and keep my room neat. It isn't so bad."

"Why didn't Anna come to the carnival with you today?"

"She doesn't come to this side much and today she wanted to stay and read. I can't believe anyone wouldn't want to go to the carnival, but she didn't. Sometimes she helps some of the other children. Not everyone can come to the carnival. I don't really know why. That's just the way it is. Luther, what did you do before you died?"

"Krissy, I wish I knew. I've been talking to George the past few days about my mother. As we talk about things, I remember what my life was like. It's sad to say, but right now I don't know much. I would hope that I would have had a little girl just like you to love and be a part of my life. I hope I can find that out very soon."

"I'm sure you had a little girl. I would just bet on it. I hope you find out soon who she is. Now I want to go on some rides. Come on, Luther."

For the next several hours, they rode every ride that was there. Krissy was fearless and held Luther's hand when she sensed he was scared. It was the best day ever for Luther. He was having so much fun, and it was all because of a little girl who came into his new life and wanted to be his friend. After their second time on the Ferris wheel, they had an ice cream cone. Luther got peach and vanilla. Krissy wanted chocolate fudge with sprinkles on top.

There was a puppet show and they sat down in the front row to watch it. They laughed and laughed because the puppets were so funny. They saw dancers and acrobats. Luther was sure there couldn't have been an inch of space at this carnival that they didn't cover. What a wonderful day.

Too soon, it started getting dark and Krissy said they would have to leave. She had to be home soon or she would get in trouble. Luther didn't want that, but he also didn't want the day to end. He wished he could spend many more days with his new friend.

They arrived back at Luther's door and Krissy went to get her scooter. "Thank you for going to the carnival with me, Luther. I had a good time and it was so much fun."

"Oh, Krissy, I had the best time. I am so glad that you stopped me and insisted I go with you. Is it very far for you to go home? Do you want me to walk you there?" Luther asked, hoping that she would let him do that. It would give him a little more time with her.

"No, that's okay. It isn't far and you can't go there yet anyway." And then as Luther bent down, she gave him a big hug and a kiss on the cheek.

"Goodbye, Krissy. I hope I get to see you again. And thank you."

"You're welcome. Maybe I can come back again sometime to see you. Maybe we can go to the carnival next year. Bye."

As she rode her scooter down the hall heading for her home on the other side of heaven, she knew he was watching her. She stopped, turned around, and waved. And with a tear rolling down her cheek, she said softly, "Goodbye, Grandpa."

The Lace Hankie

Luther felt so good. It was great going to the carnival with Krissy. He thought she was the sweetest little girl ever. There was something about her that just made its way into his heart.

As he was preparing for bed, he realized that he hadn't thought about his mother once while he was at the carnival. He knew he was having a session with George the next day. He would deal with all that stuff then. For now he was as happy as anyone could possibly be.

Sleep came easily for Luther that night. He dreamed of ice cream cones, Ferris wheels, cheeseburgers, and especially a little girl with long brown hair who stole his heart.

After breakfast the next day, Luther headed off to see George. Breakfast had been good. He had fried potatoes, ham and eggs, toast, and coffee. He felt refueled and ready for the day. Breakfasts lately had been spent with a man named Herbert. It didn't appear that Herbert knew Luther in his earthly life and that made Luther happy. That time having a meal with Joe Wozneski had been a disaster.

Luther knocked on George's door. It was opened by a young man who was at least a foot taller than him. He said his name was Sam and he was helping George organize some files. He told him that George would be back shortly, as he had a quick errand to run. Luther sat on the chair and paged through a magazine. He was just getting interested in an article on woodworking when George came into the room.

"Ah, Luther, you beat me here. Sorry, I am late. Let's go in the other room and get comfortable." Luther headed for the chair where he always sat and George sat across from him.

"So tell me, Luther, what did you do yesterday?"

"George, it was the best day ever. I wasn't feeling very good after I left you and I just wanted to go to my room. Next thing I knew, there was this little girl riding a scooter down the hall. She asked me if I wanted to go to the carnival with her. Oops!" Luther realized that he just broke a promise to Krissy. "Please don't let Krissy get into any trouble for riding her scooter in the hall. I promised her I wouldn't tell anyone."

George laughed. He knew Krissy very well and could just imagine her riding her scooter in the hall. He assured Luther that she wouldn't get in trouble. *At least not this time*, he thought to himself.

"I wasn't going to go, but she was very persuasive. Boy, was I ever glad that I went. We had the best time. I felt like a kid again. It was great. Krissy sure is a special little girl. It was my lucky day when she rode by my door and stopped to talk."

George placed his hands on his right knee and smiled. It was almost a smirk rather than a smile, as if he knew something that no one else did. Today, George was wearing brown pants and an ivory shirt. He was meticulous. He brushed off a piece of lint from his pants and finally said, "Yes, Krissy certainly is a very special little girl. I've known her for a long time now. Every now and then, she comes here and we have a nice chat. I'm glad you got to meet her and spend the day together."

"George," said Luther. "There is something that I would like to ask, if it's okay with you?"

"Certainly," answered George.

Luther wasn't sure where to begin, but he was curious about his new surroundings. "Since I've been here, I have seen lots of people. Krissy said that this is heaven and I believe that it really is. If every person who has ever died is here, this place must be really big. How can everyone possibly be here? And does that mean that famous people, like George Washington, are here too? Would I ever be able to see and meet them?"

George started to say something, but Luther wanted to continue asking him questions.

"Krissy said she lived in another part of heaven, a place where we go when we have finished talking to you. Is there a separate place for children? And what about people from other countries? I don't think I have seen anyone here who is from China or heard anyone talking in a foreign language. Does each country have their own special section?"

"Those are a lot of questions and I will try to answer them for you. Krissy is right when she said she lives in another area. You perhaps will someday be able to go there. The people you see here are from all over the world. You are seeing them as you want to see them. You are hearing them speak in the language you understand. Luther, did you read the Bible before you came here?"

"I don't know. I guess I went to Sunday school and church when I was a child. I would hope that I continued doing that as an adult. The Bible would have been read there. I'm sure I know some Bible verses."

"Luther, the book of Acts talks about devout men from every nation under heaven, each talking in their own language and each being able to understand and hear them in their native tongues. They were amazed and wondered how this could be. Was it the power of God? That's the way it is here.

"Luther, I know there are many things that you do not understand. You have been amazed and mystified. I don't expect you to understand any of this just yet. You will, I can assure you of that. You asked about George Washington. Yes, he is here. Every person who lived on earth is here. You may have met them and didn't know it. Here we are all equal. No one is better than another. We come here and learn lessons from our earthly life. Everyone before you has done that, as you are doing now. Just like the devout men in Acts, they speak in their own language and each understands the other. Luther, trust me. I promise that you will understand." And with a smirk on his face, he added, "All in due time, Luther, all in due time."

Luther looked at George and saw the smirk. He smiled, knowing he would have to be patient. He thought he was beginning to understand what George just told him. He wasn't sure how he knew, but he trusted George.

There was quiet between them for some time. George knew that Luther was trying to comprehend all this. It was confusing, even frightening, but everyone here has been where Luther is now. They have all asked the same questions. George looked over at Luther and thought he saw a calming expression on his face. Luther was finally accepting where he was and that he was safe. His journey through his earthly life would, at times, be difficult, but it was something he would have to do to finally obtain that ultimate inner peace.

Luther thanked George for answering his questions. At least he thought he answered them. There were still many things that he didn't understand, but he was going to have to leave all that up to George. If this was his eternal home, he had a long time to figure them out. Finally, he asked George why he hadn't seen any churches here. Surely in heaven there should be churches or other places of worship.

George smiled and said, "Luther, there are many places of worship here. There are churches, synagogues, temples, and others. You just have to look for them. Perhaps you will stumble across one soon. If that happens, it means that you are ready to find one. Not everyone is ready right away, but I will confirm to you that they are here.

"And now, Luther, if you are ready, we must move on with your story."

Luther nodded.

"Today we are going to talk about your father, Warren. But before we do that, do you have any questions about your mother? I know you had a lot of information to digest with all that I last told you. I want you to know that it is important that you learn about your family, even if the things I tell you aren't kind."

"I wouldn't know what to ask. She wasn't a very nice person from what you told me. I never knew her, did I?"

"There was one instance when you saw her. You were about fifteen years old at the time. She and Horace had come back to the town you lived in. Horace was going to be presented with an award, and the presentation just happened to be in the town from which he and Bertha had run away from. You were downtown selling pretzels when they walked by you. Horace bought two pretzels and offered one to Bertha. You thanked him because he gave you fifteen cents and told you to keep the change. Horace asked what your name was and you told him you went by Wayne.

"Horace then introduced himself and Bertha. He told you the pretzels were very good and he was happy to see a young man working and helping earn money for his family. When you heard their names, you felt faint. Horace said you didn't look well and made you sit down on the cement. He asked Bertha for her hankie so he could wipe your brow, which by now was very sweaty. You could tell she wasn't exactly happy about giving up her lace hankie to a street boy, but she did as Horace asked and gave it to him. You looked up at her and asked if she knew who you were. She immediately said she had no idea who you were other than a street boy selling pretzels. You told her that you were her youngest son, Wayne. She glared at you and immediately walked away. Horace walked off toward his wife and looked back at you and said that was a terrible thing to say to a fine lady like his wife. Horace dropped the hankie and they both walked away as quickly as they could. By the look on Horace's face, he knew that what you said was true—you were her son, Wayne. That was the only time you ever saw her.

"You looked down on the sidewalk at the lace hankie. It was very fancy. You noticed it had a big B embroidered on the one corner and the edges were crocheted in very pale colors of blue, pink, yellow, and green. Your first reaction was to tear it to shreds, but you decided to keep it. After all, it was all you had of your mother. In your heart, you had always hoped that someday she would come back for you and Gerald. But after that day, you knew she never would and you vowed from that day forward, you would never want anything to do with her, ever."

"So I never really had a mother then. Did my father raise us, Gerald and me? Or did my sisters? What happened to us after she left?"

"That is where we are going to start today," said George.

Warren

"Luther, you never saw your mother after that, but there were times when you were very close to her. If it is of any consequence to you, your mother was never the same after that encounter. She put on a good front, but seeing you and being faced with the reality that you actually were her youngest son had a profound effect on her. It, however, did not affect her enough to try and reconcile with you or any of her children that she had abandoned. Her lifestyle, the one Horace was able to afford her now, was too important—perhaps more important than how the choices she had made many years earlier actually affected all of you.

"But now on to Warren. If you remember, he was lying on the kitchen floor after having come home drunk the previous evening. By now Bertha was used to dragging him to bed, but that night, she was more than happy to let him lie where he was. It gave her the opportunity to finish packing and have everything ready for her departure the following morning. Bertha hoped and prayed that Warren would not wake up until after she was gone. At that point, she could have cared less what he said or what he did. He would no longer be her problem and it was good riddance to him and the life they had shared."

*****

Warren heard his daughter Marion yelling at him. At first, he thought it was Bertha nagging him as always. When he realized that it wasn't Bertha, he sat up. His head was aching, but his back hurt more after being on the floor for the whole night.

"Damn that woman," Warren said. "She left me sleeping on the floor all night. Now I have to go to work with a backache as well as a headache. And what's with all the yelling. Marion? Is that you?"

"Yes, Dad. It's me, and you better get yourself up and figure out just what's going on around here. I'm supposed to be at work in two hours and I can't leave the boys alone."

"What do you mean leave them alone? Where's your mother?"

"That's what I'm trying to tell you. Mother took off with suitcases and she took Doug and Marge with her. They left with that awful Mr. Hinderfield from next door. I never liked him and now I really don't after what he just did. Dad, are you listening to me?"

Marion was really yelling now after seeing Warren about to fall down on the floor again. Marion was hysterical at this point and overwhelmed with all that had happened in only a matter of a few minutes. Gerald was crying for his mamma. His crying upset Wayne, who in turn started crying. It was total chaos.

Marion went into the other room to comfort her young brothers. She got a glass of milk for Gerald and warmed a bottle for Wayne. He really was old enough to be off a bottle, but their mother hadn't seemed interested in weaning him. Marion now knew why.

Warren slowly walked into the living room and took Wayne from Marion. He wasn't sure why all this yelling was going on. Where in tarnation was Bertha? She was always there in the morning to feed them breakfast. But then he began to comprehend what Marion had told him. Bertha had left with the man next door, taking Doug and Marge and all they had in suitcases. Just what was she doing and where did she think she was going?

"Marion, tell me exactly what is going on here?"

"Dad, I told you. Mother, Doug, and Marge all left with suitcases. They got into Mr. Hinderfield's car and drove off. She told me I would have to take off work today and watch Gerald and Wayne." The boys by now had calmed down and were playing with some blocks.

"Marion, are you sure this Hinderfield didn't just drop Doug and Marge off at school and drop your mother off at the market? It makes no sense that she would just up and leave her house and her children. I know that we fight at times, but it just wouldn't be like her to up and leave…would it?"

"Dad, by the look on her face, I am sure she won't be back. I often thought there was something going on between her and Mr. Hinderfield, and now I know I was right. Dad, I'm sorry, but what are we supposed to do? I can't afford to lose my job and you can't stay home with the boys. I could ask Elizabeth if she would come back, but she's so happy where she is living and working now. I could ask Mildred to help, but she has her hands full with little Ralph and now she has another baby on the way."

"Mildred's expecting again?" Warren asked. "Why doesn't anyone ever tell me these things? Did your mother know?"

"Yes, Mother just found out this week. I thought she would have told you."

"I guess that's just one more secret your mother was keeping from me. Marion, can you go down the street to Mrs. Wilson's house and ask if you can use her phone? Call Wittner and tell him you can't come to work today. I'll talk to him later today and explain what's going on. I don't think he'll fire you once he hears the story. See if you can call Mildred's neighbor. You know the one who just had a phone put in last month? You know her name, don't you? See if she can get a message to Mildred that we must talk to her as soon as possible."

"Mildred's neighbor is Mrs. Kilmar. Are you going to be all right with the boys till I get back?"

"Yes, I'm fine. I'm not as drunk as your mother would want you to think. I conked out on the floor because your mother hit me on the head with a frying pan."

"Oh no, Daddy," Marion said as she ran over to him. "She actually hit you with a frying pan? I never thought she could do such a thing. I'll run over to Mrs. Wilson's and be back as soon as I can."

As Marion walked the two blocks to Mrs. Wilson's house, she felt as if someone had hit *her* on the head with a frying pan. How could her own mother do this to her father? She knew her mother had a temper, but this was going too far. Maybe they would be better off without her. The big problem was, who was going to take care of the boys? She arrived at Mrs. Wilson's and knocked on the door. When Mrs. Wilson opened, before she could even say hello, Marion blurted out, "Mrs. Wilson, I need to use your phone right away. May I please come in?"

"Why, Marion, what a pleasant surprise. Come in. Of course, you may use my phone. I hope it isn't for an emergency at your house. Is one of your brothers sick? They are such cute little boys. I could just love them to death every time I see them."

"No, Mrs. Wilson. Gerald and Wayne are fine. I just need to call my boss, Mr. Wittner, and tell him I'm needed at home today and won't be able to come to work. And I need to get in contact with my sister, Mildred."

Marion didn't really know what to say to Mrs. Wilson. How could she tell her the truth that her mother just up and left, taking two of her children and leaving the rest behind? But Marion knew when Miss Peabody across the street found out, the whole town would know. For all Marion knew, Miss Peabody could have been watching out her window and saw her mother, Doug, and Marge get in Mr. Hinderfield's car and figured out something wasn't right. It was going to get pretty ugly before long when the rumors and truths started coming out.

Marion got home in time to see her father trying to put a diaper on Wayne. Never having done it before, he had no idea what he was doing. He had planned to wait until Marion got back, but the diaper stench penetrating the room was too overwhelming. Marion quickly took over while explaining about the two phone calls she had made.

Her boss wasn't happy and told her she would have to resolve her family issues and return to work as soon as possible. Mrs. Kilmar said she would get a message to Mildred.

"Daddy, what are we going to do? Mr. Wittner wasn't happy that I couldn't come to work again today, especially after missing once before. When I told him I didn't know when I could come back, he said he wasn't going to hold my job forever. Daddy, I'm scared."

"Marion, I've known Don Wittner for many years. I'll go and talk to him. I have to leave for work now. No point in both our bosses being upset."

Don Wittner

Warren packed his lunch, something else he never did before. He changed his clothes and headed out the door. He worked for the Esso Petroleum Company and had been with them for over twenty years now. At one time, he had delivered fuel oil to homes driving a gas truck pulled by several horses. They still had some horses, but about five years ago, they purchased several motorized trucks for deliveries. Warren made deliveries sometimes, but he mainly worked in maintenance. He had a knack for fixing the trucks when in need of repairs, and he soon found himself the head mechanic. He was making a decent salary because of his experience and years of working there. It was enough to take care of his family and see to all of their needs.

He didn't own a car since work and the local stores were all within walking distance. He also saw no need for a telephone. He wanted no part of these modern contraptions, although today a phone would have come in handy. He figured if there had been one of those in the house, Bertha would have been talking on it most of the day and neglecting her family and household chores even more than she obviously did. Mrs. Wilson had told them if they needed the use of a phone, they could use hers anytime.

As he walked to work, he wondered where Bertha, Doug, and Marge were. He knew Bertha hadn't been happy, but he never thought she would leave. And leave her two babies? What kind of a woman would do such a thing? He knew it was going to be hard, but maybe it was good riddance to her. She always yelled at the girls when they were little, and it was on more than one occasion that he had to stop her from hitting them. Since today was Friday, he would go to work and then have the weekend to think and figure out what he was going to do.

Warren concentrated on his work all day, trying to put his personal problems on the back burner. Fortunately, there was enough going on at work that allowed him to do that. On his way home, he stopped at the department store where Marion worked. He wanted to talk to Don Wittner personally.

Warren approached the desk where Don Wittner's secretary sat. "Hello, my name is Warren Yeager and I would like to speak to Mr. Wittner."

The secretary was a stern-looking woman about forty years old named Katherine Jones. Katherine had never married and devoted herself to her job. She knew Mr. Wittner couldn't get along without her and she used that to bargain for raises when she felt the need. She had mousey brown hair with streaks of gray at the temple, tied back in a bun at the base of her neck. She wore glasses that sat low on her nose. She was a force to be reckoned with, as the saying went. She stared at Warren over the top of her glasses.

"Do you have an appointment?" she asked, knowing full well that he did not. She made it a point to know everything about Don Wittner, both at work and in his personal life. Mrs. Wittner was a big gossip and liked to come in and tell Katherine various things about their life.

Katherine thought she was a bore, but she listened to all her talk just in case there would be a time when the information would come in handy for her benefit.

"No, ma'am. I don't, but it is about my daughter, Marion, and I need to speak to Mr. Wittner right away."

Katherine was going to send Warren on his way without seeing her boss. After all, it was late in the day and she wanted to leave. She would have to stay as long as he was here; at least she felt she should. There was something going on in that young woman's life and she wanted to find out what it was. She knew Marion was engaged to a young farmer named Earl Miller. She was taking bets with herself that Marion had probably found herself in a family way and that was what the crisis was all about. Well, if Marion lost her job, it would serve her right for doing things she shouldn't have been doing before she got married.

Just then Don Wittner came out of his office. He saw Warren and immediately went over to him and shook his hand, saying it was good to see him again. He invited Warren into his office and closed the door. Katherine wanted to remind her boss what time it was, but the look he gave her told her she had better not say anything. In fact, he told her she could leave for the day and that he would see her on Monday morning.

Don Wittner led Warren into his office and told him to take a seat. Before Warren had a chance to say anything, Don said, "Warren, I was surprised to get the call from Marion this morning saying she was unable to come to work. I must admit I was not very happy about it because she is a good worker and always on time. But as the day went on, I began to think about her and hoped there wasn't anything seriously wrong at home or that Marion was ill."

"Well, Don, Marion isn't sick. The fact is she had to stay home and watch her two younger brothers today because my wife, her mother, left us. I was asleep when all this happened, but Marion said her mother left with two of my other children, suitcases in hand. Marion said her mother wouldn't be coming back. Don, I am still trying to figure it all out, but I find myself in a situation with two young boys, Gerald who is four and Wayne, two. They need to be taken care of and I have no one to do that. Marion agreed to watch them today and I told her to contact you. I'd really appreciate it if you didn't fire her. She was sure she was going to lose her job. I don't know what to do. I'm still in shock after what happened this morning."

Don Wittner was a handsome man with a full head of black hair. He wore an expensive gray three-piece suit and looked every part the executive that he was. He had a gold wedding band on his left hand and a diamond pinkie ring on his other hand. He had taken over the Wittner Department Store when his father retired, who had taken it over from his father at his death. Don's grandfather, Walter, started the store in the early 1800s, and the store grew to become the finest department store within a hundred-mile radius. They sold just about anything one would need to run a home, plus men's, women's, and children's clothing. Recently, they started selling shoes. Prices were reasonable and affordable for almost everyone in town. Don was an easy man to work for and he knew every employee by first name. In most cases, he knew their spouses' and children's names. He gave each employee a generous Christmas gift plus a turkey. When an employee got married or had a baby, he always sent a big flower arrangement as a gift. He thought of them as his family. His father had done the same when he ran the store and the kindness shown was returned to them many times over.

"Warren, I am so sorry. I don't know what to say. If I sounded harsh to Marion this morning, please tell her I apologize. I don't want to lose Marion as an employee, but I understand that she is needed at home. I will put her on what I am calling a leave of absence. When she is able to return to work, have her call me and she will have her job back immediately. Perhaps she would be able to come in on a part-time basis. If that is a possibility, we can make that work as well. And I might be able to find someone to help you out. My wife knows a lady who is a member of our church. She was recently widowed and has two young children of her own. Her husband died suddenly and she is struggling financially. Would you like me to ask my wife about her? Perhaps you could arrange to meet and see if she could be able to help you out."

"I appreciate all this and will be beholden to you, Don. Thank you so much." Warren left the office and headed straight for home. He was beginning to feel a little better about things. Somehow he knew they would get through this. He just wasn't sure how, right now.

Life without Bertha

When Warren got home, he found Mildred and her husband Maurice there. Elizabeth was there too, as well as Earl, Marion's fiancé. Ralph, Mildred's son, was playing on the floor with Wayne and Gerald. Mildred knew something was wrong from the message she received from Mrs. Kilmar. As soon as Maurice was finished working, they came right over. She had made a big pot of vegetable soup that day and she brought it along for everyone to eat. Elizabeth had stopped at the house to pick up some of her things that were still there, and Marion started telling them about the events of the day. Earl usually picked Marion up after work on Friday nights, and when he went to the store and was told she hadn't come in that day, he became worried and went to the house.

Warren thought it was probably just as well that they were all there. Better to get it all out in the open and let everyone know what was happening.

Marion had told them about their mother leaving with Doug and Marge. Elizabeth was sure she would be back any time now. Marion had confided to Mildred her concerns about their mother's relationship with Mr. Hinderfield. Mildred had suspected something was going on too and wasn't all that surprised to hear this. Mildred was the oldest of the seven children and she felt she knew her mother the best. They had always had a stormy relationship, and she had heard many times over from her mother about her dread of raising more children and the drudgery of all the housework.

Warren told them about his visit with Don Wittner and Marion was glad that he had been so understanding. Earl had never liked Bertha. Many times, he had witnessed her anger toward the young boys and thought it wasn't good. He was totally supportive of Marion and her need to take care of her young brothers now. He even thought that they could marry sooner than planned and have the boys live with them. He would have liked to have more time with Marion as newlyweds, but he firmly believed that family came first. He would talk to Marion about this when they were alone.

Elizabeth was crying as she sat alone by the front window. She never thought her mother could do anything like this. She was sure that Marion had misunderstood. Marion had told her before that there was something going on with Mr. Hinderfield, but Elizabeth was absolutely certain that could not be true. Her mother would never do such a thing. She felt that she had a good relationship with her mother, perhaps because she no longer was living in the house. In reality, she was feeling some jealously that her mother had chosen her sister Marge instead of her, if she really had left as Marion said.

After supper, Mildred helped Marion get the boys ready for bed. She knew she and Maurice would have to leave soon so they could get their own son home to bed. Mildred told her father that she would do whatever she could and the boys could spend time with her if needed.

Elizabeth said she had to get back to the Whitney residence to take care of the children. Mr. Whitney worked at Wittner's Department Store as a salesclerk and Mrs. Whitney was a college professor. They lived in a large home on the boulevard. Elizabeth had started working for them a little over a year ago. Initially, she would go there on her way home from school to help out, until Mrs. Whitney had talked to Bertha to see if it could be arranged for Elizabeth to live with them. Elizabeth was grateful and glad to be out of the house and away from all the drama.

That night, though, the Yeager house was quiet. The boys were in bed and sound asleep, and Mildred, Maurice, and little Ralph had left. Elizabeth left too. She prayed the whole walk back to the Whitneys that tomorrow her mother, Marge, and Doug would be back home where they belonged and things would be back to normal, at least as normal as they could be in the Yeager household. Marion and Earl sat alone on the living room couch, each deep in thought over what had happened. Earl wanted to talk to Marion about getting married and having the boys live with them, but he sensed tonight wasn't the night to bring this up. He would have to leave soon to go back home because his chores would be waiting for him early in the morning. He would see Marion again over the weekend. Perhaps then he could approach the subject.

After everyone left, Warren slowly climbed the stairs to the second floor and walked into the bedroom that he had shared with Bertha. As Warren got into bed, he realized it was the first time in twenty years he had slept alone, not counting the times he slept on the couch after coming home from the bar. He found it strange, but he didn't miss Bertha as much as he thought he would. Somehow they would get through this, God willing.

*****

"And so, Luther, things were certainly different in the Yeager household, and for the next two years, they managed. Mildred had her second child, another boy, Claude. Marion married Earl and went to live with him on the farm he had purchased. A little over a year later, their son Earl Jr. was born and they nicknamed him Sonny. Marion had gone back to work at Wittner's Department Store part-time. She would come to the house and watch you and Gerald three days a week. Both Mildred and Marion took turns taking care of you and your brother.

"Elizabeth continued to work for the Whitney family. A friend of the family introduced her to a young man named Charles and they began dating. Mrs. Wittner told her husband to tell Warren about Emma Schultz, who was very willing to help out as needed. Emma would come to the house in the mornings after her children left for school and would stay until your father came home from work. She had her own children come to your house after school. She did some cleaning and the laundry and had a meal prepared. Before long, Warren felt comfortable being home with you and Gerald and

75

actually enjoyed the quality time he was spending with his two young sons. His days of going to the bar after work were long gone."

"George, did anyone ever hear from my mother again?"

"Actually, Warren did. About nine months after she left, a registered letter arrived for him. It was from an attorney asking for his signature on a divorce agreement. Bertha didn't want anything, just the freedom to be away from Warren. Warren gladly signed and shortly thereafter was issued a divorce decree. There were times when he missed Bertha, but when he thought of what she had done, those thoughts were quickly erased. He actually felt nothing but pity for her most of the time. Obviously, the wealth that she now had in her new life was more important than her own flesh and blood. She never contacted any of her other children. Warren missed Doug and Marge and hoped that they were happy. He would have liked to see them, but he was sure by now Bertha had poisoned their minds against him.

"Three years after Bertha left, Warren asked Emma to marry him. He had become fond of her and she did take good care of his house and his children. She agreed. The family moved into her house, which was larger. It provided a bedroom for each of her children and a bedroom for you and Gerald to share on the third floor."

"So," Luther asked, "was life easier now that my father had remarried and we had a stepmother to take care of us?"

"That certainly was what everyone hoped would be the situation, but unfortunately, it wasn't meant to be.

"So, Luther, that is all for today. I will be seeing you again in a few days. We must get on with your life so that you can begin your real mission here."

"My real mission? What do you mean?"

"Another day, Luther, another day. All in due time."

Luther just rolled his eyes.

Marie

L uther found himself out in the hallway again and on his way back to his room. He wished he could remember his youth, but he couldn't. George told him he was about six years old when his father married Emma. He was trying very hard to picture his life at that age.

He realized, as he often did after a session with George, that he was now very hungry. It was close to lunchtime, so he headed toward the dining room. He had been partnered with several people at lunch, and they were always interesting to talk to. As he approached his table, he saw a woman sitting there. She was rather nice-looking with short blonde hair.

"Hello there. My name is Luther and it looks like we are going to have lunch together today," Luther said as he seated himself in the chair opposite her. He couldn't help notice the deep brown eyes and freckles on her nose and cheeks.

"Hello, my name is Marie. This is where I was told to sit, so if this is your table, I guess we are lunch partners."

"I've been working with George to learn about my past," Luther said. "Then I have some mission to do. I just learned that today and I have no idea what that is all about."

"Ah, yes, George is good at assigning missions. Everyone here has had at least one."

"If I may ask, what was your mission?" Luther asked hesitantly.

"There was a time I would not have wanted to talk about it, but I have to learn to face reality. Alcohol was my problem. It ultimately led to my death at the age of sixty-two. I thought having a drink for breakfast was the thing to do. By lunchtime, I had already had several. After I came here, I realized that I had missed so many important things in the life of my husband and son because of my drinking.

"I only thought about myself and when I would have my next drink. As a result, I developed cancer and died much younger than I should have. I left behind a husband, a son, and two wonderful grandchildren.

"When I was in college, it was all about having fun. One night, I went out and got drunk, as usual. Later that month, I got really sick, and my roommate, Sherry took me to the emergency room. The doctor told me I was pregnant. I couldn't believe it. Sherry said she heard of a clinic downtown where they took care of problems like mine. She said she would take me there if I wanted to go.

"The idea sounded good, but I wasn't sure. I was scared. I weighed all the pros and cons and realized there weren't many pros. A week later, we went to the clinic. The doctor began the procedure, and within fifteen minutes, it was all over.

"Back in our dorm room, I slept off and on and wasn't feeling very good. I guess I passed out because several days later, I woke up in the hospital. My mother was called. She was there when I woke up. Sherry was too, and she was so scared. She didn't want to tell anyone what had happened, but the doctor knew immediately. My mother was told that I had lost so much blood that I almost died. The surgery stopped the bleeding and I was going to be okay, but the likelihood of me ever being able to have children was very slim.

"After a week in the hospital, my mother took me home. Soon I started looking for a job. I was successful at finding one and was eventually promoted to a higher position. I even got to accompany the buyers to New York when they shopped for the next season's fashions. I loved it. I saved my money, and within six months, I found a small efficiency that was perfect for me. Finally, I was on my own.

"My life was in a good place until the day I got a phone call from my mother. All she said was that I had to come home as soon as possible. I rushed over to my mother's house and found her sitting there with two people I had never seen before. My mother introduced me to the couple, telling me they were my roommate Sherry's parents. Wow. I hadn't seen Sherry since the day I left the hospital, and to be honest, I hadn't thought much about her either. College and everything connected to it was all part of my past, one I didn't want to revisit.

"Sherry's parents were sitting on the sofa and Sherry's father was holding her mother's hand. Her eyes were swollen and red from crying. Finally, her father said he was so sorry to have to tell me this, but Sherry died. She committed suicide."

"I couldn't believe what I was hearing. How, when, and why? They said it was three weeks ago. She died of an overdose. This just didn't make sense. Sherry never drank; she never used drugs. She was the total opposite of me. She studied, got good grades, and stayed away from the vices that I seemed to be drawn to.

"They said they found an envelope addressed to me and wanted me to have it. I took it while trying to keep my hand from shaking. Why would Sherry write me a note and then kill herself? I excused myself and ran upstairs and into the bathroom. Slowly, I opened the envelope. It was in Sherry's handwriting. I would have recognized it anywhere because of the fancy swirl she always put on the end of each word and the little circles above her i's."

"Her letter said that she felt so guilty for what happened to me in college. She blamed herself because she told me about that clinic. She felt like she persuaded me to go and she didn't think I really wanted to. She had just found out that she was pregnant. She and her boyfriend were planning on getting married, but both were unprepared for a baby. She said she remembered the doctor saying I could never have children and now she was going to have a baby. She just couldn't deal with that.

"She killed herself because of me! I made the decision to go to the clinic. I never blamed her for what happened. Why did she do this? I sat there crying until my mother knocked on the door to see if I was all right. No, I wasn't all right.

"I ran out of the house, got in my car, and headed for the nearest bar. I sat there until they closed and I was too drunk to care. They kicked me out and told me to go home. I threw them the finger and staggered out. As I opened the door, I literally fell into a man walking by. He told me I was in no condition to drive and offered to take me home. I was too drunk to realize that getting into a car with a complete stranger in the middle of the night was dangerous.

"The next day, I went to work and the only thing I could think about was Sherry. The first place I went to after work was the liquor store. I figured I could drink if I wanted to. It was a free country, wasn't it? I would just be a little more careful of how much and when. I didn't want to lose my job. I just wanted to dull the pain I was feeling.

"A few nights later, the man who drove me home knocked on my door. He said he felt bad that we were never officially introduced. His name was Pete. I apologized for my behavior that night and said I had just received some very bad news and ended up having way too much to drink.

"He was actually very nice. He said he had been out with friends and didn't realize how late it was. He was heading for his car when I fell out of the bar.

"To make a long story short, we started dating and fell in love. I never told him about my drinking habits or what had happened in college. I found I was able to have a drink every night and still be sober. Not knowing that I was a recovering alcoholic, he didn't mind. My mother adored him. She counted her blessings the day we met, even though she had no idea how that actually happened. We were married eight months later. I continued to work at the boutique and was now the number one buyer.

"Pete and I were happy. Life was good. We travelled, had parties, and were invited out with friends. Ironically, two years later, I found out that I was pregnant. I have no idea how this happened, but I thought I should light a candle in church. It was a difficult pregnancy, but we now had this beautiful baby boy, Robert Paul.

"As time went on, my drinking became more of a problem. Pete knew what was happening and tried talking to me. We would have terrible fights. He finally decided that it would be in Robert's best interest if he attended a boarding school. The excuse was that it would give him the academic attention he needed to increase his chances of getting into a good college. The real reason was so that he didn't see his mother drunk every morning when he left for school and still drunk when he came home.

"One afternoon, my sister Ava came to see me. She wanted me to go shopping with her. Little Miss Goody Two-shoes had an alternative motive. Apparently, she and her know-it-all husband, the good Dr. Sam Willing, had talked to Pete about me and decided I needed to spend some time in rehab. She said she wanted to stop at the hospital first to see Sam's new office. I wasn't interested in his office, but I went along inside. At the door, I was greeted by my mother, husband, and Sam. The next think I knew, I was in a private room. I was furious.

"I had all kinds of sessions and therapies. When Pete came to see me, I wanted to throw something at him. I hadn't had a drink during this time and I desperately wanted one. He tried to tell me that this was for my own good. I yelled, screamed, and cursed.

"I spent six lousy months in that place and I hated every minute. They all told me I was making such good progress, but I didn't really care. All I really wanted was a drink."

"When the doctors told me I could go home, everyone thought I would be able to handle things. I knew that I couldn't drink. Pete made sure there wasn't alcohol in the house, and for two months, I was sober.

"One day, I had lunch with a friend and I watched people at the bar drinking and it brought up old memories. I was so sure I would be able to handle this. I just had to be smarter. After we said goodbye, I stopped at the liquor store. I bought one bottle, planning on having only little sips at a time so the bottle would last longer.

"At home, I poured a small glass and had my first taste of vodka in what seemed to be an eternity. It was like nectar from the gods. I poured a little more.

"For the next month, I was in heaven. I had a drink after Pete left for work, one after lunch, and one shortly before he came home. I made more trips to the liquor store because soon the bottle was empty. I always put the empty bottles in the neighbor's recycle bin. Wasn't I the clever one?

"Robert's graduation was approaching and I was looking forward to seeing him again. I drank the night before and got really sick. I wasn't able to go.

"Pete knew what was going on. He found the bottle I had hidden. He was furious. He emptied it down the drain and threatened to inform every liquor store and bar in town that they were not to sell or serve me any alcohol. I cried. I promised not to do it again, knowing full well that I had no intention of keeping that promise. He called me a disgrace and said that if he had any common sense, he would divorce me and let me live with the town drunks. Instead, he gave up. He told me if I wanted to drink myself to death, he wasn't going to stop me. And that is exactly what I did.

"Pete and I drifted apart. Most nights, I sat alone with the TV and a bottle of booze. Pete and I visited Robert at college. A year after graduation, he married Yvonne. They found jobs in Florida and moved there. Pete and I would fly down to visit, but they were not always good. I spent many days and nights in the motel room too sick to visit.

"When the grandchildren came, I wanted to spend time with them, but Yvonne really didn't want that. After Zoe was born, I started having health problems. I went to several doctors and I was finally diagnosed with liver cancer. I had surgery and chemotherapy, but it was too late. I was able to make peace with my husband, son, and even my daughter-in-law at the end of my life. I will always be grateful for that. Unfortunately, I didn't have much time."

*****

Marie looked at her watch and realized that she had been talking to Luther for well over an hour. "Oh my, I have been going on for so long. I am so sorry I bored you with my story."

Luther took Marie's hand and offered her his hankie to dry her eyes. "No, don't say that. Marie, I am so sorry to hear your story. It is so sad. I was happy to listen. I wish I could help you understand that as sad as your story is, it wasn't all your fault. Sherry's death was so hard for you, but you can't continue to blame yourself for her death.

You tried to do that your whole life and it led you down the path you took. As you said, you were able to make peace with the people who mattered the most to you. Remember that."

"I never was able to make peace with my sister. My mother tried to intervene, but Ava just didn't want to be bothered with me. She didn't come to my funeral and this upset my mother. I know I should have died that night in the hospital when I was in college. Then none of the bad things would have ever happened."

"Marie, you would never have had Robert or your grandchildren. You would never have met Pete, and you have to admit the years weren't all bad. I am so glad you told me your story. I wish I knew all of mine so I could share it. I know some, but not everything. Perhaps someday we can meet again."

"Luther, I would love to hear your story. Thank you so much for all you have said. I feel so much better." And with that, she got up. Luther watched as she walked away and felt such sadness. He went back to his room and sat alone in the dark, thinking about Marie.

Ava

The next morning, Luther woke up and found that he was still in the reclining chair in his living room. He had a light blanket over him and he had no idea how it got there. He remembered what he had been thinking about. Marie. How sad her story was. He hoped he would see her again sometime. He would have to ask George about her and see if it could be arranged for them to have lunch again.

Luther showered, dressed, and left his room to go for breakfast. The scenery outside his room had changed again. Today there was a big green field and a red tractor working the soil. He watched as it went up and down each row. He thought maybe it was planting something. He found his way to the dining room and went to his assigned table. It was set for two and he was hoping that Marie would show up. Much to his disappointment, no one showed and he ate alone.

For the next several days, Luther tried to avoid thinking about Marie. He found a golf course and three men who just happened to be looking for a fourth to play a round. Luther joined them and had a wonderful time. His partner was a man named Arthur and on the third hole he birdied. Arthur and Luther ended up winning and the ones who lost treated them to a drink in the clubhouse.

Later, Luther went swimming in one of the many pools there. It was such a refreshing feeling. He was amazed after all this physical activity he never felt tired. There was a baseball game going on in the park and he sat on the bleachers and watched, cheering for the team in red. One day, he returned to his room after breakfast and saw the TV was blinking. He didn't remember ever seeing it do that before.

He picked up the remote and pressed the on button. Suddenly, he saw George, right there on the screen.

"Good morning, Luther. I trust you are doing well today. You are a hard person to reach at times with all the activities you have become involved with. This is good and I am glad you are finding things to do here. I would like you to come to my office today and join me for lunch. I am looking forward to seeing you again." And just like that, George was gone and the TV screen went blank.

Luther guessed it was time to continue the story of his life, and he was eager to hear more about his parents, siblings, and his early years on earth. He arrived at George's office and this time was greeted by a woman named Charlotte. She escorted Luther into George's office and said that he would be there shortly. The office had turned into a dining room. Instead of the sofa and chairs that were always there, he found a table.

A few minutes later, George walked in the room. Today he wore a three-piece suit. It matched the royal blue color of the napkins that were on the table. His tie was a deep red. His hair was not tied back. It was loose and hung to his shoulders, framing his oval face. He looked very much the important person he was around here. Luther was feeling underdressed in his casual clothing. George shook Luther's hand and told him how nice he looked. At that, Luther looked and realized that he now had on a three-piece suit as well. His was navy blue and his tie was gold. The look on his face told George he had no idea how this happened. George smiled with that smirk he had.

"Luther, did you ever notice how things change around here just like that?" he asked as he snapped his fingers. "Please sit down. The first course will be here shortly."

They dined on a variety of pastas in a delicious cream sauce, as well as a salad, soup, and an assortment of breads.

"Luther, I am so glad that you were able to join me today. I was hoping we could get together again soon. We still have a lot to talk about and lots of work to do."

The meal was amazing. Luther still couldn't get used to the fact that all the food here was as delicious as it was. Luther and George finished the next several courses when George said they should take a break before the dessert would be served.

"So, Luther, do you have any questions for me?"

"Well, I have two things I would like to ask you if you don't mind. The first one is about a lady named Marie. I had lunch with her several days ago and she told me her story. It was sad and I felt so bad for her. She was obviously very unhappy about some of the events from her life. I wasn't sure just what to say to her. Before I had the chance to say much, she left. I wish I could see her again."

"Yes, Marie," George said. "She is one of the things I was planning on talking to you about. She is a wonderful person, and yes, she did have an unhappy life. I know you had lunch with her and that she told you her story. I want to thank you for being there for her. Marie has been here for a while, and she has rarely spoken to anyone about her earthly life. She obviously felt comfortable with you as she told you more than she has ever told anyone. What you said to her was just what she needed to hear. Because of you, she is now ready to move on to the next part of her journey."

"But I hardly said anything. I just listened to her tell her story."

"Luther, what Marie needed the most was for someone to listen to her. No one has ever sat with her and just let her talk. You were the first. I must admit that I wasn't sure you were the person she would open up to or that you would allow her to talk uninterrupted, but you were and for that I am eternally grateful. Marie still has a lot of work to do, but because of you, she made enormous progress. Well done, Luther!"

Luther was surprised at what he just heard. He really didn't think he did anything all that great. He just listened. He was glad that George was pleased with him. He was happy that she was able to proceed with her journey here.

"George, there is something else I would like to ask you. You said my earthly life was over, which means that I died. Did I have a funeral? Where was it, who was there, and where am I buried?"

"I am so glad that you finally got around to asking me that question. For most people, that is one of the first things they ask. They want to know how they died. It took you a little longer, but now you finally want to know. I think it would be best if I just let you watch your own funeral. Then we can talk about any questions you may have about it. How does that sound?"

Luther was a little hesitant, thinking about watching his own funeral. It seemed a little eerie to him. Luther agreed warily, not really sure what to expect.

With the snap of a finger, the room suddenly became dark. "Now, Luther, you know that you lived on earth for ninety-three years, three months, and twenty-eight days. The cause of your death is listed as heart failure. This is fairly common when someone surpasses ninety years of age. We will begin at the nursing home where you resided for three years prior to your death."

*****

The screen showed a small room with stained glass windows. There was an altar in the front of the room flanked by two white candles, which had already been lit. There were several rows of pews; a few were occupied. At the rear of the chapel was a pedestal with a leather-bound booklet people signed as they came in the room. There was a lady and man standing next to the door. Luther noticed that as people signed the book, they took a few minutes to say something to the lady. After about a half an hour, the lady and man sat down in a front row pew. A minister entered and walked slowly to the front of the chapel.

A prayer was said followed by a hymn. The minister read a scripture verse and then everyone said the Twenty-third Psalm. Luther recognized the familiar words, "The Lord is my Shepherd I shall not want." The minister asked if anyone would like to say a few words about Luther. A man stood up and someone handed him a microphone.

"My name is Leonard Simmons. I lived across the hall from Luther and Margaret in the apartment building. I remember Margaret being so nice to me, especially after my Alice died. Luther always said good morning when he saw me. Sometimes, if we happened to leave our apartments at the same time, we would go and have breakfast together. Luther and Margaret invited me over to their place some evenings and we would play cards. Luther loved to play pinochle and we would play three-handed. One time, his daughter came to visit and we partnered up. Luther loved to win. There were times I thought he cheated, but I can't be sure and it wouldn't be nice to say that here at his funeral. Thank you."

A lady in the last row stood up. "Hello, my name is Melissa Rodgers. I was one of the nurses in the unit where Luther was. I just wanted to say that I thought he was a very nice man. Most of the time, he knew who I was even if he couldn't remember my name. He always asked me for an extra dessert. He wasn't supposed to have it, but sometimes if there was an extra on the cart, I would give it to him. His eyes would light up when he saw me coming in his room with the dessert. I felt bad that he didn't have many visitors. I think he knew more of what was going on around him than he left people think. I will miss seeing him when I am working."

No one else stood up. The minister nodded to the lady in the front row; she got up and walked to the front of the room. She thanked everyone for coming. She said she was sure her stepfather would have enjoyed knowing people thought enough of him to come. She said her family would miss him.

Then the minister said another prayer. At the conclusion of the service, he announced that there would be a luncheon served in the south dining room and all were invited to come. That was it. It was over in less than thirty minutes.

*****

George turned to Luther and was watching his reaction to what he had just seen. Luther said nothing; he was just staring at the blank screen. Finally, George asked him what he was feeling.

"That lady said she was my stepdaughter and I presume the man with her was her husband. I don't remember them. What is her name? Were they the only family there? Was there no one else who could have come? That man who spoke said I had a daughter. Where was she?" Luther asked sadly.

George moved his chair away from the table and crossed his leg. He was brushing a piece of lint away from his pants leg while contemplating how to answer Luther's questions.

Finally, he said, "You do have other family members, but they obviously chose not to attend. Ava, your stepdaughter, was in charge of all your final arrangements and I believe she felt she should be there. Your other family members are part of the lesson you must learn and come to terms with here. You will learn that your daughter will become a big part of your mission. We will talk about that in times to come. Your funeral was held at the nursing home, but you were not buried in the cemetery there. Your grave is in the town you lived in most of your adult life. We will continue to watch now."

*****

The room darkened again and the screen came to life. Now there was a scene in a cemetery. It was a large cemetery with many graves. A big black town car looped around until it came to a curve on top of a hill. Parking there, the lady, Ava, and her husband, Sam, got out of the car. Ava was carrying an urn. Luther realized now that his ashes were in that urn. He had been cremated. A very small flat marker was behind a mound of dirt and the urn was placed in the ground and covered up. There was no service; no one said anything. When it was over, Ava and Sam got back in the car and drove away.

Luther stared at the pile of dirt and the small marker. It showed his name and his birth and death year. Luther wondered why he wasn't buried beside his wife. He was thinking that he must have had two wives. Marion mentioned a woman named Millie. Then he knew that he had a stepdaughter, so he guessed that he married again. What had happened to Millie? Where was she buried? And what about his second wife? He asked George to explain.

"Well, you are correct in saying that you were married twice. Millie was your first wife and she died many years before you. Shortly after her death, you married a woman named Margaret. She also died before you by four years. They are both buried in the cemetery you see before you; the same cemetery that you are buried in. Margaret was laid to rest beside her first husband, Ava's father. Millie is buried in her family's plot beside her parents. There are reasons why you were not buried beside either Millie or Margaret. We will talk about them in time. Suffice it to say, you were given the least expensive funeral that could be arranged. That was Ava's decision."

"I'm beginning to think I wasn't very well liked. For some reason, I wasn't buried beside either of my wives and other family members didn't even come to my funeral. What did I do to hurt these people? Was I that bad a person on earth?"

"We will talk about this, Luther, I promise. But now I must conclude our time together. I have a very important meeting that I must attend. Luther, see if you can remember anything at all about other people who were important in your life. You may start to sense some things and I want you to write them down for us to discuss at our next meeting. Thank you for sharing lunch with me. I'm sorry we have to end on such a sad part of your earthly life. We will talk again soon, I promise. Good day."

George stood up and walked out of the room. Luther wanted to go back to his room and just be alone. George said he should try to think about people from his earthly life. He wanted desperately to do this.

On his way back, he kept thinking about those people, Ava and Sam. Who were they? Yes, he knew she was his stepdaughter. But those names sounded so familiar. Was he starting to remember them? He was trying to recall where he heard their names before. Then it suddenly dawned on him. Marie had a sister Ava and her husband's name was Sam. Was this a coincidence or could it be that the Marie he had lunch with was Ava's sister? If Ava is Marie's sister, that means that Marie was also his stepdaughter.

Remembering

Luther was too upset to go to the dining room for his meal. He sat in his chair trying to think of all the people in his life. He was almost certain now that Marie was Margaret's daughter. He was trying to remember times spent with her. He couldn't. Perhaps Marie died before he and Margaret married. He kept thinking about his funeral. Ava and Sam were the only relatives there. He was sure he had a child of his own. He had images of a little girl with long brown hair running and playing in a backyard. Where was she? Why hadn't she come? *Did I have grandchildren?* Luther wondered. They weren't there either. Surely, I had nieces and nephews. None of them were there. What did I do in my life that alienated everyone from me?

Sleep finally came to Luther. He dreamed of a little white house with blue shutters. He was driving a big black car and he stopped in front of the house. A little girl with long brown hair was sitting on the front porch steps. When she saw the car, she got very excited. She ran to it and opened the front door and climbed inside. She smiled the biggest smile and said, "Hi, Daddy. Can I drive the car into the garage?" She climbed onto his lap and started to hold the steering wheel. Luther put his hands on top of hers and they drove up the driveway and into the garage. The little girl was giggling the whole time. They got out of the car and walked down through the backyard and into the house. A wonderful aroma greeted them and a lady was taking a pot roast out of the oven. Luther walked over to the lady and gave her a kiss. Then they sat down at the table and had their meal together. He recognized the lady; she was his first wife. He called her Millie and told her about his day. She called him Wayne. The little girl kept interrupting, saying she wanted to tell Daddy what she and Mommy did that day. Millie called her Peggy and told her she must wait until Daddy was finished talking and then she could talk. Luther began to remember this scene. Peggy finally was able to tell him about helping Mommy make cookies and that they were going to have them for dessert if everyone cleaned their plates.

As quickly as the scene came to Luther, it was gone. He was in another house now with Millie. They were sitting at the kitchen table eating supper. Peggy was there, although she was now a teenager. Luther asked her how school was and she said it was okay. She said she didn't like science class and that the teacher didn't know anything. She asked if she could go to the basketball game at the school that night. Luther asked who she was going to be with and Peggy said Nancy, her best friend.

Again, Luther found himself at this same table with Millie for another meal. Peggy was there with a young man and a little boy. After the meal Luther, Peggy, and the young man played pinochle. Peggy threw a card and immediately Luther began yelling at her. "Why did you throw that card? You have to play your ace now." Peggy told him she didn't have an ace. There was a lot of tension around the table. Luther was going to lose the hand because he miscounted the cards. Peggy was upset because her father yelled at her. She knew she hadn't played the wrong card. Luther threw the cards in the middle of the table. Finally, Peggy said she didn't want to play anymore and that she had to get Jimmy ready for bed.

Luther realized that the young man was Peggy's husband and that Jimmy was their son—his grandson. Where was he now? Why hadn't he come to the funeral? He realized his behavior, while they were playing cards, wasn't very nice. Was this the way it was all the time? No wonder no one wanted to be in his life.

The next morning, Luther awoke feeling very sad. He remembered that George asked him to write down things he remembered. He found a paper and a pen on the table. He wrote down everything he had dreamed the night before. He really wanted to know more about his wife Millie and his daughter Peggy and what had happened to them. George had said that Millie died many years before him. What had happened to her? Why did she die so young? And what about Peggy? Did she die as well? Was that why she wasn't at his funeral? But there was a young boy, Jimmy, his grandson. Where was he?

A knock on his door startled him and Henry came into the room. "Luther, George asked me to tell you that he would like to see you this morning as soon as you are finished eating breakfast. If you want, I can walk to the dining room with you."

Luther stood up and told Henry that it would be fine. He wasn't sure he was very hungry, except for information about his life. And he wondered why George wanted to see him so quickly. Was there something important that he had to tell him?

"Luther, you look sad this morning. Is anything wrong?" Henry asked.

"Henry, I am starting to remember things about my life on earth and they don't seem to be very nice. Yesterday George showed me my funeral and the only relative there was a stepdaughter who I don't remember. I just wondered where the rest of my family was."

"Luther, I believe that is the reason that George wants to see you this morning. He told me that he felt bad that your session yesterday ended so abruptly. It may seem difficult now, but you will see what your entire earthly life was like and that not all of it was negative. It is best to get some of those things out of the way first. Be patient. All in due time."

"Henry, you keep saying that, but I really want to know these things now. I am not a very patient person and I probably wasn't while I lived on earth either."

*****

George was standing at the doorway when Luther arrived at his office. He told him he was glad that he was coming to see him again today. He apologized for yesterday and said he would talk to him today as long as Luther wanted.

"George, I did what you asked and wrote some things down. I had dreams all night, and they were about my first wife Millie and my daughter Peggy. The beginning of my dream was a happy one, but the last part wasn't. Can you tell me about them?"

"Luther, we can talk about them or we can continue with your early childhood. I know you are anxious to find out about Millie and Peggy, but if we follow things in order, they may make more sense. I know this is difficult to understand, but trust me in what I am saying."

"Whatever you think is best, George," Luther said, feeling slightly disappointed that he probably wouldn't learn anything about Millie or Peggy today. But he had come to trust George and knew it would be best doing it the way he suggested.

"Okay, Luther. We left off with your father marrying Emma and the family moving into her house. Let's start there. And remember, Luther, you were called Wayne during your younger years."

Emma

Emma was a difficult person to understand. Warren noticed a big difference in her after they married. It seemed that she went from being happy, loving, and understanding to being a bickering, demanding, and selfish person. All Warren wanted was to have a happy life for his young boys. Gerald was eight years old and in school as were Emma's two children, Ephraim and Sarah. Ephraim was nine and Sarah was seven. Wayne was now six and had just started school.

Emma took good care of the family. There was always a delicious meal on the table when Warren came home from work. Every Monday, the dirty clothes were washed. Emma ironed her things and those of Ephraim and Sarah, but she never ironed Gerald or Wayne's school clothing. The children had to do their homework right after school and then there were chores. It seemed that Gerald was given more chores than Ephraim and they usually involved getting dirty. When he came into the house, Emma would yell at him to go to the basement and change his clothes so he didn't get dirt all over the house. Sarah would set the table and help with the meal. Sometimes Ephraim didn't have to do anything, and he just sat on the porch and watched Gerald as he did his designated chores.

The children rarely got along. Gerald resented the fact that he had so many chores to do while Ephraim just sat and watched. He told Warren about this, and it was brought up at the supper table one night. Emma's face turned bright red and she gave the meanest look to Gerald. She finally explained that Ephraim suffered from allergies and couldn't do the outside work because it would make him sick.

Gerald was watching Ephraim out of the corner of his eye and saw him snicker. Gerald knew this wasn't true because when Ephraim wanted to play baseball, he went outside and always walked through the hayfield near the school and he never sneezed once. Warren sat there and said nothing. Gerald felt sure his father would speak up in his defense, but he never did.

As Wayne got older, he also had chores to do. He and Gerald would go to the basement to change their clothes and then do their homework. Ephraim and Sarah did their homework at the dining room table. When homework was done, they had chores to do. Gerald had to cut wood for the fireplace, and it was Wayne's job to stack it outside the back door. One time, Emma told him to bring some wood into the house so she could keep the fire going. He brought a few logs in and accidently dropped them on the living room rug. Emma was furious. She slapped Wayne hard across the face and told him he would have to clean up the mess he had made. Ephraim sat at the top of the steps listening and laughing.

When Warren came home from work that evening, he noticed the red mark on Wayne's face. He asked him what had happened, but before Wayne could answer, Emma said that he fell while bringing in the firewood. Warren looked at Wayne and told him to be more careful next time. Wayne wanted to tell his father what had really happened, but he knew it would mean more punishment from Emma.

When Wayne was twelve years old, Emma made him go into town to sell soft pretzels. She was known throughout the town for making the best pretzels. She would fill a big basket and Wayne had to walk into town to sell them. He was told he had to sell every one before he came back home. He charged three cents for each pretzel. When he returned home Emma would be waiting with her hand held out. He would give her the money and she knew exactly how much should be there. If he was short, he would be slapped and asked where the money was.

Wayne was very good at selling the soft pretzels. He had a way with words, and people liked to stop and talk to him while buying a pretzel or two. People often felt sorry for him standing outside in all kinds of weather. During the summer, he would go to town every other day; during the winter, he only went on Saturdays. A kind lady gave him an umbrella once because it was raining. He soon learned that he had regular customers and he always made sure he greeted them by name. Mrs. White, who lived three blocks from where he stood, bought six pretzels every Saturday. She always stopped to get them before she did her other shopping. She knew if she waited until she was finished with her errands, there wouldn't be any pretzels left. Wayne realized this and decided he would make a deal with her. He told her he would save six pretzels for her and would deliver them to her home when he was finished for the day. That way, she could finish her shopping and go home a different way. She accepted his offer. She even offered to pay him ten cents per pretzel because he was being so kind and going out of his way for her.

Wayne thought that was a fair deal. And so he started a home delivery service in addition to selling the pretzels on the street. He made certain he kept the extra money hidden so that Emma wouldn't get her hands on it. He never told her about his delivery service. He would take the extra money to his room and hide it under his mattress. He planned to save as much as he could so he could run away from his wicked stepmother, as he liked to call her behind her back. Fortunately, she never learned about his secret stash of money. He never told anyone, not even Gerald.

Gerald was a wild child, always getting in trouble. He wouldn't do his homework most nights and didn't do very well in school. When the teacher told Emma about this, she would slap him and tell him he was no good and would never amount to much. Warren tried to talk to him, but that didn't do any good. Warren would take sides with Emma and Gerald would be punished even more.

The older sisters, Mildred and Marion, would visit sometimes. Warren wanted to go to visit them, but Emma wouldn't allow it. She said they were grown now and on their own and he needed to be with his family at his house. Warren, however, was always happy when his daughters came to visit and brought their children to see him. Although they were his grandchildren, he was practically a stranger to them. Some days, Emma wouldn't even let them come into the house and Warren had to visit with them outside on the porch. They would always ask how Gerald and Wayne were doing. They remembered taking care of their young brothers before Emma came along and they missed seeing them. They asked if the boys could spend a Saturday or Sunday with them sometime, but Emma always said no. Warren went along with whatever Emma said. Eventually, Mildred and Marion stopped visiting. It wasn't worth seeing how sad their father was and knowing there was nothing they could do.

When Gerald was fifteen, he didn't come home from school one day. Wayne waited for him at the corner where they always met, but he never showed up. He figured Gerald had decided to go home another way or go somewhere with his friends. When Wayne got home, Gerald wasn't there. Emma asked where Gerald was and Wayne said he didn't know. Emma slapped him hard across the face and demanded to be told the truth. Wayne kept saying he didn't know. He told her he had waited at the corner as he always did, but Gerald never showed up. Emma kept yelling until Sarah finally told her mother that Gerald hadn't been in school at all that day. They went to the same school building and were only a grade apart. She knew he wasn't there because his teacher had asked her why he wasn't in school. She told the teacher he wasn't feeling well and had decided to stay home. Sarah knew that was a lie, but she thought she would get in trouble if she said she didn't know.

Wayne was then told to go ahead and do his chores and then wash up for supper. He knew he wouldn't have time to do his homework that night. Too much was happening, for sure.

When Warren came home, Emma told him that she didn't know where Gerald was. He asked what she meant by that. She said he never came home from school and Sarah said he hadn't been there all day. Warren knew both boys left for school that morning, so he asked Wayne if he knew where Gerald might be. Wayne told him they parted ways, each going to their own school, but Gerald wasn't at the corner to walk home as they usually did.

Emma started saying how bad Gerald was and it would do him good to spend the night away from home. Maybe then he would appreciate how good he had it. Suddenly, Warren stood up, threw his fork down on his plate, slammed his fist on the table, and yelled at

Emma. He told her it was her responsibility to know where the boys were. Emma stood up and started to say something in her defense, but Warren looked at her and said, "Woman, sit down and shut up!" The room went silent. No one dared to make a sound. Warren said that he was tired of seeing Wayne and Gerald doing all the chores while Ephraim sat on his rear and watched. No wonder Gerald didn't want to come home. Why should he?

There was total silence at the table. Warren picked up his jacket and told Wayne to get his. He told Sarah to clean up the kitchen; the evening meal was now over. Sarah started crying. Warren then looked at Ephraim and told him to bring in the firewood for the night. Emma started to protest. Warren gave her a stern look and told her not to give him any more mouth about Ephraim's allergies. He said Ephraim didn't have any more allergies than the man in the moon. And with that, Warren was out the door with Wayne at his side.

The Circus

Warren had a feeling he knew where Gerald had gone. He knew how unhappy the boy was at home. Warren was feeling very guilty because he had never defended either of his sons. He had allowed Emma to do the disciplining, and most of the time, it wasn't fair.

The circus had pulled into town the week before and was preparing to leave the following day. Warren highly suspected that this was where he would find Gerald. They were offering a small wage, living quarters, and meals for hired hands to work with the circus. He knew that Gerald had heard about this because he had talked about it.

Warren and Wayne drove in silence. Wayne was afraid to say anything. He had never seen his father as angry as he had been at supper that night. He was glad that he told Emma to shut up. She was a mean woman and he didn't like her at all. He was so sure Emma was going to walk over to Warren and slap him across the face just like she did to him and Gerald, almost daily. But there was something in the tone of his father's voice that made everyone shudder, including Emma. *Served her right*, Wayne thought. As they drove, he had no idea where they were going, but obviously, his father knew where Gerald might be.

Just then they pulled into an open field across from the circus. Now Wayne knew what his father was thinking. Wayne felt Gerald was here and now he knew his father thought so too.

When the car stopped, Warren and Wayne got out and crossed the field to where someone was pulling pegs out of the ground.

Warren approached the man and asked, "Who is the man in charge here?"

The young man jumped because he hadn't heard them walking toward them. He looked up at Warren and said, "That would be Mr. Higgins. He's in the third trailer after the lion cage."

"Thank you, young man," Warren said and he and Wayne headed in that direction. They found the trailer and Warren knocked on the door. After several minutes and numerous knocks, the door was opened by a very large man dressed in black pants, a purple shirt, and suspenders. He had dark black hair and a mustache that curled up at the ends. A pipe was clenched in his mouth. His hands were large and had rings on each finger. His dark eyes stared at Warren and Wayne. Wayne shivered in fear. The man looked very scary. Wayne hid behind his father as Warren started to talk.

"Mr. Higgins? I'm Warren Yeager. I believe my son Gerald came here today looking for a job. I would like to know if that is true."

"I'm Isaac Higgins, but I don't know your son. Are you sure he is here?"

"I have a pretty good idea that he is. He didn't go to school today and never came home for supper tonight. He thinks his life at home is pretty bad, so it wouldn't surprise me that he thought living and working with the circus would be easier. Could you please check to see if he might have asked about work today?"

"Well, Mr. Yeager, we can go over and talk to the manager and see if there were any new hires today. Follow me." Warren and Wayne followed Mr. Higgins to a small tent where a man was sitting at a table looking over a ledger.

"Meryl, this here is Mr. Yeager and he's looking for his son. Did you by any chance hire anyone today?" Meryl was shorter than Isaac Higgins. It was easy to notice that even though he was sitting down. He looked a lot friendlier than Mr. Higgins, or so Wayne thought.

"I hired a boy this morning. Said he was seventeen and looking for a job. Told me he had no family and it wouldn't be a problem travelling with the circus. Said his name was Gerry. I'll go and get him and see what's going on." Meryl left and was back about five minutes later with Gerald following behind.

"Gerry, is this your pa?"

"Ah, yes, sir. It is." Gerald looked up at his father. He knew he was here to take him home. He had hoped no one would find him. The circus would leave town in the morning and he could be free from his family.

"Gerald, your brother and I have come to take you home. Sarah told us that you didn't go to school today and your mother was worried when you weren't home by supper time. You're too young to be on your own and you're needed at home. So gather your things and come along."

Warren turned to Mr. Higgins and said, "I'm sorry to have bothered you. I'll take my boy home now. He may have told you he was seventeen, but the truth is he is only fifteen. His mother has been worried and will be relieved when he returns to where he belongs."

Gerald stood his ground and said, "I will not go home and don't call that woman my mother. She's a bi—and I will never live in the same house with her again."

"Gerry," yelled Meryl, "that's no way to talk about your mother. I'm sorry, but you are going to have to go home with your father. You seem like a good kid and you worked hard today. I was hoping things would work out with you, but as your father said, you are needed at home."

"Pa, please!" begged Gerald. "Don't make me go back to that place. Emma will beat me for sure. I am tired of doing all the work while Ephraim sits on his lazy ass doing nothing. I want to stay here and work. Emma will be glad to have one less mouth to feed. The only time she will miss me is when there is firewood to cut and bring inside. Wayne, why don't you come with me? Please, Pa! Let Wayne and me start a new life where no one yells and puts us down all the time. Please!"

Everyone stood silent and waited for Warren to say something. Deep in his heart, he knew the things his son was saying were true. He knew how Emma mistreated his sons and he never stood up to her, that is, until tonight. If he left Gerald go with the circus, Emma would make Wayne do all of Gerald's work as well as his own, that is, unless he stood up to her and put his foot down—something he should have done years ago. Then they wouldn't be standing here like this. He saw the look on Gerald's face and knew he had already lost him. It would be torture for him if he had to go back home. Maybe if he gave his permission for Gerald to go with the circus, he could return in a year or so and they could start over again at being father and son. Could it be a risk he was willing to take?

"Mr. Higgins, if I give my permission for Gerald to stay with you, can you assure me he will be well taken care of? I won't let him stay if I have any idea at all that he will be abused or mistreated."

"Mr. Yeager, I run a good circus here. I treat all my employees fair. They have a warm trailer to sleep in and three good meals a day. I expect them to work hard, respect me and everyone else here, and be friendly and cordial to all the circus visitors. Meryl said your son did a good day's work today and that is all I ask. I can assure you he will be taken care of as long as he works and minds his manners. If for any reason it doesn't work out, he will have to leave."

Warren looked at his son and reached out to him. Gerald reluctantly went to his father and gave him a hug. This was something that rarely happened before.

"Gerald, I will give you permission to stay here. You heard what Mr. Higgins said about work? It won't be easy, but I understand that home hasn't been any better. I can only say that I'm sorry about that. Would you please write to me and let me know how you are? Even if you just send a postcard from the places you go, I will be content with that. Promise me you will stay in touch?"

"I will, Pa. I promise. I can't live in that house anymore with that woman. She hates me. What about Wayne? Can't he come too? Please! You know she'll make him work twice as hard."

"Gerald, Wayne is coming home with me. He's too young to go with you. If you promise to keep in touch and let me know how you are, I promise that Emma will not mistreat Wayne. It is high time I start making some of the decisions. I promise you that Wayne will be treated better and that Sarah and Ephraim will have to start pulling their weight around the house."

Warren hugged his son and felt an overwhelming amount of guilt. Deep down inside, as much as he wanted him to return home, he knew that Gerald would have a better life here. He hoped that Gerald would keep his promise and write when he could. Gerald broke away from his father and looked at his younger brother. He wanted to hug him, but he didn't want anyone to think he was a sissy. He saw that Wayne had tears in his eyes. Gerald would miss him and wished his father had let him come along. He would have taken care of him. He also wondered if they would ever see each other again. He reached out his hand and Wayne took it. He was sure Wayne was thinking the same thing.

"Mr. Higgins, I will give my permission for Gerald to stay and work for you and the circus. If you would, just remind him to write. Please take care of my boy."

"Mr. Yeager, I will. Gerald, I think it would be a good idea for you go to back to your bunk and get a good night's sleep now. We have lots of work to do tomorrow. We will be leaving at dawn."

"Thank you," Warren said. He then asked if he could have a piece of paper so he could write the address down. He wanted all correspondence to go to Mildred. He didn't want to take the chance of mail coming to his house, knowing Emma would destroy it. If mail came to his daughter's, he could find out how Gerald was. He would visit over the weekend and tell her everything.

Warren and Wayne walked across the field and got back into the car. Neither one said a word. Before they reached home, Warren pulled the car to the side of the road. He turned to Wayne and told him he must never tell anyone where Gerald was. If asked, he was to say that they looked all over town and couldn't find him. He didn't want Emma to know where Gerald was. He also told Wayne that there would be changes at home. He saw the look in Wayne's eyes and knew that he wasn't sure he should believe him. Warren would just have to prove once and for all that he was the man of the house. It wasn't going to be easy or pleasant, but Warren had to try and make amends for the damage that had been done to his children because he neglected to stand up and be the father he should have been. He had failed at his first marriage and his second wasn't much better, but the ones who suffered the most were the ones he loved the most—his children.

Changes

It was after ten o'clock when Warren and Wayne finally walked in the house. It was dark; everyone was already in bed. Warren doubted they were asleep, but it made it easier to pretend they were. Warren told Wayne to go to bed and that he would see him in the morning. Warren walked up the steps and entered the bedroom he shared with Emma. She was on her side of the bed with her back turned away from him.

The next morning, Emma was preparing breakfast when Warren walked into the kitchen. Ephraim and Sarah were already sitting at the table. Emma walked right by her husband and called up the steps to Wayne. She then poured milk in the cereal bowl sitting at Wayne's place. She brought her husband his breakfast—one egg, toast, and jelly with three slices of bacon, his usual. The children were allowed to have bacon and eggs only on Sundays. As Emma put the plate in front of Warren, she looked directly at him. She wanted to know what had happened last night, but she was afraid to ask. She had never seen him so angry and she didn't want a repeat of the last meal they had all shared together.

Wayne walked into the room and sat down at the table. He looked at his cereal bowl and started to eat. He hated that the milk was already poured; by now it was soggy. In the past, he had asked Emma to wait until he was at the table before pouring the milk, but it never happened. He figured this was just another way to show her dislike for him.

The absence of Gerald at the table was noticed by everyone. A bowl had been put where he always sat, but no cereal was in it.

Emma wasn't about to waste it if he wasn't going to be there to eat it. Finally, Emma sat down at the table and asked Warren where Gerald was. There was silence from everyone, and they all looked at Warren, waiting for an answer. It seemed like an eternity before he finally spoke.

"Gerald is not here. I don't know where he is." That was all that Warren said.

"What should I tell people when they ask about him? What should I tell the school?" Emma asked.

"You don't need to tell anyone anything. It is no one's business what goes on in this house. He isn't here and you don't know where he is or when he is coming back. End of discussion." And with that statement, Warren got up, took his hat and coat off the peg by the door, and left.

Once Warren was out of the house, Emma asked Wayne where he and his father had gone last night. All Wayne said was that they drove around town and couldn't find Gerald anywhere and then they came home.

Wayne left the house with Sarah and Ephraim following close behind. He started running to school because he didn't want them asking him questions. He was tired because he hadn't slept at all that night. It was different being in the room without Gerald there. They usually talked before falling asleep, and last night just didn't seem right without his brother. He was going to miss him. He wished his father had given permission for him to go with the circus too. He wasn't sure how things were going to be at home now. He was afraid of Emma and he didn't like the way Ephraim and Sarah talked about him. He was also sure he was going to have to do all the work around the house that Gerald had done, plus his own. He remembered his father saying that things would be different, but Warren wasn't there when he got home from school. Wayne was determined, now more than ever, to save his money from the soft pretzel sales so he could run away like his brother. He would really have to think hard about where he would go. He would have to make sure his father wouldn't have any idea and come looking for him and make him go back home.

School was okay that day. No one really asked Wayne about Gerald because they weren't in the same school building. He gathered up his books and headed out as soon as the teacher dismissed the class. Force of habit made him go to the corner where he always met Gerald. Once there, he realized that Gerald would not be meeting him today or any other day. He was all alone as he walked home.

Emma was in the kitchen making the evening meal when he walked in the back door. She didn't turn around when he came in, but told him to get the firewood for the stove. Wayne went to the basement to change his clothes and then out the cellar door to gather the wood. He wanted to ask Emma if he was still going to be selling pretzels. He needed that job so he could save his money. He would have to make it seem like he didn't like selling them. If he did that, he figured she would insist he still do it. She seemed to take pleasure in making him do the things she knew he didn't like. He was afraid to ask, but he really needed to know the answer. Fortunately, when he brought the firewood into the house, she brought up the subject.

"Wayne, you will still need to go into town and sell pretzels just like you did before. You will have to figure out a way to help with the chores that were Gerald's, as well as your own. I can't afford to lose that income. Ephraim will have to help with more chores too. I sure hope his allergies don't act up. We can't afford a doctor bill."

"Yes, ma'am," was all Wayne said. He tried to say it in a way that sounded like he didn't want to do it, so she would still insist. He was glad to hear that Ephraim would be doing some work. Wayne knew Ephraim didn't have allergies. He was just lazy, so it was a good excuse. He sure had his mother fooled with the coughing and the sneezing he managed to fake.

It was Friday and usually Warren stopped at the bar on his way home from work. Emma knew this was his normal routine, so she kept a platter of food warm for him to eat when he got home. She had Sarah set the table for the four of them and was just dishing out the stew when Warren walked in. Emma, as well as the children, all had a puzzled look on their faces. He took his hat and coat off, placed them on the peg by the door, and sat down at the table.

"Where is my plate, Emma?" he asked. "Or am I not included in the meal this evening?"

Emma jumped up and got the dish she had set aside. She seemed flustered as she placed it in front of him. "Warren, you usually don't get home this early on a Friday night, and the children and I usually eat ahead of you. We're having stew tonight and I baked a chocolate cake for dessert."

"Pass me the bread will you, Ephraim?" was all that Warren said.

By now everyone was feeling uncomfortable sitting at the table. Warren took his time eating, and when he was finished, Emma started to get up and clear the table.

"Emma, sit down. Ephraim, Sarah, and Wayne, you will remain at the table. I have a few things to say. There are going to be some changes around this house. First of all, now that Gerald is not here, his chores will have to be done by someone else. Ephraim, that is going to be you." Emma started to protest, but Warren just glared at her. "It won't hurt you to bring in the firewood. You can come home from school and put on your old clothes and do those chores. If you don't have any old clothes, I'm sure you can wear Gerald's. There are some in the basement."

Ephraim had never been in the basement. From the upstairs door, it looked dark and grungy down there. He knew it was cold too, and he hated being in the cold. He always sat closest to the wood stove to keep warm. He was waiting for his mother to say something so he wouldn't have to do this, but she just sat there. *What about my allergies?* he thought.

Warren continued, "Any other chores that need to be done will be cleared by me first. Sarah, you are not too dainty to do some of the outside work as well. Wayne, I think you have enough to do selling pretzels in town. That will be your job. Do you all understand what I'm saying?"

They all nodded their heads in acknowledgment. Clearly, it wasn't going to be pleasant around the house anymore. Ephraim and Sarah were sure that once things settled down, their mother would once again put her foot down and things would be back to normal. They just hoped that this would happen much sooner than later.

"Children, you are dismissed to do your chores and homework. Emma, stay. I have some things I want to say to you." The children got up and quickly went to their rooms. They really wanted to stay and listen, but by the tone in Warren's voice, they realized it would be better not to be anywhere near the kitchen.

"Emma, I want to make it very clear that I expect the chores to be divided fairly between the three children. I will be keeping an eye on this in case you think you want to alter them in any way. Also, I will be picking Wayne up on Saturday afternoons from town when he is finished selling pretzels. We will be going to visit my daughters, Mildred and Marion. Since they do not want to visit me here because they feel unwelcome, I will go to visit them. If they ever do decide to visit me here, they will be allowed in the house and will sit in the living room to visit. There will be no more meetings on the front porch. I have grandchildren that I hardly know because they haven't been welcomed into my home. I earn a good wage to provide for this family, which includes you and your children. The least you can do is allow me to see my older children when I want to. Do I make myself clear?"

Emma had the feeling that Warren knew where Gerald was and that this sudden change in him was all connected to whatever was going on with him. She also knew that Warren had changed, was different. He wanted to be in charge, but she also knew he really had no idea how to be in charge of a family. When he was married to Bertha, he wasn't home much and that left Bertha in charge of the house. And look where that ended up. Emma had always wanted a better life for herself and her children. When Warren came along, so desperately looking for someone, she saw her opportunity. She put on a good front and pretended she really cared for him and his two brats. He did provide a good living—that she had to admit. They were far from wealthy, but there was always enough money to maintain the house and provide food and clothing for all of them. She had even somehow convinced Warren that the family really needed a car. He had been adamant about not having one. He saw it as a waste of good money. Everything they needed was within walking distance. But somehow she was able to persuade him that the family really needed one. Now he was insisting that her children should help out with the chores. Emma wasn't happy with that, but she would appease him for now and go along with it. As for his daughters, she didn't want them in her home. The girls were all right, but their snotty-nosed children were another story. She didn't care if Warren went to visit them now and then, but she would have to put her foot down when it came to their visiting at her house. She decided the best thing to do was to go along with him for a while and wait until things settled down some. She had her plan; she would get things back to the way they were.

"Yes, Warren, I understand. I will see that things are done differently, as you wish." Then she got up and started clearing the table from the evening meal.

*****

For the next several months, the Yeager household was very quiet. The children came home from school and did their designated chores and their homework. Emma and Warren only spoke to each other out of necessity. They attended worship services together every Sunday and pretended they were one big happy family. When asked about Gerald, Warren would say that he was going to be away for a little while. Emma had a hot meal on the table every evening when Warren came home from work. Conversations around the dinner table were about chores, school, and special programs that the children were in at school or church. There was a spring concert coming up and Sarah asked if they would attend. Emma said that she would be there, of course. Warren said the he would be happy to attend as well and that Ephraim and Wayne would also go along. This, of course, caused displeasure from the boys, but Warren stood his ground and said they would be going because it was their sister who was in the concert and the family had to show support. No further discussion.

On Saturday afternoons, Warren would pick Wayne up at the corner of Fifth and High streets. Wayne had to adjust his schedule so that he had time to deliver the pretzels to his favorite customers and be back in time to meet Warren. They would then drive to see his sisters. Within the past year, Marion and Earl had bought the farm directly across the street from Mildred and Maurice. This included a larger farmhouse with more pastureland for Earl's cows. It also allowed them to raise chickens and several pigs. The sisters loved being neighbors and their children were able to play together. Mildred had four children by now and Marion had one son, Earl Junior, affectionately called Sonny.

Warren loved visiting his daughters and grandchildren and they in turn loved having a relationship with him. Wayne enjoyed being with his nephews and nieces. Mildred's oldest, Ralph, was two years older than Wayne, and they had become the best of friends. Warren and Wayne would arrive around four in the afternoon and stay for supper. It was a special time for everyone. On several occasions, Elizabeth and her husband Charles would come to visit. Family gatherings were good.

About a month after Gerald left, a postcard arrived from him. It was mailed from San Francisco, California. Mildred couldn't wait to share it with her father and Wayne. Gerald wrote that he was fine and loved being with the circus. He had jobs to do that were hard, but everyone treated him good. He felt like he finally had a home with people who actually loved him and looked out for him. Reading that brought tears to Warren's eyes because it meant that Gerald felt he had never had that before. And if Warren thought about it, Gerald was right. His own mother had abandoned him and his stepmother had abused him. Warren felt regret that he never stood up to Emma before. If he had, perhaps things would have been different. He was glad that his son was now happy and hoped that he would someday get to see him again.

Wayne missed Gerald. They had been close when he still lived at home. They confided in each other and complained about Emma, Sarah, and Ephraim. Wayne knew that Gerald had been unhappy at home, but he never thought he would just take off one day. How he wished his father had left him go with Gerald. They could have looked out for each other. He hoped he would see his brother again soon.

Warren and his children often talked about Doug and Marge and wondered where they were. No one had ever heard from or about either of them. Warren felt the pain of losing two children as much as he felt the loss of Gerald. At least he still had his three girls and Wayne.

After their evening meal, Mildred and Marion would clean up the dishes and then they would play games or sit by the piano. Marion had taught herself how to play and had a beautiful singing voice. Sometimes they could persuade Mildred to sing along. It was so much fun. Warren and Wayne looked forward to this every week and hated when it started to get late and they had to leave.

During the summer, Emma would be busy making her soft pretzels. Wayne would have to take them to town three days a week. Emma would help Ephraim with his chores so he would get done faster. It was a little easier in the winter time because Wayne only sold the pretzels on Saturdays.

When Warren and Wayne would return home from their Saturday visits, Emma was usually in the kitchen. Warren would say hello and then go to the other room. Wayne would go to his room on the third floor and prepare for bed. If there was something that needed to be talked about between Warren and Emma, it was brought up. Otherwise, each went about as if the other wasn't there.

One particular Saturday, Warren left for work as usual. He didn't always work on a Saturday, but ever since Gerald left, he did. The less time spent at home, the better. He never left until he was sure Wayne was up and ready to leave for town with the pretzels and that Ephraim and Sarah were doing their chores. Warren worked until three o'clock and then left to pick up Wayne. Then they headed to Marion's. She was making a special meal that night because it was Sonny's birthday. Warren had a package in the back seat of the car—the first present he had ever given to anyone. He wanted it to be a special day for his young grandson.

They had a delicious meal of roast beef, mashed potatoes, green beans, and gravy. Marion had a birthday cake with candles on it for dessert. They were just about to sing "Happy Birthday" when there was a knock on the front door. Earl went to answer and a few minutes later came in with a puzzled look on his face. He told Marion to come with him. Everyone was wondering what was going on and who was at the door. Then Marion came into the room and announced that they had a surprise visitor. She stepped aside and into the dining room walked a very tall, nicely dressed young man. He looked around the room and finally said hello. Warren froze in his seat. He couldn't believe his eyes. He recognized him at once even though it had been close to thirteen years since he had last seen him. It was Doug.

Doug

His oldest son Doug walked up to Warren and offered his hand. Warren stood up, and instead of giving his hand, he embraced him. He was too shocked to say anything. Father and son held each other for several minutes.

Mildred came over to give her brother a big hug and kiss. Wayne, however, had no idea who this man was. After many hugs and kisses, Doug looked around the room at the family he didn't know. Warren pointed to Wayne and told Doug that this was his youngest brother. Doug went over and shook Wayne's hand. Wayne knew he had an older brother Doug, but had no memory of him at all.

After the initial shock of this unexpected visitor, Marion brought a chair from the kitchen into the dining room and set a place at the table for Doug. They sang "Happy Birthday" to Sonny and had cake and ice cream. The younger children went into the living room to play while the adults continued to sit around the table. Everyone wanted to hear from Doug and find out how he was. And they wanted to know about Marge.

The next several hours were filled with memories and getting reacquainted with each other. Doug told them he had graduated from college and law school and was working in a town about thirty miles away. He was engaged to be married to a wonderful woman named Elsa. He had always wanted to reconnect with his father and brothers and sisters, but wasn't sure what to expect.

He said it took a little time to find where they were. He never knew that Warren had remarried and sold the house they used to live in. That was where he started his search. A neighbor told him that

Warren was now living on the other side of town, but she didn't know the address. Doug went to that area and asked anyone he saw if they knew a Warren Yeager. Several people said they knew who he was, but weren't exactly sure where he lived. Finally, someone knew Emma and told him which house she lived in. He went there three weeks ago and knocked on the door. A woman, who he now realized was Emma, answered. He said he was looking for Warren Yeager. She said she was his wife and wanted to know what he wanted with her husband. Doug only said he had some business to discuss with him and wondered when he would be available. Emma had never heard of any business deals involving Warren and wondered just what was going on. She told him that Warren was at work and wouldn't be home until later in the evening. Doug asked if he would be around over the weekend. Emma finally told him that every Saturday he went to visit his daughters and gave him an address. Doug also asked her about Wayne and Gerald, but couldn't get any additional information from her. Today was the first opportunity he had to try and find his family.

Doug told them that Marge had attended nursing school in Philadelphia and was working at a local hospital there. He wasn't sure if anyone wanted to hear about his mother, so he only mentioned that she and Horace were fine. He said when they left thirteen years ago, everything was very confusing. He and Marge were told that their father didn't want them anymore and did not want to see them and that is why they left. As the years went on, as he and Marge got older, they began to talk about everything and realized their mother hadn't been entirely truthful about the situation. He said he told Marge he was going to try to find their father and siblings. He said his mother's husband, Horace, was good to them and provided them with a very nice home and an education. They traveled a lot, and both he and Marge had been to Europe several times. They were grateful for all this, but realized their other brothers and sisters would probably never have the opportunities they were given. Doug said he told his mother he wanted to find his family and she said she didn't think that was a wise idea, but she knew there wasn't anything she could do to stop him. He did assure her that if he found them, it would not interfere with his relationship with her and Horace.

Warren was both happy and sad to hear the things Doug was saying. He was glad that Doug had been given an education and the opportunity to travel. He regretted knowing that these were things he could never have been able to do for any of his children. He felt cheated out of a relationship with Doug and Marge and would never forgive Bertha for taking them away from him. If she had wanted to leave, so be it, but to deny him his children was a terrible thing to do. He was so glad that Doug had the courage to find them and hopefully allow all of them to be reunited as a family again.

Warren told Doug about Gerald. He said they received a post-card from time to time and that he seemed happy with his life. Warren neglected to tell his oldest son the reason Gerald made the decision to leave. This was something he would regret and have to live with for the rest of his life. He only hoped that someday Gerald would come back, even if just for a visit.

Hours went by with all of them catching up on past times and adventures. Marion and Mildred put the younger children to bed. It was decided that Mildred's children would spend the night there so that Mildred and Maurice could stay and continue their visit with Doug.

As the hour approached midnight, Warren realized that he had to take Wayne home. After all, tomorrow was Sunday and he and Wayne had to get up for church. He also wondered if Emma might be worried about them. They had never stayed away this long on a Saturday night. Would she still be up or would she have gone to bed? Probably the latter, and perhaps hoping they wouldn't come home at all. These were not nice thoughts and Warren regretted having them, but unfortunately, he often wondered if there was perhaps the slightest bit of truth in them.

Doug left, promising to return as soon as he could. He would bring Elsa along next time. They exchanged addresses and phone numbers and promised to keep in touch. Warren left the information with his daughters. He didn't want Emma to know anything. She had never mentioned anyone coming to the door asking for him. She would have had no idea who Doug was, even though there was a resemblance between father and son. She had never met him or Marge and showed no interest in them whatsoever.

Warren and Wayne arrived home well after midnight. Emma had already gone to bed. Wayne went to his room and Warren sat in the living room for a while longer. He was thinking about the evening and how happy it made him to finally reconnect with Doug.

The next morning, it was difficult to get up, but both Warren and Wayne managed somehow. They would have to hurry to be ready to leave for church on time. Emma's only remark at the breakfast table was that it must have been a very long evening the night before.

Wayne looked at Warren, who only said, "Yes, it certainly was."

Gerald

"My, oh my, Luther, it is getting late," George said. "We should stop here and continue another time. I wouldn't want you to miss your evening meal tonight."

"Oh please, George," Luther said excitedly. "This is all so fascinating. I want to know if Doug ever came back to visit and if he brought Elsa. There is so much about my life I want to know. Can't we continue for a little while longer…please?"

"Luther, I feel it is best if we stop for the evening. Believe me, I am thinking of you. There is a lot of history here for you to absorb and I don't want to overload you. I want you to go to the dining room and have a nice meal and then get a good night's sleep. We can continue the day after tomorrow. And I believe there will be a surprise at dinner this evening."

Now Luther was intrigued. What kind of surprise could there be? It couldn't be a special meal, because every meal seemed special. He was sad that they wouldn't continue, although he was a bit overwhelmed with everything. His young life had certainly been far from dull, even though it certainly wasn't a very happy one either. He couldn't even imagine what his adult life was like.

Reluctantly, he left George's office and headed toward the dining room. It seemed odd, but he knew exactly the right way to go. He was slowly getting used to finding his way around, even though things seemed to change at the drop of a hat.

The dining room was just starting to fill up as he walked in the room and headed toward his table. Today there were two place set-

118

tings, and Luther was hoping that the surprise George talked about would mean he had a companion to share the meal. The tablecloth tonight was bright red with cream-colored napkins. The silverware was gold; the china was multicolored. It was actually very pretty. There was a swirl design on the plates and inside each swirl was a different shade of red. Who would have ever imagined there were so many shades of red and each one different? Three glasses were at each setting. Luther assumed one was for water, another for wine, but the third was beyond him.

Luther sat down and immediately someone came to fill his water glass. Luther asked what the other two glasses were for and was told that one was for red wine and the other for white. *Pretty classy tonight*, he thought. Just then a man walked in the room and came toward Luther's table. The man had dark hair that was long on the left side and combed over the top of his head toward the right. He was slightly taller than Luther. Luther watched him as he approached his table and thought he recognized him, but couldn't place how. Was it someone he had seen here, perhaps at the bowling alley? The man stopped at Luther's table and stood there just looking at him. Finally, Luther said hello.

"Well, I'll be damned," the man said. "It is you. They told me I was going to be eating with you, but I thought for sure that just couldn't be."

Luther was bewildered. He kept searching in his mind as to how he could have known this man. "I'm Luther. What's your name?"

"Luther? Luther? Who the hell is Luther? You're Wayne and I'm your brother Gerald."

"Gerald...I can't believe it! It's been so long. How are you?"

"Well, Luther, if that's what you want to be called, but you were always Wayne to me," Gerald said. "It certainly has been a while," he grinned. "And how am I? Well, I'm dead, just like you," he chuckled. "That's how I am. And who the hell calls you Luther? And why?"

"Well," Luther began, "I used to be called Wayne, but after my first wife died, I started going by Luther. I dunno. Guess my second wife decided she liked that name better. And yes, I know you're dead. Me too, but we're here in this wonderful place and now finally together again. I remember we were inseparable as kids. I know you left home when you were fifteen to join the circus. We used to get postcards from you and they always made everyone feel good knowing that you were okay. Then one day, they just stopped and we never heard from you again. Dad was pretty upset after you left, but he finally stood up to Emma and things were different around the house."

"Yea," Gerald said. "Well, I'm glad my leaving caused the old man to finally get some backbone. That bi—he married was something else. I never heard what happened to her or her two brats. I just know I was glad to get the hell out of there. I'm sorry you had to stay. I wanted Dad to let you come. Well, you know what he said."

"Gerald, what happened? You sent postcards from all those place and said how much you liked seeing everything. Then they stopped and you never came home. We never saw you again."

"You never saw me, but I saw you," Gerald responded. "I was at Granddad's funeral. I was sitting in the back and left before it was over. I wanted to see everyone, but I just couldn't stay. Maybe I didn't want anyone to see me. I don't know. I spent about five years with the circus and then I got into a fight with one of the new guys. He was always trying to boss me around. Hell, I had five years more experience and he wanted to tell me what to do. One day, I had finally had enough, and I waited for him outside the mess tent. I told him to back off or I was going to show him my way of handling things. The son of a bi—took a swing at me and that was all it took. I really let him have it. When we were finished, he had two black eyes and he wasn't walking too steady. I figured that would be the end of that. Boy was I wrong.

"The boss came to see me later that night and told me to pack my things and leave. He said if I had a problem with someone, I should have gone to him rather than take matters into my own hands. I wanted to throw a punch at him too, but he was bigger than me, so I didn't. I wish now I had. It would have been worth it even if he would've beat the crap out of me.

"After that, I drifted around Houston for a while. That's where we were when they told me to leave. I had enough money to get a cheap room for the night with a bar next door. The whiskey sure tasted good and I stayed till they closed the joint and tossed me out. I went back the next night and the next one too. Soon my money was gone and I couldn't stay in the motel. I was lucky to find a job at a warehouse and I worked there for the next few months. I always somehow found cheap living, which was good, because most of my pay went to the local bars. Then I hopped a train and headed east. I figured I would come home and see if things were any better than before I left. I watched the house one day and saw the old man come home from work. I wanted to run up to him, but I didn't want him to see me the way I looked. One Saturday, I watched, hoping to see you, but I guess you had already moved out of the place. After several days of this, I just figured the hell with it. I was a lost cause and would only embarrass everyone, so why bother? I saw the old battle axe one day at the market. I walked right by her and gave her a little shove. She looked me right in the eye and told me I was rude. I laughed. She didn't even know me. Then I wished I had shoved her a little harder. I would have loved to see her land on her ass. Would have served her right for all the things she did to me.

"And so I drifted around town and soon met up with a girl named Edith. Now don't get me wrong, I had plenty of women over the years. Met most of them in the bars. Some were mighty nice and liked to have a good time, if you get my drift. I never thought I would ever meet someone who I would want to get serious about. Serious was something that just wasn't in my genes. But this Edith seemed different and she didn't take any crap from me. She invited me to her parent's house for dinner one night. I tried to be on my best behavior. Her dad was a big guy, worked in the coal mine. He and I seemed to get along pretty good. Her mother was just a little thing, but boy could she cook.

"Pretty soon Edith and I were seeing each other every night. She didn't want me hanging in the bars all the time and took me to the movies and the ice cream parlor. Now I wasn't the ice cream parlor type, but I was thinking about how good her mamma cooked, and if she had taught Edith all that stuff, maybe it wouldn't be so bad. By now I had a steady job at a gas station—mostly pumping gas—but

Sam, the owner, taught me how to do some repairs. I liked working for Sam. And by now Edith was planning a wedding. It was going to be something small in her parent's backyard. Next thing you know, me and Edith are hitched and living with her parents. It wasn't the best situation, but we didn't have any money for a place of our own."

Soon, a waiter arrived at their table and served their meal. They had both ordered a fish platter. The brothers ate in silence, each in deep thought about this wonderful reunion.

Edith

After their meal, the brothers enjoyed a cup of coffee and Gerald continued his story. "So, as I was saying, Sam was teaching me more and more auto repair skills and also some carpentry work. On the side, he would go around and build additions to houses or sheds. He took me along and the extra money I made was being saved so Edith and I could get a place of our own. Her idea. As soon as I got home, she would take my pay and stash it away where I couldn't find it. What she didn't know was I would take a few bucks from my pay and stop off at the bar. She might have been my wife, but she didn't need to know everything I did.

"A few years later, Sam sold me a two-car garage building that he owned. I told Edith I was going to make it into a house for us. Every chance I had, I worked on it. Sam helped when he could. The electrical and plumbing work were the most expensive, so sometimes months went by before I could get more work done. It took me about three years, but we were finally ready to move in. It wasn't big and it wasn't fancy, but it was all ours, and we didn't have to live with her parents anymore.

"The day we moved in, Edith told me I was going to be a daddy. I wasn't prepared for that. We didn't have any extra room for a baby. I was really mad when she told me. She started crying and took off for her parent's house. I let her go. I figured she would come back when she missed me. By this time, I was starting to get used to the idea of having a kid. I wasn't sure where we would put it, but I guessed we would manage. You know that woman, Edith, was as stubborn as a mule. She didn't come home, and after two weeks, I went to find her. She told me she was going to have the baby and then head out to Ohio to live with her cousin Myrtle. I told her she would do no such thing and to get her belongings and her ass back home where she belonged. Her mamma pulled me aside and told me if I wanted Edith to go back home with me, I was going to have to apologize because I hurt her feelings being so upset about this baby. Me, apologize to a woman! No way! So I left again, sure she would come to her senses and come back home. After all, we now had our own place and she never spent one night in it.

"After a few months, I went back to her parents' house to see her. Her pa was there and he told me she got on the train two days before that and headed to Ohio. I couldn't believe it. What was with this woman? He said if I wanted her back, I was going to have to go to Ohio and probably beg. Now begging, especially to a woman, was another thing I didn't do. The only time I ever begged was to ask Daddy if I could stay with the circus. I never begged again, even when I was hungry. So I up and went home again.

"Now home was getting mighty lonely. I went to work during the day and spent the night at the bar. What was the point in going home? There wasn't anyone there except some yellow stray cat that seemed to hang around. It got to the point I stopped thinking about Edith, well, most of the time anyway. Truth was, I was really missing her, but it was obvious she wasn't coming back and I sure as hell wasn't going to Ohio. My travelling days were over.

"I spent nights at the bar and usually ended up going home with someone I met there. What the hell. I figured if my wife wasn't going to be here with me, nothing kept me from doing what I wanted. Maybe she found someone she wanted to be with. Who knew? I guess I wasn't thinking clearly, because I sorta forgot she was in a family way. I figured the way things were going, I'd have a kid somewhere that I'd never see and who would never know who I was. Maybe that would be for the best anyway.

"One Friday night, I was at the bar, as usual, and I had a cute little thing sitting on my lap. She had already told me she wanted to spend the night with me, so I kept filling her glass. She was feeling no pain and let me do all the feeling I wanted. I knew I would get lucky that night. Suddenly, I felt a big hand on my shoulder and I looked up straight into Edith's dad's eyes. Oh boy. Now what did he want? He said, 'Son we need to have a little talk outside.'

"I protested and said I was busy. Then he upended my chair. I landed on my ass and the girl sitting on my lap ended up under the table. I followed him outside. He told me I should be ashamed of myself acting the way I was. I was a married man. I tried to tell him that my married wife didn't want anything to do with me, so what was I supposed to do? He told me that the next morning I was going to be on a train heading for Ohio, where I was going to see my wife and my new baby daughter. I started to say something when it hit me that he said the word daughter. I had a daughter? I actually had a daughter!

"He said when I got there, I was going to tell Edith how much I wanted her and the baby to come home and that I was going to be a model husband and father. In other words, I was going to have to beg. He handed me several envelopes. The top one had a one-way ticket to Cleveland with an address written on it. The next one had two one-way tickets home. There was also a twenty-dollar bill included. After he handed me the envelopes, he left. I walked back into the bar thinking how many rounds I could buy with that twenty. I started looking for the girl I was with and saw her sitting on some other bozo's lap. He had his hand up her blouse and she was laughing. Boy, she didn't waste much time now, did she? I turned toward the door and walked out, heading for home. I wasn't sure I'd be on that train in the morning, but at eight forty-three the next day, the train was pulling out of the station heading toward Ohio with me on it. I had a window seat with no one sitting beside me. I wasn't exactly sure how I talked myself into going, but there I was on the train. Now I had to figure out what I would say to Edith. I didn't think to ask her pa if she knew I was coming.

"When the train pulled into the station in Cleveland, I got off and asked someone where to find the address on the envelope. The man said it was only a few blocks from where he was going and offered me a ride. I told him I was going to pick up my wife and daughter at her cousin's house. He seemed nice enough and I was

125

grateful for the ride. He dropped me off at the corner and told me the house I was looking for was the second one on the right. I walked up the steps and knocked on the door.

"A little girl answered and I asked if a lady named Edith was there. She said yes and let me in the door. A very attractive lady came in from the kitchen wiping her hands on her apron. She resembled Edith in a way, but she had dark hair, and it was pinned back into a bun at the neck. The little girl told her I was looking for Edith. She asked me if I was Gerald. I said yes. She said Edith and the baby were upstairs taking a nap. She said I could follow her into the kitchen and have a cold drink if I wanted. The little girl told me her name was Molly and that she was four years old. I thanked Myrtle for the drink and asked how Edith and the baby were.

"Before she had a chance to answer, I saw someone out of the corner of my eye. It was Edith and she was holding the baby in her arms. I stood up and we just looked at each other. Finally, Edith opened the blanket and showed me my daughter. She told me she had named her May. I was overwhelmed. I didn't know what to say. This tiny thing in Edith's arms was my daughter. I was speechless. Edith asked if I wanted to hold her. I immediately said no because I was sure I would drop her or hurt her if I even tried. She was beautiful. She had a full head of hair, black, just like mine. Edith had lighter hair, but our daughter had the color of mine. Her little fingers were wrapped around the corner of the blanket and she looked just like a baby doll. Then she moved a little and yawned. I couldn't take my eyes off her.

"Myrtle came over and took the baby and said that she and Molly would keep an eye on May if we wanted to go outside for a walk. I wasn't sure I wanted to leave her, but Edith took my hand and we headed to the front door. We walked across the street to a park. Finally, Edith said she was glad that I came to see her and May. She knew that her father had given me a ticket but wasn't sure I would use it. After all, it had been nearly six months since we last saw each other. I told her I was sorry I made her feel bad when she told me she was having a baby. I said it just threw me for a loop hearing those words. I told her I missed her and that I was hoping she and little May would come back home with me.

"We suddenly stopped walking and I took Edith in my arms and kissed her. I knew right then and there that I never wanted to be away from her again. I wanted her and May to be back in our little house so we could be a real family. Edith said she had wanted to come home so many times, but she wasn't sure how I would feel about it. She didn't want to continue living with Myrtle and Molly, but she didn't know what else to do. She said she didn't want to be a burden to them.

"We sat down on a park bench and I begged Edith to come back home with me. Yes, I begged. I realized how much I missed my family when I left and how much I missed Dad. I told her that I had fixed up the house and actually put a small addition on. I guess in my mind I was hoping it could be a bedroom for our baby, if Edith would come back. We talked for a little while and Edith told me she would come home. We agreed we would leave the next day, taking the train and using the tickets her father had given me.

Eugene

"We left the following morning. It was a long train ride and May was really fussy most of the way home. I had promised Edith's father that I would call him, collect, and tell him if and when we were coming home. He said her mother would be glad to see all three of us.

"We arrived at the station later that day and Edith's parents were there to meet us. They took us home and said they would come back the next day so they could visit with May and get to know her. They were very happy that Edith had agreed to come home with me.

"I was determined to make things work. I went to work every day and brought my paycheck home every Friday. Edith made a few changes to the house. You know how women are. They always need to add something, like a pillow or a picture. I admit that Edith made it a real home. I wasn't thrilled about the lack of sleep I was getting because May had her days and nights mixed up. Edith tried to keep her calm, but the first few months were rough.

"One Friday night, I decided to stop at the bar on the way home from work. I had been pretty good and I felt that I deserved it. I stayed longer than I should have, and when I got home, Edith was mad. She knew right away where I had been. She said she had been afraid this would happen. We had a fight and I stormed out of the house and went right back to the bar. When I finally came home, Edith and May weren't there. I figured she went off to her mama's house to tell her just what a bum I was. I slept off my hangover and then headed over to her parent's house.

"Edith's dad was sitting on the porch when I turned the corner. He took one look at me and asked me if I screwed up. I tried to tell him that this was the first time I stopped at the bar. I told him I wasn't going to make a habit of it, but I felt I deserved this once in a while. I mean, it wasn't like I beat Edith or hurt May. I just wanted to have a drink with my buddies once in a while. They were already teasing me and saying I was tied to my old lady's apron strings. I guess that is what pissed me off the most, hearing that. I had to let them know that I wore the pants in our house and not Edith.

"Then the strangest thing happened. Her dad yelled for Edith to come out to the porch. She came out and stood there with a mean look on her face. She acted like she just knew her daddy was going to give it to me real good. But then her old man tells Edith to wipe that smirk off her face and sit down. He told her that there is nothing wrong with a man having a beer or two after working all week. He asked her if the bills were being paid on time and if we had food in the house to eat. Edith just stood there, as if frozen in time. She wasn't expecting her daddy to say anything like that. She admitted we were paying the bills on time and weren't starving. And neither was little May. I would never let things get that bad where I couldn't take care of my family. Yes, we didn't live in the fanciest house, but we still had a roof over our heads and food on the table.

"Edith started to cry and ran into the house. Her dad told me she would calm down and then I could take her and May home. He warned me that if I ever got so drunk that I hurt Edith or May in any way, or if I squandered my whole paycheck at the bar, I would have to answer to him.

"Every Friday night after that, I stopped at the bar with my buddies and nothing more was said about it. Edith started visiting her folks those nights. Peace had returned to our house.

"Several years went by and now May was in school. Edith started working at the shoe factory in town. The extra money was enough for us to finally build a bigger house on a vacant lot next to where we lived. I worked on that house every chance I had. Edith's dad helped and so did some of my work buddies. After two years, we were finally ready to move in. I'd never seen Edith so happy. She was finally getting that big house that she always wanted.

"Before I realized it, May was graduating from high school and wanted to go to business school. She had turned into quite a beauty. She was tall, much taller than me. She had the biggest brown eyes. Edith's dad had died several years before and left money in his will for May to continue her education. May liked what she was doing, and after she graduated, she got a job as a secretary. Eventually, she met Johnny and they go married. Nice guy. I liked him, even if I couldn't quite grasp the idea of my little girl being a wife.

"After they got married, they moved to Baltimore. Johnny got a real good job there. Edith really missed May. She wanted to go and visit all the time. I was still working and couldn't keep taking off. So I would take her to Baltimore and leave her there for a few weeks and then go back and pick her up and bring her home. But things were changing between us. Maybe all that held us together all those years was May. With Edith away, I was spending more time at the bar.

There wasn't anybody at home, so why not? Edith wanted to stay at May's more and more. And to tell you the truth, I was just as happy she did.

"Then one day, I got a letter from Edith saying she wanted to stay in Baltimore all the time. She said she wasn't happy at home anymore. I called her that night and asked her just what she meant by this. Did she want a divorce? She didn't say yes, but she didn't say no either. I later learned she met some guy there, someone with a lot more money than I ever had or would ever have, and Edith decided she liked him better than me. May called me one night crying and told me the whole story. She said her mother had changed and even she didn't know who she was anymore. She didn't even visit May very often. She was totally smitten with this guy. May didn't like him and Johnny said he had a reputation for loving and then leaving women. Edith was just the next notch on his belt. I made up my mind I was heading to Baltimore to find out just what the hell was going on.

"She wasn't even living at May's anymore. May said Edith was now with Eugene. May said she had tried to talk to her mother and warn her about him, but Edith wouldn't listen.

"I found out where they were living and went to pay them a visit. Edith answered the door and wasn't too happy to see me standing there. She tried to slam the door shut, but I got my foot inside and barged into the house. Eugene wasn't home, which at this point was probably a good thing. Edith told me she wanted to be with him and that our marriage was over. I told her she needed to get her things and get her ass out of Eugene's house and come home with me. She would have nothing to do with that. She threatened to call the cops if I didn't leave. I went outside and waited about an hour. Edith was real nervous the whole time. She kept looking at her watch. I guess she was afraid Eugene was going to come home and that I would probably take a swing at him. She was right about that.

"Another hour went by and I had cooled down some. After waiting that long, I decided to leave. Just as I was getting in my car, a big, shiny Oldsmobile pulled in the driveway. *Must be Eugene*, I thought. He sure was slick. I could see that right off the bat. He was on the short side and heavier than I would have guessed. He was bald and had funny-looking skin. I was thinking to myself that he must be good in bed and his pockets must be filled for any woman to want to be with him. Not bragging or anything, but I was way better-looking than Eugene. I watched him as he got out of his car. He walked over to me and wanted to know what I was doing there. Just then Edith came out and told him I was leaving. She said I was trying to sell her magazines. Eugene told me they weren't interested in any magazines at the moment and I best be on my way.

"Well, son of a bi——. I figured it out now. Good ole Eugene had no idea Edith was a married woman. Edith must have forgot to mention that little tidbit while they were romping around in the sheets. I laughed to myself.

"I started to get into my car and then stopped. I turned and looked at Edith and said that if she ever wanted any magazines, she could look me up at May's. I said it was actually Bobby, May's boy, our grandson, who was selling them. And I told him I would ask his grandma if she was interested. I smiled and donned my hat at Eugene and drove off. I caught a glimpse of the look on Edith's face. I laughed the whole way back to May's. I would have loved to be a little mouse in that house to hear what story Edith was going to make up for Eugene and if he was as stupid as he looked.

"It didn't take long to find out. A week later, I came home from work and guess who was standing there in the kitchen getting a chicken out of the oven? Yep, you guessed it, Edith. I asked her what she was doing there. She said she realized how much she missed me and wanted to come home. She hoped that we could patch things up. I just stood there looking at her. I finally asked her if little ole Eugene dumped her when he found out she was a wife, mother, and grandmother. She got real red in the face and said she didn't want to talk about it. She came over to me and put her arms around me and tried to give me a kiss. I let her. I mean, what the hell.

"She moved back in and things were okay. That's it, just okay. We continued to visit with May and her family whenever we could. It was a long drive but I really wanted to see them. Little Bobby was getting bigger and was now playing ball. He was the catcher on his Little League team and, boy, could he hit. Many a time he drove in the winning run. I was so proud of him. I was happy that he was able to play ball and do things that I never could.

"Our drives home from Baltimore were usually pretty quiet. I knew Edith wanted to be there and not at our house. I didn't know what to say to her. I wanted to be with May and her family too, but I still had to work. Edith suggested that I try and find a job closer to May. I really didn't like the idea of living near a big city, but I obliged and looked at the want ads. Sure, there were lots of jobs that I could do, but the cost to live there was ridiculous. Who could afford any of those places? Even if we sold our house, we still couldn't afford to live in the neighborhood where May lived and that was what Edith wanted. Once again, I had failed her as a husband.

"At home, we talked when we had to. Most evenings we ate supper, watched a little TV, and then went to bed. I still went to the bar on Friday nights…well most Fridays…and Edith would go out with her girlfriends. Her mother had passed a few years earlier and Edith had no other family.

"One morning, I couldn't get out of bed. I wasn't suffering from a hangover, just in case you're wondering. I felt weak, and when I tried to get up, I fell down. Edith said I had to see a doctor. She had been complaining that I wasn't eating right for some time now. Tell the truth, I hadn't been feeling that good either. I just passed it off. Edith insisted I see the doctor, and when I refused, she called the ambulance. I was mad as hell when they showed up and put me on the stretcher and hauled me off to the hospital. They must have given me something to calm me down because by the time we pulled up to the emergency room, I wasn't moving.

"They examined me and said they had to admit me. They wanted to run some tests to find out what was wrong. Well, the news wasn't good. They told Edith I had liver cancer. They said it was pretty far along and there wasn't anything they could do. Edith and the doctor came in the room to tell me. I asked how long I had and they said they didn't know. Truth was, they had told Edith it would only be a few months at the most. Edith took me home a few days later.

"Edith talked to Sam at the gas station and told him I wouldn't be able to come back to work. I was too sick to even protest. Edith continued to work and somehow we managed to keep our heads above water. May, Johnny, and Bobby came to visit just about every weekend. I was glad about that. I knew I was dying, but I wasn't ready to go yet.

"Soon I wasn't able to move around much at all. Edith took a leave from her job so she could be home with me all the time. I was too sick to even wonder how we were paying the bills. I didn't know it then, but Edith had been saving money and putting it away. She always was a frugal one. Also, I think May helped out too, but no one ever told me.

"It was two months since my ambulance trip to the hospital. I went to bed one night and never woke up. And that, little brother, is the story of my life. I was fifty-seven years old when I died."

Luther was so involved with listening to Gerald's life that he didn't realize it was dark outside. They had talked through the evening meal. The staff didn't want to bother them, so they closed off that area and left them alone. Luther now knew what had happened to his brother.

*****

After Emma died, Warren lived in the house by himself until years later when he went to live with Marion, who had been widowed several years earlier. Luther and Millie would visit Warren, and if Marion wanted to go away, Warren came and stayed with them. No one had ever seen or heard from Gerald after he ran away with the circus. The family often wondered where he was. Ironically, they didn't live that far from each other. Gerald knew where his family was, but he never contacted them. He felt that he was the black sheep of the family and that they were better off not having him around. Luther now knew he had a niece. He wondered where she was.

*****

Now here sat the two brothers who had been inseparable in their youth and separated because of a cruel and wicked stepmother. Finally, they were reunited. Luther hoped they would be able to see each other a lot now that they were both here. Perhaps the whole family could be together again. Luther knew he was the last of his siblings to die, so that meant that Mildred, Marion, Elizabeth, Doug, and Marge were here somewhere. And their father was here too. He would definitely have to talk to George about this. He wanted to see his family again.

The Reunion

The next morning, Luther woke up with a heavy heart. His visit with Gerald the day before was very troubling. He was to meet with George after breakfast and he certainly had a lot to talk to him about. He wanted so desperately to find out the rest of his story. He wanted to know about his sisters. And what about Marge and Doug? He had a feeling deep down inside that he would know them, but how? He remembered Doug coming to visit that one day when they celebrated Sonny's birthday. He couldn't remember if Marge ever came to visit.

Luther dressed and headed out for breakfast. As he opened the door, a cool breeze hit him right in the face. As he looked out through the big windows in the hallway, he saw snow on the ground. The season had changed overnight. One day, it was sunny and warm and the next there was snow. He remembered going sled riding with Gerald in the park near their house when they were kids. Even Sarah and Ephraim went along. It was one of the few times in their lives that they all got along. He realized that when they were away from the house and out of Emma's sight, things were different. They had a good time playing in the snow, but as soon as they got home, things changed back to the way they normally were.

Breakfast was light today. That didn't matter; Luther didn't have much of an appetite. He had a cup of tea and some toast with strawberry jam. He was sitting at the table by himself. There weren't many people there this morning, and he wondered where everyone was. But then he didn't really care. He wasn't in the mood to have a conversation with anyone, so it was just as well that he was eating alone.

After breakfast, he walked down the hall admiring the many pictures that lined the walkway. Today there were scenes of animals—horses, cows, chickens, goats, and many more. Yesterday there were scenes of water and oceans. He wondered who changed these pictures overnight. It would take a very long time to do that since the halls were long. Luther shook his head at the wonder of it all.

He arrived at George's office and sat down in the waiting area. A young man was at the desk and said hello to him as he walked in. It wasn't long before George came out of his office. He said hello and told Luther he would just be a few minutes. George then went to the desk to talk to the young man. It sounded like he was trying to arrange a meeting with several people. George was a very busy man and Luther often wondered how he had the time to do all the things he did. He wondered if he spent time with every person here, talking to them about their lives. When did George have any time to himself? And what was his story?

Then, George tapped Luther on the shoulder and asked him to come into the other room. Luther was so lost in his thoughts that he didn't even realize George was talking to him.

"My, oh my, Luther. You really were in deep thought, weren't you? What were you thinking about?"

"Well, George, I was wondering how you find the time to do all the things you do. You have spent so much time with me, and I'm guessing you spend a lot of time with everyone else here. I wondered when you had time for yourself."

George laughed as he sat down opposite Luther. He had been asked this question by so many people here. "Luther, it is my position here to guide you to your next level. I do this with everyone. Many have already attained their goals. Some, like you, are in the process. I love my work and being able to see the final results. I want everyone to know I am always with them wherever they are. There is no greater reward for me than to love each of you and always be by your side."

Luther accepted George's answer and felt a great relief knowing that George was always there for him. It was calming to know that even when he was alone, he could feel George's presence. It was a feeling he couldn't quite explain, but knowing it was what was important.

"So, Luther, I know that yesterday you were reunited with your brother, Gerald. I was so happy when we were able to arrange that. I also know you still have many more questions for me. Shall we start our session now?"

"It was really great to be with Gerald again. We were so close when we were growing up and then he left to go with the circus. We never saw him after that and over time I didn't think much about him either. Maybe I was trying to block out that part of my life because it wasn't very good. When the times in our lives were black and dismal, it was good that Gerald and I were together. We helped each other without ever saying anything. His story was sad. He died so young. He seemed to be the outcast of the family, and now I realize that he just had some bad breaks.

"George, what about my sisters and Doug? What happened to them? I remember a little about Mildred and Marion. I saw Marion here and that was great. But I don't really know their stories. And Elizabeth…what happened to her?"

"Luther, today I have a big surprise for you. There is going to be a family reunion with all your brothers and sisters and your father. How does that sound?"

Luther nearly fell off the sofa. He could hardly believe what George had just said. It was as if he could read his mind. This is what he was hoping for. Finally, all he could say was, "Really!"

George loved it when he could deliver a surprise such as this. He knew Luther had been working very hard at remembering the events of his life. It was important for him to know his early life because it was all going to tie into the tasks he would need to do. George also knew there would be painful times ahead for Luther, but he was confident about the outcome. It was time for Luther to finish learning about his younger years. The next chapters of his life would get even more complicated.

"Yes, Luther, really. You have been working so very hard trying to remember your past that I believe it is time to bring it altogether. Will, my assistant in the outer office, is getting things set up as we speak. We haven't talked much about what your tasks are going to be. Your life story, as you are learning it, will play a very important part in how you achieve the things you need to do. We will have many more sessions as you continue this journey. Some of the events will be rewarding, but some will be difficult. You will need to find strength in both to meet your final goals."

Just then the phone rang and George got up to answer it. Luther was half listening to what George was saying and still trying to comprehend what he said about the tasks he needed to complete, plus the events of his life that he had yet to discover. What could they be? He was also thinking about finally reuniting with his family. How wonderful that will be.

George hung up and turned to Luther. "Will has everything ready and he will take you to the reunion. Are you ready?"

"Yes, I'm looking forward to seeing my family again. Thank you so much, George."

"Luther, my friend, you are very welcome. I can hardly wait for our next session to hear all about it. Now go and meet your father and your siblings."

*****

Will led Luther down the hall that was lined with the pictures of the animals. He told him they were going to a reception area reserved for special events. Luther was glad that George thought of this as special because he surely did. His mind was racing. What would they look like? Would he know them? Of course, he would know Marion and Gerald because he had seen them since his arrival here, but what about the others?

They finally turned left at the end of the hallway and through a door that Luther didn't remember ever seeing. Now that didn't mean it wasn't there before; it's just that Luther didn't remember seeing it. Strange things were always happening around here.

The door opened onto a courtyard. It was beautiful. There were flowers everywhere. A huge fountain in the middle sprayed water out of a little hole to the sounds of music. When the music was loud, the water came out faster. When the music was slower and softer, it became a fine mist. There were lights reflecting on the water as well. It was the neatest thing Luther had ever seen. Just when he thought it was going to stop, it would begin to spray upward again, and the colors would bounce off and reflect on the ceiling and walls around the room. The flowers throughout the room were magnificent. There were red, yellow, and pink roses. There were lilies as white as snow. All along one wall were orchids. Luther didn't know there could be so many different types and colors of orchids. On the opposite wall was a long table covered with a long white tablecloth. On the table were white dishes rimmed in gold. The silverware was gold. The napkins were gold with white lace around the edges. There was a centerpiece of white orchids with gold bows. It looked much like a fancy wedding reception. There were comfortable chairs around the room. They were covered in a gold brocade fabric. The floor was marble, with veins of white, black, and gold running throughout—incredible.

Will waited while Luther scanned the room. He knew from experience that everyone coming into this room had the same reaction. It really was quite beautiful. Will knew that Luther was going to be spending time with his family, many of whom he hadn't seen in years. It would be a very emotional time for all of them.

"Luther, this is where you will be meeting your family. George wants you to know that you will be allowed to stay here as long as you want. There are bedrooms right through the door on the right. Your family will be here momentarily. Meals will be served buffet style. Of course, if there is ever something that anyone needs, you only need to open the door to the hallway. There will be someone outside available to you at all times."

"This room is beautiful. I have never seen so many flowers. I thought there were lots in the dining room, but that's nothing compared to this. I'm anxious to see my family, but also a little scared."

"Luther, that is completely understandable. Remember, they are your family and they love you. It will be a wonderful time for everyone."

Just then the door opened and seven people walked into the room. "Luther," Will said, "please come and meet your family."

Luther watched as his sisters, brothers, and father walked into the room. He recognized each one instantly. Marion and Mildred walked in together, holding hands. Doug was wearing a suit and tie and looked every bit the professional he had been in his life. Gerald was next to him and he looked just like he did the day before. Gerald was trying to explain something to Doug, but Luther couldn't make out what he was saying. Marge and Elizabeth came in next. The last person to enter the room was Warren. He was a tall man, slightly taller than Doug. He was wearing dark trousers and a cream-colored sweater. Will nudged Luther and encouraged him to go over to where they were standing.

When they saw Luther coming toward them, everyone had big smiles on their faces. Warren came over and grabbed Luther's hand. "Wayne, my boy. This is one of my happiest days, seeing you again and being here with all my children. I've been waiting for you to get here. Now my family is complete. Come, let's visit with your brothers and sisters."

"Dad," was all Luther could say as he collapsed into Warren's arms. Warren's strong arms enveloped his youngest son, and he held on to him for fear he would fall to the floor. Luther looked into his father's eyes and couldn't stop the tears from falling down his face. He couldn't remember crying this much; he always thought of it as being unmanly, but right at this moment, it felt good; it felt right. Suddenly, he was surrounded by his siblings. Luther hugged each one and then went back and hugged them all again.

Will didn't want to interrupt this happy reunion, but he needed to get back to George. Finally, he said, "I am so happy for the Yeager family today knowing you will have the opportunity to get reacquainted. I must depart. Remember, if there is anything you need, please do not hesitate to ask. Bless you all, everyone." And with that, Will was out the door.

Warren directed his children to the chairs that were in the room. He instructed each one to sit according to their age. Mildred was first and next came Marion, followed by Elizabeth, Doug, and Marge. Gerald was next and then Luther, who Warren called Wayne. Luther realized that his family knew him only as Wayne and he would have to get used to that. Warren, being the patriarch of the family, sat down last and began to speak.

"My children, I am a very happy man today. I finally have you altogether. It has been a long time. Our life together as a family was brief. We had many separations, but I want you to know that you have always been in my heart and in my prayers. Many times I didn't know where you were, but I said a prayer each night hoping you were safe and happy. Life wasn't always easy. We had many trials and tribulations to overcome. I blamed myself because we weren't together, but with George's help, I now realize that not everything was my fault. I tried to do my best and sometimes that wasn't enough. I hope you can forgive me for my shortcomings. All I ever wanted was to have a family and to have the ability to take care of them and for us to always be together. Now we are here and will be for eternity. Wayne, your brothers and sisters and I have had the opportunity to be with one another in this wonderful place. We always knew that someday, when you joined us, our family would be compete. Here we are."

Mildred and Marion

Mildred spoke first. She had married Maurice. They had five children and many grandchildren and great-grand-children. After Maurice passed, she and Marion travelled together, mostly bus trips, but they enjoyed whatever time they spent together. In many ways, it was just as it was when they were younger. They had always been together back then.

Mildred wiped a tear from her eye as she looked at each of her brothers and sisters and finally said, "Wayne, you were my little brother and I remember helping take care of you after Mother left. I remember how much you liked coming to my house. I would make shoofly pies. You loved them. I had to make two and hide one so that Maurice could have some when he came home from work. You were sneaky, though. Do you remember? You would try your hardest to find anything I baked and steal some. I remember the day that Claude caught you in the kitchen. You were just about to take the biggest cookie. You told him you would share it with him if he didn't tell. Well, of course, I found out and you both got a whooping. I missed having you visit after Daddy married Emma and she didn't want you coming over. So many memories."

*****

Marion was next. Marion's favorite way of describing herself was telling everyone that she was fat, ragged, and sassy. And that she was. She had helped Earl with the farm chores and later went to work in a pocketbook factory. She was very active in her church. She had

142

a beautiful voice and often sang solos in the choir. When she and Mildred were younger, they used to sing duets in church. She and Earl had one son Earl Jr., or Sonny, as he was called. He was always getting into trouble. He was definitely spoiled, but probably because after he was born, Marion found out that she couldn't have any more children. Mildred always used to tell her that Sonny was going to get in serious trouble if she didn't make him listen. But, in Marion's eyes, and quite often in Earl's as well, Sonny could do no wrong.

When Sonny was eighteen, he joined the army and was sent to Washington State for basic training. The Korean War was raging and Sonny was ready, willing and able to go. While stationed there, he met a girl, Joyce, and they married two days later. Marion remembered the phone call from Sonny telling her he was a married man. Marion was upset that everything had happened so quickly and that she and Earl never had the chance to meet their new daughter-in-law before the wedding. It hadn't been much of a wedding, though. They found a justice of the peace and that was that. Sonny said he would bring his bride home to meet them soon. Unfortunately, that would never happen.

Three months after they were married, Sonny was shipped off to Korea. Six months later, Marion received the worst news that any mother can get. Sonny had been killed in action. Since he was married, all his personal belongings were sent to Joyce. She made all the arrangements for him to be buried in Washington. Marion tried to contact Joyce to tell her they wanted to have his body sent back home and buried there. She never was able to make contact with Joyce; all attempts were unanswered.

Several years later, Marion and Earl drove to Washington to try and find their son's grave. They held each other tight as they looked down where Sonny had been laid to rest. There was a small American flag beside the tomb stone. Etched on the stone was Sonny's name, date of birth, and date of death. A cross was carved above the letters. It was the only time they visited his grave. They came home, determined to start the next chapter of their lives, one without Sonny.

Marion now had tears in her eyes, but this time, they were tears of joy. Marion had lived to be one hundred and three years old. She outlived Mildred by ten years.

"Wayne," she said as she wiped the tears away from her eyes. "I love you and always have. I am so glad that we are altogether again and here with Daddy. The rewards we have here make up for some of the bad things that happened to us. We all faced hardships. For me, it was when the army men came to the door to tell us that Sonny had been killed in Korea. You and Millie were visiting us when that happened. Do you remember?"

Luther nodded his head and realized he now remembered that. No one wanted to believe what the army representatives were telling them. They all just sat there, stunned. Sonny had been so full of life, sometimes too much life, and now he was gone. It wasn't possible.

"Wayne, you came over to me and held me in your arms. I was crying so hard. You never let go of me. You didn't say anything, but your being there comforted me. Those were difficult times for me and Earl. I knew I could always depend on you, my littlest brother."

Luther suddenly remembered the times he hadn't always been very kind to Marion. He would call her stupid. He remembered when Marion died. Someone had asked him to help with the funeral expenses because there were no funds. He said he couldn't help, but that was a lie. He wasn't there for her at the end of her life, and suddenly, he felt so ashamed and very angry at himself. And here was his sister telling him that she knew she could always depend on him.

Elizabeth and Doug

Elizabeth was two years older than Doug. She had realized early on that there were too many children in the Yeager family. She sensed her mother's frustration after Marge was born and then more frustration after Gerald and Wayne arrived. Elizabeth was the quiet and sensitive one and didn't want to be around all the conflict in the house. She would slip out the front door and go for a walk to get away. She usually ended up at the local park. It was there that she first met the Whitney children. She was happy to entertain them while the cook, whose job was to take them to the park, could sit back and relax. The cook mentioned Elizabeth to Mrs. Whitney and said she thought she would make an excellent nanny for them. Mrs. Whitney agreed to meet with Elizabeth. She wasn't convinced a teenager would be the best for taking care of her children, but there was an instant bonding between the children, Mrs. Whitney, and Elizabeth. It was agreed that if Elizabeth's mother would allow it, Elizabeth would go to the Whitney home after school and stay there until Mrs. Whitney came home from work. She would be expected to take care of the children on several Saturday afternoons and some evenings as well. Bertha, of course, was all too happy to have Elizabeth out of the house. Elizabeth loved working for the Whitneys. It was a win-win situation for all. A year later, she moved into the Whitney house permanently. When Elizabeth was sixteen, she quit school and was the fulltime nanny for Mary and Daniel. When they were older and in school and didn't need as much supervision, Elizabeth was still there if she was needed. Eventually, she took over some of the domestic household chores.

It was a sad day for Elizabeth when Mary and Daniel were sent abroad to continue their education. Elizabeth continued to do housework for the Whitneys and also got a job at an expensive dress shop in town. She didn't know it, but Mrs. Whitney had arranged the entire thing.

When she was twenty, she met Charles and before long they were married. She no longer worked for the Whitneys, but she continued her job at Clayton's Dress Salon. Several years later, Elizabeth and Charles welcomed a son, Ronald, to their family. After taking some time off while Ronald was small, she went back to work at Clayton's. Elizabeth had a good relationship with her older sisters and was sometimes there when Warren and Wayne would visit.

On Elizabeth's sixty-first birthday, she went to her family doctor because she hadn't been feeling well. She was always tired and unable to do many of the things she always enjoyed. The news was not good. After many tests, she was diagnosed with leukemia. A year later, she passed away.

Elizabeth sat in her chair with her back erect, holding her hankie. Her legs were crossed at the ankles. This is the way Mrs. Whitney had told her a lady sat while in the company of others. She hadn't forgotten. She wasn't sure what to say now. She was glad her entire family was here. She wasn't as close to Wayne as her older sisters were, but she smiled and looked at him and told him she loved him and was glad they were altogether.

*****

Doug was sitting between Elizabeth and Marge. His life had been so different from his brothers and sisters, other than Marge. He never would have had the opportunities he had in life if his mother hadn't taken him and Marge away with her when she left their father. Doug was grateful for the education he had received and the influential friends he had. He had been told his father was a drunk and an abuser. He was told that his younger brothers were being raised by his older sisters. That's what his mother told him. He loved his mother and was always there for her. She and Horace played a very big and important part in his life, continuing on into his adult life. When Horace died, Doug was there for his mother. His wife and children were an important part of her life as well. She would spend every holiday with them. He knew deep down inside that his mother had not been entirely truthful about what had happened. He eventually visited his father, but their relationship was more like a friendship rather than father and son. Doug had always thought of Horace as his father. He sat there now, looking at his father, and realized the burdens he must have carried. Doug had gone to college and became a lawyer, working in the law firm his stepfather wanted him to. He had married Elsa and had two children. He had a relationship with his brother, but knew that Wayne considered him to be superior to him. He probably felt this way because that was the way Doug wanted it.

Doug stood and walked over to Wayne. He embraced him, out of character for him, as showing affection had never been easy for Doug.

"Wayne, I wasn't there when you and Gerald were growing up. Mother took Marge and me and we left. She had convinced us that Dad was an evil person and that she had to get away for her own safety. She assured us that the two of you would be better off and well taken care of. She told us she was afraid she would not have been a good mother to you had she stayed. I remember thinking this was really strange, but I was young.

"Suddenly, my life was filled with nice clothing and many luxuries. Mother always reminded us that now we had things we would never have been able to have had we continued to live with Dad. She said we could have had money, but Dad spent most of it at the bar. And I believed her. She was a good mother to us, but she wasn't truthful about a lot of things. As I got older, I figured some things out, but by that time, I was too accustomed to the finer things in life. I didn't believe, or didn't want to believe, the things you told me about how you grew up. I did make peace with Dad and Gerald. Mother and I had many conversations after I arrived here. I truly believe she is now sorry for the things she did. I wish everyone could forgive her, but I'm not sure that is going to happen.

"Wayne, when you reached out to me, I helped you. I guess that was my way of trying to atone for all that had happened. Elsa and I took you in and gave you a home. I got you a job and gave you money until you could support yourself. We visited each other after you and Millie married. I wanted you to get to know Mother, but you never would. It took a long time for me to realize how deep your hatred of her was and how in many ways it was justified. I am glad we are together again."

Doug and Elsa

Luther remembered and was reliving every minute of that day. Doug came home from work and found Wayne sitting on the floor playing with his daughter, Grace. Doug and Elsa told him he could stay with them. Doug even found him a job working at the paper factory in town. Wayne promised to work hard and that's exactly what he did. He never missed a day's work and was never late. He had to walk about fifteen blocks in all kinds of weather, but he didn't care.

Luther took Doug's hand and held on to it as tears filled his eyes and rolled down his face.

Luther remembered now how he had gone to Doug after he ran away from home. That day, Emma had once again poured the milk on his cereal as soon as she called him to come down for breakfast. He came downstairs to find a bowl of soggy cereal. He had asked Emma so many times to please wait until he was sitting at the table before she poured the milk, but she never did. She always had a smirk on her face as she reminded him to eat everything because food wasn't allowed to be wasted in her household. That morning, Luther looked at the cereal and looked at Emma and knew he couldn't stand it anymore. He picked up the bowl and threw it out the window. The shattering of the glass was deafening. The others at the table suddenly gasped.

Emma was about to speak when Wayne told her that was the last bowl of cereal he would ever have in that house. In his pocket was the money he had been saving from the sale of pretzels. He reached in and took out a quarter. He held it in front of Emma, opened up

149

her hand, and put the quarter in it. He told her she could use that toward getting the window fixed. And with that, he walked out the door and never looked back.

He started walking down the street. He didn't expect any of them to follow him and Warren had already left for work. Wayne walked until his feet felt like cement had been poured into his shoes. He walked into the bus station and bought a ticket to the town where he knew Doug lived. When he arrived, he walked several blocks, stopping to ask a policeman for directions to Doug's house. He learned that it was another ten blocks away. He started walking and eventually he arrived at Doug's front door. He was tired, dirty, thirsty, and hungry.

He rang the doorbell and waited. Elsa opened the door and took one look at him. At first, she didn't recognize him. "Elsa, it's me, Wayne. Is Doug home?"

"Oh my goodness, what happened to you? How did you get here? You're filthy. I don't want you coming in my house looking like that."

"Please, Elsa. Is Doug here? I ran away from home this morning. I couldn't take it anymore. Living with Emma is pure evil. I can't go back there, ever. Please! I came here to see if Doug could help me. I'll get a job and I'll work real hard. I promise. I just can't go back there." And he started sobbing.

Elsa was a short woman with dark hair pinned up on top of her head. She had an apron on over a dark green dress. She was holding a baby bottle, and in the background, Wayne could hear the sound of a baby crying. Elsa kept looking over her shoulder in the direction of her crying baby. She knew she had to get back to her.

"Doug is at work and won't be home until after five tonight. I can't stand here and talk to you, but I can't send you away either. Your brother wouldn't like that. Go around to the back of the house. There is a hose outside. Clean yourself up and come in the back door to the kitchen."

Elsa was perplexed and uneasy as to what she should do. She had heard some of the horror stories about Emma from Marion and Mildred and she felt sorry for Wayne. But he would just have to stay in the kitchen until Doug came home from work. Then he could deal with this.

Wayne did as he was told. He threw his dirty hat outside and he took off his muddy shoes. He washed his face, hands, and feet. Elsa had laid a towel on the top step for him to use. When he felt he was as clean as he could be, under the circumstances, he went into the kitchen. The aroma coming from the stove was wonderful. He suddenly remembered he had nothing to eat all day. He threw his cereal out the window and never stopped long enough to get anything to eat. He was famished.

Elsa saw the look in his eye. She was now holding a baby in her arms. Wayne knew Doug and Elsa had a daughter, but he wasn't sure how old she was. Elsa placed the baby in a nearby cradle and went to the cupboard. She took out a bowl and a glass. She went to the stove and dished out a big helping of beef stew. Then she went to the ice box, took out a pitcher of milk, and poured Wayne a large glass. She put everything down in front of Wayne and told him he could eat. He couldn't grab the spoon fast enough.

"Not so fast, young man. In this house, we say prayers before we eat." Wayne looked up at her with sheer torture in his eyes. The stew smelled so good and his stomach was so hungry he didn't think he could wait another minute. At Emma and Warren's house, they only said prayers before the evening meal.

Wayne didn't know what to say or how. Praying wasn't one of his strong suits. Sensing this, Elsa sat down, folded her hands, and began to say a blessing. Wayne's stomach was growling and he was sure the blessing would go on forever. At last, Elsa said Amen and told him he could now eat. He dug his spoon into the thick, savory stew and scooped a big helping into his mouth. It tasted heavenly. He tried not to gulp the stew down, but he just couldn't eat it fast enough. When he was finished, he drank the milk. Elsa picked up his empty bowl and went to the stove and dished out another big helping. Wayne ate every last morsel. It was the best meal he had ever eaten.

Elsa sat and watched Wayne devour his meal. She suddenly felt a pang of guilt, thinking that she had actually considered sending him away. She had no idea what Doug was going to say, but she knew right then and there they would have to help Wayne. After all, he was family.

Marge and Gerald

Marge sat in her chair looking as uncomfortable as she felt. She didn't want to be there, but these people were her family, and Doug had reminded her that it was her duty. She never felt close to Warren or her other siblings, just Doug. She actually had been glad when their mother took them and left with Papa Horace. She loved Horace. Thoughts of her real father, Warren, no longer existed. Before they moved away, she was a lonely child. She had no connections with her older sisters. They were always busy doing something that she didn't want to be involved with. She hated the fact that she had two baby brothers. Her mother was always busy with them and she felt neglected. She wanted her mother to sit with her and talk, but Bertha never had time to do that.

After they moved away, she and her mother became very close, and they were able to have that one-on-one time that Marge so desperately wanted and needed. She loved when they went shopping together. They were now able to afford the best things, and it was so much fun trying on fancy clothing. She made friends at her school with girls of similar backgrounds. All of their fathers were wealthy, like hers. She was now part of the "in crowd." She loved it. She never looked back or even thought about her other brothers and sisters. As far as she was concerned they didn't even exist. Her mother told her how Warren would hit her and was always coming home drunk. Marge thought this was horrible and hated him for the things he did. Her new Papa never touched her mother in an unkind way, and he was so much fun to be around.

Marge knew she was expected to say something. She finally turned to Gerald and began to speak. "Gerald, I understand you consider yourself the black sheep of this family. I've heard you refer to yourself in this manner. I want you to know that in actuality, I may be the true black sheep." This caused a stir among the others, but Marge put up her hand for silence and let it be known that she wanted to continue. "When Mother took Doug and me away, I was glad she did. I hated living in that old house. I wanted to do everything in my power to forget about the rest of you, and for many years, I did. When Doug told me he wanted me to get to know all of you, I didn't want to, but deep down inside, I knew he was right. After all, you are my family.

"Gerald, you apparently were always getting into trouble. Maybe you were rebelling because of the situation you were in with Dad and Emma. I know you ran away when you were only fifteen." Marge paused and lifted a lace hankie to her eyes. She wasn't actually dabbing a tear away; this was just what she always did when she wanted attention.

Gerald took advantage of the lapse in time and turned to her and said, "Marge, how does that make you the black sheep? It wasn't your fault that our mother took you and left the rest of us behind."

"Gerald, I loved it when Mother took me out of that deplorable house. I was glad that I now had the finer things in life and I didn't care one iota what happened to you or Wayne. I loved my life with Mother and Papa. Even after I found out that Dad married Emma and that life was really no better with her, I didn't care. I wanted nothing to do with any of you. And in many ways, I still feel that way."

There was a gasp from everyone in the room. They all had a relationship with Marge and the past had never been mentioned. It was assumed that Marge was now happy to be reunited with her siblings and her father.

Looking now at each one of her brothers and sisters, Marge continued, "It isn't that I don't love you. It's just that I don't feel we are on the same level. We have spent time together before we all came here, and mostly, they were good times. But you never did and still don't feel like siblings to me. It's almost like we were just friends or casual acquaintances. I know how each of you feel about Mother, and

I don't think you are being fair to her. She did what she had to do to escape a terrible life and I, for one, am glad she did."

Looking at her brother Doug, Marge said, "Doug, I know you are close to our siblings and had a wonderful relationship with them. You even welcomed Warren into your home. I know you are close to Mother, but I always had a difficult time being in both worlds. When I think of Mother and Papa, I remembered all the wonderful things we did. When I was with the others, I felt disconnected and disloyal to Mother. I guess that is what makes me the black sheep. I've been told, by many people, that I must change my attitude about this."

Looking at Warren, Marge said, "I did everything in my power not to have contact with you. I didn't want to get to know you. When we were together, I pretended that I cared. Actually, I don't have any feelings at all for you. Mildred and Marion, you were always so close. I used to envy how close you were. You never included me in your girl talks. I know I was much younger, but I just didn't feel any connection with you. Elizabeth, you were rarely home, and when you were, it was usually just to get something and leave again. Then you were gone for good. Gerald, I never saw you after we left with Mother. In fact, no one saw you ever again after you ran off with the circus. Wayne, you were just a baby when we left. I remember visiting with you and your family and you coming to visit Paul and me and Nancy after she was born.

"Wayne, your wife didn't like me, especially after your daughter wasn't invited to Nancy's wedding. I had clearly stated on the invitation that no children were invited. Millie thought Peggy was old enough to be there. This was our decision. We did not want children, and if we had allowed Peggy to come, we would have had to allow the other nieces and nephews and their families to come too. We just didn't want that. Millie wrote me a nasty letter and really told me off. She even included a 'Dear Abby' letter about the age when a child could be invited to weddings. I laughed when I read that. We didn't speak for many years. I guess when Nancy got divorced five years later, Millie had the last laugh. Truth being, I never cared what she thought about the wedding guests and actually was just as glad that none of you were there. In all fairness, I will say that when Nancy died, at the age of fifty from spina bifida, you and Millie came to visit Paul and me and showed us true compassion.

"Now we are all here. The family is complete, or so you think. One person is missing and I know that she will never be included in this or any future reunions. George tells me that this in one of the lessons I must learn here. I guess all I can say is that I will try, but I can't make any promises."

For a full minute, there was complete silence in the room. Marion and Mildred looked at each other and then at their father. Warren had his head down and they were sure he was crying. It was an uncomfortable situation, and no one knew what to do or say.

Finally, Gerald stood up. He went to the table at the far corner and poured eight glasses of lemonade. One by one, he gave a glass to each of his sisters and brothers and then one to his father. When he returned with his glass, he held it up and said he wanted to make a toast.

"This is for the opportunity to be together as a family. Each of us, in our own way, has led a different life. We have all had good times and bad times. Some of you were there to support one another and offer a shoulder. We can't change who we are now and who we were then. Whether we like it or not, we're family. I believe George set this time up for us to get to know one another again and maybe even start over. I make a toast that we try to do that."

In unison, there was a very loud, "Amen." Even Marge chimed in. Perhaps it was good that feelings, both good and bad, had been shared. Now they could go forward into their eternal life.

After the toast, Gerald turned to his family and said, "I'm glad we have this time together. The truth is I don't know most of you very well at all. Mildred and Marion, you were already grown by the time I was born. I do remember you visiting us after our mother left. We had some good times, but they didn't last very long. When Emma started taking care of us, we didn't see much of you. After she and Dad married, we hardly ever saw you. Doug and Marge, I don't remember you at all. After I left with the circus, I didn't come back home.

"Wayne, you and I were close. Maybe it was because we only had each other. Emma didn't like us and was mean to us. Dad didn't do anything to stop her. Her kids didn't like us either. So it was just us. When I ran away, I was scared—more scared for you than for me. I figured you would have to do all the work, your chores as well as mine. I hated feeling that way, but I just couldn't stand being in that house with Emma any longer.

"I wanted Dad to let you go with me, but he wouldn't. Dad promised that things would be better and I hoped he meant that. I wanted to come back, but I just didn't. I don't know why. My life was okay. I knew the beer bottle better than anything. That caused me the most problems. I lost my wife over that. Then I got sick and lost my life. I can't change the way things were for any of us, but I am glad to have this chance to see each of you and for us to get to know each other. I guess that's all I have to say."

*****

Luther—or Wayne as his family called him—looked over the room. "I'm glad we are all here too. I made a lot of mistakes in my life, and I am learning now how much they hurt a lot of people. I know I still have a lot to learn. Let's make a deal to be here for one another from now on. We are family, even though we don't know one another the way family should. Like Gerald said, the past is the past. Let's be a family."

Luther held up his glass and said, "To family, especially ours."

Everyone lifted their glass and echoed Luther's words. Yes, they were family at last.

Warren

Warren knew it was now his turn to speak. He had listened very carefully to what each of his children had to say. It was true that he knew some of them better than others. He couldn't begin to count the number of times he wished things had been different. He wanted a big family and he had that. But there were so many families within his family, and rarely, if ever, was there unity among them.

He remembered the day that each one of them had been born. His first, Mildred, was the apple of his eye. He thought he could never love a child as he loved her. Even Bertha had been excited when she was born. A year later, Marion was born and Warren knew that he loved this new baby as much as he loved his first. Two years later, Elizabeth arrived. As much as he loved his girls, Warren always wanted a boy to carry on the family name. When Douglass was born, he now had the son he always wanted. He knew Bertha didn't want any more children. She told him that four was more than enough, especially when they were all so young and home with her all day.

It was then that Bertha started complaining about all the household work. From the time he walked in the door at night until he went to bed, all he heard was nothing but complaints about screaming babies. Pots and pans were slammed around in the kitchen, with Bertha muttering under her breath about the unfairness of it all. Warren didn't understand what went on in the house while he was at work. He just wanted a nice hot meal when he got home and children sitting around the table to share a meal with him and Bertha.

That rarely happened. To escape all the noise from the children and Bertha's complaining, he would stop at the bar on the way home. That hour or so after work became an oasis to him and prepared him for what awaited when he walked in his front door.

One day, Warren came home and found Bertha upstairs in bed crying. The children were nowhere to be found. Warren became frantic thinking something terrible had happened. Bertha finally composed herself enough to tell him that the children were at the park with Marion and Mildred. Warren went to put his arm around his wife to tell her he was glad everything was okay and that he hoped she would be feeling better soon. It was then that she looked at him with such hatred in her eyes and told him she wasn't going to be better anytime soon because she was going to have another baby. She said she hated this child even before it was born. She didn't want it, but there was nothing she could do about it. She said she finally had all the children out of diapers and now she would have to start all over again. She was crying uncontrollably and Warren stood by helplessly.

Warren was really happy about the new baby, but he didn't dare say that to Bertha. He knew it wouldn't go over well. This turned out to be a difficult pregnancy for Bertha. Her mother would come to help with the chores when she could. Mildred and Marion were now given additional household chores to do. In the spring, another girl was born, Marguerite. Warren had hoped for another boy, but he was happy that little Marge was a healthy baby.

It was after the birth of Marge that Warren noticed the biggest change in Bertha. She no longer cared how she looked. Sometimes she wore the same dress every day of the week. She no longer went to church; she just didn't feel up to it. Mildred and Marion often had to take care of their new little sister when they came home from school. All Bertha did was yell. On more than one occasion, Warren had to stand in front of his oldest girls or else Bertha would have hit them with whatever was handy. He remembered telling her that she was not to lay a finger on those girls. He sensed that the girls were afraid of her, and rightly so. Bertha did what was necessary for the newest baby, but absolutely no more.

Around this time, Warren started going to the bar more often. It was too unbearable at home. When he finally did come home, he would find a cold dish of food waiting for him, or no food at all. Mildred tried to save him some leftover dinner, but if Bertha found it, she threw it away and screamed at Mildred.

In time, things in the Yeager house started to simmer down a little. Then Bertha found she was pregnant again. She miscarried the child within the first two months. Two more pregnancies resulted in miscarriages. Bertha was told she should not have any more children, but before long, she found she was pregnant again. This time, she was able to carry the baby full term and Gerald was born. Two years later, Wayne was born. By now Bertha was uncontrollable.

During this time, Mildred married Maurice and moved out of the house. Marion was engaged to Earl. Elizabeth was living with the Whitneys.

Doug and Marge were in school, but Gerald and Wayne were still at home all day and Bertha was totally fed up with babies. She deliberately stayed up late at night, waiting until Warren fell asleep. She knew if she went to bed with him, another baby would soon be on the way. She was determined there would be no more children no matter what she had to do.

Warren was now stopping at the bar on his way home every evening. He dreaded going home, and the alcohol definitely eased the pain of what awaited him. Warren knew that drinking was not the solution, but at the time, it was the only answer. Home became a place he was forced to go to. He loved his children and wanted to see them, but the loving life he had with Bertha was long gone.

Although he didn't condone what Bertha had done when she left, he knew deep down why she did it. He fully acknowledged that her leaving was partially his fault. He tried to remember the fun-loving girl he had met all those years ago, the girl he fell in love with and wanted to spend the rest of his life with. She had stopped existing. He knew he was no longer the handsome young man that Bertha wanted for a husband. Now it was too late to make amends for his actions of long ago. His job now was to reunite with his children and have a good relationship with them. He wanted nothing more than that as he looked at each one.

"It gives me great pleasure to see each of you and to know that we are together again. I know life was never easy for most of you. I am truly sorry for that and wish things could have been different. Marge, I know you don't have fatherly feelings for me, and as much as that pains me, I understand. It wasn't my wish that another man would raise you and Doug. I am no longer filled with hatred for your mother. She did what she felt she had to do. I will, however, never understand how she could leave two small children behind and just walk away. None of this was their fault, none of it. Yet they suffered the most. It hurts me to know that even in later years, she never acknowledged any of her children except for you and Doug.

"However, we can't dwell on what happened. We are here together now, and it is time to get to know one another again. And now I don't know about any of you, but I am starving and there is a table filled with food right over by that wall. Let us fill our bellies and sit down together as a family."

Warren really didn't know what else to say. He stood up and started toward the table. He picked up a plate and began to fill it. Shortly after, Wayne, Gerald, and Doug got up and filled their plates. Mildred, Marion, and Elizabeth followed, leaving Marge sitting alone. They tried to make eye contact with her, but she turned her face away.

Warren walked toward another table that had eight chairs around it. He took the seat at the head of the table and sat down. He wanted to wait until each of his children were seated so they could say a prayer together and then enjoy this feast before them. As he waited, he looked over at Marge and saw she had her back toward the table and her head lowered. Warren stood up, walked over to her, and sat down. He lifted her chin and saw tears streaming down her face. He reached out to her and wrapped his arms around her in a warm embrace. At first, it seemed she was going to resist, but slowly, she allowed herself to be held in her father's arms. Warren could hear her sobs as he held her close.

"Marge, I love you. I always did and I always will."

Marge looked up at her father as tears continued to fall down onto her cheeks. Finally through sobs, she said, "Dad, I love you too. I want to have a relationship with you and my brothers and sisters. I know that Mother wasn't perfect. She was a good mother to me and Doug, but she did turn her back on the rest of her family. I understand why she did what she did, but that doesn't make it right. I wish I would have asked her how she felt. There were times when she was extremely moody. When that happened, Horace would tell me she wasn't herself and that we should just leave her alone in her room. It usually only lasted a day or two. Maybe it was then that she thought about her other children. And maybe after a while it became easier to pretend that they never existed. I guess this is something that she will have to deal with. I've only seen her once since I'm here. I asked George about her and he said it wasn't the right time to be reunited with her. When I saw her, she was sitting on a park bench watching children playing on swings. I walked toward her and she started to stand up and she called out my name. I wanted to run to her, but George was suddenly standing beside me and told me it would not be a good idea. He said there would be a time, but that wasn't it. I have never seen her since.

"When George told me that I would be coming here today, I was angry. I didn't want to see any of you. In my mind, I only had one brother, Doug, and my parents were Bertha and Horace. I know that you are my biological father, but I don't feel any connection to you. I came here reluctantly.

"Seeing everyone here, I realize that I must change my attitude. We are family. Dad, I'm sorry I hated you for so many years and blamed you for causing such pain in Mother's life. What she did was wrong and I must learn to accept that."

Warren continued to rock his daughter in his arms, whispering that it was all right. He stood and helped Marge get up. He led her to the table and helped her put food on her plate. Then she went and sat down between Gerald and Wayne.

Warren went to the head of the table and looked at his children. Finally, he said to them, "I know some of you have already started to eat, but before we continue, let us begin this new chapter of our lives with a word of prayer." Everyone bowed their heads and clasped the hands of those on either side of them. Warren gave a short but powerful prayer, blessing the wonderful food and the love for each one present as a family.

Soon forks were swirling and glasses were being clinked together as toasts were made by everyone. They all made sure that Marge was included in each toast. Before long, they were eating and talking as a family should. At one point, Gerald bumped Marge on the hand and told her to watch what she was doing. He had that smirk on his face that only Gerald did. Marge looked at him and started laughing. Now and then, she purposely bumped his hand and would say something funny to him.

Everyone was talking about something from the past. There was laughter and delight in each one of them. The one who felt the most delight was Warren. He wasn't sure how this day would turn out, but he knew that right now his family was together and that nothing was ever going to separate them again.

Wayne

Four days went by since the Yeager family got together. They formed new bonds with one another and learned about the parts of their lives that not everyone knew. It was shortly after their last evening meal together that George opened the door and came into the room. He was overwhelmed with what he saw. This is how it was supposed to be, and he was glad that the Yeager family was now happily together. He escorted them out, and as each one left, he heard them telling one another how glad they were to be together and that they loved one another.

Luther woke up the next morning after a sound sleep. He felt wonderful. He knew his brothers and sisters and his father once again. George had told him that he would be seeing him this morning and he couldn't wait. He wanted George to know how great the past four days had been.

After breakfast, Luther went to George's office. He practically ran there with great enthusiasm and expectation. George was waiting for him and ushered him in the room.

"Well, Luther, you certainly are in a good mood this morning. Does this have anything to do with the time you spent with your family?"

"Oh, George, it was wonderful."

"I am very glad to hear this. To be honest, I wasn't sure how it was going to turn out, but I am so happy that everything went so well. You still have a lot of work to do here, as do the others in your family. I just felt that it was time for all of you to be reunited. Now you will always have that network of family to talk to. Don't hesitate to contact any one of them whenever you want. You will find their names on your TV. Just click on their name and you will connect with them immediately.

"But now we must get back to your life. We have completed your childhood and will now move on to your adult life. We will begin when you went to Doug's house after you ran away from home."

*****

Doug and Elsa invited Wayne to live with them until he saved enough money to find another place. Doug got Wayne a job and he worked hard. He impressed the bosses and, after a trial period of employment, was promoted to another department with a raise. He helped out around the house doing tasks for Doug and Elsa, mowing the lawn in the summer and shoveling snow in the winter. He entertained his niece Grace and new nephew John, while Elsa prepared the evening meal. Even Elsa had to admit that it was nice having him around.

Within a year, Wayne had saved enough money to move out. There was a boarding house a few blocks away with a room available. The rent was five dollars a month and that included the evening meal. For an extra fifty cents, Mrs. Welker did the laundry. Wayne was now employed at a garment factory, putting boxes together and stacking them to be put on the delivery trucks. Most Saturdays were spent at the plant helping to load the trucks. The boss gave each worker who showed up an extra dollar in their paycheck. Wayne didn't necessarily like the work, but it wasn't hard and it sure was better than going to school and living with Emma.

Wayne worked in that factory for five years, saving his money, and before long, he was able to buy a car. He made friends with the men he worked with and even went on a few dates with some of the girls working there. Sundays were spent with Doug and Elsa. Sometimes they would all go for a Sunday drive to visit one of their sisters. It was an added bonus when Warren would be there as well. Warren had been upset when Wayne left home, but was relieved to know that he was with Doug and doing okay.

One day at work, Wayne noticed a cute girl working in the next department. He kept looking over at her and then noticed that she was looking at him as well. Wayne asked one of his buddies who she was and he said he would find out. Ernie, one of Wayne's coworkers, was dating Hannah, who just happened to work in the same department as the new girl. Ernie told Wayne that her name was Mildred.

Wayne thought Mildred was really cute and wanted to ask her out, but was afraid she would say no. Ernie talked Hannah into arranging a double date.

Luther signed, finally knowing how he met his first wife, Mildred! Now he wanted to know more about her.

That first date went well. The two couples went to the movies and then to the corner drug store for a soda. Millie, as she liked to be called, was easy to talk to and Wayne found himself very interested in her. Before the evening was over, he asked her if he could see her again. Much to his surprise, she said yes. But she said he would have to come to her house and meet her father. Wayne was a little nervous about that, but if it was the only way to see Millie, he was willing to do it.

The following Saturday, Wayne showed up at Millie's house. He had a small bouquet of flowers for her. He didn't have the money to buy them, but when he told Elsa about his upcoming date, she reached into the cookie jar, where she kept her spending money, and gave him fifty cents. When Wayne rang the door, a young girl answered. He told her his name was Wayne and asked if Millie was there. She said she was Millie's sister and her name was Hattie. She giggled and said she would find Millie. Then a man came to the door and said that he was Millie's father. He invited Wayne into the house.

"So you're the young man who's taking my Mildred out this evening."

"Yes, sir. My name is Wayne Yeager. I work at the factory where Millie works. How do you do, sir?"

"Mildred will be ready in a few minutes. I see you've met her youngest sister, Harriett. There are two other sisters, who I believe are hiding on the steps." He said this in a much louder voice, and no sooner had he said it, they heard giggling and stomping coming from upstairs.

"Just what do the two of you think you're doing?" Millie said. "Can't you find something better to do with yourselves than to spy on what's going on downstairs? If you're so interested, why don't you just go on down instead of hiding on the landing?"

Wayne sheepishly looked over at Millie's father and thought he saw a hint of a smile. Next thing he knew, Millie was coming down the steps followed by two other girls. They were giggling and almost tripped on the last step.

"Wayne, I see you've met my father, Alfred, and my sister Hattie." Pointing to her other sisters, she said, "This is Ellie and Gladys." She looked at her father and told him she wouldn't be late and then escorted Wayne out the door.

Once outside, they heard her father talking to Millie's three sisters. He told them he was sure there was something they had to do. They quickly hurried upstairs and were watching out the bedroom window to see if Wayne and Millie were holding hands as they walked down the street.

"I'm sorry for the way they acted. They aren't used to seeing me going on a date."

"Millie, I find that hard to believe. Someone as pretty as you should have fellows fighting off one another to get a date with you."

"Well, I haven't been out much. I was taking care of my mother while she was sick. And someone had to take care of the house and my three sisters. Ellie and Gladys are old enough to help with a lot of the housework. Gladys does her share, but getting Ellie to do anything is like pulling teeth. Even Hattie does more."

"I hope your mother is feeling better now."

"Actually, she died two months ago. She had been sick for a long time and her heart finally gave out. It's been hard on us, but we're managing. My father suggested I find a job outside the house and let my sisters take over more of the chores. My father works six days a week. I can be home before Gladys and Hattie get home from school. Ellie is usually home during the day and is supposed to be doing the housework, but to be honest, I don't think she does a very good job. It isn't easy, but we are managing."

"I'm so sorry to hear about your mother. I'm sure it has been hard on all of you. I'm glad you were able to go out with me tonight. We can just go for a walk to the park and stop for some ice cream, if you like. That way, you can be home early."

"Thank you. That sounds like a great idea. It's very tiring trying to work all day and then go home and still have work to do. I usually start our supper and my father finishes it when he gets home at six. Gladys and Hattie do the dishes. Ellie usually takes off as soon as we're done eating. She says she's meeting her girlfriends, but I think she has a boyfriend and doesn't want any of us to know about it. She never brings anyone around, but that would be just like her. Do you have any brothers or sisters, Wayne? And what about your parents? Do you live with them?"

"Well, that is quite a long story. I don't think I could give you my family history on just one date. It would probably take several. I'm okay with that, if you are?" Wayne said sheepishly.

"I think that would be fine," Millie said, wondering how a family could be any more complicated than hers.

*****

Wayne and Millie had many more dates after that one, and soon it was obvious to everyone that they were a couple. Wayne took her to meet Doug and Elsa and they liked her immediately. Elsa was so happy that he had found a nice girl. She thought this was just what he needed and hoped it would lead to a happy and normal life for both of them—anything other than the way Wayne's younger life had been. Wayne shared his story with Millie and she was horrified to think that his mother abandoned him and his brother the way she did.

Within a year, Wayne knew that he wanted to marry Millie. He told her he was in love with her and she said she felt the same about him. By now, he had become great friends with her sisters. Ellie was still the sneaky one. One night, when Wayne was walking home, he saw her around the corner from her house. She didn't see him. She was just getting out of a car. She walked up the steps to a neighbor's house and waved goodbye to the young man in the car. After he left, she ran down the alley and into her own backyard, then around the house, and in the front door. Wayne wondered why she was sneaking around like that and made a mental note to mention it to Millie when he saw her again.

Wayne saw Millie every day at work but didn't have much opportunity to talk with her. She worked in a different department. Every time he saw her, he realized that he was more and more in love with her. He had finally found someone who would love him forever.

Millie and Wayne

O n September 9 of the following year, Wayne and Millie
went to Elkton, Maryland, and got married. Wayne had
asked a friend from work to go along, and a very good
friend of Millie's went along too. It was a very simple ceremony. They
found a justice of the peace who was willing to perform the wedding.
It was absolutely the happiest day of Wayne's life. He was sure that
his life was finally complete. Millie's father said they could live at his
house. They didn't really have enough money to rent an apartment,
and they couldn't live in the boarding house where Wayne had lived.
Millie's sisters weren't happy though, because now they had to share
a bedroom so that Millie and Wayne could have their own room.
Wayne and Millie continued to work at the garment factory and were
able to help with the household expenses.

World War II was going on and Wayne was expecting to be
drafted. He really didn't want to go to war, but he felt the call of duty
for his country. One Saturday, after working the morning shift, he came
home with a big announcement. He had stopped at the army recruiting office on his way home and enlisted. The recruiting officer assured
him that by enlisting, he would have more options for his future in the
military. If he had waited to be drafted, he would have no choice at all.

Millie was immediately worried when she heard this news. She
knew the war was raging in Europe, and there was a good chance he
would be sent there to fight. He assured her he would be fine and
that by the time he was finished with basic training, the war could be
over and he would be sent somewhere in the United States and she
could go with him.

When Alfred heard the news, he too had mixed feelings. He was sure Wayne would have been drafted. He had fought in World War I and he knew what it was like. He did not share Wayne's theory that the war would be over soon. He listened to the newscasts on the radio every evening, and he was sure it was going to last several more years, at least. He was also sure that Wayne would be sent overseas and would be in battle.

Within two weeks' time, Wayne was off to basic training. Millie continued to live with her father and sisters. When Wayne's training was complete, he was going to send for her and she could live on the army base with him.

Millie continued to work at the garment factory. Ellie was now dating a fellow named Ted. He had been in the army and had been to Europe. He said it was really rough over there. Gladys was ready to finish high school, and Hattie was just starting junior high school.

Wayne really missed Millie. She was finally the one stable thing in his life and he depended on her to be strong. He wrote to her whenever he could, but quite often, he was exhausted after long hours of training. At the end of three months, Wayne finished his basic training and was given a three-day pass.

Arriving home, Wayne was so excited he lifted Hattie high off the ground as she came running toward him. He gave Millie a long kiss and hugged her tightly. Public display of affection was highly frowned upon during this era, but most people ignored their feelings when it was a soldier being welcomed home by his girl.

The three-day pass flew by, and it was decided that Millie would join Wayne at the army base as soon as she could get everything organized. She quit her job and started packing. This would be her first time away from the only home she ever knew. She was going to take the train to Georgia the following Monday to start another chapter of her life with Wayne. It all seemed to be working out. Ellie and Ted were going to be married, and they would move into the house and the bedroom that had been Millie and Wayne's.

The big day came and her father took off work to take her to the train station. He knew she was a big girl now, not really a girl, but a woman—a married woman at that. He would miss her. He managed to wish her well as she stepped onto the train. Fortunately, she didn't see the tears that were welling in his eyes as he watched the train take his oldest child away from him. He wished more than anything that Catharine were still here to share this day with him. He knew she would have cried, but they would have comforted each other. He knew she was smiling down from heaven at him and would keep an eye on their oldest daughter.

*****

Life on the military base was an entirely different experience for Millie. She and Wayne had a very small apartment that was issued to service men who were married. There was a small kitchen with a table and two chairs. The living room had a sofa and chair that had been left by the previous tenants. On Wayne's next pay-day, they went to the PX and bought a lamp and a radio. The bedroom had a bed, also left by the previous tenants. The mattress was lumpy, but being young, in love, and happy to be together, they didn't seem to mind. There was a small bathroom with a tub off the kitchen. Millie had brought a few things from home. Her father let her take a few dinner plates and cups, some silverware, and a skillet. Millie had saved her last few paychecks, and with that, they were able to buy everything they needed to make this their first home.

Millie made friends easily and soon she and the neighbor were spending their days together. Millie and Sara would go to the store or take long walks. Sometimes, when Wayne and Elmer came home, they would eat their evening meal together and then take in a movie or a dance.

Tensions were always high on base. They would find out when a soldier, who had been stationed there, was killed in action. The flags would fly at half-staff and there was a solemn, quiet atmosphere for the next several days. Everyone knew that the day would come when each soldier there would be assigned to a ship and sent overseas. It was rarely talked about, but everyone knew that it could happen at any time. They were happy for the times they had while there and pretended, as best they could, that what was happening in Europe was far, far away.

Millie wrote home faithfully to her family. She told them about her apartment and the friends she had made. She said Wayne was working in the motor pool. He was fixing engines on various pieces of equipment. She said she hoped all was well with them. She was sorry she wasn't able to be there for Ellie and Ted's wedding, but then none of her family was at her wedding either. She asked how Hattie was doing in school and what Gladys was doing now that she was finished with her schooling.

Hattie wrote back the most. She was very close to Millie, who had been like a mother to her. Their mother had been sick during much of her young life, and Millie had filled the role of mother during her illness and then after her death. Hattie told Millie that Ellie still didn't help much with the housework. She said Ellie was bossy and made her do all the work when she came home from school. Gladys had a job with an insurance agency. She was dating a guy named Mark. He was okay. Sometimes he would let her go along on a date with them, but he made her buy her own ice cream cone. She had to ask her father for the money and she didn't like that very much.

Four months after Millie moved to the army base, Wayne received notice that he would be shipping out in two weeks. Suddenly, their worst fears were becoming a reality. Millie knew she would have to leave and go back home to her father. When Elmer and Sara heard the news, they hurried over to see Millie and Wayne. Elmer hadn't received his orders yet, but he knew it was only a matter of time. Sara was devastated knowing her best friend would be leaving. They sat at Millie and Wayne's kitchen table somberly reminiscing about the wonderful times they had shared together. Sara told Millie she would help her pack, but in reality, there wasn't that much to be packed. She and Elmer offered to drive Millie home after Wayne left. The women promised to write to each other and hoped that someday, when the war was over, they would get together again.

The day came for Wayne to leave. He and Millie ate their last breakfast together in their apartment. They walked to the area where

Wayne was to report. They weren't sure how long they would be allowed to be together, so they held hands and smiled, each putting on a brave face, knowing that inside each of them was falling apart. When they got to building C, Wayne went in and was given his paperwork. He then went back outside. His commanding officer told him he would be called when it was time to leave, but until then he could be with his wife.

Sara and Elmer were standing with Millie. Wayne and Elmer shook hands and Elmer assured Wayne that he and Sara would see that Millie got back home to her family. A silence crept over all of them. Other soldiers and their wives were standing near them, each unsure what the future was going to hold for them.

A whistle sounded and they knew what that meant. Over a loud speaker, the soldiers were told to get their duffel bags and then line up and prepare to board ship. Wayne turned to Millie and held her close. By now she was openly crying and wasn't able to be the strong woman she had promised him she would be. He told her that he would be fine. He was going over to Europe to show those Germans just what was what and that before long, he would be home and they could go on with their lives. He promised to write every chance he could and Millie said she would write every day.

Millie watched as Wayne walked up the gang plank and boarded the ship. As it sailed out across the ocean, she stood there for the longest time, wondering if she would ever see her husband again. Finally, Elmer and Sara took her hand and they slowly walked back to the quiet apartment. Millie would be leaving in three days. Elmer was able to get a pass so he and Sara could drive her home to her father.

Army Life

illie's father and sisters were happy that she was home again even though they knew the circumstances of her return. Millie moved into the bedroom with Gladys and Hattie and took over the household duties once again. She asked her father if he wanted her to get her old job back, but he told her she could stay home and see to the house and her young sister. She would receive a portion of Wayne's pay that could be used to help with the expenses.

And so life began again in the little row house on Douglass Street with Alfred and his four daughters. Millie became the woman of the house. She went grocery shopping and did the laundry, the ironing, and the cleaning. She assigned chores to her sisters, and for once, there wasn't any arguing about doing them. Even Ellie was doing a good job. Ted was working at the local school as a janitor.

Millie did some of the cooking, but that job primarily fell to her father. Now that Millie was there to see that Hattie got to school in the morning, Alfred was able to go to work earlier. That meant he could be home earlier in the afternoon to prepare the evening meal. Millie tried to keep as busy as she could. That way, she fell asleep as soon as her head hit the pillow. It gave her less time to worry about Wayne.

*****

For Wayne, army life was a totally different experience. It was one thing to be on the base, but being on board the ship, sailing across the Atlantic Ocean, was entirely different. It would take several days to get to Europe. The accommodations weren't the greatest and it was extremely hot. The men made the most of it, passing the time playing cards. Wayne took time every evening to write to Millie. He wasn't sure when he would be able to mail his letters, but he made a promise to himself to write to her every day if he could. The officers tended to overlook when the men got rowdy and loud. Who knew what it would be like where they were going? It was better to let them have a good time now and only step in when absolutely necessary.

Wayne knew a few of the guys from his unit. Some had gone through basic training with him. They all had a fear of the unknown waiting for them, but they put on a brave face and acted as if they were fearless.

They arrived in France and immediately started out for Germany. After several days, they arrived at their base destination. Life was fairly routine except they never knew when the enemy would strike or when they would have to go on a mission where actual fighting would occur.

Wayne settled fairly well into camp life. He shared a tent with a guy named James from Mississippi. James was all right, but he wasn't the kind of person Wayne would have wanted as a friend. James liked to brag about anything and everything. Wayne didn't know what to do to get him to shut up. Finally after several weeks of this, Wayne told James to put a sock in his mouth and shut up or he would do it for him. That didn't sit well with James and he told the other guys that Wayne had threatened him. It soon became clear that the other guys liked James and didn't take too kindly to what had happened between him and Wayne. Wayne tried to tell them he couldn't stand James' bragging any longer, and if they had to share a tent with him, they'd know what he was talking about. Shortly thereafter, Wayne had the reputation of being a troublemaker.

His letters home did not always reflect the reality of what was going on. He told Millie he had lots of friends and that he was well liked on the base. He told her that many of the other guys looked up to him and often came to ask his advice or opinion on lots of things.

He neglected to tell her that most nights he sat alone, either in his tent or in the mess tent, because no one wanted to be with him.

One day, Wayne and three other guys were sent out to do some scouting. The sergeant told them they had to get along or they would be answering to him when they got back. As evening approached, they knew they would not be making it back to base. They found an abandoned house about ten miles from base and decided they would hole up there till morning and then start back to camp.

As they sat around the table, not really knowing what to do, one of the men pulled out a deck of cards and they agreed to play a friendly game of pinochle. The other guys asked Wayne if he wanted to play. Wayne agreed and the game began. Wayne partnered with Luke and they were winning just about every hand. One thing Wayne was good at was cards. He was pleased that, at least for tonight, he was actually having fun with the guys.

After numerous hands with Wayne and Luke winning all but two, one of the guys on the other team pulled out a bottle of whiskey. He had stolen it from under the sergeant's bed. They opened it and took swigs as they passed the bottle around the table. The game was really getting interesting now as each one started feeling the effects of the whiskey. Before long, another game was over, with another win for Wayne and Luke. The other guys said they had enough and weren't going to play another game with two cheaters. Wayne and Luke laughed it off and said they were sore losers.

Larry finally broke the silence and said maybe they should get their guns out and make sure they were cleaned, loaded, and ready to use, just in case the enemy showed up. The other guys thought that was a good idea and they all went for their guns. They each had a rifle, but were issued pistols for this scouting excursion. They knew their rifles were ready, so they started cleaning the pistols. Suddenly, they thought they saw a shadow at the window. They each rose and headed for the door. They were going to kill any Nazi that dared to even come near them. Mike thought he saw something move behind the tree, took aim, and fired. Nothing happened. The adrenalin plus the whiskey was really kicking in, and now they were all trigger happy.

Larry and Luke circled the building, but saw nothing. Wayne and Mike stayed by the door. When the next shot rang out, Mike ran toward the back, thinking Wayne was right behind him. Little did anyone know, Wayne had been shot and was lying by the front door, bleeding heavily from both legs. Due to the anxiety of the moment, the effect of the whiskey, and the havoc of the situation, Wayne had no one to blame for his own stupidity as his gun discharged and shot him.

*****

George walked into the room and saw Luther sitting there. He looked pale and very perplexed. Luther had just finished watching what had happened to him in Germany. It brought back many terrible memories.

"Ah, Luther, I see that you have watched another chapter of your life. What are you thinking right now?"

"I feel sick," Luther said. "That was a terrible day for me. I was so scared. Sure I was going to die."

George handed Luther a glass of water and told him to drink it and then lie back on the couch. George waited several minutes until he appeared ready to talk.

"I thought I was going to die that night," Luther repeated, barely speaking above a whisper. "Watching that made it seem like it just happened now."

"Luther, do you remember what you told Millie about that night? And what you told other people over the years?"

"Millie found out what happened. Someone from the army contacted her. She later told me she was so afraid that I would be dishonorably discharged. I guess the same thing went through my mind. I was embarrassed."

"So, Luther, you made up the story about a German soldier raiding the house you and your buddies were in and shooting you. Then the other guys shot and killed him. Is that what you told people?" George was deliberately putting much emphasis on the question. Shouting now, George said, "You wanted to be the big war hero, getting wounded and nearly killed. Is that what you were going for, Luther?"

Luther glared back at George. Why was he bringing all this up now? What harm did it do to tell his version of the story? No one was hurt by it. For most of his life, he had been a loser, someone people would laugh at or pity. He was a nobody. Coming home from the war wounded, he was somebody. People thanked him for his bravery and his service to the country. They thanked him for protecting them and taking the bullet so they could be safe.

George finally spoke and said, "Luther, I'm waiting for an answer to my question."

Luther stood up and walked toward the door. He looked back at George, or whoever the hell he was. As he walked out, he heard George calling him. It was more like a shout, a command, but he wasn't going back. That was something that had happened so many years ago. What importance did it have now anyway?

When Luther got back to his room, his TV was on and George was visible on the screen. He went over to it and turned it off, but it came right back on. He tried again to turn it off, and again it came back on.

Luther went into his bedroom and slammed the door shut. He lay down on his bed and covered his ears with his pillow. It didn't help, because the sound of George's voice came through loud and clear. There was no escaping him. He knew it was useless to run away, and actually, where would he go? George was everywhere.

"Luther!" George shouted. "I hope you are aware that there is nowhere you can go to avoid me. You will listen to me, and above all else, I expect to be answered when I ask a question. DO I MAKE MYSELF CLEAR?"

Luther sat on his bed and slowly got up. He went into the living room and sat in the chair across from the TV. He looked at the screen and saw George. He knew he would have to answer him.

"George, I'm sorry I ran out of your office, but I don't want to talk about this right now. Maybe it was wrong to lie, but who did it hurt? My family thought I was a hero. Millie knew the truth, but I knew she'd protect me once she found out that I was going to be discharged, honorably, not dishonorably. I was going home to recover from my injuries and I wasn't going back to the war. That terrible, horrible war. Millie never told anyone what really happened. We never talked about it."

"Luther, you hurt more people than you can ever imagine, and the one person you hurt the most was your own daughter. She found out the truth, but only after hearing you tell your version of the story. You deceived her. But, Luther, this certainly wasn't the only time you lied to her or hurt her. I think it is time for you to look deeper into your relationship with her. We will talk again tomorrow."

And with that, the TV screen went black and Luther was left alone with his thoughts.

Life after the Army

Morning came and Luther had no idea how he had ended up in bed. He remembered being in his living room and George was talking to him through the TV, but that was last night and now it was morning. He remembered George saying he had lied and hurt his daughter. But he couldn't remember any of that. What did George say? He vaguely remembered his daughter. He thought her name was Peggy, but he wasn't sure. Why couldn't he remember her? Suddenly, the TV went on and there was George, again, as big as life.

"Good morning, Luther. How are you today?"

Sarcastically, Luther said, "Huh, since you seem to know everything that goes on around here, you should know that I don't feel all that great. I don't remember going to bed last night and I keep thinking about what you said about my daughter. What happened with her? How did I hurt her? So tell me, Mr. Know-It-All, tell me!"

"Luther, don't get nasty. What I tell you is the truth. You must be made aware of things as they happened and understand exactly how hurtful they were. First, I want you to have breakfast and then come to my office. Henry will be bringing a tray to your room shortly, so I suggest you get dressed now. I will see you soon."

After breakfast, Luther headed to George's office. Sitting at the desk in the reception room was someone Luther had never seen before—a woman with black hair and dark eyes. She motioned for him to come in and said she was told to take him into the other room where a screen was set up for Luther to watch. George had been called away on an emergency, but he would return as quickly as he could.

The shades in the room were already pulled down and the screen was set up opposite the chair that obviously was meant for Luther. He no sooner was seated and had adjusted the pillow behind his back, when the screen came to life.

"Luther, you have been instructed to watch the next chapters of your life. They will begin with your life with Millie after you returned from the war. As you watch, you will remember the events you are about to see."

*****

Wayne was getting off the train at the station. Millie and her sister Hattie were there to greet him. The conductor helped him down the steps, as his balance was unsteady with the crutches he was using. Immediately, someone from the crowd came over and asked if he needed any help. Wayne accepted and was escorted to a nearby taxi. Strangers were thanking him for his service and he felt many people staring at him. It was good having this attention and he felt that he deserved it. When he arrived home, the cab driver helped him out of the taxi and up the steps to the front door. Wayne and Millie would be living with her father while he recuperated from his injuries.

Wayne needed and demanded much attention now, and everyone in the household noticed a vast change in him. Before going into the army, he was friendly, nice, and seemed to care about others. Now all he wanted was for everyone to wait on him and tell him how terrible it must have been to be shot by the enemy and how lucky he was to be alive. Wayne relished the attention.

Slowly, his injuries healed and he was able to look for work. A local textile factory was hiring. Most companies were eager to hire a returning soldier, and Wayne was told he could start the following week. He worked there for eleven years. During that time, he and Millie had saved some money, and with help from Millie's father, they were able to buy their first home. The year before, they welcomed a baby girl to their family, and now it was time for the three of them to be on their own.

Times were good. Millie stayed home to take care of the baby, Peggy. Wayne was the bread winner and provided well for his family. Occasionally, he would visit his brother or sisters and their families, but most holidays were spent with Millie's family. They vacationed to Florida once, visiting Millie's uncle and thoroughly enjoying the time away from work and home. Peggy was growing quickly and was her father's pride and joy. Every day she would wait outside on the front steps for him to come home from work. When she would see the car pull in the driveway, she would jump up and down and run to the car so she could ride with him to the back of the house and into the garage. Wayne would then carry her on his shoulders through the backyard and into the house to greet Millie. Yes, those were good times.

Peggy was soon approaching school-age. The only school in the area was a one-room schoolhouse and Wayne and Millie didn't want her going there. The decision was made to move. Millie had been very shrewd at saving money, and they decided to build their own home. Wayne was making good money plus receiving a disability from the army for his injuries. They were financially stable and living the American dream. When the textile factory announced it was going to close, Wayne applied for a job at Gallagher's Plastic and was immediately hired. Although the new job meant working different shifts, it came with a big pay raise.

*****

Luther watched as his life scrolled by on the screen. It brought tears to his eyes as he watched himself taking Peggy to the bowling alley with him. Luther bowled on a company league every Friday night, and Peggy loved to go along and watch. She was so proud of her daddy every time he got a strike and was soon the team cheerleader. This was quality time spent with his daughter that they both looked forward to.

As the years went by, Wayne was overlooked for important promotions and he could never understand why. It became apparent, however, that he liked to brag about all the things he had in his life and often ended up in verbal fights with his coworkers. These were not the qualities that Gallagher's was looking for in a leadership position. So Wayne was overlooked time and time again when promotions came around.

The lunchbox incident played out again on the screen, and as he watched, he was overcome with tremendous guilt. He remembered his conversation with Joe and how his life had turned out. That time he got the promotion, but only because Joe was fired for something he didn't do. It didn't bother Luther at the time. Some of his coworkers suspected that he was involved with this incident, but they couldn't prove it. He didn't get the respect from those men, which prevented him from doing his new job efficiently. The men would talk about him behind his back. They would go out after work for a beer, but they rarely included him.

Time passed. By now he had the reputation for being a hothead, both at work and at home. He would argue with his brothers-in-law and Millie was furious about this. She knew her sisters didn't like him, but they tolerated him because he was married to their sister.

On one occasion, Millie's father had to tell him to shut his mouth. He had finally had enough of the bickering between Wayne and his other daughter's husbands. This was totally out of character for him, and Wayne had to watch what he said from then on.

Peggy was growing up and now a teenager, no longer wanting to go to the bowling alley with her father. She had her own friends, other teens her age. There were school dances and sporting events to go to in hope of seeing a special boy. Millie tried to tell Wayne this, but he would just get angry and take it out on Peggy. Soon there were more and more fights with Millie. Wayne felt she was trying to control him and keep him from talking. In reality, all she was trying to do was keep him from making a fool of himself. Most times, she didn't succeed. Soon, because of his anger, he had very few friends.

It was difficult for Wayne to understand Peggy during her teenage years. He felt she was being rebellious and he didn't like it. Often, he yelled and she would run to her room in tears. He tried punishing her when she was on the phone too long. She avoided him as best she could. When Wayne tried to have a conversation with her, it always ended in an argument. He just couldn't understand all the teenage drama. His teen years were not happy ones, and he never had the opportunity to hang out with friends or attend school functions. He had chores to do. His quick temper and unkind words only made matters worse. He had alienated his daughter. She tried to talk to her mother about this, but Millie too had unhappy teenage years. She had been forced to do most of the household chores and take care of her younger sisters because her mother was very sick. And so neither Wayne nor Millie understood the changes that were going on in Peggy's teenage life.

It didn't help matters when during an argument one day, Wayne told her he didn't know what to say to her because he had always wanted a son and was very disappointed when she was born.

At this point, George interrupted and asked, "Luther, does what you said to your daughter ring a bell with anything from your own childhood? You were abandoned by your mother, and by saying what you did, you were telling Peggy that she wasn't wanted either." Luther hung his head in shame. He didn't remember saying that or how Peggy could have felt when he did.

Peggy eventually went away to school, met a boy, and got married. By this time, Luther's relationship with her was not good at all. Peggy and her husband would visit at times, and Millie always insisted that she and Luther visit them as well. Luther and Millie by now were able to take nice trips and see different parts of the country. His bragging, however, usually meant that friendships made on those trips did not last very long. Millie knew why invitations were declined, and she felt helpless to do anything about it. Fortunately, she had her sisters.

When Luther's first grandchild was born, he was extremely happy. The baby was a boy and he loved to visit him as often as possible. Now he finally had the boy he always wanted. Peggy had hoped that this might help mend their relationship with each other. By giving him a grandson, he would finally have the boy that she was not.

The little boy, named Jimmy, often stayed with his grandparents. They would arrange vacation time so Luther could spend quality time with his grandson. Over the years, he took him to ball games, the circus, and the playground. A few years later, a granddaughter was born. She was special, yes, but not the same as a grandson.

Peggy could sense how her father felt, and although she wasn't happy that he didn't show as much attention to Krissy as he did to Jimmy, she was content to take whatever he could give.

*****

The next scene, he saw was a church setting, and this time, a funeral was in progress. There was a small white casket at the front of the church. The minister was talking about a life being taken too soon. Luther saw Peggy and her husband holding each other with Jimmy sitting between them. They were crying. Millie was sitting in the next row crying as well. This was the funeral for Krissy, Luther's granddaughter. She had been born with a serious heart defect, and one night, she went to sleep and never woke up. Luther remembered how shocked he was when the call came saying that Krissy had died. Luther and Millie couldn't begin to imagine what Peggy was going through. And little Jimmy. He loved his sister and now she was gone.

The next scene was about to start when Luther suddenly stood up and said, "Stop!" He turned to George and held up his hand. He was trying to find the words and they just weren't coming out. George paused the screen and stood to hold onto Luther because it was apparent that he was about to faint. A glass of water suddenly appeared and Luther took a few sips. He took out his hankie and wiped the tears away from his eyes. He had to ask, but he was afraid. George helped him back into his seat.

Luther said, "George, my granddaughter Krissy died. I met a little girl here and her name was Krissy. It can't be. Can it...be her?" George put his hand on Luther's shoulder. "It was, wasn't it? That little girl that I went to the carnival with and had so much fun with... it was her, wasn't it? How did I not know her? If only I had known!

If only I had paid more attention to her while she was still alive. Can I…can I see her again, please?"

"Yes, Luther. That little girl was your granddaughter, Krissy. She knew you were her grandfather, and she was upset that you didn't know her. She and I had a long talk about that, and she now understands why you didn't know her. She has been here a very long time. She is very much liked and loved by everyone she meets. She is a joy to be around. You can never get back the time you had with her on earth, but perhaps soon you will be able to spend time with her again. But for now we must get back to your story."

*****

Visibly shaken, Luther watched as the screen came to life again. He wasn't sure how he could possibly pay attention to anything after that last scene. He wanted to ask George if they could take a break and continue another day, but he knew he wouldn't get the answer he wanted.

The scenes of his life continued. A few years later, another granddaughter, Becca, was born. As Luther watched, he hoped that he had paid more attention to this child, but he wasn't sure that would be the case.

He and Millie reached a point in their lives when things were good between them. They eventually decided to sell their home and move into a smaller apartment. Wayne retired from Gallagher's and started planning a big vacation to Hawaii. Millie always talked about a trip there, but felt they couldn't afford it. He wanted to surprise her on her next birthday, which was coming up in a few months.

Millie and Wayne moved into a small apartment in the same complex as Millie's sister, Hattie, and her husband, Ed. It was nice having her sister nearby. They went shopping and out for lunch often. The couples often got together for evening meals or the other activities that went on in the building.

Wayne's temperament was much better too. He no longer had to worry about cutting the grass, shoveling snow, or any of the other outside chores he had when they owned a home. It was a nice feeling.

It gave him and Millie more time to spend together. He was preparing to retire within the next few months and was hoping that he and Millie would be able to spend time travelling.

They found comfort and companionship with each other. They had weathered many storms in their marriage, but they knew that they always loved each other. They looked forward to spending their retirement with family and good friends.

They would take Sunday drives and visit Wayne's sisters. When Wayne took vacation time, they would visit with Peggy and the grandchildren or take short trips together. Wayne was hoping that Millie would agree to go to Hawaii. It would be wonderful to just relax and enjoy each other. Yes, life was good.

One night in early April, Luther, Millie, and several friends went to a concert. It was a great night and everyone had such a wonderful time. After the show, they stopped at a local diner for root beer floats. Conversations in the car were all about the concert and plans for another fun adventure in the near future. Suddenly, there was a loud noise and no one in the car knew what happened. The car behind them saw everything and knew there was no way it could have been prevented.

There was a horrific bang and the screen went black, as did the entire room.

The Accident

Luther awoke and found himself back in his room. The curtains were drawn and the room was very dark. He was reclined in his chair, his legs stretched out. He felt totally exhausted. His mind seemed to be a total blank. Then he remembered hearing that horrible loud bang, and he knew instantly what it was. His memory immediately went back to that terrible night all those years ago. He wanted it to go away and be out of his memory so he wouldn't have to remember. He wanted—no he needed—George here. Where could he be? Didn't George say he would always be here whenever he needed him? Well, he definitely needed him right now. Luther remembered he had been in George's office and he had been watching the screen showing his life. He remembered the scene with Krissy's funeral and how painful that was.

He wanted so desperately to go back into that screen and find a happy moment and remain there. There had been happy times; he had witnessed them. Why couldn't he find one and just stay there for eternity? He didn't want to go forward. Why must he? Just what was the purpose of all this? He had already lived these events once, so why did he have to relive them again? Nothing was going to change. He couldn't undo the things in his life that weren't good. Yes, he made mistakes, but who didn't? Was there anyone here who was perfect? Well, maybe George, but he didn't count.

The events of that evening all those years ago came flooding back to him. It had been such a great time, seven friends spending time together laughing and having fun. Jim had volunteered to drive. Scott and Barbara were going to follow. Wayne was in the passenger seat, while Jim's wife Mary Ann, Ruth, a good friend from Maryland, and Millie were all in the back seat. Jim and Mary Ann lived in the same condominium complex as Wayne and Millie. They were about five years younger. Jim's car was a royal blue Ford that he had recently purchased. He was eager to show Wayne all the new features.

Ruth was a childhood friend of Millie's who had moved out of the area many years ago. She loved to return to her hometown to visit friends who lived there. On this occasion, Millie had invited her to visit for the weekend and attend a show with them.

Scott and Barbara were following Jim. Scott lived in the condominium as well. He and Barbara had recently started dating. They met at a party on New Year's Eve at Wayne and Millie's. They were both recently widowed and were enjoying each other's company. Millie was thrilled that they hit it off so quickly after meeting.

The friends enjoyed the show. On the way home, Jim made the suggestion to stop for root beer floats. He knew an all-night diner a short distance away. The women thought it was a wonderful idea. No one was ready for the evening to end. Soon they were enjoying their floats and talking about the show. Each one had a favorite part, and it was like seeing it all over again as they reminisced. Someone picked up a schedule of future shows and the women were checking out the dates. They decided they would definitely get tickets for another show before too long.

After they licked the last bit of ice cream from the bottom of their glasses, they started their trip home. Jim, once again, took the lead with Scott following. They drove for about ten miles and the passengers were getting quiet. The late hour and their bellies filled were making them all sleepy. Fortunately, Jim was wide awake and he and Luther were talking in the front seat. There wasn't much traffic, so Jim kept at a steady speed.

Scott and Barbara were enjoying their time together. They liked spending time with their friends, but they also looked forward to time alone. Scott had just asked Barbara if she was free for dinner the next night. Barbara was about to answer, when she saw a car on a side road going very fast, heading straight for the main road. She turned to Scott with a worried look. Scott had noticed the car as well and slowed down; he didn't think the car was going to be able to stop in time. Suddenly, they both realized that Jim's car and the speeding car were going to be at the intersection at the same time. *Didn't Jim see the car?* they wondered. It was apparent that the two cars were going to collide. Scott and Barbara just watched, feeling totally helpless, as the speeding car ran right through the stop sign and into Jim. There was a terrible bang, and Jim's car spun around and was pushed into the opposing lane. Thank goodness there weren't any cars coming in that direction. Scott pulled to the side of the road, and he and Barbara ran toward the two mangled cars. The driver of the speeding car was slumped over the steering wheel. The girl in the passenger seat was crying hysterically. Barbara told her to stay calm. She was going to a nearby house to call the police. Then they looked into Jim's car. Jim got out and helped Mary Ann from the back seat. Luther had hit his head on the windshield and his face on the dashboard; his mouth was bleeding and he appeared stunned. Jim looked in the back seat and it was obvious that Ruth and Millie had been seriously injured. They weren't moving. Ruth was unconscious. Millie's eyes were open but glazed, and she was obviously in a lot of pain.

Barbara ran to the first house and up the steps onto the front porch. The light immediately came on and the door opened. The man at the door said he had already called the police and asked Barbara what he could do to help. Barbara had no idea what to tell him. She knew her friends were injured and only hoped the police and ambulance would come as quickly as possible.

Even though it seemed like an eternity, it was only a matter of minutes before the sound of sirens could be heard. The police, a fire truck, and several ambulances soon arrived on the scene. Scott held Barbara close as they watched Ruth being put onto a stretcher and into an ambulance. Millie's side of the car had to be cut away from the other car. It took considerable time, but they soon had Millie out of the car and into an ambulance. The police took Jim, Mary Ann, and Wayne to the hospital in one of the squad cars. Another police car took the driver and passenger from the other car.

At the hospital, Wayne needed five stitches for his head wound. Jim and Mary Ann insisted they were not hurt. They wanted to find out how Ruth and Millie were. The two women had been taken for x-rays and were being evaluated for their injuries. The hospital wanted to keep Millie overnight for observation. Ruth was going to be admitted after x-rays revealed she had a fractured pelvis.

Around five o'clock in the morning, the doctor told Wayne he should go home and get some rest. He said he was sure that Millie was going to be okay. In fact, he thought she would most likely be discharged later that day.

Scott drove Jim, Mary Ann, and Wayne home. Jim's car was being towed to a nearby garage. Gone were the happy, laughing friends who had spent such a wonderful evening together. No one said a word on the trip home. Scott dropped the others off at the front entrance. Barbara, in tears, begged them to be sure and let them know as soon as they heard any news about Millie and Ruth.

*****

Neither Jim nor Wayne had seen the other car. Jim was watching the road ahead while chatting with Wayne. The women were resting quietly in the back seat and knew nothing of the apparent disaster heading their way. Suddenly, there was a loud bang and the car was spinning around. It felt like one of those rides at an amusement park. Jim was holding the steering wheel so tight, hoping to avoid the car from flipping over. Later, at the hospital, he noticed how red and swollen his hands were from holding it. When the car finally came to a stop, Jim's first reaction was to see how the others were. Mary Ann was trying to open her door, but her hands were shaking so badly she couldn't. Jim got out and opened the door for her, asking if she was okay. She assured him she was.

They looked over at Ruth in the middle, slumped over the seat with her eyes closed. Jim and Mary Ann looked at each other and said a silent prayer that she had just passed out. The impact of the hit happened directly at Millie's door and she received the blunt force of the collision. Her eyes were open and she was lodged in her seat. She had been forced forward and then back into the door as the twisted and mangled metal went through the car.

Mary Ann shouted out her name, and Millie, ever so slightly, turned her head toward the sound of her friend's voice. She couldn't talk above a whisper and indicated she was in a lot of pain. Mary Ann told her to remain calm and that help was on the way. Millie knew that something was seriously wrong. She heard the loud noise and immediately felt herself flying through the air and bouncing back again. She couldn't move her right arm because it was pinned to the door. She felt stabbing pain in her stomach. She was trying to say something, but the words weren't coming out. She felt out of breath. She wanted to close her eyes and fade away, but the pain was so bad she couldn't. She wanted to know how the others were. And where was Wayne? Was he hurt?

On impact, Wayne hit his head on the windshield. His face slammed into the dashboard and his mouth was bleeding. His glasses had fallen off his face and he didn't know where they were. He reached in his pocket for a hankie and wiped at his mouth and then realized that he had broken one of his front teeth. His head hurt and he felt a large knot forming about his right eye. A headache was coming on and he thought he had passed out briefly. When he became aware of where he was and what had happened, he immediately tried to open the car door to get out. It wouldn't budge. Jim had the driver's door open and he and Mary Ann were looking in the back seat. Wayne looked back and saw Ruth. He looked to her right to see Millie. He saw panic in her eyes. He called her name, but she didn't answer. Jim asked Wayne if he could crawl across the front seat to get out on the driver's side. Wayne immediately did that and wanted to get into the back seat with Millie. Jim put his hand on Wayne's shoulder and said it would be best if no one tried to move either of them. He said that help was on the way and they would know the proper way to get them out of the car.

The girl in the other car looked at her boyfriend. He was sitting back in the seat now just staring at the car in front of him. He knew he had run that stop sign and had hit them. They both got out of the car and went to where Jim, Mary Ann, and Wayne were standing. Mary Ann told them that the police were called and that help was on the way.

Shawn, the driver, asked if anyone was hurt. Jim said they were concerned about the two women in the back seat. Shawn and Marcy then realized there were others in the car. Shawn immediately apologized, saying it was all his fault. He knew the stop sign was there, but he wasn't paying attention and ran right through it. Tears were falling down his face and he was visibly shaken. He hoped the two women would be okay.

Wayne, now realizing exactly what had happened, wanted to punch this kid. "Are you drunk?" he asked. "Why weren't you paying more attention to what you were doing?"

"Honestly, mister, I am not drunk. I haven't had any alcohol tonight. You can ask Marcy, my girlfriend. We went to a movie with some friends and ended up going back to their house. We had pizza and coke. I swear. I'm so sorry this happened. I was just taking Marcy home and I guess I was going faster than I should have. Marcy's parents are pretty strict, and they don't like it when she is out late at night. I was going faster than I should have to get her home. I know that stop sign is there. I drive this way a lot, but tonight I wasn't paying attention. I am so sorry." Tears were continuing down his face.

Wayne wasn't sure about that, but figured it would be best to wait for the police to check it out. Shawn didn't appear drunk, but that doesn't mean he wasn't drinking. Jim could sense that Wayne really wanted to get into this and tried to steer him away. Fortunately, a neighbor brought some blankets and a thermos of hot coffee. They each wrapped up in a blanket and Jim encouraged Wayne to have a cup of the coffee.

The sirens could be heard, coming from the direction of the town where they had seen the show. The police saw the two women in the back seat and called for a tow truck. They were sure the cars would need to be pulled apart before they could remove the women. When the ambulances arrived, the EMTs checked Ruth and Millie's injuries. They were able to get Ruth out on the driver's side, but they didn't want to move Millie until the cars were separated. They were sure her injuries were more serious.

When the cars were pulled apart, the ambulance crew quickly eased Millie out and into the awaiting ambulance.

During this time, Jim and Mary Ann were giving their statements to the police about the accident. There wasn't much they could tell them because they didn't see the other car. Another police officer was talking to Scott and Barbara. Wayne was outside watching the ambulance leave with Millie. He wanted to get to her as quickly as he could.

By the time Ruth's ambulance arrived at the hospital, she was hysterical. She was trying to get off the gurney and the nurses were trying to keep her calm. The hospital staff were sure her injuries were serious, and she was immediately taken to an available treatment room. The doctor ordered something to calm her down. They didn't want her to injure herself any more than she already was.

Millie's ambulance arrived about twenty minutes later. She remained perfectly still while in the ambulance. She was in a great deal of pain and was trying to tell them that her stomach hurt and that she felt sick. Unsure of her injuries, they just continued to keep her calm. At the hospital, she was taken for x-rays and then to a treatment room.

They put the stitches in Wayne's head and he was given something for the pain and told he would be released. He would need to see his dentist about his broken tooth. Fortunately, there was no other damage to his mouth. He asked about Millie and was told she was being treated in another section of the ER. He asked if they would please find out how she was and to tell her that he was okay.

Jim, Mary Ann, Scott, and Barbara were all sitting in the waiting room anxiously waiting to hear any news. Each, in their own way, were playing the "what if" game. Jim told himself none of this would have happened if he had not suggested going for root beer floats. He had also considered taking a back road home, but decided the main road would be quicker with less traffic at that time of night. The women had talked to the people sitting behind them at the show. If they had left right away and not lingered, they would have been through that intersection before the other car came speeding down the hill. Scott was upset with himself because he was driving slower than Jim would have liked. If he had followed closer, Jim would have driven faster and they would have been beyond the roads where the accident happened.

They all knew it was fruitless to feel this way. No one could have predicted what was going to happen. Call it fate or karma, it happened, and no amount of hindsight was going to make it go away.

After Wayne was discharged, he was taken to Millie's room. She was lying in the hospital bed and he saw pain in her eyes. She had an IV attached to her left arm and a blood pressure and heart monitor on her right arm. He went to her and took her hand. "Millie, I'm here. How are you?" he asked. She just held onto his hand and didn't say anything. She was scared, Wayne knew. Her skin was pale.

She turned her head toward him and tried to open her mouth. It felt dry and her lips were chapped. She made a sound like she was saying Ruth. Ah, Wayne thought, she wanted to know how Ruth was. This was so like his Millie, always wanting to find out how everyone else is and not concentrating on her own injuries. Before Wayne had a chance to answer, they heard a scream from the room next door. It was Ruth. Wayne went to her and found a nurse in the room with her. He asked her how Ruth was. She was reluctant to give any information until Wayne told her that Ruth had been in the accident with him and their friends. She said that Ruth had been given a sedative and that the doctor would be in shortly and could answer any questions. He went to Ruth's side, and when she saw him, she immediately felt calmer. It was her worst fear; she thought that everyone else had died and she was the only one who survived. Wayne told her that Millie was in the room next to her and that the others were not hurt. Ruth motioned to the large bandage on Wayne's head, and he assured her it was nothing more than a cut on his forehead.

The doctor came in and asked if Wayne was a relative of Ruth's. Wayne explained that Ruth had no immediate family nearby. The doctor asked Ruth if he could discuss her medical condition with Wayne and she nodded in agreement.

"Ruth, the x-rays confirm that you have a fractured pelvis and several cracked ribs. We are going to give you something for the pain and that will also help you to relax. You will need to be admitted to the hospital. I know from your chart that you live in Maryland, and we are hopeful that in a few weeks, you will be able to transfer to a hospital closer to your home. Your injuries are serious, but not life-threatening."

Wayne said he knew her closest family member was her sister and said he would contact her as soon as he got home. Ruth nodded. It was a relief to know that even though she was hurt, she would be okay.

The doctor then went to Millie's room. Wayne followed, telling the doctor that she was his wife. Her injuries appeared to be minor. She had a broken finger and some bruises. The x-rays didn't reveal anything, but they wanted her to stay in the hospital till later that day, for observation. The doctor felt sure she could be discharged then. He advised Wayne to go home, get some much needed rest, and come back to take Millie home later in the day.

"Millie, did you hear that?" Wayne said. "You'll only have to stay in the hospital for a short time and then I can take you home. You will be able to rest there and I will take care of you."

This news did seem to make Millie feel better, although she was still in a great deal of pain. According to the doctor, this pain was from the car door being rammed into her side.

Ruth and Millie were taken to the third floor where they were going to share a room. Wayne went out to tell the others what the doctor said. They were all relieved to hear this news. They would all go home and get some rest and Wayne would return to the hospital later that day to take Millie home.

*****

Millie was aware of everything that was going on. She knew that she was in a room with Ruth. They tried to talk to each other, but it was difficult for Millie to speak above a whisper and Ruth couldn't hear her. She heard the doctor tell Wayne that the x-rays showed no broken bones, other than her finger. That was a relief. She was still in a lot of pain and was hoping the medication would soon start to work. She wanted to sleep, but didn't think she would be able to.

When she heard Ruth snoring, she was glad. At least Ruth was going to get some much needed rest.

Millie must have dozed off because a nurse startled her when she approached her bed. Millie told her she was still in a lot of pain and wanted to know if she could have more pain medication. The nurse said she would mention it to the doctor when he came in for rounds. She did not think Millie's color looked good and was concerned about her pain. It should have eased by now. When the doctor on call came in a short time later, the nurse mentioned Millie's condition to him. Doctor McClain was not the primary doctor who saw Millie earlier. He checked her and agreed that something didn't seem right. He decided to order another set of x-rays just to be on the safe side.

This time, the results showed an entirely different scenario. It was obvious why Millie was in so much pain. She too had fractured her pelvis and had several broken ribs. This certainly would change her treatment plan and she would not be able to go home later today. Doctor McClain wondered how this was missed on the earlier set of x-rays. He made a note on Millie's chart to speak to her doctor as soon as he came in.

Doctor Chambers, Millie's primary doctor, was not happy that additional x-rays were ordered without his consent. Doctor McClain told him he ordered them because she was in a lot of pain and he wanted to be certain there were no other injuries. He also felt she should have some tests to check for internal injuries. Considering the severity of the impact of the collision, it would have made sense to cover all the bases. Doctor Chambers did not feel these were necessary and did not want them ordered. Doctor McClain wasn't happy with this decision, but he wasn't in charge and he had to follow protocol. He hoped there was nothing else causing her extreme pain. He made a mental note to monitor Millie during the next few days.

*****

Wayne couldn't rest when he got home. He paced around the apartment trying to get the thoughts of the accident out of his mind.

When daylight came, he called Millie's sister Hattie. He told her what happened and asked if she wanted to go along to the hospital that afternoon. Hattie and her husband, Ed, emphatically said yes.

Other family members were notified, including Ruth's sister. Wayne gave her the details plus the name of the hospital and the doctor. The last call Wayne made was to Peggy. She was upset, of course, and wanted to immediately come. Wayne told her to wait until he brought her mother home later that day.

At one o'clock that afternoon, Ed drove Hattie and Wayne to the hospital to bring Millie home. Hattie had packed a small overnight bag with some fresh clothing plus her toothbrush, a comb, and a few makeup items. They were all anxious to bring Millie home where she could recuperate with family close by. They were also concerned for Ruth. They knew she was going to have to remain in the hospital and that was a difficult situation since her sister lived so far away.

The threesome walked into Millie and Ruth's room. Millie was lying down with her head slightly elevated. Wayne went to her and leaned down to give her a kiss on the forehead. Before he could say anything, Millie told him that she wouldn't be able to come home. She explained additional x-rays were taken and they showed she had other injuries.

Needless to say, the others were shocked to hear this. Hattie immediately went to the nurse's station to find out what was going on. The nurse told her they would have to speak to the doctor. He was not in the hospital at the time, but it was the doctor on call who had ordered the second x-rays. The nurse contacted him, and before too long, he was in Millie's room to speak to her family.

He explained to them that additional tests were taken and they showed a fractured pelvis and several broken ribs. He told them that with these injuries she would need to stay in the hospital. He was hopeful that within a week, she would be able to be transferred to a hospital closer to their home.

Hattie, Ed, and Wayne weren't happy to hear this. Ed asked why they didn't find these injuries the first time. Doctor McClain said he didn't know. When he came on duty, the nurse told him that

Mrs. Yeager was in extreme pain and he felt that further tests were needed.

Hattie said they wanted to speak to the primary doctor and was told that he wasn't in the hospital at the time. They were given his phone number and told to call his office the following morning.

Millie asked if Peggy was called and Wayne told her she was. He would call her again tonight with the latest update. He knew she would want to be at her mother's side.

When Peggy heard that her mother was still in the hospital, she told her father that she would be there as soon as she could make arrangements for someone to watch her children.

The next day, Peggy and her husband met her father at the hospital. At the sight of her daughter, Millie started crying. Too emotional to see her mother in such a state, Peggy was trying to hold back her tears. Millie was pale and had bruises on her face. Her arm hung frail with an IV attached. Peggy went to her mother's bedside and reached for her hand. It was a comfort to both of them.

When they brought in a lunch tray, Millie wanted Peggy to feed her. Peggy obliged, attentively giving her mother small spoonfuls and tenderly wiping her mouth when things got a little messy. Her mother was always so strong, and seeing her helplessly lying in this hospital bed was difficult for Peggy.

Millie continued crying off and on during their visit and told Peggy that when she got home, they were going to be a much closer family. Things had not always been good between Peggy and her mother, and there had always been a strained relationship between Peggy and her father.

Peggy wanted to talk to the doctor. Her aunt had tried several times to reach him and he never returned her calls. Peggy went to the nurse and said it was imperative that she speak to him as soon as possible. The nurse understood her frustration. She dialed the doctor's office and explained the situation to his secretary, who assured her that she would have him call as soon as he was finished with his current patient.

Much to everyone's surprise, Doctor Chambers returned the call and asked to speak to Peggy. "Your mother's injuries are more serious than we originally thought. Further x-rays revealed the fracture to her pelvis and the broken ribs. She will need to remain in the hospital for about a week and then it's possible she can be transported to a hospital near her home."

"Doctor Chambers, why didn't the first set of x-rays that were taken reveal these injuries? Is she going to be all right?" Peggy was fighting back tears as she talked to the doctor.

"I can't answer why the original x-rays didn't show the injuries. It is possible that there was a great deal of swelling in her abdomen and it clouded the picture. Fortunately, we were able to see them with the second set. Your mother is going to be fine. It will take time for her to heal, probably a month or longer until she will be able to do certain activities. She could be in the hospital for an additional week and then will need care at home. She will be unable to stand for long periods of time. Housework will be out of the question. She will need some assistance with daily hygiene. I do feel quite certain though that she will not be in any hospital for a long period of time. Do you have any further questions for me at this time?"

"I guess not, for now. I just need to be sure that she is going to be okay. I live three hours away and will need to make arrangements for child care if I must stay here. Will I be able to contact you again if I have further questions?"

"I think it would be a wise idea for you to come back once your mother is home. While in the hospital, she will receive therapy as needed. She will need the most help once she returns home. You can always call my office and my secretary will be able to contact me. Goodbye."

Peggy thought the doctor was rather curt. He didn't show any compassion whatsoever. Yes, he answered her questions, but he could have shown more warmth. Bedside manners were obviously not one of his strong suits. Peggy was still trying to comprehend everything that had happened. It all seemed like a big nightmare. Unfortunately, it was all too real. Peggy knew she had to be strong for her mother. She didn't want her mother to see her crying. She composed herself and then went back to her mother's room.

She told the family what the doctor said. She told her mother she was going to go home and return after she was home from the hospital. She wanted to reassure her that she would be there when she needed her the most.

Little did anyone know that this visit to her mother's bedside would be the last time she would ever see her mother alive again.

The Worst News

F ive days had gone by and Millie was still in the hospital. Peggy called her father or her aunt daily to get an update on her mother's condition. She was hoping that her mother wouldn't be in that hospital too much longer and would be able to be transported to the local hospital. Peggy was going to stay with her parents when Millie was discharged and help take care of her. She wasn't sure how long that was going to be. She had already spoken to several close friends who said they would be glad to help out with her children while she was away. Their father, Mike, could be with them in the evenings when he got home from work. Somehow it would all work out, although at the moment, Peggy wasn't exactly sure how.

Peggy was sitting at her desk in her office. Her children were watching TV and arguing as usual. Peggy was planning on calling her mother's room around two that afternoon. That way, the kids could say hi to their grandmother. She knew her dad would be there by then to hand her the phone. Neither Millie nor Ruth were able to reach the telephone in their room.

Around 2:15 p.m., she called the kids to the phone as she dialed her mother's room. There was no answer. Peggy thought that was strange, but perhaps her family was late in arriving, or the nurse was in the room. There surely was an obvious explanation.

At 2:30 p.m., Peggy called again and still no answer. Now she was beginning to worry. She called the hospital and asked for the nurse's station on that floor, but there was no answer there either. She tried numerous times to call her mother's room and the nurse's station and no one ever answered. By 4:45 p.m., Peggy was extremely worried and knew something was wrong. She called the hospital again and explained that she had been trying to reach her mother or the nurse's station all afternoon with no luck. After being placed on hold for several minutes, she was connected to her mother's room again. And once again there was no answer.

Peggy was feeling helpless when suddenly she felt this over-whelming chill come over her entire body. She didn't understand why she felt this way. It was a warm April day. She even had the windows open in the house to let the warm air in. And now at 5:00 p.m., she was freezing. She reached for the afghan that hung over her chair and buried herself in it. The children had gone outside to play. Mike was at a meeting and she was in the house by herself. And now, for some unexplained reason, she was so very cold.

This coldness only lasted about ten minutes, although to Peggy it seemed forever. Finally, it disappeared. She wondered what that was all about. She didn't feel sick, so she didn't think she was coming down with something. The cool breeze blowing in the office window was now starting to feel good. She thought about trying the hospital again. Momentarily, she had been preoccupied with this unusual chill.

Just then her daughter came into the house crying. She had fallen and scraped her knee on the sidewalk. Peggy took her into the bathroom, cleaned the wound, and covered it with a Band-Aid. Becca was five years old and was crying hysterically. The wound wasn't bad, but Becca was sure making something of it. A kiss over the Band-Aid miraculously solved the problem, and Becca was off and running out the back door once again.

It was now 6:00 p.m. and Peggy went back into her office to once again call the hospital. Just as she reached for the phone, it rang. It was her aunt. What she was telling her was the worst possible news. Peggy's mind refused to accept it. Her mother couldn't be dead. The doctor said she'd be fine. Peggy had just seen her. She made all these plans for her children so she could be with her mother and help her get well.

Overwhelmed with shock, Peggy could faintly hear her children outside playing as she remembered the chill that had overcome and distracted her before Becca had come in crying. Her eyes transfixed on the blanket, she ran her hand over it as her aunt explained what happened.

And then the tears came.

*****

Around one that afternoon, Peggy's father, aunt, and uncle arrived at the hospital. They found Millie's side of the room empty. They asked Ruth where Millie was. Ruth told them the doctor and a nurse came in and then they wheeled Millie out. She said they didn't say anything and she had no idea where they took her.

Wayne went to the nurse's station to get to the bottom of this. Hattie and Ed followed close behind. They asked where Millie was and were told she had been taken to the ICU about an hour earlier. Hattie asked why and the nurse said she was unsure and directed them where to go. She said they would be given more information there.

They immediately found the ICU doctor, who had just come out of the unit, and Ed was the one to approach him, asking about Millie. This doctor told him he had just left her and was still trying to figure out what was going on. He had never seen Millie before and had no knowledge of her medical condition other than what he read on her chart.

The nurse had found Millie unresponsive and called the doctor on call. Millie's primary doctor was not in the hospital at that time. Upon seeing Millie, he immediately had her transferred to the ICU. Now a new doctor was involved. A call to Doctor Chambers, the primary doctor, was made, but there was no answer. His service said he was off duty and unavailable at the time. The service was told that Doctor Chambers needed to be reached immediately because a patient of his had taken an unexpected turn for the worse. They said they would try to reach him, but reiterated that he was not on call that day.

Millie's vital signs were failing. Reading her chart, Doctor Rodomsky, the ICU doctor, couldn't understand what was happening. He felt she should be taken to surgery to find out if there were internal injuries, but he also knew she would never survive surgery with her vitals so low.

Wayne, Hattie, and Ed stood there in total disbelief. What had happened? She was fine when they visited her yesterday. And just where was her doctor? They were allowed to visit her, one at a time, for only five minutes each. Doctor Rodomsky told them they could visit on the hour. He was bending the rules by letting them each visit because he was certain this patient was not going to survive much longer.

Wayne went in the room first and looked down at his wife. She was extremely pale. He picked up her hand, being very careful because of all the wires and tubes attached. He softly said her name. She, ever so slightly, opened her eyes and looked in the direction of his voice. She tried to say something, but she didn't have the strength. Wayne noticed a tear in the corner of her eye. He didn't know what to say. He was still in shock after talking to the doctor. He told her not to worry, that the nice doctor was going to take care of her, and that before long she would be home where she belonged. Millie once again tried to say something, but just closed her eyes. Wayne hoped that what he said would happen. He couldn't lose her now. He just couldn't. They had been through so much together throughout the years, and now they were looking forward to spending their golden years together. Tears were welled in his eyes, and he said a prayer as he walked out of her room. He prayed that Millie would be all right, because he didn't know what he would do without her.

Doctor Rodomsky was talking to Hattie and Ed as Wayne approached them. He was telling them he was very confused as to what was going on. Her chart didn't indicate anything that should be causing this. He didn't want to tell them he didn't think she was going to survive, but he also felt they had the right to know. He didn't know how many hourly visits they would still be able to have with her. He was making the decision himself that he would allow them to visit her more often because of the severity of the situation. He hoped the nurses here would understand. There was only one other patient in the ICU at this time and he had no family visiting.

Hattie went in next to see her sister. It was obvious to her that Millie was not going to survive. Wayne was talking on and on about getting Millie out of this hospital and back home to the local hospital where more experienced doctors could take care of her. He was also saying that as soon as she was better, they were going to take that trip to Hawaii. Millie didn't even know anything about it. Wayne was planning it as a surprise for her birthday. That date was still five months away, and hopefully, she would be well enough to travel by then. If she wasn't, they would wait and go at another time.

Hattie wanted to tell Wayne to be quiet, but she also knew that this was the only way he could handle the situation right now. She tried to block him out and think about her sister. Ed went to the cafeteria to get coffee for everyone. He needed something to do, and Wayne's constant talking was driving him crazy. He wanted to get away from that, yet be there in case there was any change. Around 4:40 p.m., Doctor Chambers arrived on the ICU floor and immediately went into Millie's room. He didn't acknowledge Wayne or Hattie at all. In fact, he actually looked annoyed. He was dressed in a white golf shirt, as he'd been playing with friends at the country club. He wasn't happy when he had been paged while teeing off at the fourteenth hole. He had left strict instructions to his service that he was not to be disturbed. This was his day off, he was not on call, and he just wanted to play golf with his friends. The hospital, or any of his patients, were not his concern at that moment.

At 5:05 p.m., he came out of the room and started walking toward the elevator. Ed went after him and asked about Millie. He looked at him with a blank expression and asked who he was. This doctor had just pushed one too many buttons, and Ed looked him hard in the eyes and told him that they were Millie's family and demanded to know what was going on. Ed tried to explain that yesterday, they saw a woman in good spirits who couldn't wait to go home, and today they find this same woman in the ICU.

Doctor Chambers ignored Ed and then, noticing Wayne, offered him a simple, "I'm sorry," and stepped into the elevator.

"I'm sorry! That is all you have to say? What does that mean?" Ed just about screamed.

The ICU doctor was fuming. He witnessed all of this. It was unthinkable that this doctor had treated Millie's family the way he did. They deserved answers, even though he himself was unsure what the answers were. He could have, at least, showed some compassion. He was in the room when Doctor Chambers came in and heard him say that this better be worth his trip here since he had to leave before his golf game was over. He made it clear to everyone in the room that he was winning and now would have to forfeit the loss. That was going to cost him a $200 bet.

At 5:02 p.m., Doctor Chambers had declared Millie dead. He disconnected her IVs and told Doctor Rodomsky to make all necessary arrangements. He then muttered something that sounded like he was hoping he would still be able to complete his golf game. Doctor Rodomsky couldn't believe how any human being could call himself a doctor and be so coldhearted and show such a lack of compassion.

Doctor Rodomsky came over and sat with Wayne. He told them he was so sorry, but that Millie had passed away at 5:02 p.m. He had no answers as to what happened. He said she was brought to the ICU, and with everything he tried, he was unable to stop her vital signs from plummeting. He thought there was possibly internal bleeding somewhere. He told them he would have suggested surgery, but Millie would never have survived it. He offered no apology for the behavior of the other doctor. What could he say at this time that would make the situation any different?

He left them briefly to fill out the necessary paperwork. When they asked if they could see Millie one more time, he took them to her side. It wasn't protocol to allow all three of them in the room, but he felt compelled to break the rules. These people had just suffered an immense loss that they were in no way prepared for. He also was sure that this patient's death could have been prevented. He wanted to reach out and strangle her primary doctor. His behavior today was totally unprofessional. He also knew that if he told anyone, he would be the one reprimanded. After all, he wasn't her primary doctor.

Doctor Rodomsky watched as they looked down at their loved one. He couldn't imagine what was going through their minds. He needed to direct them to the main office and he wanted to do that before Millie's body was taken to the morgue. He didn't want them to have to witness that.

Wayne, Hattie, and Ed stood beside Millie's bed, looking down at her lifeless body. Each, in their own way, was wondering what had happened. It didn't seem possible, but as they looked at Millie, they knew it was all so very true. Ed put his arm on Wayne's shoulder to steady him. He thought he was about to faint. Hattie reached for Millie's hand. She had been like a mother to her when her own mother died. Millie was always there for her. Now she would no longer have her in her life. She knew she would have to call Peggy and she had no idea how she was going to say the words that she knew needed to be said.

*****

Peggy didn't understand. Her aunt just told her that her mother had died. How could this possibly be? She saw her just a few days ago and she was fine—other than her injuries—and the doctor assured her she would be better in no time. And now she was gone? She realized why at 5:02 p.m. she was so cold. She was connecting with her mother at the very time of her death. It was all so unreal.

Hattie told her everything that had happened from the time they got there that afternoon. It explained why there was no answer to the phone in her room. Peggy told her aunt she would come as soon as she could. After Peggy hung up, she sat at her desk looking out the window at her children. She was going to have to tell them that their grandmother had died. They never got to talk to her and now they would never see her again.

As soon as Mike came home, she told him the terrible news. He immediately made some phone calls explaining to his boss that he would be out of town for the week. They packed and left a few hours later for the three-hour drive to Peggy's hometown.

Millie's Funeral

Luther was sitting in his chair. All the memories of that horrible day came back to him. He now remembered everything—the day he lost his Millie.

Just then the TV went on and George appeared on the screen. "Luther, I would like to see you as soon as you can get to my office."

"George, I'm not feeling very good right now. Could I please have a little time and perhaps see you tomorrow instead?"

"Luther, I am fully aware of what is going on in your mind right now, but it is imperative that I see you immediately," George said as the TV went black.

Luther stood and tried to steady himself. He didn't want to talk to George now. He really didn't want to talk to anyone, but he knew there was no way he was going to avoid George. He had thought earlier that he needed him, but he felt that now all he needed was to be alone.

When Luther walked into George's office, the girl at the desk told him to go right into the other room. George was sitting on a chair that faced an outside window. He turned when he heard the door open and then motioned for Luther to sit down.

"So, Luther, tell me what you are feeling right now?"

"George, I just relived the day my Millie died. It was terrible. I remember everything that happened." Luther's face was red and his eyes were swollen. It was obvious that he had been crying.

"Luther, you've been crying. Do you recall how often you cried after that day?"

Luther looked at George and didn't know what to say. He started to open his mouth and George put up his hand to stop him.

George was angry and it showed in his voice. It was rare that he let his anger show, but he was angry now and he wanted Luther to know it. "Don't even try to come up with an answer, because you and I both know what that answer will be. Luther, you just cried more tears in the past hour than you did in the thirty years since Millie died." George was yelling as he stood up and looked down at Luther.

Luther hung his head and tears welled in his eyes again. George was right. He knew it. He couldn't explain why he shed very few tears after Millie died. He loved her and they were happy together, but something came over him and he didn't feel that overwhelming sadness he should have. And he couldn't explain why.

There was silence in the room for quite a long time. George walked over to the window and was looking out at the people sitting in the park. Millie was there. George had wanted to bring her into the room to see Luther, but now he thought better of that. He knew it was going to have to happen sometime, but he didn't want it to be now. He returned to the chair he had been sitting in and looked over at Luther. Right now he was a very sad and lonely man.

Luther finally looked at George. He didn't know what to say. He felt terrible. He knew George was angry with him, and he knew he had every right to be. Luther also knew that his life from the time Millie died was drastically different from the way it was before her death. There were flashes of his life that were beginning to come back to him. He just couldn't remember everything and didn't have a good feeling about what would happen next.

George pushed a button on the wall and the screen came down. Immediately, the curtains closed and the room became dark. George never said a word. The scene was Peggy and her family coming to the house the evening that Millie died. Wayne (as he was not yet called Luther) had been standing at the patio door, and he watched as Peggy and her family drove up the driveway. Peggy saw her father, and as soon as the car stopped, she hurried to him. When she got to the apartment, she saw him sitting in a chair with his head bowed and his hands over his eyes. Peggy went to him and he looked up as if he was surprised to see her. Peggy knew he had seen her and couldn't understand why he would pretend he was only seeing her now for the first time. He stood up and held her and tears were in his eyes. Peggy's eyes were red because she had been crying most of the way there. Mike was driving, and fortunately, the children had fallen asleep in the back seat.

The scene then changed to the day of the funeral. Peggy and her family rode in the funeral car with her father. Other family and friends followed. They were at the cemetery now. The burial plot was the one that Millie's father had purchased when Millie's mother died. Millie was laid to rest beside her parents. Krissy was there too.

Two days after the funeral, Mike and the children went home. Peggy stayed with her father to help him go through her mother's things. Mike would return in another week to take her back home. Peggy tried to talk her father into going home with them, but he refused. He said he had too much to do and he needed to be home. Peggy agreed to come back in a few weeks to help in any way she could.

*****

The screen went black, the lights came back on, and the curtains opened automatically. Luther continued to stare at the blank screen as if he were waiting for something else to appear. He felt numb. He wanted to return to his room and be alone. He wished George would say something, anything, just to break the silence that cut through the room like a knife.

George purposely sat in the chair watching Luther, not saying a word. He knew Luther felt uncomfortable and he wanted him to feel that way.

Finally, George stood and looked out the window. Millie was no longer there. He turned to Luther and said, "I want you to go back to your room now. I want you to think very hard about your life after Millie died. Come to my office tomorrow morning after breakfast. We have many things to talk about, and I want to get started as soon as we can. Good day, Luther."

Luther had been dismissed. In his mind, he was reliving the events that he had just watched. He had no explanation why he acted the way he did when Peggy came that night. He also couldn't explain why he didn't feel that overwhelming sadness and grief. Was he just putting on a good act or trying to be brave? No, that wasn't it. He just wanted to move on with his life.

The next morning, he arrived at George's office, immediately after he finished his breakfast. George came out of the room and escorted him to the couch. George was immaculately dressed in a yellow tennis shirt. He was wearing blue jeans, something Luther never expected to see. George had on white Nike running shoes. Today his long hair was tied back into a ponytail. Luther thought he looked like one of the young hippies he often saw at the pool at his condo.

George sat across from him with a stern expression on his face. After what seemed like a long time, George finally said, "Luther, are you ready to continue?"

Luther nodded. He had vague recollections of his life after Millie, but all too often, they were cloudy. He actually thought his life was pretty good. He was sure he was happy. He knew that he remarried and his second wife's name was Margaret. He wasn't sure what he was going to see today, but looking at George, he was sure it wasn't going to be good.

Lisa

"Okay then. Let's get started," George said. Once again, the room darkened and the screen came down. Luther watched the scene unfold in front of him. Peggy and Hattie were there and they were sorting through Millie's clothing from the closet and the dresser. Most of the things were too big for Peggy, and Millie's taste wasn't the same as Hattie's. Wayne was sitting in the living room watching a baseball game. He didn't want to disturb the women in the bedroom. He would have had no idea what to do with Millie's things. He heard them mention Goodwill and the Salvation Army, and he thought those were good places to start.

After several hours, Peggy and Hattie came out with bags of clothing. They told him what their plans were. Wayne just shook his head. He was far more interested in the ball game than women's clothes. He really didn't care what they did with them as long as they got them out of the apartment. He was already planning on rearranging the closet to accommodate his things.

*****

The next scene that came to view was Hattie and Ed in Wayne's dining room. The table had lots of papers scattered all over it. Wayne looked perplexed and was asking Hattie for advice as to what and how to handle all this. Hattie went to work and organized everything and told Wayne she would take care of all the paperwork. Insurance companies, Social Security, and numerous other places needed to be notified of Millie's death. Forms had to be filled out and a death certificate was needed to accompany each form. Wayne had no idea what to do. Hattie assured him she would take care of it. Ed suggested that he and Wayne go to the pool so that Hattie could concentrate on the task before her.

There were a few adults at the pool and a handful of teenagers splashing in the deep end. Wayne set his towel down on one of the lounge chairs and jumped in the water. Ed noticed a young woman swim over to him and they started talking. The woman was about thirty years old with bleached blonde hair. She was wearing a bikini that left nothing to the imagination. Wayne was smiling and swimming around her, acting worse than the teenagers at the other end of the pool. Ed just watched in utter amazement as this woman, Lisa, was putting the moves on Wayne. And he was playing right along with it. Ed heard Lisa say that if she had as much money as he did, she would take a fabulous vacation to Paris and buy lots and lots of expensive clothing and jewelry. Shockingly, Ed heard Wayne say that he could afford to take her there. It was obvious that Wayne and Lisa had talked on previous occasions and that Wayne had bragged about how much money he had. Ed was thinking what a fool Wayne was.

After a short swim, Wayne and Lisa got out of the water and sat at one of the tables on the other side of the pool. It was now impossible for Ed to hear what they were talking about. Lisa was surely making a play for Wayne and arranging herself so he would get a full view of her very voluptuous breasts. The view didn't go unnoticed, as Wayne's eyes never strayed from them.

Two teenage girls, who had been flirting with some boys at the deep end of the pool, got out of the water and sat near Ed. He couldn't help hear what they were saying.

"Just look at my mom over there, flaunting herself all over that old man. He must be at least eighty. Mom said he has lots of money and she was interested in finding out just how much. His wife just died and she thinks he's lonely and that she's just the one to make him feel better. She's always complaining about her lousy-paying job at K-Mart. My father doesn't pay any child support either. Can you imagine going to bed with that old geezer? Yuk! I guess she'll do anything to get her hands on his money."

Her friend just rolled her eyes and shook her head. The girls got up and walked away. Ed looked over at Wayne and Lisa in total disgust. He wondered just how stupid Wayne was. He knew he was egotistical and bragged about things he had. Yes, he had a fair amount of money and there were still some insurance policies from Millie and a possible malpractice suit, but…

Ed decided he had had enough of this and walked over to where Wayne and Lisa were sitting. He introduced himself to Lisa, saying he was Wayne's brother-in-law. Lisa looked up at him trying to decide if he could possibly have more money than Wayne. Maybe she could make a play for him too. Maybe he was a lonely widower. Ed said he was going back to the apartment. He told Wayne he thought Hattie would have most, if not all, the paperwork done by now. Wayne just nodded and said he would be along shortly.

*****

The screen went black at that moment and George looked over at Luther. He was sitting there with absolutely no expression on his face.

"Your thoughts on what you just witnessed?" George said.

"It wasn't like that. Lisa was a very nice lady who was going through some rough times. She was trying to raise a teenage daughter and getting no help from her ex-husband. She didn't have a good-paying job and was struggling financially. She was just being nice to me and I wanted to be nice to her. I felt sorry for her and thought if I could help her I would," Luther said with a sheepish look on his face.

"Luther! Who do you think you're fooling?" George screamed. "That video speaks loud and clear. Do you honestly think she was interested in you for anything other than the money that you so brazenly announced you had? Maybe someone you tell this story to will believe you, but I can assure you it isn't me. Nor was it your brother-in-law." George was angry now and even he couldn't believe how stupid and naïve Luther was. "So, Luther, what did you do? Did you take her to Paris?" George, of course, knew the answer, but he wanted to hear what Luther had to say.

"No, I didn't take her to Paris. We were only joking about that. I did take her out for dinner a few times, and I must say it was very nice. She never asked me for money. I, of course, paid for dinner. After all, that's what a man should do on a date. She wasn't interested in me for my money. She told me she always liked older men and she found me very attractive. I don't think she was just saying that. I think she meant it."

George couldn't believe what he was hearing.

"I knew she was too young for me even though she said she liked older men. I wasn't going to marry her, George. Honestly, I wasn't." Luther was trying as hard as he could to defend himself.

"Did you give her any money?"

"I offered to help her out and she refused. After our third date, I took her back to her apartment and she invited me in for a drink. I used her bathroom and put a hundred dollar bill under the soap dish. I knew she wouldn't take it if I offered, and I thought this was a good way to let her know I cared and that I wanted to help her."

George gave Luther that look—the one that Luther had come to know when he wasn't always being totally truthful. "Honestly, George, I only gave her money that one time. We didn't go out anymore after that. I didn't go to the pool much, and the few times I did, she wasn't there. I was planning on going to Europe with my army buddies and I was preparing for that trip."

*****

Luther left George's office and slowly walked back to his room. He knew he wasn't exactly being honest with George and he was sure that George knew it. The simple fact was that he really did like Lisa and he wanted to continue seeing her. He kept telling himself that he didn't care what other people would say about him. Millie's family never liked him. He always knew that, so it didn't matter what they thought. He was planning on getting Millie's estate settled and them moving on with his life. He figured Peggy would be upset, but she had her own life with her family. If she no longer wanted to accept him as her father, well that was the way it would be.

He remembered that he called Lisa and asked her out. She sounded like she didn't want to talk to him. Maybe she was upset about the money he had left in her bathroom, but he was only trying to be nice. She said she was busy and couldn't see him that night. She did say she would call him in a few days. However, a few days went by and Luther never heard from her. He never saw her again.

It was later that month that he made the final arrangements to go on the European trip to visit World War II sites. He was excited about the trip. He knew that if Millie were alive, he wouldn't be going. He was now beginning to wonder if she would have gone on the Hawaiian trip he had planned. She always talked about going, but she was afraid to travel that far away from home. Well, Millie was no longer here and he was going to live his life the way he wanted to.

Luther knew Millie's family and Peggy were not happy about his upcoming trip. They all thought it was too soon after Millie's death. Also, there were still things that needed to be done to settle her estate. There was the possibility of a lawsuit against the hospital and the doctor for malpractice. Hattie kept reminding him that he needed to see the lawyer to discuss that. Luther didn't want to deal with that now. He was totally focused on his trip.

Luther didn't like the idea that he had lied to George. He thought about trying to contact him, but decided to go for a walk instead. He needed a breath of fresh air and it was a warm, sunny day. He headed for a patio door. Opening it, he was immediately embraced with the sound of birds in the distance and the smell of some sweet flower. He started down the path toward a trail of rosebushes. All thoughts of George and Lisa were gone in a flash.

He walked at a slow pace, taking in the beautiful sights around him. There were big maple trees evenly spaced in a large open area. The lawn was magnificently trimmed and looked like lush green velvet as far as the eye could see. Every time Luther walked outside, he saw something different, and he continued to be amazed at the marvel of this wonderful place. He walked for what seemed like a long time, never once feeling out of breath or tired. Coming the opposite direction was a jogger. He stopped when he met Luther and they chatted for a few minutes. The smell of honeysuckles was present now, and Luther stopped at a bush to totally absorb himself in the aroma. It seemed that around every corner, there were different flowers, each having their own unique scent. On the other side of the bushes, he noticed a park bench where a woman was sitting, reading a book. She vaguely looked familiar, but he knew he sometimes thought that about many people here. He thought he would sit at the opposite end of the bench and see if his memory could recall her face.

The woman looked up as Luther sat down. She smiled at him and it was then that he knew who she was. He didn't think she recognized him. It was Lisa. He wanted to say something, but she returned her attention to her book. Luther kept staring at her. She looked different than he remembered. She was much older and had a big scar on the left side of her cheek. He understood her being older because it had been many years since he had last seen her. She was still beautiful and he wanted to talk to her, but was afraid.

After a few minutes, she put the book down beside her and looked at Luther. "I'm sure I know who you are. I've seen you before, but I don't think it was here. You are Wayne, aren't you?" she asked.

"Yes, I am. How have you been, Lisa? I thought it was you when I sat down, but you were very involved with your book and I didn't want to disturb you."

"I'm okay, I guess. I just recently arrived here and I'm still trying to sort things out. I have been talking with George, and it has been difficult. How long have you been here?"

"It's been a little while now. I actually have no idea because time here doesn't seem to matter much. Sometimes I think I've been here a long time, and then at times, it seems very recent. It does take a lot of getting used to. I too have been talking to George and sorting out my life. It's been difficult and challenging. I was in a nursing home until I died, and I didn't remember very much. I am learning that for a good part of my life, I haven't been a very nice person. I know I have to do some things to redeem myself. What about you?" He asked, not sure he wanted to know the answer.

Lisa went on to tell him that she got involved with a guy who was abusive. Her ex-husband filed for custody of their daughter, and she lost all visitation rights. She was so involved with this new boyfriend that she didn't even care. Her life was on a downhill swing, and before long, she was a hopeless case. Her boyfriend got her hooked on drugs, and that is what ultimately led to her death. Now she was here and was trying to sort out all the things she did wrong in her life.

Luther felt terrible. He always thought she was such a sweet girl. It was obvious that she didn't really want to talk to him, so he just stood up and said goodbye.

Frustration

George was frustrated. This was something he didn't feel often, but right now he did. Most of the time when people came to talk to him about their lives, he felt that he was actually helping them to see more clearly the good and bad that went on during their earthly life. Most felt remorse after they saw how some of their actions hurt others. They wanted to do whatever they could to repent. Occasionally, there was a stubborn case where it took more discussions and replays of their life for them to understand and see the results of their actions.

Luther was a difficult case. George had shown him most of his life by now. He was sure that Luther knew the rest of his story, even if he wasn't going to admit it. He wondered why he couldn't see and understand the things he had done. George lamented. His life story and events should have hit him like the proverbial ton of bricks, yet it hadn't.

George paced around his office wondering what he was going to have to do to get through to him. George was trying to be patient with him, but his patience was running out. He realized he was just going to have to take the matter by the horn and somehow get Luther to understand.

George sent a message to Luther that he needed to see him as soon as possible.

George sat down and rewound the tape on the screen in his office. He hoped that he would be able to accomplish something. Luther needed to move on and complete his personal tasks. George hung his head down and folded his hands. He said a prayer for guidance, wisdom, and patience. He needed to find the right words to say to Luther—the words that would change him.

*****

Meanwhile, Luther was sitting around the pool enjoying the warm sunshine. The water temperature was perfect. He didn't recognize anyone there and that was okay with him. He wasn't up for running into anyone with problems. He was enjoying watching people splash around each other. His thoughts turned to his childhood. He would have loved to be able to swim in a pool, or even the river, and splash and have fun with other kids. He never had that luxury living in the household he did. He could only imagine what his stepmother would have said if he asked if he could go swimming. She would have laughed and then slapped him across the face. She would have told him that he didn't have time for such nonsense when there were chores to be done. He probably would have been given extra work just because he asked.

Suddenly, Luther was startled by someone hovering over him. Luther looked up as he was presented with a note. *Now what?* he thought. *I haven't been here very long and already someone wants something. Why can't I just enjoy myself? I thought this place was where enjoyment and fun were supposed to happen. It seems every time I am trying to do that, someone from my past comes to tell me some nonsense story that I could care less about. Why must the past constantly be brought up? It's over and done with, and nothing can change what happened. If it wasn't that, then it was George wanting to see me.*

At first Luther enjoyed taking with George. He learned a lot about his early childhood and his mother, father, and stepmother.

He was reminded of his first wife Millie and how she died. He thought about his second wife Margaret and the things they did together. But Luther thought he was finished with all that. Okay, he now knew his story, so give it a rest and let's move on. He thought about George saying there was some kind of task he had to do, but every time he saw George, the actual task wasn't mentioned. Maybe the next time he saw him, he would just have to ask so he could do it and get on with his eternal life.

Luther reluctantly took the note from the man and opened it. It was hard to read with the sun glaring down on the paper. He needed to go back to his towel under the umbrella so he could see it. He actually thought about just throwing it away, but he knew he couldn't get away with that. Someone else would appear with another note, and it would mean getting a reprimand from George. Luther considered putting it in his pocket and saving it to read later, but knew he would face the same consequences. He was hoping the note wouldn't mean he would have to leave the pool. He was really enjoying himself.

The note read that George wanted to see him as soon as possible. *Darn! That man sure has a way of ruining any fun I am having. I'm going to take my good old sweet time getting to his office this time. After all, what's he going to do about it? I could tell him I met someone on the way, started talking, and lost sense of time. I wonder if he would buy that!*

Luther deliberately took the longest way there. He wanted to stop at his room first to change clothes, but somewhere along the way, he realized that his swimming trunks had been replaced with khaki pants, a bright red shirt, and sandals. It was still a wonder how these things just happened. Luther was just turning the corner, when George came from the opposite direction. They literally ran right into each other.

"Luther," George said in a very stern voice. "Where have you been? I sent my messenger with a note to you over two earthly hours ago. What has taken you so long?"

"Geez, George. Calm down. Do you want to have a heart attack or something? I came as soon as I could. What could possibly be so urgent? It's not like time flies around here." Luther was smirking and that made George even madder than he already was.

"Luther, you are in no position to make comments like that. Time may not fly, but time does change. There are changes that you are unaware of. You don't want to cross me or make me any angrier than I am right now. I am trying hard to change that, but if you continue to push the wrong buttons with me, you will be sorry. Now I suggest that we go to my office immediately. Luther, do I make myself clear?"

"Aye, aye, sir!" Luther said. *Boy, he's really got his dander up today. I wonder who made him mad. Why was he taking it out on me?*

Luther followed George into his office and looked around. He noticed the furniture was different. There was a recliner chair where the sofa used to be and another chair in the corner. Even the pictures on the walls were different. Luther wondered why George felt the need to redecorate. What was wrong with the other furniture? Oh well, he was the boss around here, so it didn't really matter to him.

"Sit down, Luther," George said angrily. Luther headed toward the chair in the corner, but George stopped him with a stern look. He pointed to the recliner and said, "Not that chair, this one." Luther obeyed his command and sat down. Immediately, the chair reclined into a comfortable position. Luther thought it felt so relaxing he might just fall asleep. Before he could even finish that thought, George said, "And don't think you are going to fall asleep, because I can assure you it isn't going to happen. I just want you lying down."

Luther was now beginning to worry about what was going to happen. He didn't remember ever seeing George this angry. He was trying to remember if there was something that he could have done that didn't suit George, but he couldn't think of anything offhand.

George paced around the room. He was trying to compose himself so that he could be effective. He didn't want to be angry, but he couldn't help himself. This was totally uncharacteristic of him, but the circumstances weren't normal. He just couldn't believe that Luther could be so naïve and stupid. George tried to rationalize all this. Yes, his upbringing was terrible and he certainly didn't have a good role model to look up to. But that didn't excuse his behavior. Millie was so upset when she learned of the things that he did. She couldn't believe this was the same man she had been married to. George had shared with her the story of Luther's life. Most of it she knew, but what hurt her the most was what happened after she died.

The Lawsuit

Luther just sat, reclined in the chair. He thought for a minute he might fall asleep anyway, but George's pacing kept him awake. It seemed like hours since he first sat down, and he wondered when George was going to say something, anything, just to break through the difficult atmosphere in the room.

Finally, his voice in a rage, George said, "Luther, do you remember all the events of your earthly life now?"

Mumbling and with uncertainty in his voice, Luther answered that he thought he did.

"So, Luther, you remember your first wife, Millie, and the events surrounding her death? And you remember your daughter, Peggy? And how about Margaret, your second wife, and your life with her?"

"Yes, George, I remember them. Why do you ask? Didn't we go over this before?"

George had continued to pace, but suddenly, he stopped and looked down at Luther. He knew his face was turning red and his voice was going to roar in rage, but now he no longer cared. "Luther, it would be wise of you to just answer the questions and not ask them. I have just about had it with your attitude and your behavior, and I will not tolerate it any longer. There have been a few people who have been in my office over time that have tried my patience, but you are working your way to the top of that list. I was going to continue with videos of your life, but I have come to the conclusion that it is time to move on. I have tried to give you every opportunity to realize that some of the things you did were not very nice, yet you continue to act like a stupid moron. DO YOU UNDERSTAND WHAT I AM SAYING?"

Luther tried to sit up as best he could. George certainly had his attention now. In fact, he was downright frightened. With a very sheepish expression and in a voice no louder than a whisper, he answered, "Yes, George, I do."

"Good. Then listen to me very carefully. After you made a fool of yourself with Lisa, thinking that she actually was romantically interested in you…"

Luther started to interrupt, but George quickly and with a very stern look put any verbal response he could have made to silence. "As I was saying. After you made a fool of yourself with Lisa, you met Margaret. Margaret was the extreme opposite of Lisa in one way. She was much older than you, as Lisa was many years younger. Here the opposition stops, because Margaret saw dollar signs in your eyes, as did Lisa." George could see that Luther was having a difficult time hearing this, but remained quiet.

"You sued the hospital and the doctor who treated Millie for malpractice. This was because of the treatment, or I should say the lack of treatment, that Millie received after the accident. The autopsy revealed internal injuries that resulted in Millie slowly bleeding to death. Surgery upon admission to the hospital could have corrected that and Millie would have survived. Now, Luther, you had every right to pursue this lawsuit, and after much time and deliberation, you won. It never went to court because the insurance company settled out of court.

"Luther, you bragged to everyone you knew that you were going to become a very rich man. You told people you didn't even know. You told friends of friends. And you told Lisa and Margaret. Most people wondered what kind of an idiot you were for bragging about this. I'm sure you thought it was going to finally put you in a higher standing with people, especially those who you thought felt they were better than you. The one person whom you did not tell was Peggy. Did you think she would want some of the money?

"By this time, you were no longer speaking to any of Millie's sisters. Her family went out of their way to help you. They invited you for meals so you wouldn't have to cook or eat alone. Hattie went with you to the lawyer's office. You never understood what was being said and you relied on her to translate. This, of course, stopped after you met Margaret. Did she tell you to exclude Millie's family? Perhaps she thought they would want a cut of this money.

"Your sister-in-law did all the paperwork that had to be filed. She sent form after form to insurance companies and anywhere else proof of Millie's death was needed. She went over and above what should have been expected of her. And how did you treat her? You spoke ill of her, telling people that she was only after the money. She didn't want any of the money, but she had a right to know what was going on. It was her sister who died. Millie's other family members deserved to know too. And Peggy! She definitely deserved to know.

"Because of the settlement, no one actually knew the dollar amount that you received. The newspaper reported that it had been settle in your favor and out of court. After Millie's family told Peggy what was in the newspaper, she asked you if you ever heard anything about the case. Do you remember what you told her?"

Luther didn't say anything. He was listening and he didn't like what he was hearing. George put his face inches from Luther's and shouted, "DO YOU REMEMBER WHAT YOU TOLD HER?"

Luther shook with fright. He just couldn't believe how angry George was. Finally, he said he didn't think he remembered.

"Let me refresh your memory," George said, slightly calmer. "You told her that the lawyers told you there wasn't enough evidence for a case and it was dismissed. Do you remember that now?"

"No," Luther answered.

Now George was more than furious. Luther thought he was going to strike him. Did he actually say that to Peggy? He knew that he had, even though he told George a different story.

"Yes, Luther, you did. Didn't you think she had a right to know? Didn't you think she had the right to some of that money too? That was her mother who died. Were you that greedy that you couldn't spare any? You had grandchildren who could have benefited from that money. Did you ever think of them?"

"George?" Luther said very timidly. "Maybe I thought she would spend anything she got foolishly. I'm sure I was planning on seeing that she got something."

"Luther, how much money did Peggy actually get from that lawsuit?"

Luther closed his eyes and sadly knew the answer. With tears in his eyes and a lump in his throat, he said, "None."

There was silence in the room. Luther was beginning to see where George was going with this. He realized that he was greedy with the money. Finally, he was somebody. He had money and he could compete with the wealthy people he knew. He always felt that they snubbed their noses at him. He remembered what Millie's sister said to him once. It was before the malpractice suit. He thought he had a fair amount of money and he wanted to brag to her how much he had. She snidely told him, while laughing, that she had more money than that. She humiliated him. Just who did she think she was? Well, he got the last laugh when he got the malpractice money. Now he was richer than she was and he would make sure she knew it.

The Insurance Policies

Luther told Margaret that he was going to get a lot of money and she seemed very pleased. Luther remembered her saying that she was so happy for him. Did she say that because she really was happy or because she wanted to share that wealth? It did dawn on him that after they got married, she did say that he should invest the money and not share it with anyone, including family. She said they would be able to travel and enjoy their life now. She said if he gave any to his daughter, she would probably get greedy and would expect him to continue to give her more. If he did that, there wouldn't be any left for him. Did she really say that? He wasn't sure now. And wasn't it Margaret who suggested that he tell Peggy that there wasn't enough evidence for a case? By telling her that, she would realize there wasn't any money to be had. This was all so confusing.

The truth was that he enjoyed being wealthy. He and Margaret travelled and bought expensive things. The people who had looked down on him suddenly seemed to enjoy having him travel in their circle. It took long enough, but Luther finally was somebody and he deserved to feel this way. Maybe it would have been nice to see that Peggy and her family got something. He had more money than he could ever spend in his lifetime, so what harm would it have been to share some with her? But Margaret was right. She probably would have become greedy and would continue to want more. He thought he could leave her some money in his will, and then she would have something after he was gone. But that never happened either.

Luther shifted his eyes and noticed George sitting in the chair across from him. The recliner he had been in was now in an upright position and he was face-to-face with George. George still looked mad, but he wasn't saying anything. Luther felt uncomfortable just having George stare at him.

Finally, George broke the silence that hung in the room like thick fog. "Luther, I know you lied to your daughter and told her there was no lawsuit. You thought by telling her that, she wouldn't question you about any money. And she didn't. However, she knew the truth. She knew you were lying to her. Perhaps you were too busy spending your newfound money that you didn't take time to read the newspaper. Surely, her aunts would tell her about it. Oh, Luther, she knew all the time that you had been lying to her and she never called you out on it.

"So tell me about the life insurance policies you took out on your grandchildren? You do remember them don't you?"

"I thought that was a good gesture on my part. Peggy already had one child die and I know what a struggle it was for her and Mike to pay for the funeral. I thought if I took life insurance policies out on the other children, if something like that were to happen again, they wouldn't have that same burden."

Luther could tell that George wasn't buying into anything he was saying, but it actually was the truth. Luther certainly didn't want to think that something like that would happen again, but who knew? Things happened that no one had any control over. So what was George's problem now?

George stood up and circled the room. He gazed out the window and then finally turned to face Luther. "Where did you get the money for the insurance policies, Luther? AND don't think you can give me some bull story because I know the truth. Do you understand what I'm saying?"

Luther thought about those policies. They were actually Margaret's idea. She told him that Peggy would really appreciate the fact that he was looking out for his grandchildren. But, sadly, he also remembered where the money came from. It wasn't from the malpractice settlement. While he was cleaning out the drawers in the desk, where Millie kept all her personal things, he found two savings account books. They were in Millie's name. He remembered them. There was an account for each grandchild. The one had a large amount of money in it, while the other had slightly less. He looked at the entry dates and realized that deposits were usually made after a holiday or birthday. He also noticed that there were no withdrawals. The books were started shortly after each child was born.

"I found bank accounts that Millie had started for the grandchildren. She had wanted to do this for them. I think she said it would be something they could use in the future, perhaps college, when the time came. I thought I could use that money to do something for them now, rather than just sit in an account. I didn't know what to do with them."

George interrupted saying, "Could you rationally tell me how a life insurance policy for each child could benefit them in their lifetime?"

Luther was squirming in his seat now, feeling very uncomfortable. He was trying to think of what and how to say anything that would make this seem like a good idea. "You know, George, it is always good to have a life insurance policy. I thought if I bought this for them now, the premiums wouldn't be very expensive and they could continue them after they were adults. Maybe by then they would be married and have families of their own. If something were to happen to them, it would help their family." Luther was hoping that the answer would satisfy George, but he was beginning to think that would not be the case.

"So, Luther, let me get this straight. You took the life insurance policies out on the children."

Suddenly, a screen came down from the ceiling. There stood Luther and Peggy sitting at his dining room table. Luther was explaining what he wanted to do. When he was finished, he asked Peggy what she thought of the idea. She said it was his money and he could do whatever he wanted with it. But she also said it would make more sense if whatever he was going to spend was put in some kind of mutual fund or trust so that the children could use it when they got older. Peggy knew that her father didn't like what she was saying. He then proceeded to tell her that since he was buying these policies, he was going to name himself as beneficiary.

The screen paused and George looked over at Luther. "Now, Luther, it appears that you planned on taking out these life insurance policies on your grandchildren. And you would be using the money that their grandmother had saved for their future. So if they didn't die before you, they would have these policies to do with as they wanted when they were older. But if they died before you, then you would get the insurance money. Do I have this right?"

"George, if something were to happen to them, then I would have used that money to pay for their funeral. I wouldn't have kept it."

Ignoring what Luther just said, George asked, "I guess you would have thought you could plan their funeral and do things your way since it would be YOUR money that was paying for it, right?" George was no longer furious with Luther. He just couldn't believe that someone could be this naïve. Maybe stupid was a better word.

"So your grandchildren would never actually ever see any of this money. They could never use it to help pay for college or anything else they may have needed in the future. I fail to see how this was going to be of any benefit to them."

Luther didn't say anything. He was watching the screen. Even though it had been paused, he saw the look in Peggy's eyes. It was as if she couldn't believe what she was hearing. He knew that money was not going to help his grandchildren. Peggy was right. He should have put the money in a trust. His lawyer had suggested doing that, but Margaret had persuaded him to take out the policies. She was wrong and he should have never listened to her.

The screen continued and the paperwork was completed, and there were now two life insurance policies, one in each grandchild's name. Luther was relieved that it was taken care of. He now felt that he had done something for them. And Margaret was happy too.

"Luther, when did Peggy find out that the money for those policies didn't come directly from you but from the money that her mother had been saving for the children?"

Luther just shrugged his shoulders as if he didn't know. The truth was that he actually didn't remember, but he had a feeling that George was going to tell him.

"Luther, I'm tired of all this right now. I don't know what to do with you. I need to stop this session before I get angry again. I want you to go back to your room and think about the question I just asked you. And, Luther, you better not stop to do something else on the way back. Don't bother even going to the dining room tonight. I'll have someone bring you a sandwich. We'll talk again tomorrow and I can't wait to hear your version of the story. You better heed my advice, because I will not tolerate any more lies from you. I can guarantee you will not like the consequences. Do you understand?"

"Yes, George." Luther quickly got up and left the room. He was so glad when he was out in the hall again. The actions from his past were starting to haunt him. He couldn't change them, so he wasn't sure exactly what George wanted from him. He could apologize for his actions and he guessed that was what he was supposed to do. But what about these consequences that George keeps talking about? He headed down the hall toward his room. He thought about taking a long hot shower, hoping that would clear his head. Maybe it would give him some answers. He wasn't happy about missing a meal in the dining room, though. He wanted more than a sandwich, but he guessed that was what he was stuck with for the night.

A Surprise Visitor

After Luther left the office, George paced around the room. He was feeling remorseful about the way things went. Yes, he was upset with Luther, but he had no reason to be so angry with him. After all, this was a peaceful place where people came to spend the rest of eternity. Yes, they had things they had to accomplish before they could fully reap the rewards here, but anger, hatred, and hurt had no place here under any circumstances.

George knew he had to make Luther understand his actions, but getting angry at him was not the answer. As George sat in his office, darkness filled the room. It was then that George knelt on his knees and prayed to his Father for guidance and the right answers.

After much time, George was feeling better and he was sure he knew what needed to be done. Angry dialog might be necessary, but that anger couldn't come from him. He knew what he had to do.

*****

Back in his room, Luther headed straight for the shower. It felt so good he stayed under the hot water for a good fifteen minutes. He kept thinking about the video he watched in George's office. It was haunting him. He felt confused. Did he do the right things for his daughter? It certainly didn't seem like George thought so. George was even questioning Margaret's commitment to him. The one thing that he was sure of was that Margaret really did care for him. They had a good marriage. They were both retired when they met, and with the money from the malpractice suit, they were free to travel and do what they wanted. The money was his. It was awarded to him, not Peggy or anyone else. Luther also knew that he didn't want Millie's sisters to find out just how much money he got. If he told Peggy, or even gave her any, he knew she would tell her aunts. Was that part of his reasoning?

Luther had just finished drying off when there was a knock at his door. "It's probably the sandwich I'm getting for supper," Luther muttered. He wasn't really very hungry right now, especially for a sandwich. He just wanted to curl up on his recliner and watch a good movie, or maybe a baseball game. He was trying to remember if he had ever seen one on the TV. He didn't recall.

Luther opened the door, and much to his surprise, it was George standing there. He couldn't remember any other time when George actually came to visit him. He appeared on the TV, but never in person. Luther wasn't in the mood for more talk, especially from George.

"Luther, may I come in?" It seemed like a dumb question since George could come and go anywhere he wanted. "I would really like to talk to you, and I promise I won't lecture or get angry." George knew Luther's concerns.

Luther opened the door wider so George could come in. Luther looked at George as if he were seeing him for the first time. He wondered if he ever realized just how blue his eyes were. They seemed to penetrate right through the atmosphere. Luther thought he even noticed tears.

Could George have been crying? He never would have thought that was something George would do. George appeared to be more human right now. Of course, Luther thought of George as human, but there was something different about him.

George and Luther sat on the couch. Luther waited for George to speak, having no idea what he was going to say. The lamp in the corner went on and immediately dimmed to a warm glow. Luther didn't recall that ever happening before. It was times like this that Luther thought of George as magical.

"Luther, I came to apologize to you. I was angry and I let my anger get the better of me. It is my place here to show everyone their earthly lives and how that affected others, but it isn't my place to judge and allow my emotions to get out of hand. My yelling at you didn't do either of us any good. It only caused pain and that is something that cannot be tolerated. I know better than to act the way I did. I have been helping and guiding people for a long time. It is my responsibility to help you, but I must do it in a more sensitive way. I am truly sorry and hope that you can forgive me."

Luther was dumbfounded. He didn't know what to think or say. He just never would have imagined George saying this to him, or anyone for that matter. Luther realized that he had tears in his own eyes now and a lump in his throat that was making it difficult to speak. Then, much to his amazement, as well as George's, Luther embraced George and gave him a hug. This was something that was very uncharacteristic for him. He couldn't remember a time in his life when he actually ever did that. Somehow it just felt like the right thing to do. For the first time, he was experiencing compassion and he wasn't sure how to handle it. Under any other circumstances, he would have felt that this was a feminine gesture and something he would have never done with another man. But as both Luther and George stood there embraced in each other's arms, they both felt the tension of the day melt away and peace returning to each of them.

Luther found himself saying something he rarely, if ever, said to anyone. "George, I forgive you and I too want to apologize."

*****

Luther slept soundly that night. He was at peace with himself and with George. He knew he still had a lot of work to do, but he now felt that he would be able to do everything that George asked of him. He was also beginning to realize that his actions hurt other people while he lived on earth. He especially hurt his daughter, and she was the one person he should have tried to protect and help.

Luther knew that the money for the insurance policies came from the money Millie had saved for the grandkids. He used it and it could have helped them as they got older. The money spent on the policies was wasted and no one benefited from them at all. He remembered the phone call from Peggy, when his grandson was getting ready for college. She called and asked how much money was in the account her mother had started for him. Luther lied to her. He told her there wasn't any bank account. She was so upset because she knew there was—one for each of the two kids. She asked him what happened to that money. Luther told her he knew nothing about them. She said her mother told her about the accounts. When Krissy died, the money that was in her account was put into Jimmy's account. When Becca was born, an account was opened for her. She told her father that her aunts had also given money to be put in those accounts. Luther lied to her and continued to tell her there were no such accounts. He was correct that there were no accounts, because he had cashed them in and used that money—his grandchildren's money—to buy the insurance policies. How could he have been so stupid?

When it all came down to understanding the facts of what happened, Luther knew that he had stolen the money from his own grandchildren. How could he have done such a thing? Especially when he got millions from the malpractice suit. He could have paid for their college educations outright and never missed a penny. But that wasn't what he did. Instead, he and Margaret travelled the world. Material things were bought to show that he was somebody and had money to prove it. Luther now knew what the saying "money is the root of all evil" meant. Now that he thought back on the later years of his life, just what did this money do for him? Yes, it allowed him to live a very luxurious lifestyle, to travel and buy expensive things, but he lost family because of it. His family. The ones who should have meant the most to him. He had friends and Margaret's family, but they weren't his own flesh and blood. This newfound wealth allowed him to travel with other wealthy people. But it turned him against his own family.

Luther hoped someday he would be able to tell Peggy, Jimmy, and Becca just how sorry he was for what he did. They were too young to be here, but when the time came, he hoped he could see them and tell them. He would ask George if that was possible.

Other than the guilt he felt for what he had done, he felt better. He would make amends with his family when he could, but for now he was hopefully washing away a lot of the sins he had committed while he lived on earth.

BJ

The next morning, Luther decided to go for a walk. It looked like a beautiful day and he wanted to explore some new places. First he would go to the dining room for breakfast. He never ate the sandwich that was delivered last night, after George left. Now he was famished, and a good breakfast, a new day, and hopefully a new beginning awaited him.

The blueberry pancakes were exceptional. His breakfast partner today was a young boy who had been killed in a motorcycle accident. Luther listened as he told him about the anguish his parents felt at his death and how sorry he was because he never listened to them.

After breakfast, Luther started down a path he had never been on before. He wanted to enjoy the day. The sun was shining brightly, and it felt like it was a balmy eighty degrees outside. The sweater he had worn to breakfast vanished and he was very comfortable in the short sleeve button-down shirt he was wearing. He smiled at the people he passed and said hello to most of them. Some people were jogging while others were riding bikes. Some, like Luther, were just taking a leisurely stroll.

Luther had no idea how long he had walked or exactly where he was. It still amazed him that he could walk that long without his knees bothering him. He noticed a ball game going on in a grass-covered field ahead. There was a bench there and he decided to sit down and watch for a little while. Luther wasn't sure what kind of game it was. It wasn't baseball or football. They had a smaller ball and were using some kind of long-handled thing with a net on the top. They would catch the ball in the net and toss it to another player. It looked interesting and those playing sure seemed to be enjoying themselves.

Luther was about to get up and continue his walk, when an elderly lady came over and asked if she could sit on the bench with him. Luther didn't have a problem with that. The bench was big enough for several people. Luther felt he should remain sitting for just a little while longer. He didn't want to appear rude, getting up just as she was sitting down. He nodded to her and then went back to watching the game.

After a few minutes, the lady asked him if he knew what they were playing.

"I have no idea. It isn't baseball or football. I don't remember ever seeing a game like this before, but they sure seem to be having fun."

"They certainly do," she said. "It's so nice to see young people enjoying themselves. My name's BJ. What's yours?"

"Hello, BJ. My name is Luther. I was taking a walk because it is such a beautiful day."

"Hello, Luther. It's nice to meet you. Yes, it is a lovely day. I was out walking too. I often come to this spot and sit. Sometimes I'm fortunate enough to meet someone to talk to."

Oh wonderful, Luther thought. *She wants to talk and I want to get up and continue my walk. Now I will have to sit here longer. Oh well, I guess I didn't have anything better to do.*

Maybe it will help me take my mind off some of the things George and I were talking about.

They both sat there watching the game, and Luther was just about to get up when BJ turned to him and asked him how long he had been there.

"I don't think it's been a long time. It's hard to tell around here. The days seem to roll right into one another. I've been talking with George a lot and learning about my life. Have you been here long?"

BJ had a funny look on her face and said, "George, yes, dear George. I have been talking to him too. I've been here a long time, and George keeps telling me I must learn about the mistakes that I made while I lived on earth. I don't really want to talk about those things. I had a good life and was happy. I would like to see my husband and children again, but George says that can't happen until I am sorry for the mistakes I made. Before I met my husband, I had horrible early years. I got away from that life to become a better person. I was so unhappy and then I met my husband and life was wonderful. George keeps insisting that I relive those horrible early years. I don't want to and because of that, I can't move forward."

Luther felt sorry for BJ. He knew what she was talking about. George insisted that he relive his early life too. He didn't want to do that either, but he wanted to move on and go forward. He looked at BJ and said, "I know what you mean, but if you do as George says, then perhaps you will be able to be reunited with your husband and children."

"Luther, if I may ask, what is your story?"

Luther wasn't sure he wanted to go into his life story with her. It was bad enough when he had to watch and relive it with George, but he found himself telling her about his early life and his mother abandoning the family for a man with more money.

"I don't remember my mother. My brother Gerald and I used to call our father's second wife the wicked stepmonster because she was so mean. It was so bad that Gerald ran away when he was fifteen and joined the circus. We never saw him after that. When I was sixteen, I ran away too."

BJ sat on the bench just staring at Luther. She wanted to get up and walk away, but she felt like she was tied to the bench with rope. She was unable to move. She didn't want to hear any more about his life. She reached into her pocket and pulled out a handkerchief and dabbed at her eyes.

Luther watched as BJ took out her hankie. It was pure white with a large B embroidered on one corner. The crocheted lace around the edges was blue, pink, yellow, and green. He knew he had seen one just like that before. He was trying to remember where.

Suddenly, he knew. "BJ, may I ask what those initials stand for?"

"My name is Bertha Jean. My husband used to call me BJ. It wasn't a romantic nickname, but it was his special name for me. No one else had ever called me that. It was something special between

Horace and me. I so desperately want to see him again and our two children. I…"

Luther couldn't take any more. He interrupted her saying, "You're my mother. You're the woman who walked away from my brother and me. You didn't care what happened to us. You took Doug and Marge, but what about your other five children? You disowned us. You ran off with the man next door and never looked back. You are a despicable person. How could you have done that?" Luther was yelling. His face was bright red. He wanted to reach out and strangle her. After he learned what she had done, he wanted the opportunity to talk to her and find out why she did what she did. He was sure she would have a reasonable answer. He knew that his father wasn't the greatest husband and that was part of the reason. Now he knew. She never cared at all.

Bertha tried to get up and suddenly George was standing in front of her. He simply looked at her and said, "Bertha, you will have to talk to your son now. You don't have a choice."

Bertha looked over at Wayne (that was the name she knew him by) and began to lash out at him. "I hated you and your brother from the day I knew I was pregnant with you. I didn't want you. I already had more children than I ever wanted. Your father wouldn't leave me alone and I was doomed to a life of cleaning, cooking, dishes, and children. And then more children. I couldn't take it anymore. For my own sanity, I had to get out. Horace offered me a way to do that. He wanted to take you and Gerald with us, but I said no. All you both ever did was cry and get into things. I was tired of cleaning up after you. I hated it. I didn't want to take Marge or Doug either, but Horace wanted children so badly that I finally agreed to take them. They were older, and they knew how to behave. They were in school and out of the house during the day. You and Gerald were always underfoot. I left so I could have a nice home and nice things, like this handkerchief. I had a whole drawer full of them. Horace was very generous with us. I deserved that after putting up with your father and you two brats."

George looked over at Luther and saw the pain burning in his eyes. He also saw tears. He was hearing words from the woman who gave birth to him that no child should ever have to hear. He also looked at Bertha and told her that now she was going to hear the rest of the story of her youngest son's life. She could no longer walk away from the truth.

George waited while Luther composed himself. Then he told him to tell his mother the rest of his story. Luther told her every detail about his life. He told her about every slap across the face he and Gerald received from Emma. Luther was exhausted when he finished, but he felt an overwhelming sense of relief. He was no longer angry at her. He realized that she had been denied moving forward in her journey here because of her hatred. He believed she actually loved Horace and wanted to be with him. Hopefully now she would be able to make the progress she needed to complete her mission.

Bertha dabbed her handkerchief at her eyes. She couldn't move. She felt faint. She didn't want to hear the words of this son whom she denied for so many, many years. She wasn't exactly sure what she was feeling. She didn't want to even try to think. She had put all thoughts of her life before Horace out of her mind, and now this boy, her son, was telling her just what a miserable life he had. Was it her fault? She wasn't ready to take the blame for that, at least not yet.

George went to Luther and put his hand on his shoulder. He knew that what just happened would benefit him, even though right now he was falling apart inside. It would help him progress with his journey, but now was not the time for him to realize that. He had to come to terms with the words his mother spoke to him.

George went to Bertha and helped her up. He led her down the path. What just happened would also help her, even though she was unaware of it.

Bertha turned to her son and said, "I know you hate me and I don't care. But remember one thing. You can hate me for what I did to you, but you are no better. Think about what you did to your child. When you told her you were disappointed she was a girl because you always wanted a boy, you disowned her too. Yes, I know that you told her that. I know more than you think I do, thanks to George. Maybe you didn't walk away from her, but the words were the same as if you did. Remember all the other things you said and did. Just as I must live with the things I did, you must do the same. I can only hope that it doesn't take as long for you as it did for me. Goodbye, Luther Wayne."

*****

Luther sat on the bench and watched as George led his mother away. He wanted to shout out to her, but he didn't know what to say anymore. He also knew the words she said to him were true. She as much admitted that she wasn't a good mother, but he now knew that he wasn't a good father either. He wondered if Bertha realized how much she missed in her life. She said she had a good life, but without some pretty amazing people—children, grandchildren, and by now great-grandchildren and great-great-grandchildren. Sadly, he knew that he missed out on some of these amazing people as well. He hated her and in a strange way loved her both at the same time. He wasn't sure how he could love her after what she did and what she said to him. He hoped she would find peace in her life and have the ability to ask for the forgiveness she needed, even if she didn't realize how desperately she needed it.

Luther's mind was wandering in so many directions. He knew he had hurt his daughter. He wondered how she felt about him. Maybe that's why she wasn't at his funeral. Perhaps she hated him so much she didn't want to be there.

Suddenly, George appeared out of nowhere. He sat down on the bench beside Luther. He looked exhausted. He spoke in a very low voice, trying to use words of comfort. "Luther, I am so sorry that your experience with your mother was not a good one. Bertha has been here for a long time and she just can't move on. I have tried many ways to break down her hatred for her family, but nothing seems to work. I was hoping that if she saw you, she might soften. She wants so desperately to see Horace again and she can't move forward unless she realizes how much pain she has caused so many people. Maybe hearing the story of your youth, after she left, will create some changes within her. I can only be hopeful that will happen."

Luther looked at George and just shook his head. In his mind, he was hearing the last words she said to him, how he abandoned his child just as she did. He needed to know about Peggy and how she felt about him. He turned to George and said, "I know I hurt Peggy with the things I said and did. Is that why she wasn't at my funeral? Did she hate me that much? How can I ever ask for forgiveness and atone for what I did to her and my grandchildren?"

"Peggy didn't go to your funeral because she didn't know anything about it. She learned of your death by reading it in her local newspaper. Margaret's daughter, Ava, knew how to reach Peggy, but didn't bother to let her know of your passing."

George remembered the pain that Peggy felt as she read her father's obituary in the newspaper. He knew what Peggy was feeling. There was no possibility anymore of a renewed relationship with her father. She was feeling guilt of her own for not trying harder to reconnect with him. She had been so tired of being rejected for so long that she didn't want to try, but the possibility was always there as long as he was alive. Now she knew she would never have that opportunity. She wondered if she would have gone to the funeral if she had known about it. The obituary stated that there had been a memorial service two weeks ago. How sad that Ava didn't think enough to even let her know of her father's death. Perhaps sad wasn't the right word, but Peggy didn't want to even think about it. Her father was gone and that was that.

George wanted to share that with Luther, but he thought better of it. There would be a time and place, but now was not it.

They sat there for a long time, each in deep thought. Luther couldn't get the image of his mother out of his mind. Would she ever realize just how much hurt she caused because of her actions? Luther was thinking about his daughter and grandchildren. He wished he had been more involved in their lives. He could blame Margaret for what happened, but the truth was that he didn't stand up for his family. He left her control the situation and that wasn't right. He remembered the wonderful times they had together and he wondered if she ever truly cared for him at all. Would she have loved him if he hadn't received all that money from the malpractice suit?

George looked over at Luther and felt his pain. Luther had come a long way today and unfortunately it was a painful journey. Sometimes that's the way it happened. George had no control over this. It was his responsibility to guide everyone through their earthly life so they could experience their journey through heaven.

Luther still had work to do and some of it wouldn't be easy, but George felt the hardest parts of his journey were now in the past. He had confidence that Luther was heading in the right direction.

The Letter

Luther turned to George and said, "George, what am I supposed to feel for my mother? I feel sorry for her and yet she abandoned us. I don't understand how she could have done that. But then I didn't realize just how much I hurt my daughter. What can I do about that? I wish I knew everything that happened between Peggy and me."

George knew what had to come next. As painful as it was going to be, he had to let Luther know how Peggy felt about him. He reached into his pocket and pulled out a letter. It was addressed to Luther at the nursing home where he lived. He handed it to Luther. He knew no words were needed as he watched Luther unfold the letter and begin to read it.

> *Dear Dad,*
>
> *I have thought long and hard about writing to you and finally decided that I needed to put into words things that I have been feeling for many years. I don't know if I will ever actually mail this to you, so if you are reading this letter now, you will know that I felt it was important enough to me that I write.*
>
> *On our last conversation, I was shocked at the things you were accusing me of. You said that at Margaret's birthday party, I stood up in front of everyone and said that when my mother died, Margaret asked you to marry her. I never said any*

such thing. What I did say was that you were very sad and lonely after my mother died and that when you met Margaret, I started to see a twinkle in your eyes again. I said that I was glad you had met her and that you have been able to share so many years together. I was disappointed that Jimmy and Becca and their families weren't invited to that party. They are your grandchildren. They probably would have come if they had been included.

Now I would like to talk about some things that concern me. Growing up, I never really knew exactly how you felt about me. I do remember the day you told me that you were disappointed because I wasn't a boy. I still can remember that conversation as if it happened yesterday. What you said hurt me very deeply. I had no control over the fact that I was born a girl. I remember when I was younger, you would take me to the bowling alley with you, but as I grew up, we drifted apart. Perhaps this is normal between a father and a teenage daughter, but the drift continued and we never got remotely close again. In fact, over the years, it had actually gotten worse and now is practically nonexistent. I never wanted it that way, but we can't rewrite history.

It seemed that after my mother died is when the permanent drift was apparent. I sometimes get the impression that anything and anyone who was a part of your life with my mother was something that you didn't want to have anything to do with anymore. You stopped seeing friends from the past and then you no longer seemed interested in me or my children.

I had hoped that after that, you and I would be closer. This was before you met Margaret. I do believe we were headed in that direction, but after

Margaret came along, things changed. I never expected you to be alone for the rest of your life, but it seemed that after Margaret, you decided you had a new life and the old one, and everyone in it, were no longer necessary or important to you. I remember I would call you to tell you what Jimmy and Becca were doing. I would hardly begin when you would interrupt me, telling me something about Margaret's grandchildren. It seemed that if Jimmy or Becca did something, one of her grandchildren did it bigger and better. I know you think this sounds like I am jealous, but that is not the case. I was interested in knowing about Margaret's family. I had just hoped that you would have been interested in what your grandchildren were doing as well.

You rarely came to visit me, and when you did, it was a stop on your way to or from Ava's. You never stayed long, but you made sure to let me know that you would be staying with Margaret's daughter a week or two.

When my mother died, I went with you to the lawyer to see about a malpractice case. I remember him saying that he thought you had a very good chance of winning. I know that Aunt Hattie went along on several occasions. Then suddenly you stopped asking her to go with you. I don't know if you thought she would want some money from you if you were to win, but I can assure you that was never the situation. I asked to be informed as to how it was going. And then you told me that the case was dropped because there wasn't enough evidence against the doctor. I know for a fact that was not true. They settled out of court. It was in the newspaper. A lawyer friend told me that if it was settled out of court, it was because they knew they wouldn't win and the financial reward was most likely in the millions. I don't care what the figures were, I just would have liked to have been told the truth. Why did you feel the need to lie to me? I was her daughter and I had every right to know. Did you think I wanted some of the money too? I didn't because it was nothing short of blood money. My mother died so you could have it.

Suddenly, you were taking trips all over the world and buying expensive things, and I wondered how you could afford such things. Do you think I was stupid not knowing where the money came from? You used to tell me how poor you were and how it took every bit of money you had to live. Did you think you needed to tell me this so I wouldn't ask for anything? You would tell me you lived on a fixed income. It must have been pretty well fixed to do all the things you and Margaret did.

Money doesn't buy happiness. I am not rich, but I am happy and I have a relationship with the people who are important to me. No amount of money could take that away. I hope the money you have has made you happy. You alienated your own family. I hope we were all worth it. I thought family would have been important to you and that you would have understood why. I know you didn't have that with your parents, so I would have thought you would have made a point to have relationships with your child and grandchildren. Apparently, I was wrong in assuming that.

When my children were little, my mother started a savings account for them. When Krissy died, her money was put into Jimmy's. This money was for them to use when they graduated from high school, perhaps to help with college expenses. After my mother's death, I never asked you about those accounts. I assumed they would remain intact until needed. When Jimmy was about to graduate, I remember asking you how much money was in his account. It was then that you told me there was no account. I asked you what happened to them and you got mad and told me there never were any bank accounts. I argued with you because I knew there were, but you insisted that none existed.

Shortly after that conversation, I figured out just what happened to that money. You told me you wanted to take out a life insurance policy on each of the children. I told you they already had one, but that it was your money and you could do what you wanted with it. I do remember suggesting putting something in some kind of an account for them to use when they were older. You insisted on the life insurance policies and you made yourself the owner and the beneficiary of them. You tried to tell me that you would pay the premiums until they could afford to make them.

When you told me there were no savings accounts started by my mother, I suddenly knew where the money for the life insurance policies came from. That money would never be of any use to your grandchildren. When they were older, you transferred those polices over to them, but by then the premiums were too high because quite a few payments were missing. As far as I'm concerned, this only constitutes stealing from your own grandchildren. Didn't you get enough money from the malpractice suit that you had to steal from innocent children? Unbelievable!

When my birthday came around this year, I remember opening my card from you. Imagine my surprise when I saw that the card was for a "wonderful son-in-law." I thought perhaps you had grabbed the wrong card, but that wasn't the case since you had a personal note to me inside. I guess you just didn't bother to read what you were sending, or it really didn't matter to you. When I asked you about it, you actually got mad at me. It would have been less hurtful if you had just not sent a card at all.

Another thing—the story about your army days. Here once again, you lied to me. You told me how the German soldier came to the window and shot and the bullet hit you. You told me how your buddies found him and shot him. I believed that story. Why wouldn't I? But years later, I learned the truth. You gave me all my mother's photo albums and scrapbooks, including the one she made about your days in the military. There in black and white was a letter from you telling her the real story. I remember asking you again about that incident because I was doing a family scrapbook. You told me the same story you always told me. You obviously told this lie so many times that to you it was the truth. The lie is far more dramatic and one that would allow people to have compassion for you. That lie made you feel important, like you were a war hero who was wounded and survived. The truth would have been nice, even though it doesn't have as much flair to it. Have no fear, your secret is safe with me, but if anyone would want to check into this a little deeper, the Internet today makes it very easy to do. Maybe it isn't something that you really care much about. You and I both know the truth and someday you will have to answer to a higher authority.

I feel sorry for you that you have wonderful grandchildren and great-grandchildren who don't know you. They would have loved to have had a relationship with you. They were hurt that they weren't invited to Margaret's party. They also were upset about the savings accounts that you lied about. I do believe they would have forgiven you for those things if you had bothered to make an attempt to be involved in their lives.

You have made it so obvious to me on so many occasions you really didn't want me to be a part of your life. I got the impression that we weren't good enough for you. We didn't make as much money as Margaret's children and grandchildren, and we didn't have as many degrees after our names, but we were family. You could have been proud of us too, but you weren't.

I used to give you pictures of all the kids over the years and yet they were never displayed. Your living room was filled with pictures of Margaret's grandchildren, but never yours. Didn't you ever feel any sense of guilt?

I have a very close relationship with my children and grandchildren. Fortunately, history did not repeat itself as it did with you. I would like to think that they have lost something by not being allowed to know you, but if the relationship would have been built on lies, then perhaps it is best left the way it is. From all the lies you have told me and others, I'm not sure you know any other way of life.

I hope you are happy with your life. I am sure that you think of Margaret's family as you own. You could have had more, but you made the decision to abandon your biological family and accept another. That is too bad because you have missed out on some wonderful and special people. But this is your loss. They can't really say it is their loss because they never got to know you.

There is one more thing I feel needs to be said. I know that you used to tell me that when Margaret died, she was going to be buried beside her first husband and that you were going to be buried beside my mother. Perhaps over the years, you have made other arrangements. If you didn't, I would suggest that you do. My aunts have a legal document stating that under no circumstances are you to be buried beside my mother. They own the cemetery plot and have the right to decide this.

I think that is about all that I need to say to you. I am truly sorry that things are the way they are, but I also feel that you have created this situation. For many years, I have thought about all these things and never said anything, but I can no longer keep them locked inside me. I don't expect any response from you, but if you decide to answer, that is up to you.

Your daughter,
Peggy

Guilt

George placed his hand on Luther's shoulder and said, "Come, let's walk." Luther slowly rose and walked along the path beside George. He was visibly shaken and George reached out and took his arm. He had just read the letter from his daughter. There were no words for the way he felt.

They walked in silence for a while, each in deep thought. Luther kept thinking about the things Peggy said in her letter. He remembered receiving the letter and how angry he was when he read it. He threw it away and told everyone that Peggy didn't want to have a relationship with him. It was easier that way.

George sensed what Luther was feeling. Ava had seen the letter too. She found it in the trash can. She was glad when she read it. She was hoping that he wouldn't change his mind and want to have a relationship with his daughter and her family. She had already talked him into changing his will so her children and grandchildren were the only ones named. She didn't want Peggy to have anything. She truly felt that she and her family deserved any money he had. After all, they had put up with him for all those years while he was married to her mother. Margaret had only married Luther because he told her he was about to become a very rich man. Luther had no idea how any of them felt.

George didn't want to tell Luther the truth about this just yet. He knew he was having enough trouble coping with the things that Peggy said in her letter.

They continued to walk in silence. Luther was thinking about his own life and his family now, especially his daughter. He knew that he had two grandchildren and four great-grandchildren. He had some memories of Jimmy and Becca, but he knew he wasn't involved in their lives as much as he could have been. And what about the great-grandchildren? He never took the time to see them and he could have. He never wanted to be bothered, because he was so involved with Margaret's family. She didn't want him to visit his family. She always had an excuse for not seeing them.

They spent every holiday with Margaret's family. He remembered Peggy inviting them for Thanksgiving one year. Luther told her that they were going to Ava's. Peggy asked about Christmas and he said they were going to Ava's for that holiday too. He remembered Peggy saying that she guessed he couldn't make time to spend a holiday with her if he was so busy with Margaret's family. He took her words as an insult, but now he realized that he was the one who was doing the insulting. There should have been equality with their children, but Margaret didn't want that, and he went along with it. That wasn't right, but he allowed it to happen.

George knew what Luther was thinking. He didn't want to interrupt his thoughts. George knew he was trying to come to grips with his actions from the past. He knew the more he thought about them, the easier it was going to be to complete his task here.

Luther was also thinking about his mother and the things she said to him.

Finally, George spoke. "Luther, today was difficult, I know. You had asked me once if you could see your mother and talk to her. I knew she wasn't ready for that. Your meeting today was quite by accident. I wanted you to meet her, but I was so hoping she would have changed. I'm sorry that didn't happen. In time, she will realize what she needs to do. I only hope you can forgive her for those things.

"If it is any consolation, Bertha was not always the happy person she wanted everyone to think she was. She experienced long periods of depression when no one could talk to her. Even Horace was unable to comfort her. He was sure she was suffering extreme guilt, but she was too proud to admit it. Horace loved her very much and wanted to do anything possible to make her happy. He would take her shopping and let her pick out anything she wanted. He would surprise her with expensive jewelry. He took her to Paris one summer. During those times, Bertha did forget the guilt she carried and was happy. However, those times were short-lived.

"One time, Horace thought the only way Bertha was going to return to that fun-loving girl he fell in love with so many years ago was to talk about the past. He tried, but she just crawled deeper inside herself and wouldn't come out.

"He wanted to take you and Gerald, as well as Marge and Doug, when they ran away together. He always wanted a big family with lots of children. He knew Bertha was overwhelmed with children and housework, but he would have seen that there was domestic help in the house. He would have hired a nanny for you and Gerald. He hired a housekeeper so Bertha didn't have to lift a finger around the house. It would have been so different than what her life was like with your father. But Bertha didn't want any part of it. She reluctantly agreed to take Marge and Doug because they were in school. She was secretly hoping he would send them to a boarding school in Europe.

"The last thing she wanted in her house was two toddlers, even if she didn't have to be totally responsible for them. Horace knew deep down inside that Bertha was suffering enormous guilt. It is that guilt that I have been trying to work through with her."

"George, do you think she will ever be able to do that?"

"That is a good question. I think the only answer I can give you is…all in due time."

And with that, both George and Luther smiled as they continued down the path together.

*****

Several months went by and Luther met with George every day. They continued to talk about Luther's earthly life. George was pleased with the progress Luther was making and felt he was ready for his final step in his journey through heaven. It was time.

Forgiveness

Luther was sitting in the garden. He loved this garden. The scent of the fresh flowers was everywhere, as far as the eye could see. He was feeling overwhelmed with emotion. He now knew his entire life story. He remembered everything, the good as well as the bad. He knew what he had to do. George always told him he had a mission and now he knew what it was.

There was total silence around him except for the faint sound of birds singing off in the distance. The air was still, and there was no wind. The flowers were standing tall as he sat on the park bench with his head in his hands remembering. Remembering everything. Even though there were sad times, it was a good feeling and he felt at peace.

Luther moved ever so slightly and felt the presence of someone on the bench with him. He looked over, and beside him was his granddaughter, Krissy. He hadn't seen her since the day they went to the carnival together. He smiled and took her into his arms, giving her the biggest hug.

"Oh, Krissy! It is so good to see you again. I have thought about you so many times. I've missed you. Do you remember all the fun we had at the carnival? It is one of my happiest moments here."

Krissy returned the hug and then put a sloppy wet kiss on her grandfather's cheek. She had just finished eating a Popsicle and Luther felt the sticky red residue ringing her mouth as it lingered on his face. "Yes, I remember. It was fun. Grandpa, there is someplace I must take you. Come with me."

Luther was content to just sit on the bench, but Krissy insisted that he get up and go with her. He followed her along the path to the other side of the garden. There they saw different flowers, each having their own succinct aroma. Luther watched Krissy attentively as he sat down to see what was going to happen next.

Krissy stood behind the bench. Soon a woman appeared and sat down beside Luther. It was Bertha. He recognized her instantly. Luther looked at her. Tears were running down her face. He wanted to say something, but didn't know what. Bertha held out her hand to her son. Luther looked at it, so frail and tiny. He placed his hand on top of hers and she squeezed it as tight as she could. She was just about to say something, when she embraced him in her arms. Bertha clung to her youngest son as tears continued to fall. He reached in his pocket for his hankie to dry her eyes. What he felt was something frilly and lacy. He noticed that it was the hankie that Bertha had dropped that day when Luther sold her husband the soft pretzels. He wasn't sure how it got there, but he remembered it. He had kept it all those years. It was the only thing he ever had to remind him of her. Bertha knew and remembered too.

"Wayne, I don't know how to say how sorry I am for the things I did to you. I abandoned you and your brother for selfish reasons. I have had to learn that what I did that fateful day so many years ago caused you both so much grief. I hurt you and others, as well. I think I hurt you the most. I left you when you needed a mother. I don't deserve any kind of forgiveness. I know that for many years, you hated me and rightly so. My mission here was to learn how to earn the forgiveness of those I hurt. It wasn't easy for me. I missed out on what should have been the most important things in my life. I now know that I lost grandchildren and great-grandchildren. Krissy found me one day and helped me understand everything I lost."

Bertha wanted to continue, but the tears were coming so hard she could no longer speak.

Luther felt something stir in his heart and knew it was love for this woman, his mother, the person who hurt him the most. It was time for forgiveness. There was a time for hated and a time for love, and this was the time for love. Luther thought about his own life and how he hurt his daughter and grandchildren. He hoped that some-day he would be able to see them and ask for their forgiveness.

Saying the words he was about to say were something strange to him, words he never said during his earthly life. He looked at Bertha and said, "Mother, I forgive you. We will now be together in eternity and there will be love between us."

As soon as the words came out of his mouth, he felt such wonderful joy. He also felt Krissy standing in front of them with her arms held out. Together they had one really big hug.

Krissy led Bertha down the path. There she met Horace. She was finally reunited with her husband. They embraced and held each other for a long time. Bertha finally had the peace and love in her life that she had been searching for. And a little child led her to that.

Warren was then on the bench with his son. "My son, I love you. I am sorry for the things I did that caused you pain."

Luther had already forgiven his father. Now they would always be together. Krissy came over and squeezed herself between them. They all laughed. Krissy was holding hands with both her grandfather and great-grandfather. She was happy that this day was finally here and her family was going to be together again. She had been waiting a long time for this moment. She smiled and looked up at both of them and said, "This day is better than when we went to the carnival. I'm so happy."

Warren continued to hold Krissy's hand as he stood up. Luther stood and embraced his father.

Krissy led Warren down the path next. He and Bertha nodded to each other and felt the forgiveness that they both needed. And a little child led him.

Next came Luther's sisters and brothers. They all stood together and embraced. A family cannot be torn apart permanently. They may each go their separate way, they may argue, but someday they will reunite and never more be parted. Each in turn hugged their brother. The past was over and now there would be a new beginning.

Beside her grandfather's siblings, Mildred, Marion, Elizabeth, Doug, and Marge, Krissy was jumping up and down. And finally there was Gerald. Krissy took his hand and led him to her grandfather. He was trying to pull one of Krissy's ponytails. It was a game they often played.

Krissy led them down the path, to Warren, who greeted them with love.

And it was a little child who led them.

Luther watched as his family walked down the path together. At last, they were all finally together. He knew he would be with them again soon and they would spend eternity together.

Luther knew that his mission was not quite finished. He still had some things to do.

Reconciliation

As Luther sat down on the bench again, he saw Krissy running across the grass. She ran to a woman who was very excited to see her. The woman leaned down and Krissy whispered something in her ear, and they both laughed. As they got closer, Luther realized that the woman was Millie, his Millie. He had wanted to see her so much. He remembered asking George if or when that could happen. Of course, George would always answer with that infamous line, "all in due time."

Krissy led her grandmother to Luther, by the hand. She took Luther's hand and placed it in Millie's.

Luther and Millie just stood staring at each other until Krissy tugged on her grandfather's arm indicating she wanted him to give Millie a hug. Luther got the message and reached out to Millie. She fell into his arms and they both cried tears of joy. It had been a long time since they had seen each other. Much had happened since that horrible day when Millie died.

Millie knew that Wayne, as she called him, was really scared when she died. He had felt he was once again abandoned by another woman in his life, even though she had no control of the circumstances. It came as no surprise to her that within a year of her death, he remarried. She also knew the wedge that was driven between her husband and their daughter. She had hoped that her death would make them closer, that each would realize how much they actually needed each other. But that was not meant to be. Millie learned that all things happened for a reason. She remembered talking to George about it. She didn't understand why or what the reason could be, but she trusted George's wisdom. George had to remind her that she needed patience to understand. He assured her that at some point, everything would turn out the way it was meant to be.

Was this the day that would happen? When she saw Krissy coming toward her, she knew, deep down in her heart, it was. She wanted to see her husband again. They didn't always have a happy marriage, but there certainly were good times. Unfortunately, her death ended the opportunity for any good times to continue.

Luther turned to Millie and kissed her. He smiled and told her he loved her and missed her. "Millie, I was blind after you died. I didn't know what to do. Others tried to help me and I resented that. I wanted to be strong, but I wasn't. I wanted to reach out to Peggy, but I didn't know how. Then I married Margaret and we had a good marriage, at least I thought we did. But throughout all that, I lost Peggy. We had great-grandchildren I never met. They never knew me and I could have made that happen. I became too wrapped up in my new life that I overlooked the most important people in it. Peggy wrote me a letter telling me how much I hurt her. I was very angry when I read it. I threw it away and blamed her. I couldn't see that I was the one who was at fault. I didn't want to believe the things she wrote to me. I concentrated on my life with Margaret and her family. I pretended they were my real family. I did to Peggy what my mother did to me and I was too stupid to realize it. I'm so sorry for the things I did. Millie, can you ever forgive me?"

"Wayne, when I learned the things that you did, I was angry. I told George I wanted to go back to earth and shake you. I talked to George many times about that. I think I actually talked the anger out of myself. When I learned that you were here, I asked George if I could see you. In all of his wisdom, he knew that was not a good idea. I used to hope I would run into you somewhere, but that didn't happen. It could only happen when the time was right. And only George knew when that was.

"Wayne, I had to learn things about myself that I didn't want to. I faced them and became the person I was meant to be. We can't undo what was done. We can only move on. Now we are ready to do just that. You asked me for forgiveness…yes, I forgive you."

Suddenly, Krissy appeared and took her grandmother's hand. She led her down the path where other people were standing. Millie was now with her parents and her sisters. Krissy smiled as she gave each of them a big hug. She was so full of life. She brought excitement wherever she went. Today she was with her family. And this little child brought them all that joy as she led them to each other.

Luther looked over his shoulder at his family. He knew each one of them. Krissy was doing cartwheels on the grass. Luther smiled as he watched.

Luther sat down on the bench again and saw two people walking together. As they got closer, he knew exactly who they were, Margaret and Marie. It felt strange seeing his second wife, after just being with Millie. He loved them both, each in their own way. During some of his sessions with George, he blamed Margaret for the lack of a relationship with Peggy. It took him a while to realize that he had to take responsibility for his actions. He was so involved with Margaret and her family that he didn't care about how much he hurt his own. Margaret only wanted to visit her children and grandchildren, never Peggy. And he allowed that to happen.

Peggy was right, what she said in her letter, that throughout their house were many pictures of family. The only problem was that they were pictures of Margaret's family. The only pictures of Luther's grandchildren were on a desk in the spare bedroom. Why didn't he insist that his family's pictures be displayed for everyone to see? As time went on, it was just easier to give in to Margaret, especially after Marie died. Margaret was so distraught she nearly had a nervous breakdown. She kept saying over and over that no parent should have to bury a child. He felt so sorry for her and wanted to do whatever he could to ease her pain. He neglected to remember that his own daughter had lost a child. Did he comfort her when Krissy died? No.

George helped Luther understand that he couldn't continue to blame others for his mistakes. He had to learn to take responsibility for his own actions. He remembered when he read the letter from Peggy. He remembered that he read it once and then threw it away. Out of sight, out of mind. It was Peggy who was ending whatever relationship they had, not him. So if that was the way she wanted it, then so be it. It was easy to tell everyone that his daughter didn't want anything to do with him. They could feel sorry for him and he would be blameless. But after reading that letter now, he was finally able to see that everything she said was true. He had chosen to ignore it and place the blame on her. He was just as self-centered as his mother had been. Luther went on with his life and didn't care about Peggy. He shuttered to think of the things he missed, things other people got to enjoy.

Margaret and Marie approached Luther. Marie stepped back and let her mother speak first. Luther reached for her, but Margaret moved back and wouldn't allow him to touch her. Luther didn't know, but Margaret was still working with George about issues in her life. Her mission was not completed. Luther asked how she was and she said fine. She said she was enjoying being with Marie again. She asked how he was and he said fine. He told her about his reunion with his parents and siblings. Margaret didn't seem to be all that interested. She started to walk away.

Marie looked at her mother and said, "Mother! Don't you think Luther deserves more than that? He was your husband and he loved you. In your own way, I believe you loved him too. He was a good husband to you and he was good to Ava and me and our children. It was unfortunate that his daughter and her family didn't get the chance to have a relationship with you. There was no reason for that.

"Luther, I am glad to see you again. Mother is still working with George and isn't herself today. Come, Mother, we will leave now. Luther, I'm sorry. Please do not feel sad. She will be fine and I know you will see her again sometime and things will be different. She just needs more time." Marie led her mother down another path and soon they were out of sight.

Luther did feel sad for Margaret. He was happy that Marie was with her.

Next came Emma, Sarah, and Ephraim. Emma looked exactly how Luther remembered her the last time he saw her. That was the day he threw his cereal bowl out the window. He walked out of that house and never went back. His life drastically changed that day. Had he forgiven Emma for the way she treated him and Gerald? He hadn't thought about her at all since he was here. He remembered when he learned that she had died. He felt nothing. He didn't go to the funeral. He didn't want to be there, even for his father. It was only after Emma's death that he and his father had a better relationship. Warren went to live with Marion. Earl had passed and Marion was taking care of him. Emma's name never came up. Now she was standing in front of him. What would she say to him? What would he say to her? Could he forgive her for the way she treated him?

A long time passed as they stood there. Sarah was the first to speak. "Wayne, we came today because George asked us to. I don't know what to say. Ephraim and I have talked about our home and our life together, and we now realize it wasn't good. I think we were jealous of you and Gerald, as funny as that may sound. We were sad when our father died and we didn't want Mother to marry Warren. We didn't want Mother to have to share her affection with two other children. When we saw that she wasn't going to do that, we were relieved, but the way she treated you wasn't right. You and Gerald deserved better. I'm sorry for the way things were."

Ephraim nodded his head in agreement with his sister.

Emma looked at her stepson and said, "I am sorry for the way things were in our house. As I have looked back on my life, I realize that I was a bitter woman. I was angry when my husband died. I married your father because I wanted someone to take care of me. I resented having his children to take care of. I did many things wrong in my life and I am sorry for them. I am glad that you were able to become the man you did. I realize it was no thanks to me."

Luther could do nothing more than listen and absorb at first. Finally, he spoke. "Emma, I wasn't a perfect person either. I did many things in my life that I am not proud of. Perhaps I became a man because of you. I no longer hold any anger toward you. Our lives crossed and we existed in each other's space. Maybe we can now exist in a happier place."

Then Emma did something she never did the entire time Luther existed in her space. She reached out to him and gave him a hug. It was a powerful moment. Then she took the hand of each of her children and slowly walked down the path. And Krissy led them.

Luther was sure they would never cross paths again and perhaps that was for the best. The past was the past and it couldn't be changed. Each learned something about life because of their actions. Luther sat back down on the bench again with a heavy heart. He remembered all the terrible things that happened while living in that house with Emma, but somehow they didn't hurt as much as he thought they would.

One by one, the people from Luther's life came before him. If an apology was needed by either, it was exchanged. Each learned something about life that day. His bowling team from Gallagher's came with Joe Wozneski leading them in. High fives were given. Happy times were shared. The bad times were all part of the past. They were moving forward now.

Luther was feeling happy. So many people who were part of his life were there. He greeted each one and told them how glad he was to see them. It reminded him of that old TV show, *This Is Your Life*.

Krissy came over and sat with her grandfather. She asked him if he was having a good day. He took her hand and said he most definitely was. Krissy put her arm around him and gave him another one of her sloppy kisses. She knew he had to see all these people so he could continue on his journey through heaven.

Soon, the rest of his family, including Millie, were all standing around him. It was a good day. And a little child led them to the reconciliation they all wanted and needed.

George was watching from a distance. He smiled. This was one part of Luther's mission that he had to do. He was glad that his family would now be able to all be together. He had hoped that Margaret would have made more progress with her mission by now. That would happen, all in due time, all in due time.

Luther's Final Journey

Luther was so happy having his family with him. It was a wonderful feeling knowing that they were altogether. With Millie by his side and Krissy holding his hand, things couldn't have been any better. There was so much more that Luther wanted to say to Millie, and he knew they would have the opportunity to have many long conversations as they spent eternity together.

Krissy was running around on the grass. She was so excited having her grandparents here with her. She and Millie had been together for a long time and they enjoyed a special relationship with each other.

The happy threesome spent the next several weeks together, treasuring every second of this precious time.

About a month later, Luther was summoned to George's office. He had been so preoccupied with the time he spent with his family he didn't even think of George. He was glad he would have the opportunity to thank him for bringing all this about.

George greeted Luther at his office door. He knew how happy Luther was, but there was still a very important part of his mission to be completed. He didn't want to spoil the exhilaration Luther was feeling, but things needed to be done to complete his final mission.

"My, oh my, Luther! You certainly are in a wonderful mood today. I see a smile on your face and a bounce to your step. Please come in."

"George, I have to be the happiest person here. I have reunited with my family. My mother has asked me for forgiveness, and Emma even gave me a hug. I have learned a lot from my time on earth. I also know that I have given you a hard time about many things. I am sorry for that. I know that you were only trying to help me. Thank you for sticking with me and seeing me through this journey. I have spent the past several weeks with Millie and Krissy and it has been wonderful. Thank you, thank you!"

"Luther, I am so happy that things worked out the way they did. After seeing your mother and talking to her that day at the park, she completely fell apart. It was challenging for her to see and admit the things she did wrong in her life. I always felt you were the one who could change her. Her other children tried and came close, but it was you who stirred the most guilt in her and made her see and understand things. She actually came to me and was finally able to complete her mission here. I am happy to tell you that after seeing you, she was happily reunited with Horace and they are so happy to be together."

"I'm glad that she is finally happy. I hated her for so long and I wanted to continue to hate her, but what good did that hatred do? It only made me more bitter than I already was. She made a decision in life to do what she did. I am glad that she realized her actions caused a lot of pain to many people. But she apologized for them. I believe that deep down, she was in a lot of pain for what she did, but she couldn't admit it. I am glad that she and Horace are together again."

"Luther, I am glad that you can now see that. Yes, your mother was in much pain her entire life. Her conscience finally gave out and she had to admit to the things she did.

"I do regret that Margaret has not reached that point yet. It will come eventually, but for now she has not completed her mission. Luther, I know it appears that she only married you for your money and that it was entirely her fault that you never had a good relationship with your daughter, but in all fairness to her, she was suffering long before she met you. Her first husband died young and she was forced to raise two children by herself. Margaret was never a strong woman. James, her husband, made all the decisions and took care of all the household expenses. Margaret had no idea how to pay a bill or even write a check. When James died suddenly, she was completely lost. She was forced to become an independent woman. Many people tried to help her, and some were not looking out for her best interest. She learned what she had to, but it wasn't easy and it caused much insecurity in her life. When she met you, she knew you would take over all the things that she hated to do. You became the person she could depend on. She wanted to be sure you would always be there for her. She was terrified that Peggy would step in and somehow send her away. She knew she could never go through all that again. When she realized that she could control you, she did what she thought was the only thing she could do. She created a break between you and Peggy. She must learn these things and accept them to move on. She wants to be reunited with James again. I am hopeful that all this will happen soon. Luther, just remember one thing. Margaret, in her own way, did love you."

Luther was glad to hear that. He knew that he loved her. It was different than the love he felt for Millie. He hoped that Margaret would be able to move on with her mission.

George waited a few minutes for Luther to absorb all this. He wanted him to realize that Margaret was a good wife to him and that many of her actions only came about for fear of her own self-preservation.

"Now, Luther, we must move on. There is one more part of your mission that must be completed. To be honest with you, I'm not sure how it will turn out, but I am indeed hopeful. We will have to go back to watching the screen. There are things you need to see and understand before you can complete your final mission. Are you ready? I must warn you that you will not enjoy watching a good portion of this, but the end result will be well worth it."

Luther thought about that. He had been so happy being with Millie and Krissy. He didn't want to see unhappy scenes again, but he knew he had to trust George. He hoped that he was right when he said that it would all be worth it.

"Yes, George, I am ready. To be honest, I am a little apprehensive, but I know it is what I must do."

The Realization

T he room went to darkness and the screen came to life. It was a birthday party. A young girl was just getting ready to blow out the candles. Luther started to count the candles on the cake and was sure he saw sixteen. Everyone at the party was having such a wonderful time. Somehow he knew this was Becca's sixteenth birthday party. She was so grown up. She blew out the candles and everyone cheered.

Next it was time to open the many gifts that were sitting on a nearby table. There was a small package there, and as Becca reached for it, he saw tears in Peggy's eyes. Inside the box was a beautiful necklace. It sparkled as Becca held it in her hands. This necklace was from Peggy. Luther remembered seeing that necklace before. It had been Peggy's, and he remembered that he and Millie had given it to her on her sixteenth birthday. Peggy loved it, and when she saw it, she ran over to her parents and gave each of them a big hug and kiss. Millie told Peggy that her dad had been the one to pick it out.

Luther remembered being in the jewelry store buying it. He thought it was really pretty and was hoping that Peggy would love it. Now he was watching as his only granddaughter was admiring this same necklace. She obviously loved it as much as Peggy had many years earlier.

Peggy was standing beside Becca and told her that it was something very special because it had come from her father. She wanted Becca to know that it meant so much to her. She had kept it all these years hoping that she could give it to her daughter one day. For Peggy and her dad, it had been a special bonding moment between them. Peggy remembered that happy time. Many times when things were not good between them, she would take the necklace out of the box and remember those cherished moments.

Becca knew that her grandfather hadn't been a part of her life and she often wondered why. When she would ask her mother about it, all Peggy would say was that they lived in a complicated situation and that she only wanted to remember the happy times.

Luther watched his daughter and granddaughter. He heard the words his daughter said about him. It made him sad to think that he wasn't a part of happy times such as he just witnessed. And he had no one to blame but himself.

*****

The next scene was at a school. There was a track meet going on. Luther watched as runners came around and crossed the line, winning the race. He saw Peggy sitting on a blanket talking to another woman. He heard an announcement that the 3,200-meter race was coming up. He watched as he saw his grandson Jimmy approach the starting line. The gun fired and the runners took off. When the final lap was coming up, Jimmy started running faster. Soon he was in the lead and was going strong. He heard coaches yelling and cheering. Peggy stood up and listened to the crowd screaming Jimmy's name. When Jimmy crossed the line in first place, everyone was running toward him with shouts of excitement. Peggy was jumping up and down. Then Jimmy ran through the gate and went right up to Peggy and lifted her high in the air. He had just broken the school record that had stood for thirty years. It was such a wonderful, exciting time. Luther heard Peggy say how happy she was and that his grandfather would be so proud.

Luther wondered if he knew about that. Could it have been one of those times when Peggy started to tell him something and he would interrupt her to tell her something about one of Margaret's grandchildren? How could he have done such a thing? This was a very eventful time in his grandson's life and he never even acknowledged it. Yet he heard Peggy telling her son that his grandfather would be so proud of him. Did Jimmy ever question that?

*****

Next came the scene at a wedding. It was in a beautiful church. Luther remembered this event. It was the wedding of his grandson Jimmy when he married Jamie. He knew that he and Margaret were there. Margaret didn't want to go, but this was one of few times that Luther said he was going with or without her. It was his grandson who was getting married and he wanted to be there. Margaret finally agreed to go and he thought they had a good time. As he looked back on the scene now, he knew there were so many other times when he wasn't at an important event in the life of his grandson.

When his great-grandson was born, he sent the baby a savings bond. He never made time to see him. He had the opportunity, but he made excuses not to visit. He would say that they lived too far away, yet Ava's family lived even farther away and they visited there often.

*****

Another scene came on the screen and Luther realized it was his granddaughter Becca's graduation from college. Luther had been invited to the graduation, but chose not to attend. He told her it was too far to travel, but it happened to be in the same town where Ava lived. He watched as Becca asked her mother if she should even invite him to it. Peggy said of course she should. After all, he was her grandfather. Peggy made a point of saying that if he didn't come, she was sure he had a very good reason. Becca wasn't sure she wanted to invite him, but to please her mother, she did. Becca knew all too well that her grandfather didn't seem all that interested in any of them.

Luther remembered when he got the invitation. He didn't want to go and was really not the least bit interested in the fact that his only granddaughter had just accomplished this. Margaret told him there was a piano concert that same day and that he was expected to attend it with her. He did remember that he sent her a savings bond for graduation. Actually, everyone just assumed that it came from him, because there was no card attached and no way of actually knowing for sure.

"I didn't even send a card to her? What was I thinking?"

George stopped the screen and looked over at Luther. It was obvious that he was remembering and regretting that he never allowed himself to become a part of the lives of his family. This pain was something that Luther was going to have to live with. There were tears in his eyes.

"George, I wasn't involved in the lives of my grandchildren, was I? How could I have ignored them the way I did?"

George didn't say anything. He didn't know what to say or how to say anything that would make Luther feel any better.

George knew that Luther was feeling extremely remorseful about the events he was watching. He also knew that watching these events were something he had to do. The pain he was feeling was necessary for him to complete his journey. There was one final screen that George wanted Luther to see. He knew it would be the most painful one, but the one that would help Luther the most.

Josh

Peggy answered her phone as she was running out the door. She had several errands to do before coming home to make the evening meal for her and Mike.

"Hi, Becca. What's up?"

"Hi, Mom. I wanted to give you a heads-up about something. I'm not sure how you are going to feel about this."

Peggy wondered what Becca was about to say. She didn't sound like there was something wrong with anyone or that it was anything serious. "Okay, what is it?"

"Josh came home from school today very excited. His history class has been talking about World War II. They talked about the famous people associated with that war, especially war heroes. Josh told his teacher that his great-grandfather fought in the war and that he was a hero because he had been shot. He heard that story from me. We had been looking at picture albums and there were pictures of my grandfather. He was in his army uniform and Josh asked about him. Mom, I know you told me what really happened when Grandpa got shot, but I didn't want to tell him that. So I told him the story that Grandpa always told everyone—the one where the German soldier shot him. There was a picture in the album of him in his hospital bed with both his legs in a cast. Josh thought this was so neat, not the part about getting shot, but being a war hero and helping to win the war."

Peggy listened as Becca said all this. She knew the true story of how her father had gotten shot and so did Becca. What harm did it do to let a little boy think this man, his great-grandfather, was really a war hero? Josh was ten years old and in fifth grade. He loved playing with his army men and having battles and winning the wars. Now he knew that his own great-grandfather was actually in one of those wars. The truth didn't really matter much to anyone anymore, and if Josh wanted to believe he was a war hero, then so be it. She was still trying to figure out how this involved her.

"Mom, Josh told his teacher the story. The teacher would like you to speak to his class on grandparent's day about your father and his involvement in the war. I didn't know what to say when she called me and asked if I could talk to you about it. I think she would understand if you said you didn't feel comfortable doing this, but it would mean so much to Josh."

There was silence on the other end of the phone. Peggy didn't know what to say. She was expected to talk about a man who was shot in the war by an enemy soldier. That wasn't the way it happened. She was expected to talk about a man who really didn't want to be bothered with her, her children, or her grandchildren. She couldn't tell them the truth, that he lied so many times, stole money from his family, and felt closer to his second wife's family than his own—and all because they had more money.

"Mom, are you still there?"

"Yes, I am. I was trying to absorb everything that you were saying. I would have a hard time talking about a man who did the things he did, yet I can't not do it for Josh. I don't know if Josh will ever learn the truth, but for now how can it hurt him to think this man, his great-grandfather, was really a war hero. When is this happening at school?"

"It's in two weeks, October 15. You will do it, won't you?"

"Yes, I will do it. I can't disappoint Josh. I will just have to think about what I want to say."

They ended their conversation and Peggy just sat in the car staring at her phone. She would have to really search her soul and think about what she could say about her father. She didn't want to lie. She knew the story about her father being the war hero and getting shot by the enemy would be a lie, but she didn't know how to avoid that.

And it was the story that he told everyone, so she hoped that counted as, maybe, only a partial lie.

*****

October 15 was fast approaching and Peggy was feeling extremely nervous. She had gotten out all her mother's scrapbooks and looked at the pictures of her parents and her early life. She was hoping that by looking at them, she would find the words that she wanted to say to Josh's class. She had been so preoccupied with the unhappiness in her life concerning her father that she actually forgot that there were some good times.

Finally, she sat down at her desk and closed her eyes. She prayed for guidance.

She had talked to Josh the night before, and he was so excited about having her come to his school and talk. She didn't want to disappoint him. She wasn't sure how much time had elapsed, but she was suddenly aware that Mike was standing at the door to her office. He knew what she was doing. He too had said prayers asking for the right words to come to her. He felt her struggle and yet, at the same time, felt helpless. He knew this was something she had to do on her own. He would, of course, be there that day for Josh as well as for her. Peggy looked up at Mike and smiled. She knew he was worried about her. She stood up and went to him and he enfolded her in his arms. Having his support and strength meant so much to her. He was a good man and they had a very good life together.

"Mike, I have prayed about this, and now I am going to wait until I have all the answers I need. I trust that God will be there for me and guide me in the direction I need to go. And thank you for being you and for being here for me. I don't know where I would be without you."

"My love, I am always here for you. I know that when the time comes, you will have the words you need. And Josh will be so proud."

*****

Grandparents Day finally arrived. Peggy and Mike drove to Josh's school, in silence. They both knew there wasn't much to say now. They were in deep thought. Mike noticed that Peggy seemed calm and relaxed. He knew she had spent several nights looking at pictures and thinking about this day.

When they walked into the fifth-grade classroom, Josh immediately ran to them. He gave each of them a big hug. He tugged at Peggy's arm and guided her to where his teacher, Mrs. Whitman, was sitting.

"Grandma, this is my teacher, Mrs. Whitman." Peggy shook her hand and said she was very happy to meet her. Mrs. Whitman said that Josh had been so excited about this day that it had been hard to keep his attention on his schoolwork. She thanked Peggy for agreeing to speak to the class. The program opened with the class singing a song, a funny song about grandparents. The children were all excited and laughed when the silly words were sung. Mrs. Whitman welcomed the visitors to the class and told them they were going to have a special guest talk to them. She told the adults that they had been studying World War II and that the class had been exceptionally interested in how life was all those years ago. Then the teacher looked over at Josh, signaling him to stand up. He walked over to his grandmother and held her hand.

"This is my grandma and her dad was in in World War II. He was my great-grandfather. My grandma is going to talk about him today."

Peggy smiled at Josh as he led her to the front of the room. She looked over at Mike who gave her a thumbs up. She felt calm and knew she would be able to do this. Speaking in front of people was not something that she was used to doing, but she felt calm. She knew she would be able to do this.

"Good morning, everyone. And how are you today?" There was a murmur of hello's and some saying fine.

"Josh told me that your class was learning about World War II and he asked me if I would talk to you about my father. His name was Luther Wayne Yeager. He didn't have a very good life as he was growing up. After he met my mother, things were much different for him. He was happy and all the sad things that happened to him as a young boy didn't matter anymore. He worked in a factory and that is where he met my mother.

"The war in Europe was going on. There was fighting and people were scared. My mother used to tell me that her father would sit by the radio each night to listen to the news. There were no TVs back then. He wanted to know what was happening overseas. He had fought in World I and he knew it wasn't very nice. My grandfather was worried that our country would somehow get involved with this war and he didn't want to see that again.

"On December 7, 1941, Japanese planes attacked the U.S. Naval Base at Pearl Harbor, Hawaii. Many American soldiers were killed and battleships were destroyed. The president of the United States said that date would live in infamy. That means it would be a day that everyone would always remember. It was the day that our country was attacked and now we would be involved with this horrible war. The day after this attack, Pres. Franklin Roosevelt announced that the United States was declaring war against Japan.

"Shortly after this attack, the leader of Germany declared war against our country, and we now would be involved with the war that was going on in Europe as well.

"My father knew that he would be drafted and would have to go to war. He decided to sign up on his own, and within a few weeks, he became a U.S. soldier in the army. After he went to basic training, where he learned how to shoot a gun and be a soldier, he went by ship to Europe. He was scared and never knew when the enemy would attack.

"One day his commanding officer sent him and three other soldiers out into the hills of Germany to look for enemy camps. They didn't find any, but they were sure there were German soldiers nearby. My father and his army buddies found an abandoned house and they stayed there overnight. They would begin their hunt for German soldiers again the next morning.

"Suddenly, shots rang out. My father and his friends grabbed their guns and went outside to find out what was happening. My father ran toward the trees thinking someone was there. Another shot was fired and my father was hit in both of his legs. He stayed very still because he didn't want his friends to come running. He was afraid the enemy would shoot them too.

"Soon my father's friends realized that he was not with them and they went to look for him. They saw a German soldier standing over him, ready to shoot him again. They immediately shot the German soldier and rushed to my father to see how badly he was hurt. When they saw the wounds in his legs, they knew it was serious. They carried him into the house and immediately called for help. It took a while, but finally help arrived. They put my father on a stretcher and they went back to the camp. It was a long way and my father was in a lot of pain. He thought of my mother and wanted to keep his strength up as long as he could. He had promised her he would come back from the war so they could be together again.

"At camp they took him to the makeshift hospital and operated on his legs. The doctor wasn't sure they would be able to save them. They had to make arrangements for him to be sent to a hospital where he would be able to get better medical care.

"The other soldiers stood watching as he was put on a military plane to be taken to a hospital in England. They all said a prayer that night that he would be okay.

"My father had to have several surgeries on his legs, and fortunately, the doctors were able to save both his legs. He spent many months in the hospital where he had to learn how to walk again. He would then be on a ship and brought back to the United States. The doctors on the ship did whatever they could to keep him comfortable. They hoped he would not have a setback on the long ocean trip back home.

"My mother learned about this several weeks after he was shot. She was so scared. When she found out where his ship would dock, she immediately made plans to be there.

"Once back in the United States, my father was sent to Walter Reed Hospital in Washington DC where he would get more therapy. He spent many months in that hospital.

"Finally, the day came when he was allowed to go home. My parents took the train from Washington and my grandfather met them at the station. It was difficult for my father to walk, so the porter on the train helped him as best he could. When other people at the train station saw that a soldier was trying to get off the train, they ran to him and helped. They didn't know how he got shot, but this was an American soldier who was fighting a war to help bring peace to our country as well as the world. Several men who had served in World War I saluted him as he was helped to a nearby taxi. They thought of him as a war hero.

"After months of continued therapy, he was able to walk without the help of a cane. He found a job at a local factory. Several years later, I was born.

"My father didn't talk much about the war. It was a very scary and painful time in his life. He was a good man. He and I had a special bond as I was growing up. I would wait on our front porch for him to come home from work. He would stop the car and I would get in and we would drive to our garage together. Then he would carry me on his shoulders into the house where my mother was making supper. He was on a bowling team, and I would go with him every Friday night and cheer on the team. These were special times for us and ones that I will always remember.

"My father died several years ago on July 4. It was an appropriate day because it was the day we celebrate our independence as a country. He helped fight for that continued independence for our freedom. He will always be a hero to me. Thank you."

Then Peggy showed the class pictures of her father. There was one in his uniform and another of him in the hospital with both of his legs in casts.

There was a round of applause from the other grandparents as well as the students in the class. Peggy went back to sit beside Mike. He smiled at her and reached for her hand. He was so proud of her. He knew how much she had struggled with this and she was fantastic. She told the story of a soldier at a terrible time in the history of our country.

Peggy felt at peace after this. She knew the circumstances weren't quite the way she told them. But she knew that despite how he was shot, it was a scary time for him. Somehow she felt that special bond that she and her father had again. Somehow she knew that her dad was smiling down on her.

When the class ended, Josh ran to his grandmother and gave her another big hug. He thanked her for telling her story.

*****

Luther sat in his chair staring at the screen, which by now had gone black. He didn't know what to say. He just watched his daughter tell his story—the story he always told everyone even though it wasn't accurate. He heard her compassion as she spoke to his great-grandson's class. She could have refused to talk. She could have even told the truth. The class most likely wouldn't have thought of him as a war hero if she did. But she told a story of a man she loved and admired. He remembered their special bond too. Somewhere along the way, he lost it. Other things became more important to him, and he sacrificed his family for material things. Money is the root of all evil. He remembered when he thought of what his mother did, and all for money. He was no better. Tears welled in his eyes.

George sat quietly with him and left him with his thoughts. There were no words he could say now that would make Luther feel any better. It was difficult, but something he had to do. George knew that Luther was now ready for his final task. The pain of watching Peggy would remain, but forgiveness was finally here. It was the lesson that Luther had to learn. His life's story was difficult, but it was now time to concentrate on the good, the happy, and the love that was most often left unsaid. Yes, Luther was ready.

He went to Luther and escorted him back to his room. And just like a father did for his child, George tucked him in his bed and quietly left the room.

Luther slept. His dreams were of those happy, cherished memories with his daughter. He felt a connection to her again. He wasn't sure how this could be, but he knew his feelings were real.

Salvation, Repentance, and Prayers

Luther woke the next morning feeling refreshed. He remembered his dreams and how happy they were. He relived the wonderful times he spent with his daughter. He felt enormous grief that he had treated her the way he did. He wanted to be able to make it up to her, but he didn't know how. He was here in heaven and Peggy was on earth. He wondered if he would have to wait until she died and came here before that could happen.

He got dressed and went to the dining room for breakfast. He was so surprised to see Krissy at his table. How wonderful was this? As soon as he saw her, he rushed over to where she sat. Krissy looked up and smiled.

"Hi, Grandpa. What are we going to have for breakfast this morning?"

"Krissy…oh, Krissy. It is so good to see you. I'm happy that you are here. What brings you to this side of heaven today?"

"Well, I wanted to have breakfast with you, and I asked George if that would be okay. He said he thought that was a great idea, so here I am."

Luther smiled, thinking about this special little girl and how glad he was that she was in his life now. He gave her a tap on her hand as he asked what sounded good for breakfast.

"Well, I was thinking about pancakes and bacon. What do you think?"

"Krissy, that sounds terrific. And with lots and lots of maple syrup on top."

Krissy had a puzzled look on her face. "What other way would we eat them?"

As they ate their pancakes, they talked about meeting all the people in Luther's life. He was glad that he and Millie were together again. They spent lots of time with Krissy. At night, Millie and Krissy had to go back to their side of heaven and Luther went back to his room. He knew there was something else he had to do before he would be able to join them. He wasn't exactly sure what it was. He needed to talk to George about it.

When breakfast was over, Krissy said she had to go back so she could do her chores. She got up and gave her grandfather a big hug and kiss. Her lips were still smeared with maple syrup and Luther felt her sticky kiss.

They said goodbye and Krissy went jogging down the path. Luther decided he would go for a walk as well. He stumbled across a road that he had never seen before. He wasn't sure how he could have missed it, because he thought it was the way he went to George's office. Once again things changed right before his eyes.

It was another beautiful day as he walked along the path. He listened to the birds chirping in the trees. He was feeling pretty good, especially after having breakfast with Krissy.

As he went around a curve in the road, he thought he heard singing. It was the music of old familiar hymns—the ones he remembered from his childhood. He followed the sound and soon saw before him a big white church. He remembered seeing a church once before, but he didn't go inside then. Today, he felt drawn to this place. He remembered George telling him that there were many churches here, but he would only see them when he was ready to. He knew he wasn't ready before, but today he just knew he wanted to go inside.

As he entered, he realized a church service was going on and a choir was singing. He sat down near the back of the church and listened. The voices of the choir blended together and sounded wonderful. He had heard the Mormon Tabernacle Choir sing once and thought they were amazing. There was no comparison; this choir was magnificent.

When the choir finished, a man stood up in front of the church and said, *"To the choirmaster, a Psalm of David. The heavens declare the glory of God, and the sky proclaims his handiwork."* He too had been moved by the music. He said this as he quoted Psalm 19.

The minister stood in the pulpit and began his sermon. He talked about forgiveness and earning salvation. He said that Christ died for our sins and we must turn from them. It is called repentance. What matters is the attitude of our hearts and our honesty.

Luther was mesmerized by the words the minister said. He knew he had sinned while he lived on earth. He faced all the things he did in his talks with George. He knew he had made great progress, but there was still something that had to be done. When the service ended, Luther remained sitting in the pew. He wanted to talk to God. He wanted to pray. He bowed his head and thought about what he wanted to say.

"Dear God, I know that I have sinned and I ask for your forgiveness. I feel repentance in my heart. I need Your help to fulfil my final task here so that I can move forward in my journey. I understand that my repentance won't eliminate the consequences of my sins. I have hurt people in my earthly life. I have met these people and they have forgiven me. I too have forgiven the people in my life who hurt me. I wasn't sure I would be able to do that, but with Your help, I did. The one person I have hurt the most is my daughter. I heard the words she has spoken about me and they break my heart. Even though I abandoned her, she still spoke kindly of me. I want her forgiveness. Praying to You now, I realize this is my final task. I know that with Your help, I will be able to accomplish this. Amen."

Luther sat in the church for a long time. He prayed in a way he never remembered praying before. He knew he took praying and asking for forgiveness lightheartedly while he lived on earth.

Slowly, he rose and left the church. The sun shining down on him felt good. He felt better than he did before. He wasn't sure how, but somehow he felt things were going to be okay. He felt that Krissy being there for breakfast with him was an omen. She was the glue that held all of this together. He remembered the Bible verse from Isaiah that talked about wild animals lying down together with other animals and a little child leading them. That's what Krissy did with his family. He knew she would be the connecting link. She's the little child who would lead him to find the answers and take him on his final journey through heaven.

Peggy

❦

eggy left the dentist's office with a smile on her face. A good
checkup and clean teeth, just what she wanted to hear. She
headed north on Field Avenue toward her exit. There appeared
to be a traffic jam ahead and Peggy was carefully following a detour
around a minor fender bender. Before she knew it, she had missed
turning onto her exit and would now have to go all the way to Route
44 to catch the bypass.

Heading in that direction, she realized that she would be driving
right past St. Mark's Cemetery. Most of her family was buried there.
On a whim, she drove through the entrance and headed toward her
family's plot. It had been several years since she had been there. She
always felt that cemeteries gave her the creeps and visiting a head-
stone was not really visiting the person buried there. She always made
arrangements with a local florist to have flowers put on her grandparents', her mother's, and Krissy's graves.

She found the graves and stood before the marble headstones.
Her grandmother was the first to be buried there. She died in 1939
and Peggy never knew her. She always wished she had. She enjoyed the
relationship she had with her grandchildren, and it would have been
nice to have had a grandmother in her life. She never knew her father's
mother, because she disowned most of her family many years ago.

Her grandfather was buried between her grandmother and her
mother. He had been a very important person in her life. He used to
take her and her cousin to baseball games and they always had such
a good time. They would take the train to Philadelphia and then a
trolley to the stadium.

Peggy looked down at her mother's grave. How tragic was her death. She and her mother had become great friends as each got older and enjoyed spending time together when they could. At the time of her death, Peggy lived several hours away and didn't see her mother as often as she would have liked. She wanted to be there when her mother got home from the hospital, but tragically, that wasn't meant to be.

Krissy's grave was next. It was many years since her death. That was the worst possible day of Peggy's life. For many years, she blamed God for taking her little girl. Why was he such a cruel God? How could he do such a thing? Did he think she wasn't a good mother? She knew that wasn't true; she was a good mother. In time, she accepted God's will and her life continued. She thought about Krissy every day and remembered that funny, busy, full of life little child who brought so much joy to everyone she was around.

Peggy knew her father was buried at this same cemetery. She didn't know where his grave was located. She had been thinking about him lately, especially since the day she spoke about him at Josh's school.

As she was getting back into her car, she suddenly felt the urge to visit his grave. She would have to go to the cemetery office in hopes that someone would be there to tell her where his grave was located. He was supposed to be buried beside her mother, but after the way he treated her family, that didn't happen.

As she parked her car, a lady was just locking the office door. Peggy immediately went to her and told her it was very important that she find out the location of a grave site. The secretary told her the office was closed and she would have to come back the next day. For some reason, she felt an urgency in finding it now. She didn't want to come back. She explained the situation in hopes that she would agree to help her. Reluctantly, the secretary went back into the office to try and locate it and fortunately found it within a few minutes. She didn't ask, but wondered why a daughter wouldn't know where her own father was buried. It wasn't really any of her business. She was glad she was able to help.

Peggy thanked her for taking the time and proceeded to that part of the cemetery. It was on top of a hill, just off to the right. The secretary told her there were many graves there, so she was just going to have to walk up and down and look for it.

She parked her car and looked over all the graves in that section. How would she ever be able to find it? There must have been at least fifty graves.

She started walking toward the ones on the left side, but suddenly felt like someone was pushing her in the other direction. She even turned around to be sure that there wasn't anyone there. For some reason, something was forcing her to start in the opposite direction.

There were several large tombstones in this area, but none with the name Yeager. There were many small, flat stones and some covered with overgrown grass. She was going to start in the front row, but she fell like she was being pushed again, toward the rows in the back. She walked down the last row, and as she started toward the next one, she saw her father's grave. The flat gray stone was on the corner, barely visible. It had sunk in the ground slightly and had dirt and leaves on it. Etched in the stone were the following words:

Luther Wayne Yeager
1919–2012

Nothing more. No mention of either wife. It was as simple as could possibly be. *What a pity*, Peggy thought. Obviously, it was the cheapest funeral that could have been had. Her father had money. Didn't he preplan his funeral? He should have. This was Ava's doings, she was sure. Even though she didn't have a relationship with him, he deserved better than this. She wondered what happened to the money he had. She doubted it was all spent. Ava probably figured out a way to see that her family got it. Peggy never wanted his money. She really only wanted to have a relationship with him and to know that he loved her. She remembered telling him in the letter she wrote to him that it was nothing short of blood money, only there because of her mother's death.

Peggy looked down at the tiny grave, running her fingers across the etched words in the stone, and felt extreme pity and anger. If she had known about his death, she would have done things differently. Tears welled in her eyes as she looked down.

Being here at her father's grave site, she became very emotional. Her mind was remembering everything about him. Their relationship started out as love when she was a small child, misunderstanding as a teenager, and confusion and hurt as an adult. Her thoughts went back to her birthday and the card he sent her saying "Happy birthday to a wonderful son-in-law." She called him just a few days later on his birthday and asked him about it. He got angry and told her she should just be glad she got a card.

The day after his birthday, Marion, his sister, died at the age of one hundred and three. Peggy called to tell him. He didn't seem to be very upset about it. He said they wouldn't be coming to any funeral because it was too far to drive. Peggy thought that was strange because it never was too far a drive to visit Ava.

When Aunt Marion died, there were no provisions for her funeral. Everyone thought it had been preplanned. Peggy and her cousins said they could each give something, but it would have been a financial struggle for most of them. Someone mentioned Luther. Everyone knew he had the money and were sure he would help. Aunt Marion always said she could depend on her little brother to help her out and she knew he would always be there for her.

Another cousin called him to ask if he would be willing to help with the funeral costs. He became so angry. He told her that he lived on a fixed income and didn't believe she didn't have any money. It was explained to him that anything she had went directly to the nursing home. He said he needed proof that she had no money.

Two of his nieces were furious when they heard this. How could he be so coldhearted? They each wrote him a very nasty letter telling him exactly how they felt about him. One taped two pennies at the bottom of her letter, saying that was her two cents' worth, and maybe he could use them since he lived on a fixed income.

Peggy remembered always asking her father to come and visit. He usually found one excuse after another. On one occasion, Peggy asked if he could visit, watch Becca play baseball on her school team, and stay overnight. Surprisingly, he said that he and Margaret would come. Peggy prepared a nice meal for everyone. They would then go to the game together. When Luther and Margaret pulled into the driveway, Peggy went out to greet them. Luther got out of the car and immediately said, "We ain't staying. It's too damn hot."

Peggy was flabbergasted. Yes, it was hot, but her home had air-conditioning. She looked at him and said, "Well, hello to you too."

Luther and Margaret stayed about an hour and said they were going to Ava's house. Peggy asked about dinner and the game. Luther just grunted and said they were leaving. Peggy was so upset she vowed never to invite him to her house again.

Peggy never forgot the insurance policies and the lies he told about them. She was furious that he could steal money from his own grandchildren when he got millions from the malpractice suit. When she realized she just couldn't take his attitude and lack of feelings for her and her family any longer, she decided she would write to him. She wanted to tell him exactly how she felt. She poured her heart out in that letter. What did she have to lose? If he felt any remorse after reading the letter, she hoped he would find it in his heart to ask for forgiveness. If not, then she was better off not constantly being hurt by him.

Peggy never heard from her father after that. She remembered reading about Margaret's death in the local newspaper. She thought about her father, but she didn't contact him. Perhaps she should have, but she just wasn't prepared for anything he might say to her. Several years later, she was reading the paper again and there in bold print was his obituary. Peggy felt a stab in her heart. Her father had died and no one even contacted her to let her know. It said the funeral had already taken place at the nursing home where he lived. The internment had been private with a burial at St. Mark's Cemetery. Obviously, she was not wanted there.

Peggy sat down on the ground next to the small grave. She started remembering the good times. She smiled as she thought about the July 4th parade when he hoisted her on his shoulders so she could see over the crowd. And later that night as they watched the fireworks, he put his hands over her ears so they wouldn't be so loud. *I must have been about five or six.* When a thunderstorm came in the middle of the night and the lightning scared her, he would get in her bed and hold her so tightly, whispering that it was okay and he wasn't going to let anything hurt her.

Yes, there were good times. She was so focused on the bad times that she forgot about them. Now they were wonderful memories swirling inside her head. Her father did love her, even if he had a difficult time expressing that as she got older.

It was now time to put the past to rest. It was time to let love return. The fifth commandment from the Bible said to "honor thy father and thy mother." Peggy needed to do this, despite the past. The circle of their lives should be completed. Peggy knew that throughout all the hurt, she always loved her father, even when she wasn't sure how he felt about her.

She looked up as she felt a cool breeze come over her. Just then a feather fell on his tombstone. A sign from heaven? She felt a drop of moisture on her hand. It wasn't raining, so where did that come from? Peggy knew. She smiled as she felt her father's presence. She knew he was there and that all was good between them again. She looked up and smiled. *Dad, I love you and always have.* She thought she felt a sloppy wet kiss on her cheek. Something was there, but she wasn't sure what. Krissy giggled and hugged her mother. Peggy couldn't see her, but she felt her presence and knew it was Krissy.

And a little child embraced them with the love that seemed lost, but had always been there.

*****

There were tears in Luther's eyes. His daughter had forgiven him for all the terrible things he did. He loved her so much and felt that love returned to him. Krissy came running toward her grandfather. She grabbed his hand and led him down a path he never saw before. When they crossed the horizon, a rainbow illuminated the sky. It was the most beautiful place imaginable. *"What no eye has seen, nor ear heard, nor the heart of man imagined."*

Krissy was leading him. This little child led him to his new home.

He felt a powerful arm around him and heard the words of the Father. *"Blessed are the pure in heart, for they shall see God. Truly, I say to you, today you will be with me in Paradise."*

George smiled.

Luther accomplished his mission. His journey through heaven was complete.

The End

About the Author

Moser lives with her husband on a large working dairy farm. A "city girl," she moved to rural Pennsylvania when she married and that in itself is a story waiting to be told. She and her husband share four children and six grandchildren. Amid all that family raising, in a pinch, she can be found feeding the baby calves or even helping milk the cows. Moser can rightfully say she has entered a life totally different from "the city" and wouldn't trade places with anyone else.

To keep her hands in the "literary world," she writes a monthly column, "Down on the Farm," for a local newspaper, often sharing her personal experiences down on the farm, which are entertaining and informative.

Writing has always been a personal catharsis for Moser. Writing *A Journey through Heaven* began as a simple personal quest to forgive her father for past behavior. Moser was in search not only for a way to forgive him but also to believe that he forgave himself. The writing process has been a healing one for Moser. She did not intend to write a book, but as each story came to life, she knew she had to share the pain and the healing with others so that they too could start their own journey.

CPSIA information can be obtained
at www.ICGtesting.com
Printed in the USA
BVHW071052241219
567672BV00001B/1/P

9 781098 008642